OCT 20

P9-CMV-918

THE
THREE
MRS.
WRIGHTS

ALSO BY LINDA KEIR

Drowning with Others

The Swing of Things

THE
THREE
MRS.
WRIGHTS

A NOVEL

LINDA KEIR

LAKE UNION
PUBLISHING

This is a work of fiction. Names, characters, organizations, places, events, and incidents are either products of the author's imagination or are used fictitiously. Any resemblance to actual persons, living or dead, or actual events is purely coincidental.

Text copyright © 2020 by Linda Keir
All rights reserved.

No part of this book may be reproduced, or stored in a retrieval system, or transmitted in any form or by any means, electronic, mechanical, photocopying, recording, or otherwise, without express written permission of the publisher.

Published by Lake Union Publishing, Seattle

www.apub.com

Amazon, the Amazon logo, and Lake Union Publishing are trademarks of Amazon.com, Inc., or its affiliates.

ISBN-13: 9781542019705
ISBN-10: 1542019702

Cover design by Shasti O'Leary Soudant

Printed in the United States of America

For Mark Stevens

Chapter One

LARK

What's in a name? I say everything.

—"How I Lied about My Name and Discovered My Truth,"
a TED Talk by Jon M. Wright

Hotel bars were not Lark's scene. Fairly or unfairly, she associated them with balding, fiftysomething bros who ordered their second drinks while halfway through their first ones, and who one-upped each other's sports injuries while name-dropping vacation spots to prove who had the fattest wallet and the biggest penis. Their jobs would be equally uninteresting: management consultant, investment adviser, salesman.

Granted, at twenty-six, she had very little experience, so she was mostly just guessing. And yet here she was, in an honest-to-god hotel bar in the godforsaken town of Buffalo, New York, and she had to admit the place was living down to her imagination. Last updated in the early 1990s—so around the time she was born—the place held a sad handful of couples and singles, and the guy nearest her, the one twisting a heavy gold watch around his meaty wrist, looked like the third-generation owner of a regional waste-management company. A cheesy lounge trio would have provided welcome comic relief, but instead the piped-in music was soft rock from her mom's teenage years.

She was consoling herself that she'd be on her way home to sunny LA tomorrow afternoon when *he* walked in.

He was tall and fit, with wavy brown hair that would look overdue for a haircut on anyone else. On him it somehow framed his face perfectly. As he made his way to the bar, Lark had the fleeting thought that he didn't belong there—nobody truly belonged in a hotel bar in Buffalo, but he looked a cut above the rest of the customers. He was wearing jeans, a blue sport coat, a casually wrinkled white shirt, and brown leather shoes that cost more than any purse she'd ever owned. She looked away as he scanned the room, definitely not wanting him to catch her staring.

Also, the bartender, buzzed hair and gap-toothed, was in front of her, tribal tats curling up his forearms and disappearing under his rolled shirtsleeves.

"What can I get you, miss?" he asked.

"Vodka and soda with a lemon." One quick drink and then back to her room.

He nodded seriously and turned away to pour it. *Miss* sounded a little too formal coming out of his mouth, but maybe he felt like he had to compensate for the tattoos by overcompensating on the professional front. Maybe he regretted the clichéd ink, among other poor life choices, and was dedicating himself to mixology. The hotel bar was his apprenticeship to growing a bushy beard and opening his own craft cocktail joint.

She gave a quiet snort, amused at her ability to invent a life story for a random stranger who probably was nothing more than he appeared to be. When she looked down the bar, the brown-haired man caught her eye and gave the briefest smile, as if amused she was amused, before looking away.

The bartender brought her drink, centered it on a napkin, and with a flourish scooped brown-and-orange snack mix into a tiny bowl before moving down the bar toward the brown-haired man, who was already in conversation with two middle-aged women. Within a minute, the four of them were laughing, and all four had drinks, even the bartender, who had apparently been purchased a shot by the brown-haired man.

Lark hated schmoozers but had a grudging respect for the skill. She simply couldn't understand how some people made a thousand easy friendships without wondering where they'd lead or how long they'd last. Her plan for tonight, after enjoying her token drink in a token hotel bar, was to turn in early and be at her best for the pitch meeting that had brought her to Buffalo in the first place.

Except that she stayed for a second drink, watching in fascination as the brown-haired man made friends. He had an undeniable magnetism, and it was painfully obvious that both women would have slipped their room keys into his pants' front pockets if he'd given them the slightest provocation. They were probably his age or a little bit older, and he was probably—what, forties?—but he wasn't flirting with them. He was just . . . charming them. He didn't seem to be making an effort to keep it going, though, and eventually, with obvious regrets, the two women paid their tabs and left. Waste Management had already gone, too, and when the bartender went out into the room to bus some tables, Lark and the brown-haired man were alone.

Seeing to feel her looking at him, he turned and caught her. As a startlingly warm blush seared her face, he smiled, nodded, and turned back to the TV.

Why isn't he hitting on me? thought Lark, an embarrassing thought she'd tell no one ever. After all the needy drama that defined her relationship with Dylan, she definitely wasn't looking for anything, but she knew she was attractive, knew her face and breasts and blue-streaked shoulder-length black hair had an effect, mostly because men were so bad at disguising their interest.

Something she was apparently bad at, too.

Was she interested? Or was the second vodka soda simply doing its work?

"Keep staring at me and you're going to have to buy me a drink," the brown-haired man finally said, his eyes still on the TV and a sly smile in his voice.

Fuck it, she thought. Hotel bar in Buffalo. Have a drink with a good-looking man.

Sliding off her stool, she pushed her drink down the bar, leaving a snail trail of condensation behind, and sat down next to him.

He turned, grinned, and offered a hand to shake. "I'm Trip."

"Lark. I guess both our parents liked four-letter words."

That made him laugh. He had full lips, appealingly imperfect teeth, and a few threads of silver in his thick head of hair.

"Four-letter words are an essential component of parenting."

She wasn't about to ask him whether he had kids.

The bartender was back, hands spread on the bar, grinning like he thought he knew something.

"I'll have another," she said, pushing her half-full, half-melted drink toward him because she really didn't want to overdo it. "And whatever he's having."

As the bartender went away, Trip leaned in ever so slightly.

"I was wondering how long it would take you," he said, not quite making eye contact.

"You're pretty sure of yourself," she told him. What was it about him that made her lean in, too?

He shrugged. "Don't take that the wrong way. Nobody wants to spend an evening in Buffalo alone. Certainly no one should."

"Well, why didn't you say hi first?"

Trip studied his bottle of beer, rotating it slowly with his fingers. "Because I'm attracted to strong women. I wanted to see if you were one."

Her loss for words coincided perfectly with the bartender's return. Fortunately, Trip thanked him in a way that clearly disinvited him from joining the conversation, and the bartender sidled away and picked up his phone.

"What brings you to Buffalo?" he asked, angling his body so he was close but not intrusively so.

"Games," she blurted.

"Games?" he asked with a wry smile.

"I'm a . . . board game designer. A Hunter-Cash scout spotted one of my prototypes at a toy fair and invited me to come in and pitch it to them. I have a meeting tomorrow."

"So you'd be selling your idea to them?"

Lark sipped her drink. It was stronger than the last one, so either the bartender was pouring with a free hand or simply layering the vodka on top, hoping for a bigger tip. Which was a move she could appreciate from her waitressing days.

"I'm not sure they'll make an offer," she answered finally. "But that's why I'm here."

"Tell me about it," he said, looking actually interested.

Lark always hated this part. Sketching ideas, building prototypes, and watching people's kids interact with them was so much fun she never felt time passing. Pitching her creations to people who understood investment, marketing, and sales—and Trip looked like he came from that world—always made her feel dry mouthed. Like a kid who really didn't know how the world worked.

On the other hand, this was perfect preparation for tomorrow.

"It makes science fun for middle schoolers," she said after taking a deep breath. "I designed it specifically for girls, because I always wanted to be a scientist, but I struggled with math and science in school."

"So you created the tools?"

"I worked with some grad-student friends at UCLA who are studying how girls learn and came up with a board game that's also a chemistry set."

"Interesting concept."

He was doing a perfect job of listening even if his main goal was to get into her pants—the thought of which didn't sound nearly as bad to her as it should.

"There are very basic, nontoxic agents that combine in different ways to create different outcomes. The game itself is kind of like Life, where you're navigating a career, only here you're trying to become a successful scientist. At key points you win things you get to pour into your beaker. And when you complete the game, you get the activating ingredient that does something simple but cool, like making the solution change color, or give off a puff of smoke, or suddenly crystallize."

She liked the way Trip waited until he was sure she was done before he spoke. And when he did say something, it was another question, not a piece of advice or an excuse to turn the conversation back to himself.

"Can you play it more than once? Seems like it might be one and done."

One and done. Lark felt a pleasant shiver with the thought.

"There are different possible outcomes each time, and enough supplies for four players to play six times before you have to order a replacement pack or an upgrade. Most board games are only played several times after they're purchased anyway, so some parents may feel satisfied even if their kids only play once or twice."

"What do you call it?"

"Activate! There's probably a better name. I kept playing with the word *solution*, but I couldn't figure it out."

"Does it work?"

"Every time."

He tipped his beer bottle back and swallowed, then picked at the label while nodding thoughtfully. "I don't really know the market, but it sounds like a terrific idea. And from the sound of your voice, I sense you might have a hard time letting it go."

As if she had the financial freedom to turn down a reasonable offer. Now she was getting nervous about pitching, and she really didn't want to think about that right now.

"What do you do?" she asked.

Finally, he locked eyes with her. His brown irises were warm. "I could tell you, but I think we'd both be bored. And bored is the last thing I'm feeling right now." He paused. Smiled. "How about I tell you in the morning?"

∾

Lark woke panicked, her mouth dry and her head faintly throbbing: Was it her room or his? How much time did she have before her meeting?

A glance at her phone reassured her she had plenty of time, and a look around told her they were in her room. Her carry-on, never unpacked, lay neatly across the luggage caddy.

And Trip, whose last name she still hadn't learned, lay next to her, his breathing light and even. His clothes were draped over the chair on his side of the bed.

She had friends who would have felt a stab of shame: they may have proudly worn pink Pussyhats but still had internalized the patriarchal preaching that girls didn't do one-night stands. Lark was different. Her mom, a freethinker who'd written a book in the 1980s about feminist theory—a mostly forgotten tract for an academic press, but still a book—had told her since age sixteen that there was nothing wrong with having sexual desires and acting on them, as long as it was safely done. Which it had been. Twice.

What she'd *expected* to feel was a sense of having completed a dare in service of a story she might tell her roommate, Callie. She'd fucked a handsome salt-and-pepper guy in a hotel in Buffalo, of all places, and it was awesome. Anonymous hotel-room sex and the guy had actually been a considerate—no, incredible—lover.

What she was actually feeling was something different. Kind of— *god, don't think it*—a glow. A tingly combination of satisfaction and the lust for more.

She rolled onto her side so she could study him more closely.

He opened one eye. "Morning, Lark," he murmured, shifting toward her.

And not that a guy deserved credit for remembering her name, but at least he wasn't afraid to use it.

In the gray light seeping around the edges of the drapes, he looked a couple of years older than he had last night, and she could see there was a lot more salt in his stubble than there was in the hair on his head. His hair was flat on one side and wild on the other. But those eyes, crinkled around the edges.

That smile.

He threw back the covers and, with his fingers, traced the tattoos visible just over her left hip, then nudged her onto her stomach so he could see the full-color scene on her back. The whole thing—Mauna Kea and the rolling waves of the Big Island, done by an artist who specialized in the Japanese style—had cost three years and thousands of dollars but had been worth every sting and every cent. Trip, as far as she could tell, was uninked.

"I didn't get a good look at this last night," he murmured. "It's amazing."

"My dad grew up in Compton, and my mom grew up in Hilo," she told him, rolling back on her side. "I was born in Honolulu, but we moved to LA when I was little. A piece of my heart will always be in Hawaii, but I'm a California girl."

He grinned. "You're not like any California girl I've ever met."

She didn't even answer, just worked herself toward him, felt his insistent stiffening, and plucked another condom from the nightstand before climbing on top. Lark was not usually one for morning sex, for kisses laced with morning breath and for sheets smelling of sweat and alcohol. And they didn't kiss. Where last night's sex had been hot and frantic, despite his consideration, this morning they started slow, continued slow, and kept it going until she thought she was going to lose her mind.

If she was being honest, the thing that put her over the edge was the eye contact. Those penetrating brown eyes locked on hers and never looked away, never gave her a moment to suspect he was thinking about another girl or the meetings he had to have scheduled this morning. His eyes, his smile, and the achingly slow crescendo as they moved in unison.

He finished first but she was close, riding him, grinding against him, gripping his arms tighter and tighter until she finally came, surprising them both with a cry of relief and delight that quickly became happy laughter as she collapsed against his chest.

"Morning, Trip," she whispered.

They ordered room-service breakfast and Trip signed it to his room, explaining to the bellhop that yes, he knew which room he was in at the moment. Wearing robes, they set the tray between them, fluffed up the pillows, and reclined while they worked their way through coffee and orange juice, toast, and mixed fruit, with a side of eggs and bacon for Trip. The toast was cold and the fruit was hard and flavorless, but Lark wolfed it down, hungrier than she'd been in months.

She remembered her last breakfast with Dylan, the day she'd finally told him to move out. He'd been stringing her along for months as their relationship deteriorated, always insisting he was just about to land a job or sell his screenplay, until she began to suspect he hadn't been trying at all and had simply been hoping she would have a change of heart. At their usual Saturday-morning spot, he ordered french toast smothered in syrup with a side of sausage patties—the same thing he'd had every single time for two and a half years—and she suddenly realized he would never change. She wanted a larger world, and he was content on her couch.

Despite Callie's insistence that Lark pursue what she called "rebound sex," last night and this morning represented her first intimacy since Dylan. It was both a huge relief and a dramatic improvement.

"You said last night you'd tell me in the morning what you do for a living," she said, after washing down a bite of toast with orange juice.

"Can we just say I work with money?" he asked, sipping coffee.

She shook her head. "Not good enough. You could be an accountant or a bank robber, for all I know."

He chuckled. "Lots of people who work in the financial field are bank robbers, even if they don't wear masks. Fortunately, I get to give people money more often than I take it away."

"How does that work?" Lark asked.

"I made a little bit of money running a hedge fund, but I didn't love the work. Now I'm a venture capitalist."

Lark felt her stomach drop a little. The whole time she'd been blathering on about her big idea, she'd been talking to someone who knew the ins and outs of business better than she ever would. It was like being on a hidden-camera version of *Shark Tank*. He'd probably dismissed her as someone who had no idea what she was doing.

"Although I prefer the term *angel investor*," he added. "It makes me sound a lot nicer."

She liked the way he reached out and absentmindedly touched her hair as he said it, as if he wasn't really thinking about what his fingers were doing.

"And who are you investing in here in Buffalo?" she asked.

"A tech start-up that has a real chance of crashing within eighteen months."

"So you're passing?"

"My plan was to hear the rest of what they have to say before I fly back this afternoon."

"Where to?"

"Chicago. You?"

"LA."

"Lovely Lark from LA. One of these days, we'll need to get on a last-name basis. What time are you pitching?"

"One thirty. I have a five-thirty flight."

"Plenty of time."

"For what?"

He lifted the tray, their plates half-empty but both of them obviously finished, and carried it over to the desk. "To see the sights."

"Of Buffalo?"

"I hope you like hot wings." He unlocked his phone and began typing with his thumbs.

"I'm vegetarian—well, pescatarian."

He glanced up and grinned. "Of course you are."

"So you have a meeting this morning?" she asked, cringing at the way it reminded her of Dylan, who would ask misleading questions instead of just coming out and saying, *I wish you could stay.* By the end, she was responding not to his words but what she assumed he meant, which to a stranger would have sounded like a mash-up of two unrelated conversations. Which wasn't totally inaccurate.

Trip came over and kissed her firmly on the lips, looking into her eyes the whole time.

"I just canceled. I told them there's an emergency and I have to leave right away."

"But there isn't?"

"The real emergency is my need for a shower," he said, kissing her again.

Opening the nightstand drawer, he put his phone inside and closed it before heading to the bathroom, dropping his robe on the way.

Meticulous, she thought distractedly, half hoping to see some blue-ink tattoo on his back, something corny like a lizard or a Woody Woodpecker but a sign he'd had a wild side in college. His skin, however, was unadorned. The good news was, despite some weathering that proved he was indeed older than her, his skin was taut, his midsection was pretty flat, and his butt wasn't half-bad.

Lark waited until he had the shower going and steam was wisping over the curtain before she dropped her own robe and went to join him.

～

"So where are we going?" she asked as Trip put the car in gear. They had both checked out of the hotel, and her bag was nestled next to his in the trunk of his rental car. He had been coy about their destination, asking only if she was up for an adventure. She was.

"Road trip."

"What about your flight?"

"It's a really short road trip. But I rebooked on the three o'clock."

"And where are we going?"

"You'll see. Want to put some music on?"

The radio stations were all awful, and by the time she got her phone synced with the car and had selected some music she thought Trip could handle, she had figured out their destination, because the signs for Niagara Falls were hard to miss. Most of the hotels on Niagara Falls Boulevard were the usual chains clumped at every interstate exit ramp, but there were still a couple of down-market budget motels advertising honeymoon suites.

"Don't people wait until after they get married to come here?" she asked sarcastically.

"It's either this or hot wings, Lark. Buffalo's attractions are many, but they aren't endless."

They parked, bought tickets, and drank bad coffee while they waited for the next departure of the *Maid of the Mist*. Trip apologized and stepped away for a few minutes to make a work-related phone call and send a few quick emails. Lark stared out at the river. It was chilly and gray, with a slight drizzle, and it looked as though the boat was going to be practically empty.

When he came back and suggested they wait at a nearby café table, Lark wasn't sure how they should sit. Across from or next to each other? Should they hold hands? She would have been happy however but didn't want to push things. Trip solved the problem by sitting next to her, comfortably nearby but not right on top of her.

"Last night, when you saw me looking at you, what did you think?" she asked.

"I thought I probably reminded you of someone you knew," he said lightly.

"You don't remind me of anyone I've ever met," she told him, half quoting his line from earlier that morning.

"Glad to hear it."

"You're also lying."

He turned and looked at her, cocking an eyebrow. "I like to think I make a unique impression."

"I think you know exactly what effect you have on people."

"You give me too much credit," he said, smiling.

She kissed him. "But I like that you're humble."

Finally, it was time to board the boat. They walked up the short gangplank, accepted bright-blue ponchos from a bored-looking steward, and made their way to the front, where they'd been told they'd have the best vantage point.

They made small talk, commenting on the scenery and the other tourists as the boat moved away from the dock.

When the falls came into view, Trip asked, "So what will you do if they pass on your idea?"

"Get some gig work to tide me over. Decide which toy fairs I want to go to. Think about updating my website. Keep pitching."

She didn't bother to explain she'd charged this whole trip on a credit card that was already carrying a significant balance. Paying that off would be a victory in itself.

The volume of the cascading water forced both of them to raise their voices.

"Maybe you're not thinking big enough," he said, leaning in so his mouth was close to her ear.

"Big for me would be to license it myself, but I don't have much of a track record, so if they like it and they offer to buy it outright—"

"Do you want to sell it to them?"

"I have other ideas. And who knows? Maybe this one's no good, and it's better to let someone else take the financial hit."

"Do you really think the idea's no good?"

"Honestly? No, but I need investors and stuff. My parents certainly don't have that kind of cash. My mom teaches community college, and my dad is the operations manager for a construction company."

"What if I offered to be your first investor?"

She could now barely hear him over the roaring falls, but she would have had a delayed reaction even in a quiet room. Her excitement at the words was tempered by a sudden stab of suspicion.

"Are you serious?" she asked, hardly able to process his words.

Trip nodded.

"We just met, and now you want to give me money? I like you a lot, Trip, but . . ."

But what kind of guy offered someone money in the morning? What kind of girl took it? Her head was spinning, and the motion of the boat and the noise of the falls made it even harder to think clearly.

"But what? Tell me what you're worried about."

"You're kind of freaking me out. Is this what you do? You just hand out checks?"

The falls were fully in view, frothing white cataracts that held the rapt attention of the two dozen other people on board. But Trip stared only at her.

"If I could front you something, ten or twenty thousand to start, would that give you the breathing room to take yourself seriously?"

Lark shook her head. "Yes, of course. But is this a date or a business meeting? I have no idea if I want to see you again—if you want to see me—so adding money to the equation just makes it weird."

"It's only weird if we make it weird. The business side of the arrangement will be just that."

"And the personal side?"

"Totally separate."

Lark stared at him, unable to process it.

He squeezed her shoulder and kissed her cheek. "Zero pressure. Think about it. And see what happens in your meeting later. But don't miss the view."

They turned and looked as the boat sailed into the mist boiling off the falls. Her face and fingers felt cold and raw, but inside she was burning up.

Wrapping their arms around each other's crinkly plastic ponchos, they hugged tightly as the water poured down around them.

As the boat chugged away, a ray of sun broke through the clouds and made a dazzling rainbow, prompting oohs and aahs and scattered applause from the other passengers.

"That is gorgeous," said Trip. "Do you want to take a selfie? I understand if you want to keep this private."

She took a breath, considering. "I'm single. You're . . . you're single, right?"

"As can be."

Feeling light and happy, laughing, she nodded. They took selfies with both of their phones. Trip shared his on Instagram, which he confessed was new to him—he had "never been much of a social media guy but decided to try"—and she shared hers on Instagram and Twitter. Neither of them was on Facebook. They followed each other on Instagram and then stowed their phones before the water ruined them completely.

Her caption, because she wanted to play it cool and not give too much away, was, *Sometimes you go to a business meeting and end up on a boat with a new friend.*

She didn't see his until she was waiting at the gate for her flight to board.

People say you can't find the end of the rainbow. Not true.

Chapter Two

Jessica

It's not who you are now, but who you have the guts to become.

—"How I Lied about My Name and Discovered My Truth,"
a TED Talk by Jon M. Wright

Spontaneous. Adventurous. Intrepid.

Three adjectives no one would ever have associated with Jessica Meyers.

Calculating, cautious, and *circumspect* had always been her jam.

Yet here she was in Chicago, for the first time ever, creeping around the truck that blocked the one open spot on the street in front of her new place in Lakeview. The building, a converted three-story warehouse made of rough gray stone, was a far cry from the charming redbrick walk-up she'd envisioned. Then again, after Jon told her he'd signed the lease, she had promised him she wouldn't google the address, that she'd let the whole experience unfold *spontaneously.* And why not? The last year and a half had shown her that sometimes life's unpredictability was better than anything you could plan for yourself.

Jessica pulled into the lot behind the building, which seemed far too small to accommodate every resident. The only two open spaces were located beneath a sign warning: **ASSIGNED PARKING ONLY! WE TOW IMMEDIATELY!** Stopping in front of the dumpster, she jotted a note saying she was moving in, flipped on her hazards, grabbed a laundry basket full of clothes, and hoped for the best. Despite the circumstances and the blustery weather, it was hard not to be hopeful as she took the key out of her purse. Jon had overnighted it to her in a box gift wrapped with a repeating pattern of colorful little houses and tied with a bow.

The tag hanging from the key was scribbled with his adorably illegible writing:

The key is to let your heart rule your head.

He knew her too well.

Little about her current reality tracked with the life plan she'd written in fifth grade for a class assignment. The essay, which she'd titled *What I'm Destined to Be and Why* (it had earned her an A-plus), had ameliorated an already budding concern about her future by providing an easy-to-follow blueprint: *Good grades in high school! Harvard, Stanford, Yale, or best possible college! Medical school! Doctor who helps kids with cancer!!!*

Other than a storybook wedding, which her recklessly confident grade school self had planned for the day after med school graduation—having failed to take into account the aching loneliness that endless study, impossible hours, and the grind of residency would exact on her ability to find a suitable mate—Jessica had followed her childhood plan to a T.

And then Jonathan Wright III, MD, PhD, had come along and shattered her painstakingly curated black-and-white reality, offering an opportunity to cross the last item off her list in an entirely different way than she'd imagined. Charming, brilliant, and rich, he'd recruited her for his hush-hush start-up, a private-equity moon shot developing an easy-to-swallow diagnostic tool to detect childhood cancers before Stage 0 and save untold thousands of young lives.

Though she'd been attracted to him the moment she'd first laid eyes on him, the idea they might actually fall in love had been the furthest thing from her mind. Sitting in an auditorium at the Mayo Clinic in Phoenix while he shared his audacious vision, she'd been focused on his brilliance. A chance meeting at the reception following his lecture had sparked a connection that was undeniably electric. The days they'd spent together were the most alive she'd ever felt—the weeks apart made that much harder once she knew what she was missing.

And then, without warning, he'd said, "Come to Chicago. I need you here. I need you in my life."

Dangling the promise of both student-loan-payoff-level money and the chance to work on a team developing the technology to diagnose childhood cancer before it even happened, he had talked her into withdrawing her acceptance from a fellowship at Duke.

She had been looking forward to meeting Jon at the door of the apartment where they would begin their new life together—until this morning, when he'd texted, *Meeting's running long. I have to take a later flight, but I'll call when I'm on my way. XO.*

As she had replied from the road to ask for a more precise ETA, she realized her off-brand USB cord, which worked only intermittently anyway, had stopped charging entirely somewhere near the Iowa-Illinois border. The phone had died before she could hit "Send," and she'd made the rest of the drive to Chicago accompanied only by the voices of rural radio stations.

Jessica hated to cross the threshold without him, but as she entered the gleaming white lobby and noted the modern artwork, sleek furniture, and slate-tile floor, she was too excited to wait. Besides, she probably had fifteen minutes to get her car unpacked before it was ticketed, towed, and incarcerated in some sort of Chicago parking prison.

She rode the elevator to the second floor. Having spent the first few years of her thirties living in a worn beige block of apartments in a cookie-cutter Arizona development, she'd been craving character and charm, and probably would have picked out something different. On the other hand, she didn't miss the musty, commingled odor created by years of cooking and human habitation. She also liked the wide hallway, the high ceiling, and the two skylights that illuminated the path to 205 despite the overcast afternoon.

There was a note taped to the door.

For a moment, she wondered if Jon had arrived before her after all and had some sort of surprise planned. Maybe a romantic scavenger hunt leading to what was destined to become their new favorite coffee place?

As she took another step closer, she realized the logo at the top of the page had also been painted on the truck blocking the front of the building: Chicagoland Rent-to-Own.

Please call our office to reschedule your furniture delivery.

"Shit!" echoed down the hallway as she dropped the laundry basket by the door and veered into the nearby stairwell. All her furniture was thrift store and hand-me-down IKEA, so she'd gifted it to an incoming resident at the hospital and kept only what she could fit in her car. Jon had promised to furnish their new apartment and make arrangements with the movers.

Jessica knew he was starting from scratch, too, but *rental furniture?*

Another question for her growing list.

She flew down the stairs and sprinted across the lobby, but as she burst through the front door, the truck was already moving away down the block. She raced after it, the gusty wind and spattering raindrops chilling her skin.

Thanks to Chicago traffic, perhaps the first and last time she'd think *that*, the truck slowed to a stop fifty feet away.

Jessica caught up and rapped on the window.

"I just missed you!" she said, pointing back toward her building. "Apartment 205!"

The driver looked at her in surprise before cracking the window. "We had the code to the building but no key to the unit. We tried to call."

"My phone is dead and my boyfriend is on a flight," Jessica told him. "Would you come back? Please?"

His hulking partner, who looked like a former football player whose muscles were turning to fat, shrugged and said, "Gotta be done by six."

"It'll take us five or ten to get back around the block," added the driver resignedly.

"I really appreciate this," Jessica said, glad she had cash for a tip and a few minutes to take in the apartment before they arrived.

She headed back, detouring into the parking lot to check on her car and grab her finicky charger and a couple of boxes. She reentered the warm lobby and called the elevator, which arrived quickly—another promising sign.

Finally, she put her key in the door and entered her apartment. *Their* apartment.

It was simply stunning. A cozy warm-gray entryway opened into a big airy space, with a white open-concept kitchen/dining area (complete with quartz countertops and stainless steel appliances) on the left and an oversize living room on the right. Between them, metal-railed stairs led to an open second-level hallway that overlooked the living area and two-story floor-to-ceiling windows.

Jessica made her way to the upper level, where there was a roomy master bedroom with both a walk-in closet and an en suite bathroom with a double-sink vanity. The other doors along the hallway revealed a guest bedroom, a laundry closet with washer and dryer, and a full guest bathroom. There was even a charming office nook complete with a built-in desk.

While she was flipping a light switch that didn't seem to work, the movers arrived. She let them in and showed them around while still taking everything in herself, from the dramatic dark floors to the genuine wood-burning fireplace.

"Layout seems self-explanatory," said the big guy, whose uniform name patch identified him as Darnell.

"We'll start bringing everything in," said the driver, a.k.a. Steve.

"I have a few more boxes to bring up, and I need to move my car," she told them. "I'll leave the door open so you can come and go."

"Hurry back, so you can tell us where you want everything."

Since everything they were about to bring in had been chosen by Jon, she hoped he'd be arriving soon. She fished a charging block out of her bag, plugged it into a wall outlet, and fiddled with both ends of the USB cord.

No luck.

She went down to get another load from her trunk before the movers came back.

It was raining harder now, so she moved the car to the building's back entrance and shuttled the remainder of her worldly belongings inside.

Permanent parking? moved to the top of the list of her questions for Jon as she circled the block, looking for a spot that was both open and free of resident-only restrictions. She finally found one two blocks away.

She grabbed the jean jacket she'd left on the passenger seat, covered her head, and ran back to the building. Picking up two suitcases, she was grateful she'd included some bath towels among the few household items she'd brought.

Jessica reached the elevator at the same time as the movers and squeezed in with them.

"It says we're supposed to have two club chairs, but there were three on the truck," Darnell said, handing her a manifest.

She examined the list of furniture as they walked down the hall together and entered the apartment.

"I need to call my boyfriend to find out what he ordered. Do you have a USB cord I can borrow to charge my phone?"

"Sure, but I don't think it's going to help," Steve said, flipping a nearby light switch up and down a few times. "Your utilities aren't on yet."

"They were supposed to be," she said.

Darnell handed her his phone.

She thanked him, dialed Jon, and got his voice mail.

In what she hoped was a breezy tone, she left a message inquiring about the furniture order, asking if he knew when the power was scheduled to go on, wondering when he thought he would arrive, and suggesting where he might find parking when he did.

Then she dialed ComEd to see about the power.

She waited on hold long enough that she was able to direct the movers while they positioned an admittedly attractive navy blue, mid-century-style velvet couch and two tweedy charcoal club chairs in the living room. When the customer-service representative finally came on the line, he informed her that the power was indeed scheduled to go on today, but she needed to be patient because it was October first.

"Why does the date matter?" Jessica asked.

"October first and May first are the busiest days of the year in the Chicago rental market," the rep said, in a tone suggesting Jessica was the only person on earth unaware of that fact. "There's always a backlog."

For the next hour, she brought up boxes and began to unpack while overseeing the placement of two area rugs, a distressed-wood dining room table with six upholstered chairs, a master bedroom set featuring a sleigh bed, matching dressers and nightstands, and accent lamps she would very much have liked to turn on given the intensifying gloom outside.

She didn't know what to expect for the guest bedroom but assumed Jon would have chosen bunk beds in whichever configuration worked best for his three kids—a son, Logan, who was in grade school; Paige, a middle schooler; and high schooler Ava. When the movers brought only a single queen mattress, she felt, she had to admit, a sense of relief that he wasn't planning overnights anytime soon. In the abstract, she loved children. She was absolutely passionate about treating and curing sick kids. But she had never really known how to be anything other than a medical professional diagnosing and treating their symptoms. As an only child who'd never done a single hour of babysitting, she had no model or instinct for cooing to a baby, handling the incessant questions of a fourth grader, or disciplining a teenager who'd blown curfew. The very thought of doing those things made her nervous. She knew she would figure out how to be with Jon's kids, but she was more than content to wait awhile.

Having made the executive decision that the third club chair was sent in error, Jessica signed the delivery order, gave the movers a healthy tip, and sent them on their way. In the sudden quiet, she felt lonely, and more than a little worried. Jon hadn't appeared yet, and the rain had turned to sleet. She pictured cars sliding off the Chicago expressways—or into each other.

She had to charge her phone. Dashing out to a nearby Walgreens she'd seen earlier, just this side of the elevated tracks where trains rumbled overhead, she literally ran the whole way but still got plenty wet. Thankfully, they had not only USB cords but a functional outlet right outside the restroom.

With the first sign of a charge, her phone began to ping wildly. There were texts from Jon, the movers, and her mother, who wrote, *Are you there yet?? Can't relax until I know you're safe.*

She went straight to the messages from Jon.

Back in Chicago, but Annie Wilkes is in rare form. Halfway to you but had to pull over to mediate a family situation via group chat. Ugh. Wish I didn't have to engage but don't have a choice.

Despite her annoyance at the delay, she couldn't help but chuckle. Jon often referred to his estranged, soon-to-be ex-wife, Holly, by the nickname Annie Wilkes—the "hobbler" from *Misery.* The two of them had been living separate lives for years, but he had to maintain a certain air of business-as-usual with the family or she went off the rails—sometimes for days.

Don't worry about the power, we'll keep each other warm until it comes on, he added. *Also, there are only supposed to be two chairs.*

There were more updates as he covertly texted her while dealing with a situation that must have been severely taxing his patience, especially today.

Glad I'm not out at the house. Can't run away on broken ankles ;-p
Have to keep reminding myself I'm doing this for the kids.
OK, I'm on my way.

Jon was patient, kind, and generous to her, and an utterly devoted father. Jessica had endured the entrances and exits of multiple stepfathers in her life and understood the emotional toll of divorce only too well. Her mother always swore that a new "beau" was the only way to truly move on. Hopefully, *Annie* would find someone soon.

While her phone was still plugged in, Jessica needed to let her mother know she'd arrived safely—or she'd no doubt have the Illinois Highway Patrol out looking for her. As she was texting to let her know the trip had been smooth, the apartment was amazing, and photos would have to wait until she could fully charge her phone, a new text alert pinged.

I'm here. Where are you?

∼

Textbook Jon, Jessica thought as she opened the door and saw the warm, flickering light of a pillar candle set in a previously unnoticed alcove by the door. Three more candles lit the way from the breakfast bar to the living room, where a fire was already starting to heat the chilly room.

Jon met her at the bottom of the stairs, also candlelit, and took her newly purchased umbrella before greeting her with a long, passionate kiss. "Welcome home."

The way he had transformed the cold, dark apartment in such a short time was nothing short of magic.

"Welcome home yourself," she said, kissing him again.

"It's been a long day," they said simultaneously before laughing together.

"I'm so sorry I wasn't here to help," Jon said, wiping a raindrop off her cheek. "I hated to miss it. Will you let me make it up to you?"

"I'll think about it," she teased him, taking in the bottle of champagne, two glasses, and what appeared to be half the takeout section of Whole Foods, all laid out on a blanket in front of the hearth.

"Let me start," he said, removing her damp jean jacket, "by getting you out of these cold, wet clothes." He moved on to her blouse, kissing her skin beneath each button as he unfastened it.

She shivered more from desire than cold, particularly after he unbuttoned her jeans, pushed them to the floor, and paused to admire the leopard-print bra and matching panties she'd bought in anticipation of this moment.

"My brilliant brunette bombshell."

Jessica had grown up thinking she was merely ordinary, nice-enough looking but with nothing to make her stand out. In recent years, however, introversion and interminable hours had bred an aching loneliness that left her wondering if there was actually something inherently objectionable about her.

Until Jon came along and convinced her otherwise.

Instead of tearing off her panties and ravishing her, the next thing she knew he was wrapping her in a delightfully warm blanket he'd placed nearby.

"I'm starving," he said, flashing a wry smile. "And if I had to wager a guess, you're even hungrier."

"Famished," she said, her voice suddenly husky.

"Just how I like you," he said, firelight sparkling in his eyes. He took her hand and led her to the picnic he'd created.

As they worked their way through a delicious hodgepodge of everything from cheese and crackers to lemon-herb salmon, they paused to make toasts to Jessica's arrival in Chicago, to Jon's great taste in apartments—and to their future together, both personally and professionally.

Jessica bit into a dark-chocolate-dipped strawberry and lifted her glass. "And here's to attractive rental furniture."

"I'll drink to that," Jon agreed, clinking her glass and looking around. "It's nicer than I expected."

"I guess I sort of assumed you were bringing your own furniture when you said you had the basics covered, though."

"I thought I was," he said, shaking his head. "Annie Wilkes definitely felt otherwise—strongly enough that she had her lawyer inform me. I decided to save my battles for something more valuable than a couch, some chairs, and a bed or two."

"Are the kids doing okay?" Jessica asked, wishing her motive were entirely altruistic and not a slightly sneaky way to inquire about the guest bedroom setup.

"That's what she was raging about today," he said, his voice cracking a little. "She insists they won't be staying overnight anywhere. Looks like I'm going to have to spend more time at the house than I expected, at least for the foreseeable future."

"I want you to be there for them," Jessica said. She should have felt worse about this development than she did. "Things will change once a judge realizes how wacko she is."

Jon looked as though the weight of the world had been lifted from his shoulders. "You're so fucking awesome."

She felt ever-so-slightly guilty about his grateful smile. "I know how important you are to your kids."

"I have no idea how I could function without you," he said, raising his glass. "To us."

They toasted, kissed, and toasted again.

"I hope you didn't have to run out of there empty-handed," Jessica said. "Did you bring anything with you at all?"

"I have a few things in my car," he said. "I'll grab them later."

"Oh shoot," she said. "Where did you park?"

"In the lot."

"You better move now. You'll get towed."

"Not from one of our spaces."

"We have parking?"

"Right next to each other, just outside the back door."

"I parked two blocks away thinking—"

"No need to think right now," he said, putting down his champagne, taking her hand, and pulling her toward him.

"Why didn't you tell me?"

"Why don't you tell me what you'd like me to do to you?" he asked. "I've been hard as a rock since I saw that incredibly sexy bra and panties."

Chapter Three

HOLLY

But being bold doesn't mean there won't be risk—strap
on that helmet.

—"How I Lied about My Name and Discovered My Truth,"
a TED Talk by Jon M. Wright

Appearances were important, which was why Holly never went riding in jeans and an old T-shirt but always put on riding pants, boots, a formfitting jacket, and a helmet. Yes, she knew that made her a caricature to her neighbors and even her kids—Barrington Hills Horse Lady—but she had a bigger agenda than impressing the local dunderheads or her own easily embarrassed children. The horses she rode needed all the positive PR they could get.

As luck would have it, this morning offered its own reminder of why she did what she did. After a raw, unseasonably cold handful of days, the sun had come out, the air had warmed and stilled, and early October was showing its kinder side. Holly supposed they might be in for a spell of what she was sure they were no longer allowed to call Indian summer. Shortly after dawn, while Jack was still in bed and

Galenia was cooking breakfast and packing lunches for Ava, Logan, and Paige, Holly had stolen out to the stable, saddled her blaze-faced bay, Wags—named for his twitchy tail—and cantered around the pasture a few times before deciding on a slightly longer ride.

They were clopping alongside the all-but-empty road when they were both startled by the nearly silent passing of Theresa Yadao's silver Tesla. Wags spooked, crow-hopping and nearly throwing Holly, who even as she fought to keep him under control still saw Theresa shaking her head, her eyes invisible behind huge black sunglasses.

Reining Wags in, Holly patted his neck and cooed to him as the Tesla glided away like some sinister hovercraft. Then, without thinking, she gave her horse a gentle nudge with her heels, flicked the reins, and shouted, "Hah!" as she galloped off in pursuit.

Like a dog chasing a car, Holly had no idea what she'd do if she actually caught Theresa. But the entitled bitch had scared her horse, and Holly was pissed off. Maybe she wanted to give Theresa a scare, too—or at least a piece of her mind.

She almost caught the car, but Theresa saw them coming in her side-view mirror, and instead of slowing at the stop sign, she sped up, rolled through it, and turned left, her car disappearing into the gently rolling hills. No doubt on a coffee run. Maybe an early yoga class. The adrenaline still surging in her veins, Holly imagined riding into town, tying Wags to a parking meter as if she were in some western, and slapping the Frappuccino out of her enemy's hand. Better yet, slapping *her*.

But no. Of course not. Holly slowed again and turned the opposite direction. Ironically, if she'd been able to use the bridle path she and Theresa were warring over, she wouldn't have been near the road at all. Theresa and her husband, Larry, had bought a sprawling colonial on ten acres of prime pasture—but the only animals to use that grass were two massive, shaggy Bernese mountain dogs who barked at cars and horses and left massive piles of poop that were never picked up. The Yadaos, upon learning the previous owners had granted the village an easement at the back of their property for a planned bridle path extension, had tried to reverse that decision, citing their need for privacy and decrying what they viewed as an ironically socialist land grab by a few wealthy elites.

Never mind the fact that they were all wealthy elites—why else would they live where they did?—this left Holly with a larger question: Why move to horse country if you hated horses?

Holly and Jack had moved here specifically for Holly's horses, so she wouldn't have to commute out of the city every day just to ride and care for them. And her horses needed love more than most: before she found them, they were castoffs, unwanteds, candidates for rendering or zoo meat. She'd never understood the obsession with Arabians and Thoroughbreds when there were so many beautiful, unloved animals just waiting for a patient owner to bring them back to full health and fitness.

Besides Wags, she had Alderman, a formerly obese quarter horse who was finally shedding the gut acquired by years of poor diet and neglect. There was Royal, her underfed paint, who still wouldn't let anyone ride her. Silk Purse and Sow's Ear were two quarter horses she'd rescued from a situation of extreme neglect downstate—Holly still shuddered when she pictured the owner's home, which had been even more disgusting than the confined horses' stalls. And Mini-Me, her miniature, had formerly been owned by a family under the misapprehension that it was a house pet, not an actual horse. (Although, truth be told, Mini-Me did live in the backyard, not with the rest of the horses.) Easy Rider, a Tennessee walker, was her only horse who'd never faced adversity, but she had always thought it wise to have a mount for guests—and her husband.

Jack was not a horse person but joked to their friends that he was a "Holly person," and over the course of their marriage had not only tolerated but encouraged her lifelong passion, from their move to what passed for the country in Greater Chicagoland to his significant financial support of her charity, Horse Stability, which last year had raised more than $400,000 to support horse rescue and adoption. Holly had long hosted school groups so kids could meet the horses and take brief rides on the gentlest ones, but her amazing volunteer, Brian Fredericksen, had encouraged her to dream big and plan carefully. Horse Stability's new ten-year plan included a short bridle path connecting Holly's barn directly to the local park district riding center, an after-school program where teens learned to gentle and work with rescue horses, and, finally, a stable on Chicago's South Side, bringing a taste of the country to kids who never left the city limits.

Sometimes it seemed as though the smallest victory would be the hardest one to achieve: extending the bridle path behind the Yadao mansion. If she was really going to offer her rehabilitated horses for community use, it only made sense to connect her own land to the village's riding center and the network of public and private trails beyond. But the Yadaos were doing everything in their power to keep that from happening.

The short gallop and the rising sun had her scalp sweating under her helmet; a quick glance at her watch made her realize she had to turn around if she was going to see the kids before they headed off to school. Jack would probably miss it: his East Coast trip had lasted several days longer than he'd told her it would, and she'd already been dozing off when he'd arrived last night. If past form was any indication, he'd sleep until midmorning, spend an hour working out, and then head to his office in the city.

Which was fine. Between a half day of seeing patients at the pediatric clinic, lunch with a friend, and after-school chauffeuring duties, Holly had more than enough to fill her day. She saw kids only two days a week at the practice she'd founded and always looked forward to it. She dealt mostly in annual checkups and sick visits, counseling parents on coughs, colds, fevers, acne, and head lice. Boring and pleasantly routine.

Wags had clearly been unsettled by both the encounter with Theresa and Holly's impulsive decision to give chase—something she now regretted both for the horse's sake and ongoing diplomatic efforts with the Yadaos. She baby-talked him all the way home, even singing "I Ride an Old Paint," a cheesy song that was all she could think of on the spur of the moment. He calmed somewhat, although behind her she could feel his tale swishing erratically from side to side.

As she led him through the gate to their paddock, she saw Alderman waiting stubbornly by the feeder for her to fork out some hay, and Royal shaking flies off her head in a far corner. Silk Purse and Sow's Ear trotted together, the siblings still playful, as if they couldn't believe they'd finally escaped confinement. She couldn't keep them all, of course, but she took satisfaction in the time she spent with them and the fact that they'd leave her for good homes.

And, sadly, there were always more poor and neglected horses to replace them.

Leading Wags into the barn and then to his stall, Holly took off his bridle and put on his halter. She tied him to a ring and, feeling hot, hung her helmet and jacket on a peg outside before removing his saddle and pad. Working the currycomb along his neck and flanks, she continued to coo to him, reassuring him that all was well, and there would be no more surprises in his day.

When the comb slipped out of her hand and landed in the straw by his back legs, she didn't even think about it as she bent down to pick it up, keeping one hand on his broad, muscled flank. In an instant, Wags spooked, turned, and kicked with his back hooves, one of them pounding the side of the stall so loudly it sounded like a gunshot, the other glancing off her temple.

She fell hard and stared confusedly at her hands in the straw while Wags bucked and whinnied above her. Only when another hoof landed on her thigh and made her shout in pain did she wake to the danger and start crawling away.

Thankfully, she'd left the stall door open, so she was able to slip out and push it closed from the outside. She reached up dizzily and slid the bolt home, then collapsed again, sitting with her back to the stall door. Inside, Wags snorted and turned restlessly.

"Wags, why?" she croaked, knowing her feeling of betrayal was senseless, that horses were all instinct, and it was foolish to ascribe human emotions to them. The fault was hers and hers alone, for not being more careful, for assuming he'd progressed further than he had.

She'd been injured before—usually with horses, once in a car accident—and was familiar with the sense of unreality, the confusion caused by the adrenaline. But this felt like something different. Her decision to walk out of the stable was immediately countered by the realization that she was still sitting on the floor; her intention to rise to her feet was stymied by a sudden feeling of near immobility.

After reaching in her pocket for her phone, she stared at the lock screen, unable to remember her passcode, before putting it away.

A word came to mind, flitting away before she could grab it: *concussion.*

No. She was just stunned. She needed to give herself a minute.

Retrieving her phone, she looked at the time: 7:10. She resolved to give herself ten minutes before getting on with her day.

At 7:22, Holly came through the back door, leaned heavily on the wall, and struggled out of her riding boots. Checking her appearance in the small mirror above the key hooks, she saw Wags had kicked her hair wildly askew but that her face was marked only by dirt, not bruising or blood. Her thigh throbbed with pain but took weight: with concentration, she could walk more or less normally. Fixing a smile on her face, she went into the kitchen, where Logan and Paige were finishing their meals at the breakfast bar. Three lunch sacks were zipped and waiting

on the end counter, and Galenia was loading the dishwasher, clattering the dishes in a way that made Holly wince.

"Morning, children," she said as brightly as she could manage. "Where's Ava?"

"Rabbit green urn," said Paige.

"I didn't get that," said Holly, confused and a little frightened she was mishearing things.

"Behind you," said her sixteen-year-old, entering from the hall and stuffing her lunch sack into an already overloaded backpack. She looked up from her phone. "God, Mom, what's with you? You look super pale."

"I do?" Holly asked. "I guess I'm feeling a little off. You're ready early."

"Riding with Sienna. She and Zoe want to study for the algebra test."

"Are you ready for the Shakespeare quiz, too?"

"Yes. Bye, Mom."

And with that, her oldest daughter dashed away, raven curls bouncing on her shoulders, key chain, water bottle, school lanyard, and headphone cord all dangling from her backpack.

Holly dropped onto a stool next to Logan and patted his hand, thinking she probably shouldn't get behind the wheel of a car right away. "Galenia, can you drive this morning? I'm not feeling well, and I think I need to lie down for a few minutes."

"That's fine, Mrs. Wright," said Galenia.

"Paige, do you have practice today for *The Music Man*?"

"He's a what? He's a what? He's a music man!" Paige sang energetically.

"Very funny." At least she'd heard that clearly. She kissed Paige and Logan on the tops of their heads and made her way through the dining room, into the living room, and lowered herself onto the couch. She would be fine, she was sure—Wags's hoof hadn't caught her square—but for the moment she thought it safest to remain upright and keep her eyes open.

The sound of Galenia getting the kids ready and out the door came to her as if down a tunnel. Her thoughts were flitting between Wags, Theresa, the after-school schedule, and Jack when the door slammed and finally the house grew quiet. She could feel her pulse throbbing in her aching thigh. *Ice,* she thought.

~

When she woke up, Jack was coming down the hall, talking on his phone. She must have drifted off, after all.

"I'm not paying you to find problems," he told someone. "I'm paying you to make them go away. Call me when you have."

She was struggling to sit up when he passed the living room doorway. Seeing her, he slid his phone into the pocket of his University of Chicago hoodie. He was still unshaven.

With effort, she smiled and pushed her hair back from her face.

"Why aren't you driving the kids?" he asked.

"I have a little bit of a headache, so I asked Galenia to do it."

Stretching, she swung her legs onto the floor, feeling a throb and noticing that her right pant leg was almost painfully tight. Her thigh was swelling. Her head was no longer pounding, but something told her not to move her neck too quickly. She felt fragile.

"Holly, what's wrong?"

"Wags," she told him, resigning herself to the truth. "I startled him in the stable, and he kicked me."

The look on his face was blink-and-miss-it, a small cloud sailing past the sun. Irritation, not concern.

"Where?"

She touched her temple.

He sat down and pulled his chair close. "Jesus, Holly. You weren't wearing your helmet? Look at me."

"I wore my helmet while I was riding," she said weakly.

"Well, that's fucking awesome," he muttered.

They locked eyes, and she knew he was staring at her pupils, checking to see if they were dilated or one was larger than the other.

"Did you black out or lose consciousness?" he asked, working through the concussion protocol.

"No," she answered.

"Do you remember everything that happened before and after he kicked you? Tell me."

She did remember and thought she did an excellent job of re-creating the scene for Jack, right down to the unreality of staring at her hands on the stable floor.

"Your speech isn't slurred," he said, nodding in satisfaction. "Any sensitivity to light or noise?"

"A little," she admitted.

"Did you throw up?"

She shook her head and realized she shouldn't have.

"Your head hurts," he said gently, touching her head with his fingertips and circling until he located the point of contact. "You're going to have one hell of a bump."

He stood and strode briskly out of the room. The freezer door snapped open, and she heard the rattle of ice cubes. Despite the reason, she enjoyed having his full attention. It was so rare these days.

He came back, screwing the cap onto an ice bag and handing it to her. He sat down, settled back in his chair, and studied her while she held the ice to her temple and felt the cool relief.

"You could get a CT scan, except I don't think there's a fracture, and bleeding seems unlikely. But we need to keep a close eye on your symptoms. Are you seeing patients today?"

"Just a few," she said.

"Cancel them. Take it easy."

"I will," she told him, knowing she wouldn't but liking that he wanted her to.

"He didn't kick you anywhere else, did he?" asked Jack suddenly.

"My leg, but it's fine."

He rolled his eyes. "You should have gone into mixed martial arts. You'd have been great at taking a beating."

He noted the swelling but was polite enough not to point out the obvious: she needed to ice that, too. Holly felt a warmth in her leg that could have been the injury but could also have been a wish that he would put his hand on her thigh and touch her tenderly.

"How was Buffalo?" she asked instead.

"A two-day trip that ended up being four? Remind me not to work with family foundations in the future. One of the brothers was having way too much fun dangling two-point-five mil over my head," he said. "And I *still* don't know if he's on board."

"Sounds like a pissing contest. Don't you usually win those?"

He grinned, and something stirred inside her, more than just fleeting arousal. Longing? Regret? After twenty-one years of knowing him, nineteen of those married, sometimes it was difficult to separate the two. Sometimes when she was riding, she liked to engage in a thought experiment. If she had known then what she knew now, would she still have made the same decisions—still put Jack's career first, still stayed married?

"Sometimes the way to win a battle isn't with a full-frontal assault," said Jack, laughing.

"You mean a charm offensive."

"Charm is never offensive, but once that fails, it's time for a strategic retreat. The fact that I acted like I don't need their money is the very thing that will make him insist I take it. You know, if I had realized I'd have to spend so much time in places like Buffalo, Scranton, and Phoenix, I might never have set out to cure cancer."

Which was a joke he'd made dozens of times before.

"I thought you said you wouldn't have to go to Phoenix every month anymore."

"No, that's right. I'm bringing some of that business in-house," he said.

"The kids will enjoy having you around more often," she said, idly wondering whether it was a business relationship that had ended or the other kind.

"And I'll enjoy that, too. But it's not like I'm suddenly off the road. I'm considering partnering with a West Coast lab to run some of our testing, and I'm going to spend some time at their facilities."

Remembering a previous West Coast project, Holly recalled the longer flights and hotel nights that had kept Jack away for additional weeks every year.

"So it's a wash," she said.

"It's an attractive proposition, but we're still in the courtship phase," he told her. "I have no idea if this one's going to work out or not."

Chapter Four

LARK

If you want something badly enough, you have to be in control of the process.

—"How I Lied about My Name and Discovered My Truth,"
a TED Talk by Jon M. Wright

Back home in LA, Lark knew she should have been over the moon to receive an offer from Hunter-Cash. And had that offer arrived before her encounter with Trip, she probably would have answered with an enthusiastic yes and signed the contract the same day—succumbing to the pressure of rent, credit card bills, student loans, and Callie. Especially Callie.

Callie had been completely on board and supportive of Lark's fling with the handsome older man. After all, she'd practically been pushing Lark into hot guys' laps ever since Lark broke things off with Dylan. But Callie stopped cold when Lark admitted she'd told Hunter-Cash she needed time to decide—hoping Trip would come through in the meantime and allow her to keep Activate! for herself.

"You spent money you don't even have to fly out there, they offered you money on the spot, and you told them you'd *think about it*?" groaned Callie as she drove Lark home from the airport that day. "Thirty thousand bucks goes a long way when you're living on credit."

"But thirty thousand bucks is all I'd ever get. Hunter-Cash wants to own the game, but Trip said he'd invest in me. What if it's my million-dollar idea?" countered Lark, ignoring a sick feeling and the scary thought: *What if I'm wrong?*

"I love you, Lark, but it just seems crazy to be talking about a million-dollar idea when you owe six figures in student loans, five figures in credit card debt, and four figures in rent and utilities."

Neither of them said anything as Callie gave her full attention to a lane change on the 405; Nebraska born and bred, Callie was as cautious a driver as she was fiscally responsible.

Lark couldn't blame her roommate for looking out for her. She had already been questioning her relationship with Dylan and planning to live with Callie when Dylan got fired from his entry-level job at a big consulting firm. In a moment of weakness, Lark had allowed him to move in, regretting the decision after Dylan said losing his job was "probably for the best, so I can focus on screenwriting." Callie had been forced to make other living arrangements until Lark had finally gotten Dylan out the door.

If anyone wanted to shoot holes in Lark's ability to make good decisions, nobody had more ammunition than Callie.

Moreover, while Lark told Callie almost everything, she couldn't admit that part of the excitement of being with Trip was his aura of effortless wealth. That he could so casually offer to invest ten or twenty thousand in her ideas suggested that he knew how these things worked and he knew how to help her make more. She had no intention of milking him for cash—the words *sugar daddy* made her want to vomit—but she thought she could learn a lot from him. Possibly including how to be a part of that high-stakes, moneyed world. So.

"There's nothing wrong with waiting a week or two," she said, once Callie had successfully merged onto Venice Boulevard. "For all Hunter-Cash knows, I could have a lawyer reading the fine print. I could have other offers."

"Do you know how much every week costs you in interest?" asked Callie. "Because I do."

"And do you know how much more money I could make if my game takes off, if *my company* takes off?" countered Lark.

"You have no idea if Trip's offer is real," said Callie, whose five-foot-nothing height forced her to peer over the steering wheel like a grandma. "You have no idea if he's real. You didn't even get his last name."

"He's real," insisted Lark, still able to summon the feeling of his stubble on her cheek, the soreness of her thighs.

Hoping desperately she was right.

That had been a week and a half ago. Since then, her contact at Hunter-Cash, a friendly but pushy guy named Zachary, had emailed her twice, asking whether she'd come to a decision and not too subtly hinting they were ready to move on.

Lark and Trip had texted just infrequently enough and just vaguely enough that Lark was starting to wonder if Callie was right about everything.

She had pored over his Instagram feed a half dozen times, looking for clues, but there wasn't much to see. He'd told her he was new to it, and he clearly wasn't lying. Following 178, 37 followers, and some of those were businesses in the cities where he'd checked in. Most of his twenty-three pictures were just hotel room views: *Good morning, New York! Looking good, Chicago! Hello, Phoenix!* Like a newbie, he was working his way through all the filters and editing options, color-saturating his skyline shots to the point of overkill. She found it endearing—his real-life suaveness definitely didn't translate to social media—if not at all revealing. And his Instagram handle, Triphammer312, told her little. She was pretty sure his last name wasn't actually Hammer. Because of course she'd googled it.

After a late-afternoon budget session during which Lark admitted she would have to start waitressing and driving Lyft again if she didn't accept the Hunter-Cash offer, Callie had proposed they stay in, watch Netflix, and cook their own dinner to save money. Listlessly, Lark agreed, meanwhile composing two different messages in her head. The first was a short text to Trip: *Did you mean what you said about investing in me, or was that just bullshit?* The second was an email to Zachary at Hunter-Cash that included the words, I am pleased to accept your offer. She couldn't bring herself to send the former, so she figured she'd probably send the latter in the morning.

Callie was chopping veggies for a stir-fry in the kitchen, and Lark was trying to will herself off the couch to help when her phone pinged.

It was Trip. *You free?*

She picked up and thumbed back. *To talk?*

For a date. I'm in LA.

What, now???

Picking up a rental. Meet me at Soyokaze?

Instead of replying, Lark jumped up, ran to the kitchen, and held her screen in front of Callie's face.

"Oh my god!" said Callie, seeming genuinely excited for her.

"Right?" said Lark, getting ready to answer *YES*.

"But you're not meeting him there," said Callie, putting a hand on Lark's arm.

"I'm not?"

Callie, left-handed, was still holding a knife, somehow managing to look protective of Lark and threatening toward Trip. "No. He's picking you up here. So I can meet him."

Lark felt a slow smile spread across her face as she bent over to give Callie a hug, wary of the blade. It didn't hurt anything to satisfy her roommate's curiosity and, truth be told, made Lark feel a tiny bit safer.

"Great idea," she murmured, breaking away and texting her reply. *Can you pick me up?*

His answer didn't come right away. In fact, it took long enough that she had circled the apartment three times, staring at the phone and waiting for the little bubble that indicated he was typing a reply.

Sorry, dealing with the clerk. Of course! Give me your address and I'm on my way.

Lark and Callie looked at each other, grinned, and then started jumping up and down. Then Lark stopped, looked down at her sweatpants and her POWERED BY PLANTS T-shirt. She touched her hair and felt the snarls.

"I've got to shower," she said, heading for the bathroom. "Sorry about dinner!"

Her hair was clean and dry, and she was wearing jeans and a cute silk top showing just a hint of cleavage. Underneath: matching bra and panties from Victoria's Secret, just in case. A wisp of the perfume she'd splurged on and never gotten to wear because Dylan had scent-sensitivity issues. Lark loved it because it made her think of lying in a king-size bed in Hawaii with the balcony doors flung open and the smell of fruit, flowers, and surf drifting in from outside. Even though she'd been born there and her mom was Hawaiian, she'd been back only a handful of times after they moved to the mainland when she was eleven. Her biracial father, born and raised in Compton before he shipped out in the navy, felt more comfortable in California. Amazingly, her parents were still together and living happily in the Valley, something few of her friends could say about theirs.

Callie sat on the couch, eating stir-fry with a fork, watching Lark pace.

"You know, this is better than TV," she said.

"Stop it."

"Do you mind if I record you? This would make a killer GIF or Boomerang."

"He's here," said Lark, peeking out the window and then throwing herself into a chair.

Callie grinned mischievously.

"Don't interrogate him," warned Lark.

"Who, me?" asked Callie, a Midwestern model of innocence.

It was a quiet evening and the windows were open, so they could hear the engine shut off, then his footsteps as he came up the walk of their 1930s courtyard apartment complex. He paused on the step, probably double-checking the unit number, then knocked softly.

Lark locked eyes with Callie, then went to the door and threw it open. Truthfully, she was worried she'd be disappointed, that her one-night stand in gray Buffalo would look out of place in sunny California. She was afraid he'd look older than she remembered, and that the silvering fox she'd described to Callie would be embarrassingly threadbare on second viewing.

And at first she couldn't tell. All she saw was a huge spray of tropical flowers. Then Trip's head peeking over.

"Can I come in?" he asked, grinning.

"Hi! Yeah," she said awkwardly, stepping aside, stunned at how the flowers seemed to have materialized from thoughts she'd been having only minutes ago.

He kissed her cheek as he came in. "For you."

"This is my roommate, Callie," Lark said, moving aside so he could see her.

Callie waved from the couch. "Hiya."

"I hope I haven't interrupted your plans," said Trip, taking in the situation and looking, charmingly, a tiny bit awkward.

"Well, we were going to watch season three of some true-crime show, but somehow I'll manage without her," said Callie, none too subtly looking Trip up and down.

Trip glanced at Lark, a look she couldn't interpret as meaning anything but *Your roommate seems awesome.* Weirdly, it made her feel a sense of pride in Callie, her freckled face and upturned nose, her boyish-cut sandy hair, her ordinary, sensible goodness. The fact that Trip took one look and approved of her meant more than it probably should have.

He still hadn't handed over the bouquet. Cradling the vase in the crook of his left arm, he yanked a handful of flowers out of the vase and gave them to Callie, their stems dripping all over the coffee table.

"Well, these are for you, Callie," he said before turning and giving the rest of the still-lovely arrangement to Lark. "And *this* is for you."

Now that he wasn't obscured by a floral display, she was relieved to discover she found him just as handsome as before, if not more so. He was dressed casually but neatly in chinos and a blue patterned shirt—the fact that the shirt was tucked in and his pants were belted the only things that hinted he was a Midwesterner.

"It's good to see you, Lark," he said.

"Good to see you, too," she said, feeling like her smile might rip her face wide open.

As they stood there awkwardly, Callie looked like she was enjoying their discomfort a little too much.

"How long are you in town for, Trip?" she asked, something Lark wanted to know, too.

"Just two nights, I'm afraid. Meetings all day tomorrow, flying out Thursday morning."

"Lark said you're a venture capitalist?" she probed.

Trip laughed and held up his hands: *guilty.* "It's not as entertaining as they make it out to be on TV."

Lark put the flowers on the breakfast bar as Callie continued to question the new man in her life.

"What kinds of things do you invest in?"

"I typically find my opportunities in health care, but I like to keep my portfolio diversified. I've been known to dabble in real estate development and even entertainment if the project is right."

He sounded almost sheepish, as if reluctant to seem like he was bragging. In contrast to Dylan, who made his dreams of working in film and TV sound precious and unique.

"Where are you staying?" Callie asked.

"Four Seasons," said Trip.

Callie nodded, satisfied. "Just in case I need to know where to find her in the morning."

"Callie!" blurted Lark, horrified.

But Callie just opened her palms, a picture of innocence.

Trip laughed. "And on that note . . . shall we go?"

"I am hungry," said Lark, shaking her head but wondering whether Callie was right. Bringing an overnight bag sent the wrong message, so instead she excused herself, found a rarely used purse, and put a toothbrush and a clean pair of panties inside. If she was going to do the so-called walk of shame, at least she'd do it in a fresh pair of underwear.

As she snapped the purse closed, her mind strayed to later in the evening, when she hoped Trip would be slipping off the panties she was currently wearing.

Moments later they were rolling down the block in a convertible BMW.

"Living the dream, huh?" she teased him.

"Renting the cliché," he confirmed. "But why not? There's frost on the ground back in Chicago."

~

Lark liked good food but could rarely afford it, and she certainly had never set foot in Soyokaze, regarded by many as LA's best sushi omakase restaurant. She had heard of it, as status-conscious Angelenos were always careful to name-drop, and she remembered one college classmate telling her *I sat next to Bradley Cooper at Soyokaze last night* with studied casualness. Lark was determined to savor the experience and took in the many small luxuries with pleasure, from the team of hostesses who greeted them with warm formality to the garden-like restroom where she went to check her lipstick and send a hurried text to Callie.

I think dinner for two here is going to be one month's rent!

Returning to the dining room, she noted that it was almost spartan in its simplicity: eight diners sat at an L-shaped counter, where the shaven-headed chef, his gestures deft and economical, was aided by two assistants. Trip had somehow gotten them seats on the short side of the L, making a very public situation feel almost private. Lark was surprised to see several of the remaining half dozen diners tapping and swiping on their phones, as if paying four figures for a meal was merely routine.

Trip looked comfortable but far from blasé.

"Sake?" he asked as she settled into her seat. A chilled bottle was waiting next to two small cups.

"Sure," she told him.

"We're celebrating," he said, pouring hers and then his own.

"We are?" she asked as they clinked and drank. The sake was like nothing she'd ever had before. Intriguing.

"We most definitely are." Then, before she could press him on the details, he said, "I love how you had Callie check me out."

"That was embarrassing, but I assure you, it was her idea."

"She's obviously a good friend."

"The best."

Even in the bright light from the chef's work area, Trip's dark-brown eyes were bottomless pools, the pupils impossible to tell apart from the irises.

"And do I pass?" he asked.

"I think it's pretty obvious you pass. That was quick thinking with the flowers."

"I hope you aren't upset that I destroyed the bouquet," he said, looking genuinely concerned.

"Are you kidding?"

"I really don't want to screw this up, Lark."

He reached for her hand under the counter. She gave him a squeeze, surprised at how suddenly vulnerable he looked. It threw her, so instead she responded lightly.

"You don't seem like you're very good at screwing things up, Trip," she said as the chef placed the first dish in front of them.

Consisting of one slice of fish wrapped around a mysterious other kind of fish, with a small mound of caviar on top, it was so simple and beautiful it made her want to laugh. It also clearly made one of the other diners want to Instagram it—a server promptly appeared at that man's shoulder with a polite but firm "No photos."

Trip's was already in his mouth, and he chewed with a look of serene contentment. "You have to eat it within ten seconds," he informed her.

"I do?"

He nodded toward the chef, who was already assembling the next one-bite course. "He says that's how it's meant to be tasted."

"Clearly you've been here before," said Lark, finally taking a bite and understanding why all the other diners were smiling. It was incredible.

"One other time. To reward myself for striking out on my own."

"So what are you celebrating tonight?"

"I have a contract for you. There's a copy in my pocket. I'm not going to ruin the moment by whipping it out now, but it's been vetted and approved by my lawyers, and all it needs is your signature. We're celebrating the start of a very promising business career."

Suddenly the soft surroundings took on a sharper tone. Lark almost jumped when a server silently appeared beside her and removed her plate.

"I haven't even read it, Trip—and you want me to sign it tonight?"

To his credit, he looked surprised, too. "Tonight? Oh, god no. No, no, no. I'm not trying to rush you into anything."

"Phew." Lark relaxed and sipped the sake.

"Take it with you, take your time. Have someone check it out. This is not anything . . . weird."

She chuckled. "Only weird if we make it weird, right?"

"Right," he said, looking relieved. "You'll keep intellectual property rights, you'll own your trademarks, your ideas, your company. I'll get a modest slice of any net profit once my original investment has been paid back. And I reserve the right to invest more money before anyone else can. I believe in the game you've created. I believe in you."

"Before this conversation goes any further, I have one condition," she told him coolly.

"Name it."

"I need to know your last name."

His face was like an open book as she read his response: surprise, again, at what she was asking; disbelief that he hadn't already told her; and happiness that he could grant her request.

"Mitchell," he said with what looked like relief.

"And Trip is a nickname, so what's your real first name?"

"Jonathan, but I don't think I've ever been called that by anyone but a teacher on the first day of school."

"Trip Mitchell," she repeated, weighing it, trying to decide if the first name–last name combination matched up with the man sitting across from her. It didn't, exactly, but then how many people would have guessed *her* last name?

"Now yours," he added, smiling.

"Robinson," she told him.

"Mrs. Robinson, you're trying to seduce me," he said with a chuckle. "Aren't you?"

"What?" she asked, puzzled.

"Old movie reference. Sorry, moving along."

He was clearly embarrassed, but she felt a little dumb for not getting the reference, too. She decided to google it later and watch the movie before he came to town again.

The chef offered the second dish, a tiny black dumpling decorated with gold leaf, of all things. People paid money to eat money here, apparently. Lark and Trip ate theirs simultaneously, *mmm*-ing in approval as they savored the salty, smoky taste of eel. The sudden silence was awkward and surprising and went on just a little too long. Then they both reached for a jellied seaweed salad at the same time and got their chopsticks tangled up. Lark laughed loud enough that all the diners and even the chef looked their way.

"Now this is weird," she said, still giggling, once they no longer had everyone's attention. "Nice, but weird."

"How do you mean?"

She took a deep breath. "I mean, we've been naked together, and we're going into business together, but we hardly *know* each other. I just learned your last name. I mean, it's all really exciting, but I don't know where it's going, and I'm worried that we don't even know how to talk to each other."

"Then let's talk about ourselves," he said as one of the ever-attentive servers removed their plates and dabbed at a nonexistent spot on the gleaming, buffed wood countertop.

"So we just tell our whole life stories?"

"I'm in no rush."

"It feels . . . forced."

"Then tell me something big about yourself," he said as the chef and his helpers began assembling what looked like lumps of crab in broth, cupped in actual crab shells perched atop tiny cylindrical hibachis. "Tell me what scares you most in the world."

Lark didn't know what to say. Well, sure, with Dylan she had been afraid of being tied to someone who wouldn't grow up, and she was worried she'd never pay off her student loans, but neither of those seemed big enough to answer Trip's question. Which was a good one: if you knew someone's deepest, darkest fear, you'd know them more intimately than if they recited a list of biographical facts.

While they ate the next course and refilled their cups of sake, she stalled by telling him about her family and how she'd grown up in a loving household where she'd been encouraged to be independent even when she secretly wanted a little more parenting.

When he pressed her again, all she could come up with was a litany of everyone's real-world fears: climate change, fascism, nuclear war. The fear that none of what she did mattered because the world was slowly playing itself out. But even though those fears were real, in a way they didn't feel real, because she herself had never felt the direct impact of any of these global-size problems.

But Trip listened, nodded, cared. If she had only one sentence to describe what made him different from every other guy, it might have been: *He never talks over me.* It was almost spooky. As she heard herself go on, even though she had some doubts about what she was saying, she felt stronger because she was able to say it. And maybe there wasn't anything wrong with struggling to articulate these problems, anyway: issues that big *should* be hard to articulate.

When she finished, he looked at her, then took a swallow of the sake he'd been ignoring. "I'm not convinced," he said.

"What do you mean?"

"I hear genuine concern, but not fear. I don't think you're afraid of anything. I wish I were like you."

"Good thing it's your turn," she told him.

He chuckled. "I should have had an answer ready before I asked such a big question."

"Bad planning."

He thought about it through the next couple of courses—perfect sashimi arrayed on an ice sculpture, shabu-shabu with tofu and vegetables they swirled in hot broth in the order dictated by the chef—then fiddled with his chopsticks while he spoke, as if it were easier for him to share while he concentrated on something else.

"This is going to sound unbelievably corny, Lark. I've been in relationships—I've even been married—but I've never found my soul mate. I guess my deepest fear is not finding that person."

"Not finding your true love," she said.

He nodded and looked down, bashful about his admission.

Her heart pounded. It was beautiful and a little scary, like going ninety miles an hour and driving with one hand—on a cliff-top road with a beautiful view.

Delicate bowls of black sesame ice cream covered with black truffles were placed in front of them. Instead of reaching for his spoon, Trip reached out and placed his hand over hers. He parted his lips to say something and then seemed to think better of it.

"Ten-second rule," he said instead.

Lark could hardly taste her dessert, and it was still incredibly delicious.

Chapter Five

Jessica

Don't let anyone see how you make the secret sauce.

—"How I Lied about My Name and Discovered My Truth,"
a TED Talk by Jon M. Wright

Hearing the lock unlatch, Jessica pushed open the tinted-glass door and stepped into a sleek all-white lobby. The only color—a pale-blue shadow—emanated from the Cancura logo spanning the back wall above the security desk. Jon's frequent references to his company as a "start-up," plus Jessica's drive through the bustling, trendy West Loop, had led her to expect something a little more low-key. Instead, she'd had her name checked against a clipboard before parking in a lot ringed by tall black fencing, then presented herself to a video intercom at the front door. The building itself was a four-story brick warehouse identified by address only.

She had rehearsed her introduction, hoping her lofty new title would roll easily off her tongue—*I'm Jessica Meyers, the director of medical monitoring and consulting*—but that had been unnecessary so far. Her name had been enough for the guards in the parking lot and lobby, both older gentlemen who looked every bit the retired cops they probably were.

"ID?" this one simply asked, scrutinizing her Arizona driver's license much more carefully than any TSA agent ever had, even running it under a black light. If this was how visitors and new hires were received, Jessica wondered how full-time employees were authenticated before entering the belly of the beast: key cards, laminated photo IDs, fingerprint and retina scans, or all of the above?

"I'm supposed to see Olivia Zsofka," she said, offering the name of Jon's executive assistant while the guard squinted at the state-seal hologram.

Then again, he seemed to know that already. Turning a touch screen toward her, he picked up the phone. "I have Ms. Meyers here to see Olivia."

Jessica Meyers, she tapped into the electronic register. Under *Title*, she resisted the urge to add, *Girlfriend of Jonathan Wright*.

While she waited on a chrome-and-white-leather couch, feeling like an impostor, her chest tightened with panic and doubt. Throughout her residency, Jessica's career fantasies had centered on an oncology fellowship followed by private practice. And then Jon had materialized in her world with his magnetic charm and a rationale that couldn't be denied: *Why spend your life fighting battles on your own when you can join me and win the actual war on cancer?*

Their connection at the reception following his Phoenix presentation on the cutting-edge nanotechnology he'd developed—where he claimed to have noticed her in the crowd—had been immediate.

He'd been entirely accessible as he joined a group of residents so they could ask further questions, all of which he answered thoughtfully and patiently—especially hers.

"I'm curious about the results of your clinical trials."

"You and me both," he said, checking his phone. "I'm expecting a call from the director of one of the nephroblastoma studies any second."

"You're that far into development?"

"Things are happening at a mind-blowing speed."

That had been more than apparent during his talk, when he'd immediately captured the audience's attention by leading off with, *Years ago, I had a simple idea: What if detecting childhood cancer was as easy as getting kids to take chewable vitamins?*

Then, for a laugh, he'd crunched and swallowed a Flintstones vitamin, joked about how he preferred the orange flavor to grape, and delivered the kicker. *My company, Cancura, is about to make this a reality. Health-care professionals can give their patients the world's most sophisticated diagnostic tool to eat alongside their cereal. A short time later, our patented Revelate device will deliver the results without so much as a needle poke. What we're talking about here is painless detection, long before the disease produces a single symptom. Cancer is curable when we catch it early enough.*

"Won't the kids' teeth or stomach acids destroy the nanobots or whatever they're currently being called?" asked a male resident with a superior air.

Jon had dispatched the question by saying, "We're talking about particles that are much smaller than atoms. Have you ever gotten an atom caught in your teeth?"

That got a laugh.

"Where are you headed from here?" he'd asked when suddenly it was just the two of them. She felt stunned to even be in his orbit.

"I'm doing an oncology fellowship at Duke."

"Too bad. I have a feeling you'd be a perfect fit at Cancura." He smiled. "But I meant for lunch."

Their relationship, working and otherwise, began at that moment. The romance was less of a whirlwind and more of a tornado—they'd gone to his hotel room that very night, where the sex was amazing and the intimacy even more so. Clearing his schedule and hers after spending a leisurely morning in bed, Jon proposed a hike to the top of Camelback Mountain, something Jessica had never gotten around to doing despite her years in the city. They timed it for sunset, and as she watched lights winking on across the valley with Jon holding her hand tightly, she had a profound sense of how narrow her world had been as she zealously pursued her goals.

Having recently separated from Holly, Jon visited as often as his schedule allowed. In their rambling conversations, they discovered their deepest bond was their belief that with enough hard work even the most intractable problems could be solved. When he asked her to come to Chicago, she said yes almost before the words were out of his mouth, even though her email to Duke took her a day to write and left her queasy when she hit "Send." By canceling on such short notice to join Jon at Cancura, she was sacrificing her academic reputation, but for the sake of a medical breakthrough that could—would—change the world.

When it was time to make her announcement in the doctors' lounge of the hospital, she had an unexpectedly hard time owning it. Even though her new annual salary would be three times what any fellow would be earning and would make a huge dent in her ungodly student loans, she couldn't help feeling she'd jumped the queue. As she told the other residents about her surprising career move, she played up the clinical aspects of the position, imagining their whispers after she left: *Why the fuck did she even apply for a fellowship if she was going to end up working at some start-up?*

She couldn't very well add, *Because I'm a doctor who fell in love.*

~

Instead of Olivia Zsofka, a tall, slim man of roughly forty with dark, closely cropped hair and a trimmed beard came through another frosted-glass door behind the security desk.

"Marco Ruiz, director of sales," he said, extending his hand.

"Jessica Meyers," she said, returning his handshake and his smile.

"Olivia handles all our onboarding, but she's under the weather. I'm afraid you're stuck with me."

"And you're stuck with me," Jessica said, thinking Marco couldn't have been happy to have a new hire foisted upon him. "Sorry to hear Ms. Zsofka isn't feeling well."

"Morning sickness."

"That can really knock you out," Jessica said, hoping she sounded like an all-around team player, as suggested in the article she'd read in preparation for her detour into the corporate world, "How to Rock Your First Day on the Job."

"Do you have kids?" he asked, escorting her through the door and down a hall of windowless doors secured by key card locks.

"Treating them has been more my priority than having them," Jessica said, partly to address the unspoken universal question when hiring a woman in her thirties, but mostly because it was true—that was, other than the de facto stepchildren she was likely to have sooner rather than later. "So, no."

Luckily, he was a man, so he simply nodded and didn't say, *You don't want kids. Really?*

And she didn't have to offer some variation of, *My childhood wasn't altogether conducive to the role modeling necessary for successful parenting.*

At the end of the hall, they took an elevator to the top floor. When the doors slid open, she was relieved to see the offices were not all like something out of a high-security science-fiction movie set. Austere, yes, but nicely furnished, and with occasional touches of color.

"Welcome to Cancura," he said. "Where medicine and miracles meet."

If the slogan was cheesy, the building was anything but. While it was the opposite of open-plan—she quickly felt lost in the endless hallways, corners, and security doors—Jessica marveled as Marco guided her through the chef-run cafeteria. She gazed out the ample windows at the striking Chicago skyline as he listed the must-tries (the mediterranean chicken pita, pad thai, and chopped salad with shrimp) and what to avoid (*anything vegan, but that may just be me*). There was a state-of-the-art fitness center, a childcare center with two tasteful breastfeeding rooms (*in case you change your mind someday*—there it was), and a small theater where Cancura hosted bands, comedians, and motivational speakers. Marco also rattled off the amenities within a one-block walk, which included a convenience store, a dry cleaner, four restaurants (one of them with a Michelin star), and an athleisure store that offered a generous employee discount.

"If there were sleeping accommodations, I don't think I'd have any reason to go home," Jessica joked as they boarded the elevator again to go down one floor.

"They're in the basement," Marco said.

"But of course," she replied.

"You know how lab rats love to burrow and build nests deep inside the bowels of a building," Marco deadpanned.

"And work nonstop," she said with a smile. She'd certainly spent untold hours in various labs over the years and felt comfortable among test tubes and beakers.

The elevator stopped on the third floor.

"Ready to see where the real magic happens?" he asked with a small smile.

Despite her nerves, she pictured something amazing—the medical-research-lab equivalent of Willy Wonka's chocolate factory, a floor-spanning space where a hundred lab-coated workers moved with a sense of happy purpose. Where the potential of ambushing humankind's greatest killers in their nascent stages provided its own source of illumination.

Instead, they entered a warren of hallways and locked doors, their labels far from illuminating. DISCOVERY. TRANSLATION. INNOVATION. OUTCOMES.

Now it was Jessica's turn to be deadpan. "Truly magical."

"Everyone wants to cure cancer, but nobody thinks about the level of security that requires," Marco said with a chuckle. "It's not that we don't want to share our work with the world, but Jon's investors committed their cash with the understanding that they get to own the process."

Which, she thought with a twinge of sadness, might be the only way a true breakthrough could happen.

She could practically hear Jon's voice in her head as Marco swiped his key card to open a door labeled simply **RESEARCH**.

No one should ever have to look into the eyes of a child's parent and say, "I'm sorry, we've done all we could do." Ever again.

"I thought you might want to see your new domain as our first-ever director of medical monitoring and consulting," Marco said.

Jessica felt her cheeks flush. Jon hadn't mentioned anything about the position being new.

"Definitely," she said in what she hoped was a breezy tone, as sweat trickled from the nape of her neck down her back. Thankfully, she'd also heeded the article's advice to *take it up a notch, no matter the dress code* and worn a suit jacket. Concealing nervous perspiration certainly fell into their rationale of *the better you look, the better the first impression.*

Maybe Jon had anticipated her nervousness and intentionally decided not to tell her she was the first director of medical monitoring and consulting. But there was nothing she hadn't told him. Nothing they hadn't shared with each other. She knew he was weirded out by mice and so always avoided Phase 1 trials. He knew she'd grown up with a succession of stepfathers, that she'd always been shy and bookish, and that she had a tendency to sweat when she felt intimidated, out of water, and faced with meeting new people—all of which were an unavoidable part of her career pivot.

Marco guided her around one of the many labs. After quickly listing mandatory OSHA regulations in a flight attendant monotone (*avoid open-toed shoes, flip-flops, tennis shoes, or porous shoes*) he spent more time discussing security protocols. No materials were to be removed from the lab without logging and approval (she was the one responsible for approval, which made her sweat a little harder); work performed in the lab was not to be discussed outside the secure, locked area, even with colleagues who were allowed inside the secure, locked area; and, surprisingly, employees were discouraged from naming their employer to anyone except immediate family.

"It's like working for the CIA, except we don't assassinate dictators," Marco said, putting his hand on a sleek gray device. "And the machines *we* hook people up to save lives."

"Is that a Revelate?" Jessica asked.

He nodded. "This is actually an older model. Jon is challenging the team to make each generation smaller."

Roughly the size of a bread box, the plastic case was a pearlescent gray with soft-blue lights and cables leading to a monitor, a keyboard, and a flexible arm cuff.

"If it had a controller, I might think it was a gaming system," Jessica said.

He laughed. "With a seven-digit retail price."

She liked him, which helped her relax. A little.

Marco introduced her to a research coordinator named Janet and a lab tech named either Brennan or Brendan. Due to a fortuitously timed meeting, she managed to avoid being introduced to an onslaught of people she'd soon come to know well but whose names and titles she would surely jumble until she did.

"Don't think you're getting by without paperwork," said Marco, finally taking her down to the second floor, which resembled a more conventional office suite. "We don't have much of an HR department, but Olivia left you a checklist."

En route, they passed by a glassed-in corner office with a name plaque reading JONATHAN WRIGHT III, MD, PhD but nothing to delineate his dual titles as president and CEO. She admired the modesty of this egalitarian approach.

"You already know our charismatic, largely absent but always fear-less leader," Marco said.

Jessica was glad she was following him and avoiding eye contact. "I'm so grateful to Dr. Wright for this amazing opportunity. Ever since I was a little girl, it's been my dream to be part of the cure."

She smiled weakly when he turned and raised an eyebrow, wishing she hadn't gushed.

Jessica and Jon had agreed to maintain a professional, discreet dis-tance at the office, not only to avoid any hint of favoritism but to keep their relationship utterly secret—at least until Jon had all the details of his divorce ironed out with the volatile "Annie Wilkes." To that end, he had scheduled a quick business trip to the West Coast for her first day. Jessica knew it made sense for her to get settled on her own, but now that she was here, she wished he were, too.

As Marco led her toward a cluster of cubicles, she looked for her name on one of the gray panels. She almost walked past him when he stopped at a glass-walled office.

There it was: JESSICA MEYERS, MD.

The momentary charge she felt stepping into her own blessedly title-free office—complete with supplies, business cards, a computer troubleshooting guide from IT, security badge and key card, and even a box of Cancura-branded chocolates—was tempered by the single-spaced, bullet-pointed checklist lying on her keyboard.

- Test system log-in
- Review company policies on intranet dashboard
- Choose health insurance and life insurance plans
- Complete payroll, 401(k) enrollment, Federal and State W-4 forms
- Confirm your Form I-9 has been processed
- Fill out direct deposit, Equal Employment Opportunity, and Self-Identification forms

- Read, sign, and date nondisclosure agreement and noncompete agreement

"Sorry Olivia isn't here to walk you through this, but it should be mostly self-explanatory," Marco said, checking his phone. "Whatever you do, don't leave without signing the nondisclosure agreement. Jonathan's been known to fire people who didn't take care of that."

Jessica stared at him. "You're joking."

"I am," he said with a smile. "Probably. Good luck. I'm just at the end of the hall if you need anything."

～

Thank god it was company policy for employees to wear visible name badges, even if they were first name only. At a cafeteria lunch surrounded by people Marco assured her were "mostly" from her department, the mental gymnastics of following the friendly but nonstop banter of her new colleagues threatened to make Jessica tumble to earth.

"The new-hire paperwork took me all morning," she told the table during the first lull, hoping to steer the conversation toward something they could all relate to. Everyone hated paperwork, right?

"I came here from pharma, and believe me, this is *nothing*," said a red-haired woman named Yulia. "The record was two days and four phone calls to HR. It took one guy a full week, so they fired him."

"Well, that makes me feel better," Jessica said, hoping she didn't have a stem from her spinach-with-strawberry-and-goat-cheese salad in her teeth.

"Best way to avoid that problem is to cut out the middleman and eliminate the HR department entirely," said Marco.

"That's progress," said a brunette named Lori, slicing a butternut squash ravioli neatly in half.

"Can we go after lawyers next?" Brennan-not-Brendan said, taking a sip of his cola.

"Easy, comrade," Marco said. "My partner is a lawyer."

"Where did you train, Jessica?" asked a serious, glasses-wearing Arjun between bites of a chicken parmesan sandwich.

"I went to med school at University of Arizona, Tucson," she said.

"I thought you were from Minnesota," said tiny, otherwise silent Janet.

"Jon said you did your residency at Mayo," Arjun said.

"Yes, but in Phoenix," Jessica clarified.

The simultaneous *ohs* and informed nods suggested they were disappointed she hadn't come from the Minnesota campus. She resisted the urge to rattle off the various papers she'd coauthored, including a particularly noteworthy study about childhood acute lymphoblastic leukemia—or name-drop anyone from the lab at Mayo where she'd done research.

An attractive woman with shoulder-length blonde hair and an obscured name tag had been tracking their conversation as she approached the table and sat down. "Jon announced he was creating the position, and the next thing we knew he was raving about you, the perfect candidate he'd found to fill it."

"Isn't she pretty?" whispered Philip loudly from Jessica's left. He was an unusually tall, odd-looking man who could have been anywhere from thirty to fifty.

"Very," Jessica whispered back, simultaneously weirded out by his unprofessional observation and bothered by how attractive the woman actually was.

"You're just out of residency, right?" the woman continued.

As everyone quieted in anticipation of Jessica's answer, she fought the impulse to blather out the details of her fortuitous meeting with the brilliant, disarmingly handsome Jonathan Wright III, MD, PhD. Instead, she focused on the advice she'd read: *Lunch on your first day is a critical time to build relationships. Your past experience is not as relevant as you think it will be.* "I was headed to an oncology fellowship at Duke, but nanotechnology is the future of medicine. It just made more sense to join this team and be part of history than to do anything else."

The group nodded in agreement.

As the blonde woman's badge popped into view, identifying her as Kate, Philip once again whispered into Jessica's ear. "You're pretty, too."

"Thank you," Jessica mumbled awkwardly.

"You have almost no wrinkles."

I'm only thirty-four, she didn't say, wondering how old Philip thought she was. "Good genes, I guess."

"Philip is absolutely brilliant but definitely marches to his own beat," Marco whispered from her right side. "We've got a few others like him. But don't worry. You'll get used to ignoring his intrusive questions and odd comments before you know it."

~

Jessica made her way back to her new desk and was wondering what, exactly, had just happened when a text alert pinged.

Nice job navigating the lunch bunch.

Jessica couldn't help but wonder who exactly was reporting on her to Jon. Marco? Kate?

Says who? she responded.

You're a perfect fit.

I'm not sure that's true.

Well, you have a point. I'm thinking of Philip here.

Why didn't you tell me I was the first?

If I did, I'd be lying, now wouldn't I?

Ha! Seriously. I'm the first director of medical monitoring and consulting?

Seriously you are brilliant, beautiful, and I knew from the moment we met that you and your big brain belonged at Cancura. Near me. With me.

You're not even here.

Oh, but I am.

Meaning what?

Look in your bottom left desk drawer.

She tugged open the drawer. There was a long rectangular box inside with a bow on top.

Close the door to your office before you open it.

What's inside?

Just do it.

She got up and quietly shut the door. She questioned the abundance of caution when she opened the lid of the box and saw a lab coat bearing the Cancura logo and JESSICA embroidered on the breast pocket.

When she lifted the jacket out of the box, however, a tissue-wrapped gift sealed with an Agent Provocateur sticker slid to the floor. She peered through the glass wall beside her door to make sure no one was nearby and tore open the paper to find a stunning, sexy white silk bodysuit with an intricate floral design—size 34C.

OMG! she typed back. *I can't believe you did that!*

We have a very specific dress code for our first ever director of medical monitoring and consulting.

So I see.

Looking forward to seeing that myself!

Jessica hung the lab coat on the hook behind her door, wrapped the bodysuit in the tissue, and tucked it into the oversize leather tote the magazine article had deemed crucial for carting home *the first-day paperwork and corporate swag.*

She only wished there had been advice on how to manage first-day-on-the-job arousal due to unsolicited—but very welcome—advances from the boss.

Chapter Six

HOLLY

Hold your enemies close but romance your allies.

—"How I Lied about My Name and Discovered My Truth,"
a TED Talk by Jon M. Wright

Holly acknowledged Theresa and Larry Yadao with a curt nod and a tight smile before taking her seat in the front row on the opposite side of the aisle in the Village Hall. She wished the attendees of this meeting of the zoning board of appeals would behave like guests at a wedding and choose sides based on who they were there for, because that would have made it so much easier to read the room. Still, despite being a relative newcomer to Barrington Hills—she'd lived there only fifteen years, unlike some of her second-generation neighbors—she felt confident that the recently arrived Yadaos were more like a groom whose out-of-town family couldn't all be bothered to show up.

Fairly confident, anyway.

Truth was, this was a pivotal meeting for the bridle path extension behind Chez Yadao. One year ago, the equestrian commission had approved the proposal, and a few months later, the plan commission had also approved it and kicked it up to the board of trustees for a vote—which would have been a rubber stamp had not the Yadaos, recently closed on their home, suddenly taken an interest in village affairs and requested a delay until they could mount an appeal. Never mind that they should have done due diligence while buying their house. Now, after various maneuvers, including legal threats and online petitions (Holly's had 337 signatures to the Yadaos' 42, she noted proudly), here they were for a crucial decision: Would the board uphold the original decision and refer the matter to the trustees for a vote—one that now felt less certain to come out in Holly's favor—or would they grant the Yadaos time to try to revoke the easement attached to their property? The truly galling thing was that the six-yard-wide swath in question was already outside their fence.

A throb at her temple reminded her of the headache that had come and gone all day, accompanied by periodic bouts of spaciness. And although her hearing was fine, once in a while words seemed scrambled. On her way in from the parking lot, she could have sworn she heard someone say, "Jelly and egg man," which simply couldn't have been correct.

Brian Fredericksen slid into the front row next to her. "Sorry I'm late."

With five minutes until the gavel dropped, Brian wasn't actually late, but he was also the kind of dad who coached his AYSO soccer team with motivational-poster mantras like, "Early is on time and on time is late!" Neatly bearded and unconventionally handsome, he was an ex–real estate lawyer who'd stayed home with the kids to support his CEO wife's career and now volunteered wherever his daughters' interests were concerned. He himself was uncomfortable on horseback, but his wife had done competitive dressage in her teens and twenties, and now both daughters were horse crazy. After meeting at the riding center several years ago, where his daughters' hearts had melted over Holly's unloved animals, Brian had, over time, become Holly's unpaid but essential legal adviser, communications officer, and development assistant for Horse Stability. She was as grateful for his easy companionship as his enthusiastic help.

"How are we looking?" asked Holly, not wanting to turn around to read the room.

Without hesitation, Brian did just that, scanning faces, nodding at several people, and doing a quick head count. "Not bad. I emailed, texted, Facebooked, and tweeted this morning, trying to get the numbers up. I'm sure we'll get a few more, even if they're a little late."

Holly glanced over at Theresa, who was watching them intently. Brian grinned and gave her a thumbs-up, which caused Theresa and Larry to go into a huddle with their lawyer.

"Who does this?" complained Holly pointlessly. "It's like moving to Taos and telling everyone there are too many art galleries."

"Either way, they're outnumbered," Brian reassured her. "Dane said he'd speak, and so did Mary Rose. I think we can count on Danielle, Cooper, Angie, Nikita, and probably Shirin. Plus whoever shows up and wants to talk but didn't get in touch. Even if they keep people to two minutes, we should be able to dominate the comment time. I honestly don't know who wants to stand up against horses in this town."

"Besides the obvious parties, of course."

"Of course."

As he scrolled on his phone to see whether anyone had retweeted his call to action, the chairperson rapped his gavel, calling the meeting to order. Brian reached over and gave her arm a squeeze. Her head throbbed again, and suddenly Holly felt distracted and unprepared, unable to concentrate as the chairperson asked the board to approve the minutes of the last meeting before laying out the agenda of the meeting before them.

"As I'm sure most of you are here to speak for or against the proposed riding trail extension, and as none of the other matters before us are urgent, I propose we table all other discussion until our next quarterly meeting and focus solely upon the arguments for and against the riding trail. I understand both sides have lawyers . . ."

Brian squeezed her arm again. "We've got this," he whispered.

~

She had allowed Brian to talk her into a quick celebratory drink, even as she hoped they weren't celebrating too soon. The board of appeals had ruled in their favor, but they still faced a vote by the trustees—next month at the soonest—allowing the Yadaos more time for threats and shenanigans. But she owed him at least a drink for his efforts. The testimony had been overwhelmingly in support of the bridle path extension.

"Cheers," Brian said, raising his IPA as their waitress departed.

She lifted her glass of white—the safest option where headaches were concerned—and clinked it against his bottle.

They had ended up in a sports bar because, at 9:15 on a weeknight, the restaurants with a good wine selection were already closing. Only an hour from downtown Chicago and things got downright provincial. In general, she didn't mind—except for the wine, which tasted like the box it was dispensed from had been stored in the sun.

"You're doing a lot of good work for the community," she said.

"As are you," he said.

Brian really was a good guy. And while stay-at-home dads in Barrington Hills were still subject to occasional snide remarks from women as well as other men, Holly knew he'd been very successful in the business world. He brought an easy confidence and competence to parenting, something she wished she didn't find so appealing.

"We should probably talk about the gala," she said suddenly.

"Whoa, Nellie."

He was right—it was the wrong moment, and yet the annual fundraiser for Horse Stability would be here before she knew it. What had once been a catered party in her home during which Holly made a plea for donations had now become a black-tie ball at the Chicago Cultural Center opposite Millennium Park. In the former public library, under the world's largest Tiffany glass dome, attendees would pay $250 per plate for an elegant dinner accompanied by live jazz. Before, during, and after, she would work the room, targeting the donors and influencers—with a little help.

"I'm sorry, I shouldn't bring it up after you just sat through a two-hour board hearing," she said.

Brian sighed cheerfully. "Everything seems to be on track. A couple of the VIPs are hemming and hawing about whether they'll really make it, so we may have to make a couple of last-minute invites to ensure we don't have any empty seats. I assume Jack will be there."

The truth was, her husband was always the most important guest at the Hay Bale Ball. Not only was he good at guilting big-name, big-money donors into attending, but he had a knack for getting them to commit to gifting more than planned. The latter skill was, after all, how he'd managed to turn Cancura into a buzzy and extremely well-capitalized start-up in only seven years. But Brian's seemingly offhand statement was freighted with meaning: last year, for the first time ever, Jack had missed the gala, and follow-up donations were weaker than the previous year.

"It's on his calendar," said Holly. "Last year was unavoidable. He had to be in Phoenix for work."

Brian drained his bottle, caught the waitress's eye, and signaled for another. "If you're not worried, I'm not worried."

Holly forced down some of the wine. Not allowing herself to dwell on Jack and his absence.

"What's Jack's secret?" Brian asked abruptly.

Holly coughed, thinking she had misheard. "For . . . fundraising?"

"I don't mean that." Not looking at her.

She waited, not wanting to speculate about what he did mean.

His second beer arrived, and he took a healthy drink. "Obviously the guy has something special if he has you." He exhaled hard. "I just don't know how people do this, to be honest."

"Do what?"

Still not looking up: "I love my wife—I do. But we don't spend much time together anymore. And I really like spending time with you. I just . . ."

Now that she knew where he was going, she didn't move or speak, not sure she wanted to encourage him. Not sure she didn't.

". . . wish things were different. That we could be more to each other than we are now." Finally, he looked at her. "I just wanted you to know."

"What am I supposed to do with that, Brian?" she asked.

Thinking, *Run around and have an affair? Do to my husband what he's done to me?*

"I didn't mean . . . or maybe I do. I don't know." He looked away. He started to say something else and then stopped.

"I have to go," she said, her heart pounding, fumbling in her purse for money and leaving too much on the table.

Chapter Seven

LARK

*Don't be afraid to step into something new. Or break
ties to the past.*

—"How I Lied about My Name and Discovered My Truth,"
a TED Talk by Jon M. Wright

Lark had never allowed herself to be blindfolded before. Even as a girl
playing pin-the-tail-on-the-donkey, the idea that everyone else could
see what she wasn't seeing had just been too much for her. Or maybe
it was a lack of trust, knowing that people were watching her go the
wrong direction and laughing about it instead of helping. How could
they do that to each other?

And yet here she was, wearing a blindfold for the first time in her
life, surrendering to Trip, hypersensitive to his gentle touches as he
guided her down the sidewalk. He'd returned to town that morning
promising another big surprise. She'd had her eyes covered for the half-
hour drive in the car, too, and despite a general feeling they were headed
downtown, with each turn she lost more sense of direction until, for all
she knew, they were on their way to the Valley or nearing Long Beach.

"I still can't imagine a surprise big enough to make it worth all this," she told him, trying to feel her way forward as if her feet were fingers. From the way he was tugging on her, she could sense his impatience, but there was a limit to how fast she could go. Completely blind, she couldn't shake the sensation that her next step was going to land her in a deep, dark hole.

"It'll be worth it," he promised, guiding her forward. "And trust me: not only are there no obstacles in front of you, there's nobody else around."

He gave her a quick kiss on the back of her neck. She shivered pleasantly and moved forward just a little bit more quickly.

"Okay, we're going inside," he told her. "Lift your feet."

Cool air flooded out as a door opened and they went through. He led her into an elevator, and a rising sensation—and a single beep—told her they'd gone up one floor.

"Out and to your left," he said, now with his hands on her waist.

They walked a little way down a carpeted hallway.

"Now stop."

She did, then complied as he rotated her body ninety degrees to the right.

"Ready?"

Lark laughed. "Are you kidding? Let's get this over with already!"

Trip lifted the blindfold, and she stood blinking in front of an office door. With her name on a little plastic placard beside it.

LARKSPUR GAMES, LLC
LARK ROBINSON, PRESIDENT & CEO

"Larkspur?" she asked.

"It's a flower," he explained. "If you don't like it, we can change it to whatever you want before we get the actual paperwork done."

Paperwork? she wanted to say. She had so many questions.

"Your keys, Madam President," he said, offering them with a mock sense of ceremony, as if his open palm were a silver platter.

She stared at the keys, then at the plaque, then at Trip, at a loss for words.

"Is something wrong?" he asked, looking suddenly worried.

"I can't pay for this," she managed to say.

He shook his head. "I did not think that would be the first thing out of your mouth. I'll explain in a minute, I promise."

Lark put thoughts of her ballooning debt on hold as Trip explained which key was for the front door of the building, which was for the back door, which was for the bathroom down the hall, and which one unlocked their office suite.

"Where are we, by the way?" she asked.

"Culver City," Trip said. "Fifteen minutes from your place with traffic. I drove around a little bit to mess with you."

"It definitely worked."

All her reactions were a few beats behind, but slowly she started to get excited as the door opened to reveal a large reception area where, on a desk, a vase displayed three large stems covered with small pink flowers.

"Let me guess," she said. "Larkspur?"

"You got it," he said. "This area can host a receptionist and a couple of other employees until you outgrow it and need more space. You share a kitchen and restrooms with the other offices on this floor. Are you ready to see your office?"

She was. Behind door number one was a medium-size room whose tinted-glass windows gave a view of the Helms Bakery District sign. The office furniture was contemporary, almost generic, but everything looked ready to go. The phone on the desk even had a steady red light indicating an active line. As a joke, Trip had hung a framed motivational poster, the classic kitten in a tree captioned, *Hang in there, baby.* She appreciated the kitschy touch.

"You can replace that with whatever you want, as long as it fits your decorating budget, which I'm obligated to tell you is minuscule. As your chief investor, I demand fiscal responsibility."

Lark turned a slow circle, picturing herself hard at work at the desk—imagining the office filled with employees—and trying to process the change from working with her feet up on the couch. Wondering how much it all cost.

Then, finally, not wanting to look ungrateful, she launched herself at Trip and wrapped him in a tight hug, kissing him deeply. When they broke it off, she said, "The poster stays. Now tell me how this works, exactly."

He grinned and released her. "Why don't you have a seat at your desk?"

Playing along, she pushed him down into one of the guest chairs and then did her best to slink seductively into the expensive-looking task chair behind the desk. She put both feet up on a corner, steepled her fingers, and cocked an eyebrow, enjoying feeling like an executive interrogating an underling.

"Damn," he said, grinning. "You even look the part."

"Explain yourself, Mitchell," she growled.

"It's simple," he said, slouching comfortably. "You need a business address. You also need a place to work that reminds you you're the real deal, not an amateur in sweats on the couch."

She tried to interrupt, but he shushed her.

"I also need a West Coast office. I'm sick of coffee shops, and those coworking spaces are even worse. They're all dog friendly, they play terrible music, and half the people in them are wannabe movie producers hoping you'll overhear their phone conversations. I'll take the other private office here, but the rest of the space is yours. We'll carry the expenses on my books for the time being because I can use the write-off."

She felt mildly deflated—this wasn't really her office, after all?—but he anticipated her objection before she could raise it.

"Your name is on the door," he said. "The phone number is listed to Larkspur or whatever you want to call your company. The lease will be in my name, but trust me, I'll stay out of your way."

"And if I want you in my way?"

He grinned. "You're the boss, Ms. Robinson."

∽

Lark had signed the business agreement several days after dinner at Soyokaze, witnessed by Callie and notarized by a clerk at a funky corner store that also sent faxes and rented mailboxes to some of the neighborhood's more transient characters. Trip told her to take as long as she wanted and had encouraged her to have her lawyer look it over, as if she had a lawyer. Not wanting to pay the hourly expense for a legal opinion, she instead read the whole thing repeatedly, word by word, until she felt convinced there were no clauses hiding bad intentions on Trip's part. Truthfully, the mere fact that he encouraged her to use a lawyer convinced her he was on the up-and-up.

Yes, he was offering half the money Hunter-Cash had put on the table. But he was allowing her to keep her game, encouraging her to aim higher, and seemed convinced she'd be profitable. He told her he planned to use his first-investor clause liberally to pump more cash into her operation. In return he was asking for only 20 percent of the profit after recouping his expenses—and now he wasn't even charging her for office space.

Lark had checked him out online, of course. There wasn't much to find, but she had learned this was by design. While running his hedge fund, he'd explained, he worked with a small, handpicked group of clients who knew him by reputation. Once he became a so-called angel investor, he had every reason to fly below the radar, because no one was more popular than someone with money to burn. He'd been too busy to bother with Facebook and Twitter, and was still hardly a regular on Instagram. He had a neglected LinkedIn page and a bare-bones website with a contact form, and he showed up only a few other times on Google. Lark thought it showed a refreshing lack of self-promotion, and even Callie, who continued to half-heartedly play devil's advocate, was slowly being won over.

I'm looking forward to meeting this mystery man, Lark's mom had texted.

Over lunch at a nearby sandwich shop, Trip asked her what she thought was the next step for Larkspur Games.

"Well, I've never had a formal business plan, but I've studied what's worked for a lot of other first-time game designers . . ."

He nodded in vigorous agreement.

". . . and you'd be amazed at how many of them have successfully launched with Kickstarter."

Trip made a face like he'd bitten into something unpleasant. "Those are direct sales, right? Individual people essentially preordering your game?"

She nodded.

"In a way those people also become investors—and as your primary investor, I'd like to encourage you to think even bigger. What if we spent the next month working on a business plan that includes production, manufacturing, distribution, and marketing? I can definitely help with the distribution angle. I have a friend who knows retail and can set up pitch meetings with the biggest distributors, like Alliance, when you're ready. Even better, someone at Target owes me a favor. Do you want to see Activate! in all the big-box stores?"

Lark put down her black-bean-and-avocado wrap. She was hardly tasting it, anyway. "Yes, of course. I'm just not sure I know how to think that big."

"It's a new market for me, but we can learn it together."

"Why are you doing this?" she asked.

Trip sipped his iced tea. "On the one hand, it's because you have an amazing idea that I think is about to go big, and I can't let the opportunity go by."

"And on the other?" she asked, resisting the urge to reach across the table for his hand.

"Because you're fucking awesome, and I want to spend more time with you," he said hesitantly. "I'm really falling for you."

She didn't trust herself to say anything back, because she was falling for him, too.

They spent the rest of the afternoon visiting both small, independent game shops and large retailers, examining which games were sold, who manufactured them, and how they were displayed. In a smaller shop in Santa Monica, Trip interviewed the owner with an easy familiarity and a way of persistently homing in on the right questions to ask. Similar efforts went unrewarded at the big-box stores until they actually located a floor manager with some insight about what happened to unsold products and how games were ordered and stocked.

Trip took dozens of pictures on his phone and used speech-to-text to take copious notes after every encounter. When they called it a day five hours later, Lark was energized by the possibilities.

"I spent two years working on my game to make it perfect, but I never researched retail," she told him as they drove back to her place.

He shrugged. "You've been developing the product, so your focus has been on that. Now that you're a business owner, it makes sense for you to learn this stuff. It's new to me, too. We'll learn more from going out into the field and talking to people than we ever can behind a desk."

Hungry again, they headed back to Lark's place, planning to order in. Callie was out for the evening at a Spanish class, so they'd have the place to themselves for a while. Trip hadn't slept over yet because the privacy and luxury of his hotel rooms had been far more appealing to her than having him at her tiny apartment. *But if this thing between us is real,* Lark thought, *then it shouldn't always be on his terms.* Maybe tonight was the night.

When they pulled up in front, however, her mood changed instantly.

"Oh no," she said.

"What?" asked Trip, eyes on the rearview mirror as he carefully backed his rental—an Aston Martin this time, because it made him "feel like James Bond"—into an empty spot.

Dylan was sitting on the front step next to a vase of flowers and a burning Mexican love candle. Even worse, he was tuning his guitar. Clearly inspired by one of the John Hughes movies he could quote chapter and verse, he was planning some kind of grand gesture to win her back. A flicker of admiration—she hadn't thought he had it in him—was quickly snuffed out by horror and embarrassment. In baggy cargo shorts and a logo T-shirt, with his mop of hair in need of professional attention, Dylan looked like a ghost from college past.

"It's Dylan, my old boyfriend," she said, turning to watch Trip's reaction.

And what would it be? Judgment of her, derision at Dylan?

Putting the car in park and turning off the engine, Trip finally looked over. His only visible reaction was a rueful smile. "Well, that's awkward," he said.

Dylan had no idea he was being observed, having merely glanced at the luxury car and instantly determined it was not Lark's ride.

Lark's stomach fluttered with indecision. She had no idea what to do. Thankfully, Trip decided for her.

"I guess I should meet him sometime," he said, opening his door and climbing out.

Dylan's expression at seeing Lark cross the lawn with Trip was one of complete bewilderment. His hands froze on the guitar. Clearly, he hadn't planned for this scenario.

"Who's this?" he asked Lark abruptly as they drew near.

"Trip Mitchell," said Trip, offering a hand to shake. "You must be Dylan."

Dylan stared at Trip's hand until Trip finally let it drop. Then he stood up abruptly, hitting the candle with his guitar and making it wobble, almost knocking it over.

"Why are you here?" asked Lark, painfully struck by the difference between the two men. Trip wasn't quite old enough to be Dylan's father, but he was definitely a man to Dylan's boy.

"Who is this?" repeated Dylan.

Trip had maintained his cool and still hadn't offered a single clue as to his true thoughts. Instead, with a glance at Dylan and a warm, direct look into her eyes, Trip took a step back.

"I think I'd better leave you two alone," he said. "Lark, will you be all right?"

She nodded, unspeakably grateful for the way he was handling it. "I'll be fine."

"Good to meet you, Dylan," he said, moving backward across the lawn. "I'll call you later, Lark."

Lark and Dylan regarded each other as the car door slammed, the engine came to life, and Trip rolled slowly away down the block. Her mind strayed involuntarily to what Trip had said at dinner was his greatest fear: not finding his soul mate. Missing out on true love. She had told Dylan she loved him without ever fully feeling it. She'd said it out of a sense that it was the expected thing. Her feelings for Trip were already so big they were scary. Having witnessed her parents' lifelong love affair had given her the belief that love at first sight was a distinct possibility—but it had never occurred to her it might happen so soon. Was she ready? The prospect was both thrilling and terrifying.

Dylan searched her eyes hopefully as he raised his guitar. "I wrote a song for—"

"Don't sing," she told him, reaching for her keys. "Come in and we'll talk. I'll blow out the candle."

Chapter Eight

Jessica

What is truth? Truth can be less important than trust.

—"How I Lied about My Name and Discovered My Truth,"
a TED Talk by Jon M. Wright

Jessica had always believed success came from achieving excellence through preparation, not winging it. One month into her job, and she was definitely successful—but only at praying she would soon have a clue what she was doing.

Instead of seeing patients, she now *provided monitoring and consultation* for those who directed studies of the patients she'd trained to treat. Which largely meant she shuffled paper. At least so far. The only person who could truly advise her about what she was actually supposed to be doing happened to be her boss, roommate, and lover. "I didn't just bring you here because I'm in love with you," he'd whispered one harried afternoon, after she'd spent the morning writing and revising a report she worried didn't even make sense. "I have all these people working for me who excel at specific things, but you're the only one I trust implicitly to help me oversee the big picture."

From then on, when Jon gave her something to review and approve, which was constantly, she read the material assiduously before attaching her name but didn't dare do anything more than correct stray typos. She wasn't about to test his belief in her by admitting she should have done that fellowship first and that she was in over her head.

Marco had been an absolute godsend as he helped her navigate the inevitable on-the-job pitfalls: *Don't fuck with any lab protocols until you okay it with Arjun. Lori understands organizational structure better than anyone other than Jon. Philip is your go-to guy for any kind of analysis—but don't chew gum around him because he can't handle repetitive noise.* Marco's friendship and candor, particularly over lunch in the on-site café, had gone a long way to helping her settle in. Still, it wasn't as though she could ask him what, exactly, she had been hired to do.

Now Jessica Meyers, MD, director of medical monitoring and consulting, had little choice but to sculpt her role from the head-spinning job description Jon had provided. At least one task—*review and sign off on documents with respect to medical relevance*—was straightforward. When she wasn't signing off on the endless files that came to her virtual desktop for approval, she was *collaborating with management*, awaiting Jon's infrequent arrival in the office (in order to *interact with her primary academic thought leader*), and trying to figure out how to *organize and lead clinical development advisory boards*. This task was more difficult than it seemed: Yulia got too competitive with Arjun, so they had to be split up; Janet, while brilliant, rarely posited an opinion unless she was angry; et cetera, et cetera.

Some days, she half wondered whether her position had been copied and pasted from a job posting on a recruitment site. She almost wished it had been, so she could call whoever had gotten the same position at another company and ask, *How do you know when you've figured out what you're supposed to be doing?*

Whenever she thought about what she was missing in the three-year fellowship she'd abruptly declined, she assuaged her small stabs of regret by telling herself that, instead of merely becoming a medical practitioner, she was part of a team of brilliant scientists building something so monumental it would change medicine forever.

Today, Jessica finally had the breakthrough she'd been waiting for: a moment of genuine insight proving to Jon, and more importantly herself, she actually had something to contribute. The fact that Kate, the head of clinical trials—who'd legitimately but far too publicly questioned her credentials—was to be the first recipient of the director of medical monitoring's actual *monitoring* made it that much sweeter.

Jessica considered herself competitive, not vindictive or jealous, and certainly had no intention of doing anything more than flexing a little *identify program risks and create and implement mitigation strategies* muscle.

Not wanting to make her inquiry look like a power play, she didn't call Kate down to her office but instead made the trip up to the third floor. As she exited the elevator and entered the restricted area, known affectionately as Area 51, her presence was not acknowledged by the small army of lab techs. Kate, however, spotted her immediately and was halfway across the lab before Jessica reached her work area.

"Do you have a minute?" Jessica asked with unaccustomed confidence.

"For?" Kate asked brusquely.

"Maybe we should talk in your office?"

"No need." Kate didn't seem to take the hint that she might not want to be questioned in front of her staff.

Jessica lowered her voice. "I have some concerns about variations in some of the most recent leukemia biomarker trials."

Out of the corner of her eye, she saw one of the lab techs glance over before quickly refocusing on his task.

Kate folded her arms.

"The data shows wide fluctuation in the results between our in-house and outsourced testing," said Jessica, holding up the printout she'd brought as evidence.

"I'm aware," Kate said with a dismissive sniff. "Those results come from a lab we're no longer using due to their poor quality controls."

"Why aren't we doing all of our diagnostic work in-house?"

"Everyone outsources to corroborate their findings," Kate said, as if the very words were exhausting.

"But we're outsourcing some of the initial testing, too. In one trial, we did all of it in-house. In another, we subcontracted all of it. And in the third, some of the samples were tested in-house and some were sent out."

"Even a place as well funded as Cancura can't do everything in-house."

Jessica moved several inches closer, not wanting to broadcast what she was about to say. "If we outsource the initial findings as well as the corroboration, aren't we leaving ourselves open to errors by others?"

"As long as they're all tested according to the same protocols, there's nothing to worry about," Kate said flatly.

"I can't believe we're having this issue at this stage of the—"

"At this stage of the process," said Kate, interrupting, "some of us have already been working on this for *years*. And it's all under control. Now, if you'll excuse me."

She stalked away. Jessica collected herself and then turned to go, acutely conscious of how hard the lab techs were working to ignore what had just happened.

And wondering exactly what it was that had set Kate off.

~

Jon dropped his bag in the entryway and stepped into the kitchen, where he gave her a kiss that almost made their time apart worthwhile.

"Missed you, Jessie," he said.

"Missed you, too," she said, pouring and handing him a glass of wine.

"Good call," he said, noting the new stemless glassware she'd picked up on the way home from work. "It's getting to be full service around here."

"You know it," she said with a smile. "How was LA?"

"Not bad. And as far as Holly knows, I'm still there. I fudged my return date so we could have some uninterrupted time."

"Very clever. Like a mental health day."

"Truthfully, I do have to go back again next week to finalize details."

He'd gone out there twice now to meet a small group of extremely wealthy potential investors, two of them big celebrities. Citing a non-disclosure agreement, he wouldn't divulge their names, no matter how hard she tried. "Did you say hi to Kim and Kanye for me?"

"You're getting warmer," he said, pulling her close. "What smells so good, besides you?"

"Korean short ribs and rice."

"Sounds awesome."

"It will be." Jessica was about to add that she'd been able to time dinner perfectly, thanks to the modern marvel that was the Instant Pot, but didn't want to risk sounding like a ditzy housewife. Besides, she needed to talk science over dinner and preferred not to share the spotlight with a kitchen gadget.

Even though they had agreed business was to be conducted only at the office, to avoid cross-contamination with their secret and satisfying home life, Jessica had spent the day planning to break that rule. If they were a normal couple, she reasoned, she would have been able to come home and proudly share the problem she'd discovered, vent about her coworker's reaction, and then ask for advice on dealing with fragile egos in the cutthroat world of cutting-edge health-care start-ups.

"So," she said, once they'd sat down together at the table she'd arranged with place settings they'd bought on a romantic outing to Crate & Barrel. "I made an interesting discovery today."

"What's that?" he asked, taking a bite of tender short rib.

"I was going over our testing protocols and was wondering why our recent leukemia biomarker trials had such different results. The in-house diagnostics conform closely to the numbers we report in our investor materials, but it looks like some of the outsourced testing fluctuated wildly."

"What?" he said, not seeming to track what she'd just said.

"Kate told me it was because of a lab that had—"

"You went to Kate about this?" he asked, color seeming to drain from his face.

"Not before I reviewed everything I could find multiple times," she said, feeling her confidence wane. She wasn't about to add that she'd emailed Philip the data to confirm that she wasn't imagining the discrepancies. To which he'd responded, *This is really outside my purview.*

"What exactly did Kate say?" Jon asked.

"That we broke ties with that lab, that everybody outsources, and the rest of the results are well within the accepted margin of error."

"She's right," he said. "They are."

"I . . . I . . ." Jessica had a hard time swallowing while Jon angrily drained his wineglass and threw his napkin down on the table.

"Don't ever go to Kate or anyone else when you think you see a potential flaw or any other fucking thing," he said coldly. "We stay in our lanes at Cancura."

Jessica's head swam. It was as though Jon, her loving, smiling Jon, had been replaced with somebody she hardly knew. And given her job title, how exactly had she veered from her supposed *lane*? "I thought it was important."

"You couldn't wait a few hours until I got home?" he snarled, pushing his chair back and tromping upstairs before she could will herself to move. His voice echoed off the lofted ceiling. "Goddamn it!"

Jessica sat there, stunned. They'd never before been the slightest bit annoyed with each other. She'd never seen him mad about anything except Annie Wilkes's shenanigans—and even then he was usually able to laugh it off. Suddenly he was furious at her for simply doing her job?

While he stomped around the bedroom, slammed the door to the bathroom, and, from the sounds of water in the pipes, took a hot shower, she put her head on a place mat and cried.

Fifteen minutes later, the door to the bedroom opened.

Jessica didn't lift her head.

He came back downstairs. His footfalls were soft as he crossed the room to her. She didn't respond as he put his hands on her shoulders and gave them a gentle squeeze.

"I'm a total dick," he said, sounding truly remorseful. "You've spent the past four weeks doing a really good job with practically no guidance. I had no right to react the way I did."

She didn't want him to see her mottled, tearstained face, probably imprinted with the pattern of the place mat, but she finally looked up.

"There are mitigating factors you couldn't be aware of, given your short time on the job," he said, tracing the tracks of her tears with his fingertips. "Those trials are key to getting the Revelate approved by the FDA. Your questions are good but could inadvertently derail the process. Come to me the next time you have something tricky to discuss with Kate or anyone else. Let me be the messenger."

"I can't know what you don't tell me," she said, still feeling uneasy but relieved to be cut out of communications with Kate.

"I know and I'm sorry," he said.

"Jerk," she said, mainly because she'd already started to absolve him. Also because he was wearing only a towel around his waist, and despite her anger, she was also aroused. "Why did you go off on me like that?"

"Frustration," he said, kissing her tenderly. "To be honest, Kanye missed the meeting, and Kim wasn't as wowed as I'd hoped. Maybe I'll just have to rope in some bigger celebs."

As she relaxed back into her simpler role as Jon's girlfriend, she made a mental note to add *discover all mitigating factors* to her job description.

Chapter Nine

HOLLY

Life's a performance. Make it convincing.

—"How I Lied about My Name and Discovered My Truth,"
a TED Talk by Jon M. Wright

"Say, 'Aah,'" Holly instructed.

"AAAAH!" blurted the adorable, towheaded seven-year-old Maeve.

Wrinkling her nose at the aroma of Cheerios, apple juice, and unbrushed teeth, Holly clicked on her otoscope and gently used the tongue depressor. It was important not to move too quickly: once, a little boy had flinched at exactly the wrong moment, activating his gag reflex and starting her day in the worst possible way.

"I ignored it for a few days," said Maeve's mom, Cynthia, "but she keeps complaining, and I'm wondering if it's a problem with her immune system. Or maybe an allergy we don't know about. God knows her vaccinations are all up to date, so it can't be, you know . . . something like that."

Tossing the tongue depressor in the trash and clicking the speculum into place on the otoscope, Holly gently tilted Maeve's head back so she could peer inside her booger-encrusted nose. Then she instructed Maeve to turn her head left and right so she could look in her ears. In only a single generation, parents had gone from assuming the best on most childhood maladies to anticipating the worst. The way moms compared diagnoses during playdates when Holly's own kids were little, she'd gotten the impression that some of them felt left out if their kids didn't have at least one food sensitivity.

"Hmm," she said, just so Cynthia would know she'd heard her.

Putting the ear tips of the stethoscope in her ears, Holly placed the bell on Maeve's back.

"Breathe in and out for me. Nice, deep breaths."

Maeve obliged, heaving like a horse after a fast lap around the track.

"Now cough."

The little girl coughed so lustily Holly couldn't help but smile. She might have a career on the stage.

"Good job, Maeve," said Holly, draping the stethoscope around her own shoulders.

"What do you think?" asked Cynthia anxiously.

I think I could have been a surgeon, thought Holly wryly, a joke she often told herself when the pediatric stakes were particularly low. She and Jack had been on track for stellar medical careers but had both wanted a family. Neither liked the idea of having a nanny raise their kids. And when Holly became unexpectedly pregnant with Ava shortly after her residency, the issue was forced sooner than either of them anticipated. To his credit, Jack hadn't asked her to abandon her career, but he didn't exactly volunteer to stay home, either. The compromise left her with most of what she wanted—close relationships with their three wonderful kids, a part-time pediatric practice that allowed her to put her skills to some use, a lovely home, and, of course, Horse Stability—none of which would have been possible without Jack's insistence on founding Cancura despite her initial reservations.

"I think," she told Cynthia with a smile, "that we are looking at a case of the common cold. Her fever is slight, the irritation to her throat is minor, and the congestion in her nose and lungs seems consistent with a cold. It can take seven to ten days, or even more, for the symptoms to abate. In the meantime, give her plenty of rest and fluids. If the fever goes up, you can treat it with Tylenol, but it doesn't seem to be bothering her at the moment."

Both Cynthia and Maeve seemed slightly disappointed by the news. It was a familiar reaction: patients came to the doctor because they wanted medicine and a quick cure, not to be told things would work themselves out in time. Definitive answers and miraculous solutions for illnesses that so far had neither—that was exactly what Jack was on the verge of offering to the world. As a pediatrician, the idea was almost too heady for Holly to imagine. Even as the wife of Jonathan Wright, it was still beyond comprehension.

"Thank you so much, Dr. Wright," said Cynthia unconvincingly. Then, as Holly opened the door for them, she added: "I almost forgot to mention it, but my husband saw your husband on a flight to LA earlier this week. He was too far away to say hi, unfortunately."

"Don't you mean San Francisco?" asked Holly.

"Definitely LA. I know because Aaron texted me a picture of Hugh Hefner's star on the Hollywood Walk of Fame."

"Jack travels so much, I can never remember," said Holly.

Had he really said San Francisco, or was she misremembering?

~

San Francisco or LA?

The question nagged at her for the rest of the morning and lingered into the afternoon as she went to the office to check on Horse Stability business, then ferried Logan to soccer practice and Paige to a final rehearsal for the eighth-grade class's opening-night production of *The Music Man*. Jack flew thirty to forty times a year, and she was long past asking him to email his itineraries.

Certainly it was no big deal to ask him to remind her which city he'd traveled to. But the more she thought about it, the more she began to think even asking made her sound suspicious—and she *was* suspicious—so the wording was everything.

Remind me again—did you go to San Francisco?

She'd missed her window to text this morning, as he was now surely on the flight home, determined not to miss Paige's performance as Eulalie Mackecknie Shinn. And really, what was wrong with waiting until he returned to ask, *How was San Francisco?*

Or should she ask, *How was LA?*

A trick, a trap.

Unless the fault was her own. The headaches were still coming and going, and ever since Wags had kicked her, she'd been highly attuned to her own mental calibration, watching herself for gaps in memory and errors in logic. Finding more than she cared to admit. Wondering whether nothing had changed and she was just scrutinizing herself more—or whether everything had changed. She still didn't want the MRI. Didn't want to know.

It was late afternoon when Jack saved her the trouble.

I'm going to miss it. Tell Paige I am SO sorry.

What happened? she texted back.

Cracked windshield, if you can believe it. On the plane. We were all on board waiting to go. We sat there for an hour and then we all had to get off.

In SFO or LAX?

The next two flights are completely booked so I won't be home until tomorrow. I'll see the show tomorrow night.

Impulsively, she typed: *Give me your flight number when you have it and I'll come get you.*

Thinking she'd at least know where it was coming from.

Thanks, but no need. My car's at O'Hare.
OK.
Sorry it worked out like this. Love to the kids.

~

She didn't have time to brood on it. Her parents, who in retirement divided their time between Lake Geneva in Wisconsin and Longboat Key in Florida, arrived early, just as Paige texted that the tech crew was having some problems and everyone had to stay at school until the performance—but could she please bring dinner for the cast and crew? Deputizing Grandpa Walt and Nana Charlotte to collect Logan from soccer, Holly phoned in a rush order for thirty sandwiches and headed to the restaurant to pick them up while Galenia prepared dinner for the rest of them at home.

While she was waiting, she texted Ava, *Don't forget Paige's show.*

Oh boy, answered her adoring eldest daughter.

Be there, commanded Holly, not anticipating or receiving a reply.

As she marched down the auditorium aisle, weighed down by two huge bags of food, Holly noted the frenzied activity around her. The kids' moods oscillated between panic and euphoria, while the drama coach, his assistant, and several parent volunteers tried to keep everyone on task.

"Thanks Mom bye!" yelled Paige, barely pausing as she ran lines with a scene partner.

Duty done, Holly headed home for a rushed meal with her mom, dad, and a sweaty Logan, who had to be browbeaten into taking a shower. Which, naturally, took an eternity.

They were waiting for him in the entry hall, taking turns calling his name with rising humor and exasperation, when her dad asked, "I presume Jack is meeting us there?"

95

"Oh shit, I completely forgot to tell you: his plane had a cracked windshield."

"That sounds serious," said her mom, looking alarmed.

"It was before takeoff," she reassured them. "But he couldn't rebook until tomorrow."

"Where is he?" asked her dad.

"San Francisco," said Holly, utterly without conviction.

"That man sure goes a long way to bring home the bacon," her dad said brightly. "I wish I had his business smarts, not to mention his stamina."

"Thank god you didn't marry that painter," chuckled her mom, a tired joke referencing a guy she'd dated in college with zero intention of marriage, but who had committed the crime of inviting her to a group show for his painting class. To be fair to him, he'd had zero intention of becoming a full-time artist. Told and retold in the telephone game of family lore, the episode eventually became a sliding-doors moment in which she was saved from a life of bohemian squalor by the arrival of Jack. The part they didn't like to joke about was how Jack's Cancura success had rescued her old-money-without-the-money family's finances.

Her dad pulled back his cuff and checked his watch, a gesture she'd seen a thousand times but that, standing in the entry hall waiting to go, made her flash back nineteen years to when he'd done it as they waited in the vestibule of Fourth Presbyterian Church while organ music swelled in the sanctuary.

Jack was in place by the altar, she knew, her dad having peeked inside and given her a thumbs-up. That was reassuring to know after Jack's performance the previous day, when he'd been incommunicado until his late and somewhat unsteady arrival at the rehearsal dinner. Jack's best man had reassured Holly's maid of honor, who passed it along, that Jack had gotten epically drunk at the bachelor party and simply needed all day to sleep it off. Jack convincingly echoed that story once he finally arrived, though he'd refused to answer any questions about the party itself, claiming he had been "sworn to secrecy." Throughout the evening, he was engaged and loving, nothing but a model—if slightly hungover—groom.

But she had never forgotten the first time she laid eyes on him at the rehearsal dinner. How, when he saw her looking at him, his eyes flickered away for a moment and his face was utterly blank. For a single second he had looked like a different person, one who was beyond annoyed to see her. And then suddenly he was his usual charming self again. It was over so quickly she was sure she'd imagined it.

It was the first time she'd ever had that undefinable sick feeling in the pit of her stomach. His aura of unpredictability had drawn her to him, but she had assumed it wouldn't last forever, thinking of marriage as a process of discovering each other and knowing each other completely. If only she'd known he was always going to feel unknowable and just barely out of reach.

"If you don't come down right now, Logan, we are going to be late!" thundered Grandpa Walt.

After a few thumps and bumps and a door slam, Logan came running down the stairs, hair wet but otherwise presentable in a polo and khakis. They hurried out the door, argued about who was driving, and then piled into her dad's Lincoln Navigator for the two-mile drive to school.

I'm here, texted Ava. *Where are you?*

On our way. Your brother had to shower.

Not Holly's greatest parenting moment to lay the blame on the little brother, but Logan's age-appropriate aversion to showers had been a source of great amusement to all of them.

Congratulations. Eye-roll emoji.

Your father's flight was canceled, Holly added.

I wish I had a good excuse too, wrote Ava.

It's not an excuse, scolded Holly.

Whatever. If he doesn't have to be there, I don't see why I have to.

We'll see you in five minutes, wrote Holly, telling herself not to engage further.

The parking lot was full, something her dad verified by slowly rolling down every row before he succumbed to reality and parked on the street. As they walked a few hundred extra yards, there were enough other stragglers that Holly was reasonably sure they wouldn't miss the curtain, but much less confident about finding seats. She didn't want to have to stand in the back, if only to avoid hearing her parents' postshow complaints about aching legs and backs.

Unexpectedly, Ava saved the day.

Up front, she texted as the four of them entered the crowded auditorium.

Her disgruntled teenage daughter had had the gumption to save four seats, third-row center, no doubt having to defend them against the predatory horde of camera-toting parents.

"Thank you," whispered Holly as she squeezed past Ava, resisting the urge to plant a big kiss on the top of her head.

Taking her seat at the end of the group, she realized with surprise she was seated next to Cynthia, who, Holly suddenly recalled, also had a son Paige's age.

"How's Maeve?" she asked, to be polite.

"Home with ginger ale and her iPad," Cynthia said.

Her husband sat on the other side, scrolling intently on his phone. Holly couldn't remember his name, because he rarely brought the kids, but his presence felt like a rebuke.

"Is Jack still in LA?" asked Cynthia.

"Who knows?" Holly murmured, ignoring the surprised look on Cynthia's face and opening her program. As she pretended to read it, she felt a tap on her shoulder and turned around.

Brian. Smiling warmly.

"I didn't see you," she said.

"I just sat down. Easier to find a seat when you just need one."

"I guess I forgot your girls are in the show."

"Tech crew. Sound and lighting." He laughed uncomfortably, noting her cold demeanor. "I'll be spending the next two hours thinking of ways to compliment them on their work."

Holly didn't ask where his wife was. She knew the various answers by heart. *On the road. At the office. Just couldn't get away. Putting in a ton of hours.* His admission over drinks had been jarring, but she was definitely sympathetic to his plight. She felt badly about shutting him down so harshly, but she'd been flustered.

"Looks like we're about to get started," he said as the houselights started to go down.

His hand was on the back of her seat. Thankfully, her parents were fully absorbed in trying to remember how to silence their cell phones and didn't notice.

She looked into his eyes, which she'd always thought were blue, and realized they were actually green. "We'll see."

Chapter Ten

LARK

People will have questions, so own your story and keep it straight.

—"How I Lied about My Name and Discovered My Truth,"
a TED Talk by Jon M. Wright

Lark was having trouble breathing. Her arms were quivering. Her thigh and stomach muscles burned. Below her, Trip continued thrusting, his hands on her hips, holding her in place and making sure they stayed in rhythm. His eyes were locked on hers. She'd lost track of how long they'd been going as one song on her playlist bled into the next. She was so close . . .

God, it was good.

She wasn't inexperienced but had never experienced anything quite like this.

His handsome face . . .

Suddenly, she was almost there.

He could tell. "Yeah?" he asked simply.

She nodded, closing her eyes briefly to focus on the feeling, to make sure it didn't slip away. When she opened them, he was still looking at her. Waiting for her to finish so he could, too.

The best part lasted longer than she could have imagined.

After they both used the bathroom and had a drink of water, Lark lay back, listening to her music in his hotel room with an idle thought that the mattress and sheets were better quality than anything she'd ever owned—but probably not as good as what Trip had at home. Which he'd said was a neglected condo in a downtown Chicago high-rise.

He was sitting on the edge of the bed with his back to her, texting or emailing. His phone breaks were frequent. *Business,* he said. *Always business.*

She often felt like she had to compete with his phone for his full attention.

"I want to go to your place sometime," she told him. "Just for a weekend or something."

He didn't answer right away. Then, after he finished tapping out his message, he locked his phone and put it facedown on the nightstand. He flopped back on the bed.

"No, you don't," he said, smiling.

"I just said I did."

"I've never had anybody visit me there."

"You mean, none of your girlfriends?"

"I mean nobody, ever," he said, lightly running his thumb over her hip and down the outside of her thigh. "After my divorce, I just rented the first place I found. It's nice. Great view. But I never decorated— I haven't even had a friend over for a beer to watch a football game. Frankly, the place depresses me."

Lark saw two red handprints on his biceps where she'd gripped him tightly when she came. She wondered if he'd noticed when he was in the bathroom.

"Why don't you just pay someone to decorate?" she asked.

He looked thoughtful. "I'm not sure, honestly. At first I thought I was just going to be there for a year or so, kind of a transitional phase. But the transition somehow became the new norm. Permanent impermanence."

"It's starting to feel a little weird," Lark confessed.

Trip frowned. "What do you mean?"

"I mean, it feels like you only exist in my life—I don't exist in yours. You've been here three times but I haven't been to Chicago once." The words coming out of her mouth surprised her, but they were true. It was like she was suddenly articulating things she'd been half thinking and half feeling. "You even opened an office here."

"I told you, I need a West Coast base of operations."

"That's bullshit, Trip. You could have an office anywhere. You may be tired of doing it, but you can work out of hotel business centers. Your hotel room. You haven't spent more than a few hours at your new office. I mean, what's going on?"

Trip stared at her, then rolled onto his back, looking up at the ceiling. "You sound suspicious."

"I'm not suspicious, I'm confused."

He rubbed his face and breathed in deeply. Exhaled.

"What's going on is you," he said.

"That doesn't help, Trip," she said, although the fact that he'd stated it so plainly literally made her heart flutter.

"I want to be with you. I want to be *here*, with you," he added.

"Is it the sex?"

"The sex is fucking awesome," he admitted, turning his head and grinning.

"Is it my game?"

"I think it's going to be a big success. I'll be happy if I can play a part in that."

Lark sat up, folded her legs, and pulled the sheet over her shoulders.

"It's more than any of that," he continued. "But I'm doing my best not to rush things. Especially after your experience with Dylan. I know what it's like to be in that place, Lark. I remember giving up on the idea of love, even hoping I'd find it. And I want you to trust what we have."

Love. That word again. It made her feel off-balance.

"If you want me to trust you, I need to know you," she said. "I really know nothing about you. I fucking googled you, and there's hardly anything. And let's face it, your Instagram isn't exactly a personal record."

Trip laughed, turning fully toward her. "I admit I'm not good at that. What do you want to know?"

"Everything."

"Then everything it is."

"Really?"

"Shoot."

She shot, firing off questions as fast as she could think of them. Where was he born? Dayton, Ohio. Did he grow up there? Mostly. Did he have any siblings? A brother. Where did he go to college? Indiana University. What did he study? Biology and economics. What extracurriculars did he do in college? At this question he just laughed and said, "Tell you later." What was his first job out of college? Associate broker trainee. When did he meet his ex-wife? At a meat-market bar in Manhattan. What was she like? Successful, driven, already wealthy. What went wrong? Pretty much everything. ("I could tell you what went right in ten seconds," Trip said ruefully.) How long had they been divorced? Officially, five years; unofficially, longer. Had he had other serious relationships since then? Seriously underwhelming, mostly. Mostly? He'd dated some wonderful women, but none of them were the right fit—until now.

It was intense, getting so much information so quickly, but also exciting. Far from eliciting jealousy, hearing about his exes gave him depth and made him seem three-dimensional. Though what had initially attracted her to him was that he was a blank slate, Lark realized that simplistic view was the very thing that would have kept them from forming something meaningful and real.

At the same time, she noticed that his answers about his family were by far the shortest. He almost seemed to be avoiding the topic.

"Why don't you want to talk about your family, Trip?"

"I don't talk about them with anyone."

"Why not?"

He sat up slowly, folding his legs and mirroring her position except not bothering with a blanket or sheet. When he finally started talking, it seemed like he had come to a decision. Uncharacteristically, he didn't look her in the eye.

"My parents were killed in a freak accident when I was fifteen," he said. "A semi turned right from the left lane, crushing the front half of the car. I was in the back seat."

"Oh my god," Lark said, feeling sick.

"My brother, Mike, was already out of the house, and we lost touch," he continued. "I spent my high school years in Muncie, Indiana, living with an uncle who didn't particularly want the job of being my parent, and I had a hard time making friends."

Glancing at her, he added, "I feel like I shouldn't be telling you this."

"Of course you should," she said, feeling a surge of empathy. "I'm so sorry."

His brown eyes shimmered.

"It was what it was, and I don't dwell on it, because the bad things also bring the good things, you know? It all helped make me who I am. I had a high school counselor who saw something in me, and he became a mentor, helping me get my grades up and apply for colleges. I was such a bad student that I couldn't believe it when I got into Indiana University. I moved to Bloomington and worked two jobs to cover what my financial aid didn't. That's why I laughed when you asked about extracurriculars."

"I can relate," she told him. "I had to work through college, too, even though I forced myself to make time for rec volleyball and a Spanish conversation club, just to meet people."

"I wish I'd been that well rounded," he chuckled.

She reached out and took his hand, thinking it was the first time she'd ever seen him vulnerable. It was remarkable given the depth of his pain.

"I got a summer internship at a tiny brokerage in Bloomington, where I caught another break . . ." he continued. "Jesus, listen to me. I'm giving you my résumé."

"Exactly what I wanted," Lark told him, wanting to be as good a listener to Trip as he was to her. And it *was* interesting to learn he hadn't been born with a trust fund.

"The short version is that I got another lucky break. The guy who ran the place was named Joe King, and he became another mentor to me. He convinced me to get my MBA instead of taking the first job I was offered. My grades at IU were great, and I was still poor, so I was able to get into the University of Chicago's business school. That's where I discovered the power of knowing well-connected people. That's where things really started happening for me."

"And now you're an angel investor."

"That term makes us sound like nice guys who just make everybody happy, when in reality it's almost an oxymoron." He squeezed her hand. "But I've been extremely fortunate in my business career, and I've always looked for opportunities to pay back what I was given."

Men are so strange, Lark thought. Dylan had been so eager to show her his best qualities, so relentless in highlighting them that after only a few months there were none left to discover. Meanwhile, his inability to work hard and fulfill his ambitions had grown more apparent by the day.

Then there was Trip, who seemed content to listen to her and never wanted to talk about himself, but who had a story as compelling as anyone she'd ever met. Who'd suffered horrible hurt as a young man but managed to carry himself with an unbelievably appealing confidence. Who'd come from almost nothing and given himself almost everything.

Except love. He was dropping hints about it but seemed to be worried about pushing her too far, too fast. Thinking of her feelings, not his.

Suddenly Lark was lifted on a tidal rush of feeling, a euphoria that physically warmed her and made her downright giddy.

He saw something change in her face.

"What?" he asked wonderingly.

She leaned forward and kissed him on the lips.

"I love you, Trip Mitchell," she said.

Chapter Eleven

JESSICA

When your name is at the top of the org chart, there's only one person who needs to know everything: you.

—"How I Lied about My Name and Discovered My Truth," a TED Talk by Jon M. Wright

Jessica wished there were some way she could avoid Philip on her route to the coffee station. So tall and gawky his shiny, slightly rectangular forehead cleared the upper edge of his cubicle, Philip and his compulsive need to voice his unfiltered inner monologue harried passersby like a one-man gauntlet. As she went for her first cup, he'd told her, *You look good in blue, but I prefer that gray dress you wear on Wednesdays.* The remark left her wondering if she actually did wear her gray Calvin Klein dress only on Wednesdays. She didn't want to engage with him any more than she had to, which was why she waited for him to go to the men's room before she zipped down the hallway, quickly refilled her mug, and hustled back to her office.

She almost made it.

"Jessica?"

She had no choice but to stop, turn, and brace herself for whatever uncomfortable and starkly honest brain fart he was about to let loose.

"I'm finished comparing those results you emailed me."

"Darn it," she said, relieved that he was actually talking about work but kicking herself for failing to confirm that he hadn't, in fact, done anything with them after saying they were *outside his purview.* "I forgot to tell you not to worry about it."

"Why not?"

"For one thing, we've broken ties with the lab that provided the outlier results."

"And for another?"

"Come into my office," Jessica said, ushering Philip down the hall.

He even moved awkwardly, as though his limbs were new and he still hadn't read the manual.

Once inside, Jessica closed the door. After Jon's surprising blowup, which had been followed by an evening of epic makeup sex, he'd shared some information that was supposed to be for her eyes only. She had no choice but to show it to Philip now—somehow she just knew he would keep asking until she did.

"Jon was aware of the consistency problem with the lab in question, so he employed an additional outside lab to run another series of tests on the exact same samples." She handed him a copy of the data Jon had emailed to her. "The latest testing matches our in-house results precisely."

Philip rubbed the spot on his arm where she'd touched him while guiding him through her door. "Curious."

"How so?" she asked, hoping his answer corresponded to the data in question and not the fact that her hand had briefly made contact with his body.

"These numbers are literally identical to the blood tests used as controls. Even with the same patients, and the same Revelate machine, there are typically minute variations."

Jessica stared at the printouts, comparing fine-printed lines of data. Seeing that what he was saying was true. It was as though the in-house results had literally been copied.

"It's possible they've done some upgrades to the Revelate I wouldn't be aware of," Philip said, adding quickly, "I'm sure that's it."

"If so, why wouldn't Jon have told me?" asked Jessica.

Philip rubbed his arm again, making Jessica wonder if she'd given him a new and long-lasting tic. "Maybe you haven't noticed, but around here, most things are on a need-to-know basis."

Jon had made her promise she'd come to him about anything, big or small, and said he'd never overreact again. He'd flown in early this morning and was currently in the office, though he was leaving early for Barrington Hills to see his daughter's play and make nice with Holly in advance of an upcoming court date.

Jessica felt bad for Jon and his kids. He'd admitted that part of his stress was also due to the concussion Holly had been claiming she'd suffered and which she'd used once again as an excuse when she conveniently "forgot" to tell him his daughter's opening-night performance in *The Music Man* was going to be on a Thursday instead of the traditional Friday night.

Jessica reassured him, telling him he was a great dad and that any disappointment Paige felt about his missing the premiere would be immediately forgotten once she saw him in the audience tonight. Still, she hated sending Jon back into enemy territory knowing Annie Wilkes was lying in wait, plotting further manipulations. At some point, the woman needed to accept that her marriage was over and move on. If not for her own sake, then for her kids'. They were ultimately the ones hurt most by her petty games.

They all needed to move on.

As Jessica headed toward Jon's office, she allowed herself to imagine the glorious day his divorce finally became final. Knowing Jon, he wouldn't call her from the courthouse but would instead plan a surprise celebration at one of Chicago's best restaurants or, better yet, a romantic weekend away—maybe somewhere like California wine country. He'd arrange a private tasting, where they'd toast his freedom and the end of the stress that had kept him from being completely present, before planning a future around loving each other and working together on behalf of humankind.

The Pierre and Marie Curie of childhood cancer . . .

She couldn't help but grin at the possibilities and the magnitude of their life's mission. That was, until she rounded the corner and spotted him sitting on the corner of his desk with a charming smile. Had he not been so deep in conversation, he would have looked up and their eyes would have met through his office's glass wall. Instead, he continued to chat and laugh with Kate. Silken-haired, blue-eyed, brilliant Kate, who couldn't be questioned directly by anyone but him. And, unlike the brief moment in which Jessica had touched Philip on the arm to usher him into her office, Jon's hand lingered on Kate's shoulder.

Jessica backed away, now praying he wouldn't notice as she scampered toward the safety of her office.

He didn't.

~

Jon wasn't a flirt. He didn't ogle attractive women or chat up pretty waitresses. He always gave Jessica his full attention. More than that, he was always professional. Jessica had simply gotten jealous because she'd never seen him interact in such a relaxed way with another woman. And Kate wasn't just any woman—she was a highly respected coworker who'd been at Cancura since the beginning. And work was work. If they were going to succeed both professionally and personally, Jessica needed to be pragmatic and tactical, not immature, emotional, and groundlessly suspicious.

Given that Jon often skipped lunch in favor of a noon workout in the fitness center, Jessica decided a friendly gym chat—with no specific mention of Philip or Kate—was the best way to navigate the situation.

Not that there was a situation.

"Hey, you," Jon whispered conspiratorially as she climbed on the elliptical machine beside his in an otherwise empty corner of the fitness center.

"Hey," she said, setting the timer for thirty-five minutes.

"I was just thinking about you."

"Were you?" Doing her best to sound casual and unconcerned.

"Kate stopped by my office this morning."

Jessica winced at the sound of her name on his lips but was relieved he'd broached the subject and she didn't have to. Or had he seen her approach his office, after all?

"I brought her up to speed on the new lab results," Jon said. "I hadn't told her or anyone else about it because I wanted to be sure the process was as pure as possible."

"How did she take it?"

"She was delighted to learn our testing is as accurate as we'd hoped. Per your concern, I'm authorizing funding to increase our in-house capacity."

"That's great news," she said, happy for a win and leaving Philip's concern about identical test results for another day. "Wasn't Kate peeved that you kept something that important from her?"

"You certainly have a handle on her," he said, as if she really did.

Not quite knowing what to say next, Jessica worked out beside Jon in silence for a few minutes, breathing harder as the resistance increased on the elliptical's hill program.

"Hey," she finally said. "Am I missing anything where Kate is concerned?"

Jon slowed slightly. "Like what?"

"I don't know. You seem . . . I don't know . . . particularly protective of her or something."

Jon raised an eyebrow. "I have to keep her happy. Every time I turn around, some top research outfit or pharmaceutical company is trying to wine, dine, and steal her from me."

"From you?" Jessica said before she could stop herself.

"Jessie," he whispered in the sweet way he usually reserved for home. "I'm going to have the same problem with you before I know it."

"Is that what you say to all the lady doc—?"

"Don't be sexist, it's against company policy," he said, flashing the smile that had gotten her upset in the first place. He looked around to make sure no one was listening. "You have absolutely nothing to worry about where Kate is concerned. You know that, right?"

"I do," she managed to say, feeling ever so slightly choked up. "I do."

"Now stop dawdling," he said, reaching over and increasing the resistance on her machine.

As he did, she noticed a large bruise on his right biceps. Actually four smaller, fingerprint-shaped bruises grouped together. She glanced over at his left and saw what looked like a thumbprint on his inner arm.

"What's that?" she asked.

"What's what?"

"On your biceps. Those bruises."

He glanced down and shook his head. "Jujitsu."

"Jujitsu?"

"One of the potential investors is a martial arts fanatic with a fucking dojo in his house. I had no choice but to suit up for a lesson, during which I got tossed around like a rag doll."

"Ouch," Jessica said, examining the bruises again.

"No pain, no gain. Right?"

Chapter Twelve

HOLLY

*You are the problem solver. Always have your white
horse saddled and ready.*

—"How I Lied about My Name and Discovered My Truth,"
a TED Talk by Jon M. Wright

Holly hated having to check up on Jack, even though she told herself she was confirming her memory as much as his story. She'd finally admitted the kick from Wags had given her a concussion, and even if her stupid pride had kept her from having it properly diagnosed, she still didn't think it mattered much because the headaches were gradually abating and her spacey moments were becoming fewer and farther between. If only it weren't for the nagging uncertainty introduced by Cynthia during Maeve's appointment—and the unsettling thought that, if Jack had lied, there had been a witness—she might have let this one go.

San Francisco or LA?

After the successful opening of *The Music Man* at Paige's school, and the trip for ice cream suggested by her parents (which Ava ghosted, Paige politely endured, and Logan enthusiastically embraced because, face it, eleven-year-old boys can't stop eating)—after finally saying goodbyes and good nights and settling back in bed with a glass of wine, Holly had opened her laptop to find the answer.

Jack was a miles-and-points monster, so there was only one possible airline. And checking that airline's scheduled direct flights from San Francisco to Chicago, Holly found . . . nothing. No flights had been flagged for cancellations or delays. Everything was right on time. Los Angeles it was.

Except when she checked direct flights from LA, it was the same story. No significant delays.

The momentary relief Holly had felt evaporated.

She stared at her phone. Considered texting, *Where are you?* It was two hours earlier on the West Coast. If he was on the West Coast at all.

Had he for some reason decided to fly a different airline? That unlikely possibility occupied her for another hour and another glass of wine while she tried all the major carriers. Jack wouldn't fly a discount airline under any circumstances. He would rather have walked.

By the time she finally closed the laptop, her head was throbbing.

And then today he had arrived in late afternoon like a conquering hero—after putting in an obligatory half day at the office. Ava, Paige, and Logan all happened to be home and greeted him in the foyer like a scene out of *Father Knows Best.* Holly had served enough years as the stay-at-home parent to know she would never receive such a hearty welcome, but that didn't mean it didn't rankle. He had gifts for all of them, of course, and flowers for Paige, insisting he had heard rave reviews of her opening-night performance when, in truth, he couldn't have known a thing unless he'd asked someone other than Holly.

Which, come to think of it, she couldn't entirely rule out.

Paige *had* been terrific, of course, singing in tune, delivering her lines with almost no mistakes, and getting quite a few laughs.

Holly bided her time while Jack squired Paige back to school for that night's performance, then dutifully gathered Ava and Logan in response to his postshow text message: *What a show! Paige told me it was even better than last night, and I believe it! We're all going out to celebrate at the Anvil Club.*

The kitchen will be closed, she texted back.

Not to us, he answered. *I'll make a call.*

Sounds good, she wrote, knowing there was no point dragging her feet.

She couldn't help but note the lack of complaint from both Ava and Logan when she pulled them away from their respective screens and told them the plan. Jack had the same effect on investors as he had on his own family: everybody got with the program.

Apparently, the manager of the Anvil Club was on board, too, greeting them with a smile as they arrived. A few evening drinkers were watching a Blackhawks game in the bar, but the dining room was empty except for Jack and Paige, waiting at a corner table—and Brian and his wife, Nancy, who were just leaving.

"Finally found a sitter we like!" said Brian abruptly as he realized they were headed toward each other.

"Good for you!" said Holly, sounding a little false, even to herself.

Nancy smiled and said hello. Even though they crossed paths from time to time, she'd always struck Holly as distant.

"If you need a backup, you can always ask Ava," she added, sensing her eldest's eye roll without seeing it. Ava had been an enthusiastic babysitter at fourteen but was now over it.

Ava and Logan continued on to the table where their father and sister waited as Nancy headed for the door. Brian lagged behind, and Holly guessed it was just because he didn't want to seem brusque.

"Jack went to see the show tonight, so we're all celebrating," Holly told him, just to say something. "We'll be sure to toast the sound and lighting, too."

Brian chuckled. "I'm afraid that's more than we did."

"How's Nancy?" she asked.

"Busy. And Jack?"

"You know it. Home from California, anyway."

Brian broke the awkward silence that followed by saying, "Look, Holly, I'm sorry if I was out of line—"

"It's okay," she said, as quietly as she could.

He glanced ruefully over at Jack. "I just had to—"

"Not. Now," she practically breathed.

Brian nodded and then walked quickly out of the room as Holly collected herself before proceeding to the table. Nothing had happened, yet Holly couldn't help feeling somehow caught. Why should she, though?

Fortunately, Jack was oblivious and in an exceedingly good mood. He held forth during the meal, shining the spotlight on each of the kids in turn and making sure it wasn't all about Paige. A round of drinks and desserts was followed, improbably, by plates of sliders because Logan's hunger somehow turned infectious, and they all agreed that why, yes, they *would* like a second dinner—*Why, yes, I would* repeated until it became a catchphrase likely to last into next week.

She waited until the hubbub died down and the kids were all showing each other things on their phones before she said, quietly, "There was no cracked windshield, was there?"

"What?" he said, smiling as though he hadn't heard her.

"The cracked windshield, your canceled flight. I checked United, American, and Delta. Even Southwest and Alaska. It was silly, I couldn't remember if you were coming from San Francisco or LA, so I looked for the canceled flight."

He should have been outraged. *You were checking up on me?*

He could have said, *Why didn't you just ask?*

"I was in San Francisco *and* LA," he said without batting an eye. "Back and forth. Crazy week on the shuttle. The flight with the cracked windshield was private. My LA investor had to send his plane to Chicago anyway and told me to hitch a ride."

"But you said *rebook*," countered Holly weakly.

He gave an amused frown. "Sorry, poor choice of words. I couldn't wait for them to repair the fucking plane, so I needed to book a commercial flight. I meant *book*."

"Oh."

How many arguments—not that this even qualified—had ended with Holly doubting herself, no matter how sure she was of her position? How could she confirm his story, she wondered, and would she even try?

He slid closer to her on the banquette they were sharing. "I missed you," he said. "I'm sorry my travel has been crazier than usual lately. Are you up for a nightcap?"

Which, between them, had never meant a drink in a public place.

An hour later, the kids were in their rooms, the hall lights were out, and Jack was removing Holly's panties with agonizing slowness. These days they probably had sex only once a month, if that, and yet she marveled that he was still always able to make each lovemaking session a genuine occasion. Before undressing her, he had dimmed the lights as far as they would go and put on some hip new music. She didn't know how he found the time to try new bands, but she liked it. It made her feel younger.

She'd had several relationships before Jack, plus a handful of one-night stands, and one thing all those men had in common was a sense of urgency. They couldn't seem to wait to get her naked and were even faster to roll over or leave afterward. Jack had never been like that. He liked to set a mood, lingering over her body, drawing the act out until she just couldn't take it anymore. She had always been able to count on his full attention—and the eye contact that still had the ability to make her melt.

And melt she did.

Afterward, he rolled her onto her stomach, straddled her, and gently kneaded her neck and shoulders, lazily tracing long lines down her back with his fingertips until she was practically Jell-O—and almost asleep. Eventually, he climbed off and padded to the bathroom. Drowsily she heard the toilet flush and then water running as he brushed his teeth. Needing desperately to pee before she drifted off, Holly got up, found a robe, and joined him in the bathroom, which was lit only by the night-light. She swatted him on his boxer-clad butt as she made her way to the toilet.

Then she stopped. Turned on the vanity lights.

"What the hell, Holly," he protested, blinking in the sudden glare.

Dark purple bruises marked his biceps on both arms.

"What are those?" she asked, pointing.

Taking the toothbrush out of his mouth, he looked down, seemingly bewildered.

"They look like handprints, Jack."

Holly had just now lain compliantly beneath him, opening her legs, her hands on the small of his back, on his butt. If he had put his full weight on her, squeezing her arms . . . she might have identical bruises.

Shit shit shit.

"They are handprints," he said, putting his toothbrush down and rinsing. "I was rock climbing with this trust-fund baby in LA. He got his inheritance when he turned thirty, which was last year, and he's spending it pretty much the way you'd expect. Including a world-class rock-climbing wall in his three-story atrium. It was his plane, actually."

Holly sank onto the toilet seat, unable to bring herself to believe him. And now she couldn't pee, either.

Jack chuckled. "He's sitting on a hundred million dollars and needs somewhere to put it, because his financial adviser says he has enough toys. He thinks he's some hot-shit extreme-sports athlete, but he can barely ride a skateboard, and he can't belay for shit. Fortunately, he had a pro helping out who was wearing a harness and just fucking grabbed me, both hands, so I didn't fall."

Who knows? thought Holly. *It could even be true.*

He looked at her, waiting to see if she believed it or if he needed to go further.

She gave him a tired smile. "I'm glad someone was there to catch you."

"Me too," he said, grinning. "It would have been a long way down."

"Go on to bed. I'll be there in a minute."

He kissed the top of her head and left, closing the door behind him.

Holly stared at the wall. It was happening again. She should have known better than to think it would ever stop.

Chapter Thirteen

Lark

Don't lose focus. Your success or failure can hinge on the tiniest detail.

—"How I Lied about My Name and Discovered My Truth," a TED Talk by Jon M. Wright

Lark stepped out of the elevator and took the escalator down to the lobby, resting her wheeled carry-on bag on the step behind her, tucking the canvas tote containing the Activate! prototype under her arm. The adrenaline of her first solo meeting with a major buyer had yet to wear off, and she felt as though she were floating. She couldn't wait to get to the hotel and call Trip to give him the blow-by-blow.

Stepping off the escalator, she marched purposefully through the lobby of Target HQ, but before her momentum carried her through the front doors, she stopped: snow was now swirling down the Minneapolis street, and she was woefully unprepared for the elements. The cashmere scarf she'd unearthed in a drawer did little to insulate the thin business suit she'd purchased for the trip. She only wished she'd had the foresight to add a stylish wool overcoat or even a puffy winter jacket she could pull on at a discreet distance.

Trip had told her the hotel was a short walk away, but she didn't want to be found frozen in a snowdrift, either. Plucking her phone out of her slim, also brand-new briefcase—and making a mental note to avoid bringing three bags to her next meeting if she could help it—she called an Uber. Remembering Trip's own words, she made it an Uber Black.

Anytime anyone might be watching, make sure you look like you don't need the money.

It was highly unlikely anyone would note whether she climbed into a Jaguar XJ or a Toyota Yaris, but he was probably right that it was worth spending a few extra dollars to maintain appearances. Her ride was still five minutes away, so she Instagrammed a quick photo of a whimsical clock in the lobby and captioned it, **Right on target.**

When the car came, Lark's sprint across the sidewalk convinced her she'd made the right choice. It felt like the temperature had dropped ten degrees while she'd been in her meeting. How did people *live* here?

"Let me guess," said the friendly driver in an accent she couldn't place. "You are from Florida?"

"California," she admitted with a laugh.

"I knew it was somewhere warm! Do you want me to take you to the North Face store?"

"I won't be here long," she assured him.

The hotel was only six blocks away, a distance the philosophical man made seem much farther by telling her how many other drivers wouldn't have taken such a short fare, but he didn't mind because, when you thought about it, everybody needed to get where they needed to go, you know? She wished she had requested the quiet-car feature, because she wanted to process her thoughts and his small talk wasn't helping. As it was, she barely had time to check her phone and note that Triphammer312 had already liked her photo. *That* warmed her up a little.

Suddenly, she was at the hotel. As the sensibly dressed doorman opened the car door, Lark thanked the driver, thanked the doorman—refusing his offer to carry her three small bags—and hurried inside.

She had planned to check in, freshen up, and leave her bag in her room before the meeting, but a delayed flight had meant she'd needed to go straight to Target. Now, as she waited to check in at the hotel, she enjoyed playing the businesswoman: the suit, the bags, the car. Since no one could see the tattoo covering her back, only the blue streaks in her hair gave her away.

Truth be told? She liked the role. Having money to spend was nice—it was great not having to take a shared ride or sleep in a cheap Airbnb—but more than that, it made her feel purposeful. Even powerful. Being slender, multiracial, and decent looking, Lark was more than used to being talked down to, objectified, and dismissed. If she had been wearing ripped jeans and a formfitting T-shirt instead of professional attire, she knew the drivers and doormen wouldn't have stepped so quickly, and the receptionist at Target certainly wouldn't have assumed she was there for an important meeting. So.

The desk clerk looked her way. "Next guest?"

"Lark Robinson," she said as she approached. "I'm checking in."

The clerk tapped her computer, frowned, and looked up. "I'm not seeing anything under that name."

Lark checked the hotel's name and address in her calendar—she was in the right place—before realizing the likely problem: Trip had a weakness for earning airline miles and hotel points.

"My boyfriend made the reservation and probably put it under his name: Trip Mitchell. Or maybe Jonathan Mitchell."

Nodding, the clerk tried again. "I see a Jonathan Wright and a Jonathan Yerbinski, but no Mitchell."

"You're completely sure?" Lark asked.

"I'm sorry. Nothing else is coming up, and we're booked solid," said the clerk with a meaningful look over Lark's shoulder at the growing line behind her. "Vikings-Packers."

With a growing sense of unease, Lark left her place in line and found a quiet place to call. Trip had talked her into staying overnight, reminding her just how far Minneapolis was from LA.

Only now it looked like she might be sleeping in a hotel lobby or an airport gate.

Fortunately, he picked up on the first ring.

"How'd it go?"

"Great," she told him. "And Alanna says hi. I mean, she didn't make a commitment on the spot, obviously, but she absolutely loved the game. She invited an intern in, and we all played it, right there in the conference room. I was terrified that for some reason it wouldn't work—"

"It did, of course."

"—but, yes, it worked perfectly. We even played a second round so they could see a different outcome. I was there for almost three hours! She said she would present it at the buyers' meeting. They order with a six-month lead time, so we shouldn't have any problem with production."

"So far, so fucking good."

"I learned some useful stuff about their distribution setup, too," continued Lark, her words spilling out, wanting to prove she hadn't missed anything. "We're going to have to decide soon if we want to produce in China or Germany."

"Cost or quality. Let's get an order before we decide," said Trip.

Finally, Lark paused. She looked at the briefcase and tote she'd leaned against the roller bag at her feet in the hotel lobby.

"There's only one little problem," she told him. "I'm at the hotel, and they don't have a reservation in my name or yours."

"That's not good," he said after a moment.

"And they're all booked up for a football game—"

"I'll handle it," he said. "Go into the bar and order yourself a drink. By the time you're done, I'll have things straightened out."

"You sound pretty confident," she said, doubting him but feeling better anyway.

"Just get that drink. Have one for me, too. I'll call you when your room is ready."

She took a deep breath. "Love you."

"Love you, too."

Ending the call, she pulled her bag into the crowded restaurant adjacent to the lobby. With an impossibly high ceiling and acres of exotic wood and patterned glass, it was a far cry from her last hotel bar in Buffalo. A hostess greeted her, asking Lark whether she'd prefer the bar or a table; after a quick glance at the former, Lark asked for a table. She didn't want to juggle her bags on a barstool, and she didn't want to risk being hit on, either.

Even though being hit on turned out pretty well the last time, she thought to herself with a smile.

It had been two months, and the memory of that amazing night was still enough to make her blush and involuntarily clench her thighs.

The hostess led her to a table, and Lark arranged her bags and sat down on a banquette with a view of the bar. A number of solo business travelers, all male, hunched over drinks and thumbed their screens. One of them, tall and shaven headed in a shiny charcoal suit, looked up and made eye contact, his eyebrows going up either in surprise or invitation. She hoped it was involuntary.

In response, she scrutinized the happy hour menu the hostess had dropped on the table, and when the server glided up, Lark ordered a vodka soda and a wild-mushroom flatbread. By then the man's attention was again on his phone, allowing Lark to take in the scene unobserved.

A business trip was still a novelty to her, something to savor. For the weary road warriors at the bar, she imagined it was something very different: a blurred routine they would hope to break with any diversion possible. She thought with a twinge that Trip traveled more than anyone she'd ever met, and even though he remained engaged and alive, surely he'd felt the grind of being alone in a strange city. He had to have worked his charms on other single women in other hotel bars.

And that was fine. Lark's mom had raised her to believe men's and women's bodies were their own, and what they did for pleasure was nobody's business. Sex wasn't love. Trip could lay no claim to her sexual past, nor she to his. What was happening between them now was new for both of them, shared by nobody else.

Her mom hadn't even batted an eye at the age difference—though she did suggest, "Let's not be too specific about that to your father, at least for now." Lark wanted to introduce them soon, but she and Trip already had so little time to themselves that she planned to wait for one of his longer visits.

Her drink came quickly, and she took a refreshing sip, watching in amusement as the guy with the shiny head jumped up and offered his seat to a woman, ordering her a drink before she'd had a chance to sit down. Lark lifted her phone and pretended to look at it, trying to make her surveillance less obvious. Anyone glancing back would see a hip, young businesswoman checking her email and wonder why she was in town. Would anyone in a million years have guessed she was selling a tabletop game to a chain store?

Thank god for Trip's insane list of connections. He'd told Lark he'd met Alanna, the Target buyer, more than a dozen years ago, when they'd both been in finance. Attractive and roughly the same age as Trip, Alanna had asked how he was doing, and Lark couldn't help but wonder if they'd been romantically involved. Not that she cared. And Alanna certainly hadn't shown any signs of having a still-smoldering crush. Trip was just so damn likable that everyone wanted to help him. Maybe that was his big secret, even though he'd never said it succinctly: *Make everyone love you.*

She had just taken her first bite of flatbread when her phone vibrated and Trip's name appeared on the lock screen. After chewing and swallowing as quickly as she dared, she answered.

"You're all set," he told her. "It must have been a problem with their website. I was on a flight when I booked it, and the internet was going in and out."

"But they said they didn't have any rooms," said Lark, puzzled. "How did they magically find one?"

Trip laughed. "They always have rooms."

Reminding her that not all businesspeople were created equal.

"When you're ready, check in under my name," he continued. "And when you turn out the lights, imagine I'm there with you."

Lark, suddenly missing him, promised she would.

Chapter Fourteen

Jessica

You can't control every narrative, but you damn well better try.

—"How I Lied about My Name and Discovered My Truth,"
a TED Talk by Jon M. Wright

Taco Tuesdays lured everyone out of the deepest recesses of Cancura and up to the fifth floor, where they joined the line at the café by eleven thirty. Any later, and the most popular varieties—korean chicken, thai shrimp, and middle eastern lamb—would be sold out. By twelve thirty, there was little chance of scoring even a spoonful of classic carne asada.

"Craziness," announced Olivia Zsofka from the condiments table, where she grabbed a dangerously spicy-looking bottle of hot sauce.

"Complete and utter," Jessica agreed as she spooned cilantro and sliced red cabbage onto her shrimp tacos. "But I suppose that's what you get when the employee café is practically Zagat rated."

Olivia chuckled. "If Jon could make that happen, you know he would."

"I don't think I've ever seen him in here," Jessica allowed herself to say, despite the fact that Olivia was Jon's executive assistant.

"Not on Tuesdays, anyway," Olivia said. "Too hectic."

Because everyone piled into the café at the same time to score their favorite taco combinations, the dining area transformed from a lovely, Zen-like gathering space into an adult, all-science-nerd version of a high school cafeteria. The Innovation group (what Jessica now knew to be Cancura-speak for product development) took over the tables by the windows. Translation (a.k.a. marketing) crowded into a group of four-tops by the condiment and silverware stations. Discovery (advanced trials, better known as Area 51) commandeered the two long community dining tables.

"I have a table and an extra seat if you want to join me," Olivia said, pointing to a nearby two-top she'd reserved with a black sweater.

"I'd love to," Jessica said, following her to the beverage station. While she filled a glass with ice and sparkling water, Olivia helped herself to a splash of every flavor from the organic soda machine.

"Please, no judgment," she said. "I call it a 'natural suicide,' and it's one of the only things that helps my all-day-long morning sickness."

"Whatever it takes," Jessica said sympathetically as they headed for the table. "I hope you're feeling better now than you were when I first started."

"Definitely on Tuesdays," Olivia said as they sat down, and she proceeded to douse her tacos with the bottle of hot sauce. "For whatever reason, spicy food settles my stomach, too."

As Olivia took a bite, winced from the heat, and quickly took another, Jessica enjoyed a decidedly more temperate bite of shrimp. She tried to decide whether making a throwaway comment—*It'll all be worth it in the end*—would prompt a line of questions she definitely didn't want to answer.

No kids of my own. Stepkids. Sort of.

We met while I was in school.

He's in biomedical technology, too.

His name? Um . . .

At that moment, however, Philip walked by the table as he scanned for a place to sit.

"The Area 51-ers shouldn't commandeer the community seating area the way they do," Olivia said. "No one else feels comfortable taking any of the open chairs."

"There certainly doesn't seem to be a lot of cross-pollination between departments around here."

"You'd be surprised," Olivia said. "Everyone works such long hours, paths cross more than you might imagine. And then there's the coed, interdepartmental softball team. They get pretty rowdy after the games. From what I hear, one of the clinical research coordinators and a new girl in marketing ended up getting jiggy in a car outside a local tavern."

Jessica snorted. "That has to violate something in the Cancura non-disclosure documents."

"Only if they were talking about work, which I doubt very much."

Jon had said Olivia was cool, smart, funny, and great at her job when she wasn't puking her brains out. Jessica wished she didn't have to keep her distance. But anything else was just too risky, at least for the time being.

"I feel sorry for Philip," she said, watching as he resigned himself to standing with his tray balanced on the corner of a nearby counter.

"He's been kind of lost since Graham left the company," Olivia said.

"Who's Graham?"

"His BFF from data analysis."

"I thought the idea was to insulate everyone from the outside world, keep them so fat and happy they'll never leave."

"A Silicon Valley start-up dazzled him with the promise of sunshine and stock options. Jon was peeved, to say the least." Olivia took another bite of her taco.

The comment was perfectly timed given that Kate, whom Jon apparently placated at all costs to keep her from being poached, had just made her way from the line into the dining area.

"Komodo Kate," Olivia whispered conspiratorially.

Jessica stifled a giggle. "Komodo . . . ?"

"Her bite is notoriously lethal," she said.

"I'm aware," Jessica said. "I questioned her on something entirely legit given our positions and responsibilities, and she didn't take it well."

"By all accounts she's a brilliant scientist, and Jon respects and depends on her more than almost anyone, but she's definitely got the ego to go with."

"I guess it's comforting to know she's equally brusque to others."

"Typically straight guys who feel compelled to mansplain in her attractive presence," Olivia said.

They watched as the crowd parted, and a prime seat materialized the moment Kate arrived at the Area 51 tables.

"You don't suppose it's possible Jon has a soft spot for Kate that goes beyond his . . . professional admiration, do you?" Jessica asked, hoping she sounded nonchalant.

"Around here, nothing surprises me," Olivia said. "But I do know one thing for sure: Jonathan Wright is completely devoted to his wife."

"That's so sweet," Jessica said, hoping she sounded sincere—and wondering what Olivia would think when the truth finally came out.

Chapter Fifteen

HOLLY

Rebranding is rebirth.

—"How I Lied about My Name and Discovered My Truth,"
a TED Talk by Jon M. Wright

Arriving later than planned at Village Hall, Holly parked quickly and hurried inside, eyes watering from the cold north wind. Brian wouldn't be joining her, because one of his daughters had a stomach bug and Nancy was stuck in traffic. Despite the awkwardness that had followed his recent declaration, Holly missed having him by her side. She still trusted him—and trust was suddenly in very short supply.

Seeing the Yadaos on the right-hand side in the exact same seats as before, Holly sat on the left, in the front row. The seats were sparsely occupied. Since the board of trustees would not be taking testimony for or against Holly's issue, simply voting yes or no on last month's board of appeals' recommendation, she and Brian hadn't bothered to rally the troops again. The seven trustees were talking quietly on the short dais, shuffling papers and sipping water as they prepared to begin. Something about seeing the backs of heads as she came down the aisle triggered another unbidden memory of her wedding day, and she scarcely noticed when the board president gaveled the meeting to order.

The memory this time was of her dad's expression when he glanced into the sanctuary to confirm Jack was in place by the altar, standing next to his best man, Craig, who in the years since had disappeared from their lives. The look on her father's face was of cheerful reassurance, but in his eyes she'd seen sadness, a final recognition that it was too late to steer his daughter to safety.

Grandpa Walt and Nana Charlotte adored Jack now because his money and success had buoyed not only their daughter but themselves. Their shares of Cancura stock, purchased on the first day of the IPO at a rock-bottom price, had year after year exploded in value, allowing for an early and comfortable retirement with two elegant homes completely paid for. But did they remember what they'd originally thought about Jonny Wright? Despite his lofty-sounding given name of Jonathan Mitchell Wright III, he was from a perfectly ordinary family in a perfectly ordinary part of Bloomington, Indiana, the only child of an insurance salesman father and a stay-at-home mom. Jonny himself was an on-again, off-again student who dabbled in community college before finally grinding out a BS in science at IU and suddenly deciding to become a doctor.

To this day, Holly had no idea how he'd managed to gain admission to the University of Chicago, though it was likely the first time he'd found a major success with what was now his trademark blend of networking, self-promotion, chutzpah, and silver-tongued eloquence. However he'd managed it, he came quickly into his own, gaining a reputation as a brilliant student beloved by his professors and envied by his peers. Holly, also toiling away in med school, heard about him before she met him—he had a reputation for working hard *and* having fun, the latter activity terra incognita to U of C grad students, and it didn't hurt that he was handsome—and, upon meeting him, wondered, *What's his secret?*

She, after all, came from the right schools and the right family and still felt like everything was a struggle. He made it look so easy. When he flirted with her at a poorly attended school-sponsored mixer, one of U of C's periodic attempts to pretend they encouraged their high achievers to have social lives, she was smitten. Maybe it could be easy for her, too.

Her parents were not smitten. The guy she'd been dating, the one they now referred to derisively as "the painter," had actually been their preferred choice. He was a swimmer, a straight-A student in economics, and, more importantly, he came from an old-money North Shore family with a mansion overlooking Lake Michigan. The fact that he'd minored in visual arts and dedicated meaningful time to his painting hobby became a source of ridicule only after Holly had dumped him for Jonny. Jonny wouldn't start going by "Jonathan or Jon, Jack to my friends" until he began his residency, when he'd suddenly announced the change and stuck to it without a single slipup, even going so far as to pretend not to hear when people addressed him as Jonny.

At the front of the room, the board had by now approved the minutes, stated the agenda, and moved on to the proposed budget for the coming year. A stooped man with a permanent glare she recognized from previous meetings was out of his seat before the president finished speaking.

"What I want to know is, why are we wasting money on solar panels for the community center when we can get electricity from ComEd for six cents an hour?" he groused. "It's going to take ten years to pay off the investment, and I'm guessing we'll have to replace the suckers by then."

Involuntarily, Holly glanced over at Theresa Yadao, who was looking right back at her. This was going to take a while, and despite their entrenched opposition on the bridle path, they at least had this annoyance and delay in common. Holly wondered whether she should give a wry grin, and was just about to, when Theresa looked impassively away.

Bitch, she thought.

Her mom and dad had not been overly proud of their daughter's doctor-in-training boyfriend. "We're already going to have one doctor in the family," said her mom. "Why do we need two?" They remained suspicious of Jonny-turned-Jonathan through his MD, even his PhD, seeming to think for years that he was out to glom on to their family name—never mind that the name wasn't worth much in actual cash anymore. Only after Jack had quit practicing medicine to found Cancura, immediately making headlines and earning a handsome profit, did they finally stop holding him at arm's length and embrace him like a son.

By then, however, there were fewer and fewer embraces between Holly and Jack.

She never shared details about his dalliances with her parents, never confided her worries that his dubious personal ethics might extend to his professional life. If anything, she defended him more vigorously, wanting them to believe their initial assessment was wrong. Wanting it to *be* wrong.

And they had been wrong about his designs on their family. If only they hadn't been so right about his character.

After the rehearsal dinner and against her better judgment, Holly pried the story out of her bridesmaid, who had dated one of Jack's groomsmen and was still close enough to get the scoop. Holly naively thought it would have been a stripper or a hooker or something equally cliché and grotesque that could nonetheless be overlooked in the context of peer pressure and the bachelor party ritual. Apparently, however, in one of the many bars they'd drunkenly trawled that night, Jack had taken the initiative to hit on—and disappear for the rest of the night with—a random Rush Street "skank." Or maybe not a skank, maybe a perfectly nice but equally drunk girl, the word deployed in an effort to spare Holly's feelings.

And how had she felt? Angry, upset, embarrassed, certainly. But when she thought about calling off the wedding at Fourth Presbyterian, the reception at the Ivy Room in the historic Tree Studios (to which she and Jack would be transported by horse and carriage)—all of it paid for by her parents at a cost they could then scarcely afford—she couldn't help but feel she was overreacting. It wasn't the right time to confront Jack. He'd been drunk, savoring a last night of freedom. Guests had already arrived from all over the country.

And so she let herself be carried along, wanting to believe a certificate of marriage and two gold rings would change everything.

And it had. He'd been a model spouse until Ava was born. Maybe even Paige. He was too busy getting Cancura up and running—with Holly often at his side—to get into much of anything else. It wasn't until they'd moved to Barrington Hills and she'd stepped back from both Cancura and full-time medical practice, embracing the role of three-quarter-time mom, that she'd started catching him in lies about where he had been. New Orleans when he said he was in Houston. DC when he said he was in Atlanta. But what then? Burn it all down for her own hurt feelings? Holly discovered she was more pragmatic than that.

She also had her limits.

Finally, it was time for the board to vote. Holly had no idea which way any of the trustees were leaning, but it seemed straightforward enough. The board of appeals had recommended, by a vote of four to one, with one abstention, to approve the bridle path connector. Brian assured her the trustees rarely overruled their recommendations, but she wouldn't be satisfied until she'd seen it through.

The president, a square-faced, silver-haired village lifer with a brusque manner and a permanent tan, cleared his throat. "Moving on to the matter of the planned bridle path extension. As this matter was previously approved by the equestrian commission and the plan commission, and additional public comment was taken during a previous meeting of the board of appeals, we move again to a vote to approve the recommendation made by that body."

Theresa stood up suddenly. "Mr. President, I respectfully would like to inform the board that a vote to approve the connector will be met with legal action by my husband and myself. We believe the process has not been fair and transparent and that Holly Wright has unduly influenced the board of appeals recommendation. We will sue."

Holly was utterly flabbergasted. "Everyone who spoke at that meeting did so voluntarily."

"Excuse me," said the board president. "The floor is not open for comment."

"I'm done," said Theresa, sitting down and surveying the room with a prim smile.

There was confusion on the dais as board members covered their microphones and leaned back to confer about this bombshell. Theresa's statement may have been against the rules, but they had clearly heard it and were unsure how to proceed.

Holly stood up. "Please speak into your microphones. We have a right to hear the discussion, as this is a public meeting, not an executive session."

They didn't react immediately. One of the board members was whispering heatedly while the others listened with concerned expressions. With a sinking feeling, Holly knew the mere threat of legal action had intimidated the budget-conscious board, who wouldn't want to spend village money defending even a frivolous lawsuit.

"Call the vote, please," said Holly, remaining on her feet.

Reluctantly, the trustees uncovered their microphones and fell silent, exchanging wary looks.

"There has been a motion to postpone the vote," said the president with uncharacteristic uncertainty.

"I think you owe it to us to vote," insisted Holly, expecting to be shushed any minute.

The president looked at Holly, then at Theresa, thought for a moment, and then gave a weary shrug. "We'll take a voice vote. Please say yea or nay."

"Yea."

"Yea."

"Nay."

"I abstain," said the most worried-seeming board member.

"I abstain also," echoed another.

"Abstain."

The board president, who held the final vote, surveyed the room. If he voted yes, Holly would win. If he voted no, there would be a tie and a stalemate of unknown duration. What he actually did was something Holly had failed to imagine.

"I, too, abstain from voting," he pronounced. "Lacking four votes, we have failed to reach a quorum, and the matter must be considered unresolved. The board will revisit this at a future time."

She was out of her seat and in the aisle, head down to avoid eye contact with Theresa, before the gavel banged. Pushing through the outer doors, she stumbled to her car and climbed inside. She started the engine to power the heat but left the transmission in park.

Pulled out her phone. Punched autodial.

Heard his voice at the other end.

"Am I about to hear the sound of a champagne cork popping?" he asked.

"Two votes in favor, one vote against, four abstaining," she said tersely.

A brief silence, then: "What the hell?"

"Just when they were about to vote, Theresa stood up and threatened to sue the village."

"She can't do that," Brian said, anger coloring his voice.

"She was out of order, but it's not like they could unhear it. The board members shit themselves—well, five of them, anyway. I can't imagine they'll call a vote again until after the next elections."

"What did Jack say?" asked Brian finally.

"I haven't told him yet."

They were both quiet for a moment. Across the parking lot, Holly watched as a few people left the village hall and made their way to their cars.

"Well, I'm glad you called me, then."

"About that night . . . I'm sorry we haven't been able to talk about it more," she said. "I'm sorry if I was abrupt. You and I have a lot in common, and it makes me nervous."

"I'm glad you're nervous," he told her. "I am, too."

"But that doesn't mean—"

"It just means we both want to be in each other's lives."

"Yes, I suppose it does," she said.

Chapter Sixteen

Jessica and Lark

Are you agile enough to be in two places at once?

—"How I Lied about My Name and Discovered My Truth,"
a TED Talk by Jon M. Wright

"Give me your hand," Jon said to Jessica.

"I think I'd better hold on to the handrail," she told him as they approached the metal landing.

"Trust me."

"I'm ninety-four stories above the sidewalk, about to climb onto a glass contraption that's going to hang me off the side of the building. Trust is about all I've got right now."

"The glass in question is almost as strong as this steel," Jon said, thumping a nearby pillar on the John Hancock tower's observation deck. "If you're going to play tourist in your new hometown, you have to check one of our iconic skyscrapers off your list."

"If you say so," she said, smiling so Jon would know that despite her fear of heights, she was enjoying the weekend staycation he'd kicked off yesterday afternoon with a delightfully unexpected email.

Jessica,

By all accounts you've been working your ass off since arriving at Cancura and have barely gotten to see anything the Windy City has to offer. As your designated greeter and tour guide, I plan to rectify this unfortunate situation starting tonight. You are to meet me at Lou Malnati's on Randolph Street at six o'clock to sample Chicago's famous deep-dish pizza. Your weekend will feature attractions and activities including, but not limited to, riding the Ferris wheel on Navy Pier, meeting Máximo the titanosaur at the Field Museum, taking selfies at the famed Bean, and many more surprises along the way. Attendance is mandatory.

Signed,
Your Admiring Employer

Friday night had been, for lack of a better word, a complete orgy of tomato sauce, bubbling cheese, and Italian sausage, washed down with an equally abundant amount of beer. They'd come home too delightfully overfed to even think about making love.

Until morning, that was.

"We've got a big day ahead," Jon had whispered in her ear before kissing his way down her neck, stopping briefly at her breasts, and continuing on toward her open legs . . .

"Oh my god!" Jessica yelped as the TILT device emitted a hydraulic hiss and they cantilevered thirty degrees out. It was, she imagined, exactly what someone would feel in their first moment of falling off a building.

"Attagirl," Jon said with a laugh, just like he had during their brief but entirely satisfying morning sex session. "Don't forget to enjoy the view."

Jessica closed her eyes for a few harrowing seconds and then willed herself to open them. Still too fearful to stare one thousand feet straight down, she instead looked out at the nighttime skyline. The city—which she already knew to be equal parts charming, crowded, beautiful, gritty, world-class, and thoroughly Midwestern depending on the day or even the moment—was spectacular. Illumination streamed from tens of thousands of windows, and a cheery holiday glow rose from Michigan Avenue, making Chicago more than rival Paris as a city of lights. Just east of Lake Shore Drive, a golden moon glowed on the black surface of Lake Michigan, whose calm emptiness providing a stunning juxtaposition to the pulsing grid spreading out in every other direction.

"Let me guess, you got the idea for the Revelate by looking out at this city and envisioning making the impossible, possible," she said.

"Not a bad line," he said. "I just may use that."

"Feel free," she said, forgetting to be afraid as he gave her a quick lesson in Chicago geography, pointing out notable buildings, streets, and expressways, digressing to explain the engineering feats that had allowed a primitive settlement in a marshy area to become a towering metropolis. Jessica was always amazed at how much more knowledge he took in than was necessary—her Jon was truly a renaissance man.

He grinned ruefully, abruptly breaking off his lecture. "Sorry about that. Sometimes I don't know when to quit."

"I like it," she said. "What an amazing city. What an amazing day."

And it had been, as they rode the hop-on, hop-off double-decker all around the downtown area, often the only riders on top of the bus as they snuggled beneath a fuzzy wool blanket Jon had the foresight to bring along. They climbed off whenever Jon deemed something *unmissable*, giving Jessica plenty of opportunities to warm her numb nose and ears. His enthusiasm for things he'd surely seen dozens of times—he gushed like a kid as they viewed the dinosaur bones at the Field Museum, downright dawdled in front of the Macy's window displays, and even asked a German tourist to take their picture in front of the silvery Cloud Gate, or "Bean"—was massively endearing. Best of all was the sheer amount of unhurried time they had together. Just the two of them.

"I can't imagine how today could be better," Jon said.

If she were being entirely honest, however, she could. Shortly after they'd finished scarfing down a late-afternoon snack of Chicago-style hot dogs with all the trimmings, Jon got a text.

He'd looked irritated as he began tapping away on his phone.

"What is it?" she'd asked.

"Nothing," he'd said.

She could tell by the furrow between his eyes that it was definitely something. "Let me guess: Annie Wilkes is on a weekend hobbling jag?"

"Directed at Ava—at least, according to Ava," he'd said with an annoyed sigh he quickly covered with a smile. "But I'm pretty sure I already have it under control, so let's get rolling. We should at least walk through the new exhibit at the Museum of Contemporary Art. Then, as soon as it's dark," he added, pointing up at the John Hancock, "we're headed straight up there."

Now, as they leaned over the city, she could see the very spot where he'd pointed upward. Then there was another hydraulic hiss as they were once again levered upright.

Jon's phone pinged as they climbed off the platform and onto the observation deck proper.

"I'm ignoring it," he said, putting an arm around her as they headed toward the bank of elevators. "Let's get a drink upstairs."

∾

Lark had been so sure of herself when she'd booked her ticket. And during the four-hour flight, she'd been so excited she'd hardly been able to sit still, her attention wandering between a podcast, a paperback, and a few episodes of a show she'd been streaming. This was exactly the kind of grand gesture Trip loved to make—what could be more delicious than turning the tables on him?

She'd come up with the idea in bed, the morning after she'd told Trip she loved him and he'd said the same three words with a look of wonder and relief. She'd bugged him about visiting each time he left for the airport, and he'd made a variety of excuses, but what it came down to, she was sure, was some kind of weird embarrassment about his rental apartment. Maybe it was as boring as he claimed, or maybe it was actually filled with boxes. Or perhaps it was messy and just didn't fit with the cultivated image he preferred to project.

Whatever the reason, she didn't care. In fact, she secretly hoped his place would be a little bit of a dump, just to make him a little less perfect. Shortly after returning to LA from Minneapolis, where she had tortured herself with the idea that she was practically next door to Chicago (even though she knew it wasn't quite that close), she pulled the trigger and bought a ticket, planning to deliver herself as an early Christmas present.

Trip would be spending Christmas Eve through New Year's Day with his brother Mike's family, treating them to a luxurious cruise to Saint Kitts and Nevis. Though he didn't talk much about Mike, Lark knew the two of them had begun the slow process of reconnection a half dozen years ago. Mike was now a drill-press operator in Lima, Ohio, and the cultural differences between the two of them were huge, but Trip lit up when he talked about playing uncle with his two teenage nephews.

As much as Lark wished Trip were taking her to the Caribbean, too, she wouldn't have wanted to share him or to disappoint her own family by breaking their plans. Truthfully, it still felt too soon to bring him home for the holidays. Next year would be a different story.

This time, she was prepared for the weather in Chicago, with a puffy down jacket, UGG boots, and a faux-fur hat with hilarious earflaps. Not exactly sexy but she didn't figure they'd be spending much time outside.

Standing in line for a rental car with her thumbs poised over her phone, she couldn't suppress a grin. It was time to find out whether Trip was truly as spontaneous as he seemed.

You free? she texted, using the exact two words he'd deployed during his surprise visit to LA.

He didn't answer right away. In fact, she'd initialed the clerk's tablet with her forefinger and was halfway across a wind-blasted parking lot outside O'Hare when his response finally came through. She had hoped his response would be, *To talk?*—proving he remembered their exchange word for word and that he knew instantly what was up.

Instead, he wrote, *What's up?*

She located her assigned car, slid behind the wheel, turned the key in the ignition, and cranked the heat before she answered: *For a date. I'm in Chicago.*

Are you serious? he wrote after a brief pause, with no emojis or anything to indicate whether he was pleased, displeased, or merely surprised.

She forged ahead. *Picking up a rental. Meet me at Bavette's?*

Though she hadn't known anything about Chicago's dining scene, online searches had informed her that reservations at this hip, romantic steak house were booked months in advance—which made her only more determined to pull it off. Daily calls during which she'd become first-name-friendly with the maître d' had finally paid off when, relenting, he'd called her back to inform her of a prime-time cancellation with a week's notice to spare. It was hers, and now theirs.

She synced her phone to the car, opened Google Maps, and waited. She knew the restaurant's address, but she didn't yet know his.

I wish you'd told me.

She caught her breath, froze, and felt a jolt of adrenaline as for the first time it occurred to her that she might have made a big mistake.

Unfortunately, I have a business dinner I can't cancel . . .

Waves of feelings crashed over her. Disappointment. Embarrassment at her presumptuousness. Regret at wasting all those calls to Bavette's.

. . . but don't worry! This is going to be FUCKING AWESOME. I'm so happy you're here.

Her eyes misted over as warm relief trickled into her body.

He gave her the address of his building and told her the doorman would be expecting her. He wished he could leave the dinner early, he added, but real money was involved, so dessert, coffee, and even a nightcap were distinct possibilities.

But it will all be worth it knowing I'm coming home to you, Lark, he concluded. *I love you so fucking much.*

She could more than live with that. And they'd have dinner somewhere nice tomorrow. So what if it wasn't a surprise anymore?

The drive downtown was almost as slow as anything she'd experienced in LA, giving her time to watch Chicago's skyline growing taller in the windshield, the glassy buildings wreathed by exhaust and glittering red in the setting sun. She'd never been to the city and couldn't wait to see some of the sights with Trip tomorrow. Lark liked to see all the touristy stuff on a first visit but imagined that double-decker buses and boat rides would have to wait for warmer weather. There would still be plenty of museums, stores, and restaurants—not to mention one-on-one indoor sports.

After getting off the expressway, she navigated choked city streets, including a twisting, video-game-like detour through a sunken street with the improbable name of Lower Wacker Drive, before resurfacing in the heart of the city. Trip's condo was in a silvery high-rise a block from Michigan Avenue, where there were so many pedestrians and so many things to look at that she missed the garage entrance, and it took her ten minutes to get around the block again. Finally, she parked, found the tastefully decorated lobby, and gave her name to the doorman, who provided her with a spare set of keys and gave her the unit number.

"In town for long?" he asked as he buzzed her in.

"Just the weekend," Lark said.

He grinned. "Hope they don't work you too hard."

Which was a weird thing to say. But a doorman probably saw so many people every day that his small talk was on autopilot. He probably didn't even think about half the things he said. As the elevator whooshed upward, Lark once again tingled with anticipation: no, Trip wouldn't be there to greet her, but she would finally see where he lived. She could take her time taking it in before giving him a warm welcome home.

Maybe wearing just her fur hat and boots.

The thought made her laugh. He deserved some sort of surprise tonight.

The first thing she noticed was the view. Twenty-seven stories above Millennium Park, the wall-to-wall, floor-to-ceiling window drew her right across the living area, where she pressed her nose against the glass and saw lawns and a concert pavilion white with snow, traffic on what must have been Lake Shore Drive, and an abrupt black edge where Lake Michigan began. In summer, in sunlight and thronged with people, it would be truly amazing.

The second thing she noticed was how clean the apartment was. And the third thing she noticed was how it seemed practically empty. Trip's description had made it sound as though he lived amid unpacked boxes, but not only were there none of those, there were very few personal touches whatsoever. The gleaming kitchen appeared to be unused.

The living room furniture was crisply upholstered and crumb-free. And, when she ventured down the hall into the bedroom, which had an equally stunning view, the bed was neatly made. No clothes on the floor. No photos on the nightstand.

Feeling like a snoop but unable to help herself, she opened the walk-in closet and was relieved to find clothes she recognized as Trip's—and more in the bureau drawers. Several pairs of shoes, fewer than she'd expected, were polished and neatly aligned.

He clearly hadn't been lying when he'd said it wasn't much of a home. Then again, without someone to share it with, why should he have made it homier? He was on the road constantly. She thought with an affectionate twinge of how she'd always thought he was just being nice when he told her how much he loved spending time at her funky, worn, and definitely lived-in apartment. His own place was so sterile, maybe he meant it wholeheartedly.

Well, she could help him warm it up.

I made it! she texted, keeping it brief because he was at dinner. Then she added, *Can't wait until you get home. XO.*

That would be hours from now. She watched her phone for a few minutes, hoping he would send a quick answer, but there was no reply. If he was wooing investors and talking about millions of dollars, it really wasn't fair to expect one. Reluctantly, she called Bavette's and canceled the reservation, relieved it wasn't her new friend, the maître d', who answered.

Looking through the window again, she pondered hitting the street and finding a cozy restaurant for a solo dinner but found herself dissuaded when a shopping bag, caught in a fierce gust of wind, shot past the window.

So. Delivery it was, then.

∾

"There's something I need to tell you," Jon said to Jessica over cocktails and oysters in the Signature Room on the ninety-fifth floor. "It's about Kate."

Her stomach dropped even more precipitously than it had on TILT. "What about her?"

"She's involved with Arjun."

Jessica, having expected Jon to say something very different—that he and Kate had once had a fling—was confused and didn't know what to say.

"She and Arjun have been together for nearly two years," Jon continued. "But you can't breathe a word to anyone."

"Of course I won't," she said, finally feeling relieved. "But why is it such a big secret? Neither one of them is married or anything, right?"

"They work together very closely and don't want any whispers about romance to take anything away from their scientific integrity."

"Won't we have the same problem eventually?" she asked.

"That's why we're keeping it quiet," he said, stroking her knee under the table. "Until eventually."

Which is when, exactly? she thought but couldn't quite bring herself to say. "Why are you telling me this now?"

"For one thing, I wanted to put your mind at ease. I work very closely with Kate, too, and I don't want you thinking anything could be going on between us. I wouldn't blame you if you've wondered."

"I won't anymore," Jessica said. "What's the other thing?"

Jon looked down at the table. "I'm afraid you're going to be as disappointed as I am right now."

"What are you talking about?"

"Ava called while you were in the bathroom. She and Holly are at each other's throats."

"No!" Jessica blurted. She had promised herself she'd be the epitome of a patient and loving girlfriend while he settled his affairs so they could be together, but apparently her patience had worn thinner than she realized. "This is our special weekend, and I don't want you to—"

"Ava says that Holly claims she broke curfew twice, but both times she was home when she was supposed to be. Also according to Ava, Holly is insane and won't believe her and is refusing to let her go to homecoming. Ava is threatening to run away if she doesn't."

"It's just another manipulation," Jessica said. "You know it is."

Jon took a long pull of his beer. "But what if it isn't?"

Jessica folded her arms, too angry to speak.

"I have no choice," said Jon, pleading his case. "I have to deal with the situation to keep things from going nuclear."

"You know," she said, at last, "I went into this knowing it was going to be complicated for a while, and I think I've been completely understanding when it comes to your children."

"You've been amazing, Jessie."

"I haven't said a word about the fact that we live together and I have to pretend I don't know you at work. I recently had to sit there and smile while Olivia made reference to your perfect marriage."

"Oh god. I'm so sorry."

"In the meantime, I'm going home alone to my mom for Christmas while you play happy broken family with your crazy soon-to-be ex-wife, and I haven't complained once. I don't even know what, if anything, we're doing for New Year's. And most importantly, I have no idea when the hell you're actually going to be divorced."

"Soon, I promise," Jon whispered. For the first time since she'd known him, he looked like he might be about to cry.

"I went into this knowing it was going to be hard, but sometimes . . ."

"I know," he said. "I know."

"And what about tomorrow? It was supposed to be a staycation weekend with just the two of us, not a day and a half interrupted by texts reminding me that you're not really all mine." Her voice cracked. "Not yet, anyway."

"Jessie. Babe . . ." Jon dabbed the corners of his eyes with his napkin. "I promise our weekend together isn't over, come hell or high water."

"We're talking about Annie Wilkes here. Likely as not she'll find a way to deliver both."

Sniffling, they both chuckled at that.

"I already bought tickets for something tomorrow, and we're not missing it."

"No matter what?" she said.

He gripped her hand. "No matter what."

⌇

Lark was dozing on the couch when Trip finally arrived. Caught off guard, she hadn't even cleared away the Styrofoam clamshell of tofu pad thai, hadn't brushed her teeth, and certainly hadn't stripped down to fur hat and boots. Some surprise she was turning out to be.

Fortunately, Trip looked delighted to see her. He crossed the room and settled into the couch next to her, then drew her in for a lingering kiss that allowed her to taste the beer he'd been drinking.

"Surprised?" she said after they broke it off.

"Completely," he confessed. Despite his obvious happiness, he looked tired. His eyes didn't quite have their usual sparkle.

She pushed a stray lock of hair back from his forehead. "I'm sorry if it's bad timing."

"And I'm sorry I wasn't free," he said. "If there was any way I could have gotten out of it—"

Now she put her finger on his lips. "Let's both stop apologizing."

He grinned. "So when I tell you I'm too tired to go back out, I should be completely unrepentant?"

"Exactly."

While they watched TV, Lark rubbed Trip's shoulders until she realized he was asleep. The evening hadn't gone in any way like she'd planned, but there was still something comforting about being in Chicago, at Trip's place, warm and cozy while the cold wind howled outside. She liked watching him sleep and realized she almost never had the opportunity: on the West Coast, in her time zone, he always woke up hours before she did.

Eventually she faced a dilemma: cover him up on the couch or wake him up and take him to bed? With a warm flush, she realized how she could make the evening memorable after all. With Chicago's glowing night sky behind her, she undressed slowly, watching Trip's chest rise and fall. Then she climbed on the couch, straddled him, and began to give him something to dream about.

Sunday morning, Trip seemed refreshed as he took her to breakfast. As they walked through the Loop, she loved the way the L cars clattered overhead on ancient-looking iron tracks, the way Chicagoans leaned into the wind and moved with grim determination. *Weather makes a difference in people,* she thought. No wonder Trip was such a force of nature.

His phone buzzed several times during breakfast, each time chipping away at his calm.

"I'm sorry," he said, picking it up to send a quick message. "One of the businesses I invested in is cratering, and the other major backer is losing his shit."

"Aren't you worried?" she asked, suddenly concerned that it might also be bad news for Trip.

He shrugged. "Some of my investments are high risk, which is why I'm extremely diversified. High risk, high reward—but they can't all be winners."

"What about Activate!—is that high risk?"

Trip pushed his plate aside, reached across the table, and took her hand. Looking into her eyes, he said: "That is what I'd call a blue-chip investment."

Unfortunately, the other investor wouldn't be calmed and demanded a lunch meeting. Looking truly crestfallen, Trip assured her it shouldn't take more than a couple of hours—his partner in this particular venture lived in Chicago, and they would be meeting at an office nearby. Not wanting to add any more pressure on Trip, Lark tried not to let her disappointment show and promised him she'd be fine on her own.

"I'll call you the moment I'm free," he promised. "And then we'll really have some fun."

And then he was out the door, leaving her to contemplate the remains of their meal and ponder what to do with her morning.

Jessica woke up and searched online until she found a florist with Sunday hours. She drove halfway across the city to be there when the door opened. After the friendly clerk made his way behind the counter, she asked for a "cool apology arrangement for a guy." She'd let her emotions get the best of her and had to make amends.

He reappeared with an arrangement of white roses, peruvian lilies, blue delphinium, baby's breath, seeded eucalyptus, and assorted greenery.

It couldn't have been more perfect.

On the card she wrote:

Jon,

I hope it went OK last night. It's important to me that you are there for your kids when they need you and I feel badly for suggesting you should have been with me instead of them. I'm sorry.

I love you,

Jessie

She got home, set the arrangement on the kitchen counter, and went upstairs to use the computer while she waited for him. He'd told her he would be there no later than ten forty-five, which gave her just enough time to answer a few emails before he arrived. She triaged her in-box and was unsubscribing her personal account from a Phoenix gym's promotions list when a new work email popped up.

From: Marco Ruiz

Subject: Your mission, should you choose to accept it

Before she could read it, Jon's keys jangled in the front door. She quickly slid back from the computer so he wouldn't see her, but she could watch through the interior glass window overlooking the living room as he entered the apartment.

Not having spoken or texted with him since last night, Jessica felt nervous as he dropped his keys on the table in the entry hall and stepped into the kitchen. He looked puzzled until he recognized his name on the card. Then an expression she couldn't identify clouded his face, making her wish she'd had the presence of mind to apologize as quickly as he had after his one travel-weary loss of temper.

The cloud passed as quickly as it appeared, however, and he looked up and smiled broadly.

"You know," he said, his voice loud enough to be heard anywhere in the apartment. "No one's ever gotten *me* flowers before."

"Maybe no one's ever needed to," she said, coming out of the office and putting her hands on the railing. "I was such a jackass."

"Don't talk about yourself that way," he said. "I could never be so patient if the tables were turned."

"Forgive me?"

"There's nothing to forgive. You have every right to feel the way you do."

An hour later, as they enjoyed Improv Brunch at Second City and the performers ad-libbed a hilarious musical about, ironically, teenagers, it was as though there'd never been any tension between them at all. After the show, they drove to the Shedd Aquarium, laughing about how they both thought dolphins were overrated and bonding over a shared fascination with manta rays. After Jon handed his keys to the valet, and while they were ascending the steps, he took his phone out of his pocket, glanced at it, and grimaced before putting it away again.

"Are you keeping it on vibrate now?" Jessica asked.

He nodded.

"What is it this time?"

"Ava just wants me to know that everything is going to shit again with her mother," he said wearily. "I'm sorry."

"Don't be." Instead of feeling irritated, Jessica resolved to appreciate the fact that she had a partner who cared so much about the people in his life. "Is action required?"

"Not just yet."

They had passed through admissions—naturally, Jon was an aquarium sponsor with VIP privileges—and were gazing at the huge Caribbean Reef tank when, this time, her own cell phone vibrated.

"It's Marco," she said, looking at the lock screen.

"By all means, take the call," he said, nodding approvingly. "The man's working on a Sunday!"

Laughing to herself about the endless complications of dating the boss, she answered. "Hi, Marco."

"You haven't gotten back to me," he said brusquely.

"Sorry," she said. "I've been out since morning, and I haven't had a chance to—"

"Read my email," he said. "Now!"

"Hang on," she said, putting Marco on speaker while she pulled up her email.

Jon read along over her shoulder.

Jessica,

I am in Omaha and American Healthcare Systems is going to sign a contract with us tomorrow. We will need someone to oversee the Revelate rollout in their clinics across the country. I believe that someone is you. Call me when you read this.

Marco

"Are you still there?" Marco asked.

"Wow," Jessica said.

"AHS is the fifth-largest hospital system in the country, and they think the Revelate can help them hit number one."

Jessica tried to get her head around this sudden development. Marco had mentioned a possible deal, but she'd had no idea it would happen so soon or that he would ask her to be directly involved. And while this new assignment clearly belonged to the monitoring aspect of her job, the prospect of such a huge and outward-facing role was both flattering and paralyzing.

"We don't even have full FDA approval yet," she said to Jon as much as Marco. "Do we?"

Jon nodded enthusiastically.

"We do?" she exclaimed before Marco answered, forgetting for a split second that he had no idea who was standing beside her.

"Just got approval on Friday afternoon for leukemia biomarker testing," Marco said, not seeming to notice her gaffe.

"OMG!" she said as Jon smiled broadly.

"Your job will be to liaise with administration and help integrate the Revelate into their protocols. Scaling up like this will help us accelerate our nationwide launch exponentially."

Jon gave her a silent fist bump.

"The thing is, I need you to get on a plane tonight," Marco said.

"Tonight?"

"The signing came together faster than expected, and we don't want to be the ones to slow things down. They're understandably eager to meet the person who's going to head up the Cancura team. I'm booking you on a six o'clock flight from O'Hare."

"I do have a few questions. More than a few."

"All of which I'll answer when I pick you up at the airport," Marco said.

"I guess I'll see you soon," she said, feeling breathless and a little bit dizzy.

Moments after she ended the call, Jon's phone vibrated with a message alert from Marco.

"Clearly you and Marco have been conspiring," she said.

"Let's just say, I know you've missed having patient contact."

"I do, but . . ."

"I want you on the front lines. The face of Cancura."

"Are you sure I'm—?"

"Brilliant and beautiful? Definitely."

"You're not bad-looking yourself," she said, blushing. "I don't want to leave you, though."

"And I don't want to be away from you, but with some creative scheduling, I bet we can work out how to spend more time together than we do now."

"I'll believe that when I see it."

"I guess I'll just have to rise to the occasion," he said with a wink.

"That's all well and good, but if I'm really going to catch that plane and impress our new clients in the morning, I need to get home and pack."

"Not so fast," he said. "You at least have to see the eels that change color and sex. They transform from blue-lined males to solid-yellow females."

"But I—"

"Boss's orders."

~

Lark wandered gallery after gallery in the sprawling, neoclassical Art Institute, seeing everything from old armor and weapons to Renaissance masters to I-could-have-made-that modern art. She saw paintings she'd only ever seen as postcards: Edward Hopper's *Nighthawks*, Grant Wood's *American Gothic*, and Vincent van Gogh's *The Bedroom*. It was awe-inspiring and a little bit overwhelming. Suddenly, she realized more than two hours had passed, and her feet were killing her. Stopping at a little café for some coffee, she checked her phone for messages that weren't there. Resisted the urge to nudge him. Called her mom instead.

"How's Chicago?" she asked. "I hope he's giving you the grand tour."

"Cold but beautiful. I'm on my own right now because he had a work emergency come up."

"You must be disappointed."

"We'll be getting together soon. The museum is amazing."

"Send pictures?"

Lark promised she would. After a half-hearted spin through a couple more rooms, Lark realized her brain couldn't handle any more profundity, so she left the museum. Michigan Avenue, festive with wreaths and red bows, was filling up with holiday shoppers and tourists. The air had suddenly become milder, and fluffy snowflakes began to fall, making the whole scene look like a gently shaken snow globe. On the steps beside her, the Art Institute lions both sported enormous wreaths, so she took a selfie, sent it to her parents, and posted it to Instagram.

As if on cue, Trip texted: *Ugh, so sorry. My guy here is shitting bricks. Need to talk him off the ledge or we're both going to lose more money than necessary.*

That sucks! she wrote back, adding a frown emoji and fighting a pang of irritation.

Could be another hour, he wrote. *So sorry. I'll make it up to you. I love you.*

Don't worry, I'm fine. I love you, too.

Can't believe you're in Chicago and we're not together. Gotta run.

As she dropped her phone back in her coat pocket, she thought with frustration how much time she'd already spent alone in Trip's apartment. Then, in a nearby shop window, she saw the perfect gift to give him for Christmas.

It ended up being two hours before Trip called and told her to meet him under the Macy's clock at State and Washington. She got there quickly and soon realized it was a popular meeting point as group after group of Chicagoans found each other and proceeded to join the line for the Macy's window displays. The ringing bell of a Salvation Army red kettle volunteer was just loud enough to make her back up—right into the arms of Trip, who wrapped her in a grateful hug.

"Finally," he said.

"Are you all mine now?" she asked.

"All yours."

Snow was still falling lightly as they viewed the cheesy but fun window displays, then went inside the store along with about a million other people. Trip bought her a fun but inexpensive watch she admired, a pair of nicer earrings, and a sexy, beautiful dress he made her promise to wear to dinner.

Then, bags in hand, they went two blocks to a German-style Christmas market that was absolutely thronged and utterly charming. There they shouldered through crowds to view handmade glass Christmas ornaments and snack on warm pretzels and steaming-hot mulled wine. The sun set unbelievably early, but when the Christmas lights came on, everything looked festive and delightful. For the first time, Lark allowed herself to wonder what came next with Trip—if they'd ever stop doing things long distance and pick a place to be together. Would he want her to live in Chicago? Could she live in Chicago?

Maybe.

When they went back to his apartment to change for dinner, she followed him through the door, biting her tongue and waiting for him to see her gifts. He walked past the first one, then stopped and did a double take after the second one. Lining the entry hall were six framed photos of the two of them in LA. She'd uploaded them to Walgreens from her phone, selected one-hour printing, and then found pretty matted frames at an old-fashioned photo shop under the L tracks. The clerk at the shop gave her picture hooks, which she'd banged into the wall using a coffee mug that had miraculously not chipped.

She watched Trip carefully, hoping she hadn't overstepped.

His surprised expression was slowly transformed by a wide grin. "Fucking. Awesome."

"I want you to see us together every time you walk in," she explained.

"I'm glad I will," he said, kissing her. "I don't know why I never thought of this."

"You think of practically everything else," she said, kissing him back. "Where are we going to dinner?"

"Perhaps you've heard of a place called Bavette's?"

Chapter Seventeen

HOLLY

Your family is your greatest asset.

—"How I Lied about My Name and Discovered My Truth,"
a TED Talk by Jon M. Wright

Mini-Me was rubbing his nose against the sliding glass doors again. His shaggy winter coat and long mane were dusted with snow—with those big brown eyes, the effect was heart melting, especially on Paige.

"Mom, can we *please* let him in, just for a little while?" she pleaded. "He looks so cold out there!"

"He's fine, and he's not a house pet," Holly said for the umpteenth time. "He's got a nice warm shed with fresh straw any time he wants to stop begging."

Paige pouted, her fingers on the glass like a girl separated from her prisoner boyfriend. "I honestly don't even know why you got a pet-size horse if we can't have him inside."

"We rescued him precisely because someone thought he was a pet," Holly reminded her. "The poor guy hadn't been outside in months. He is a horse and needs to be treated like one. Even if he would fit on our couch."

"Can I at least give him an apple?"

"Make it a carrot," Holly said.

Jack was frowning at his tablet, seated in his favorite chair. If he had even heard the exchange, it didn't appear to register. At least he was home for once. The kids were used to his frequent absences, but this past fall it had seemed like he was going for a new record.

While Paige went to collect her hoodie, slippers, and a carrot, Holly sipped hot coffee and folded her legs under herself on the couch. Her laptop battery was dying, but she was making so much progress on the Christmas shopping she didn't want to get up. Thank god for one-day and same-day delivery. This was the first year the Wright clan had not gone downtown on the first day of winter break to do their Christmas shopping, and when Jack originally suggested skipping it, Holly had been incensed, thinking of it as some kind of family Waterloo. But after Ava and Logan sided with their dad, and even Paige's support turned out to be lukewarm, Holly faced the facts and gave in, thinking at least she and Jack still had their standing New Year's Eve reservations at the Union League Club.

What she would not admit to any of them was that staying home was actually a relief. She missed their traditional breakfast at the Walnut Room, of course, and skating in Millennium Park, but those brief pleasures had always been followed by hours of logistical nightmares as they separated, regrouped, and separated again, hauling ever-larger bags of gifts she wasn't sure any of them truly wanted.

And today was going to be busy enough as it was: Brian and an event planner were coming over shortly to meet about the fast-approaching Hay Bale Ball.

Hearing Logan thumping down the stairs, Holly called to him, "Logan, honey, could you grab my laptop charger from the kitchen desk?"

But he either didn't hear her or, just as likely, ignored her. He kept thumping all the way down to the basement, where he would put on his headset and play games with kids he'd met online. She fervently hoped they were kids.

The day may not have been as picture perfect as their usual holiday kickoff, but it was nice having everyone home. Holly enjoyed a full and slightly chaotic house, up to a point. Two weeks from now, she knew, she'd be grateful to have Galenia back on the premises and Jack back at work full time. Not that he ever was at home full time.

Holly heard the front door open as Ava came in with Sienna. They had been out driving around, going who knew where and doing who knew what. Holly tried not to pry, though she did occasionally confirm Ava's stories with her friends' parents. Even the best kids from the best homes were liable to have some secrets.

"Hi, Mom. Hi, Dad," said Ava as they breezed into the kitchen, their sneakers leaving wet prints on the hardwood floor.

"Hi, Mr. and Mrs. Wright," said Sienna. "I mean, Doctor and Doctor."

"Hi, girls," said Jack, glancing up. "And what mayhem have you been wreaking in the snowy streets of Barrington Hills today?"

They looked at each other—less a conspiratorial glance than a *What do you say to that?*—before Ava answered, "Nothing much," and began raiding the snack cabinet.

"Oh!" said Sienna, remembering something. "I saw you, Dr. Wright. Downtown yesterday. Or maybe Saturday."

Jack cocked an eyebrow. "Where was that? You should have said hi."

"I would have but you were with somebody. I didn't want her to think, 'Who's that crazy chick yelling at you from across the street?'"

"I don't mind if people think I'm friends with crazy chicks," joked Jack.

"It was in front of Macy's," clarified Sienna.

Holly felt a throb in her forehead. "Who were you with, Jack?"

"It must have been our director of medical monitoring and consulting. She's new to Chicago, so I took her to lunch and reminded her she's welcome to enjoy the city. She's been working pretty much seven days a week."

"What's her name?" asked Holly.

"Jessica Meyers," he said, looking impatient to get back to his reading.

The girls were now looking at something on Ava's phone, something a friend had posted that was worthy of a few *Oh my GODs*.

"That was nice of you," said Holly airily. "On a weekend."

Jessica Meyers.

"I thought so," said Jack.

"Where did you take her?"

"Atwood," he said without missing a beat.

Which was across from Macy's.

"And then you looked at the window displays," she continued.

He shrugged. "How could we not? She's new here."

Suddenly Sienna was back in their conversation.

"She looked super hip and cool," said Sienna. "I loved her blue hair. If I could style like that, maybe I'd want some kind of big corporate job, too."

"We look at the résumé more than the wardrobe," said Jack with a shrug, lifting his tablet again.

And just like that, the girls had grabbed a bag of chips and two mineral waters and moved to another room.

"How's she working out?" asked Holly.

He didn't look up. "Who?"

"Your new director of whatever."

"Well, I only hire rock stars, so she fits right in."

"I wish you had office parties so I could get to know your staff."

"That's actually a great idea. We'll do something this summer. But you know you're welcome at the office anytime."

"I know."

Paige had apparently gotten distracted by something, most likely her phone, but now finally returned with a carrot, which she had thoughtfully peeled. Mini-Me hadn't moved, and condensation from his nostrils clouded the glass. He perked up when he saw the carrot, though, and Paige had a hard time squeezing past him once she'd opened the door.

"Shut the door, we're not heating the yard," called Jack. To Holly, he added, "God, I sound like a total dad."

Hearing the doorbell chime, Holly clicked "Submit" on a cart full of gifts and closed her laptop.

"Expecting someone?" asked Jack.

"I told you—Brian."

"That guy," he said with a chuckle meant to imply he was not in any way a threat to Jack Wright.

She went to the front door and opened it. Brian was waiting on the front step with rosy cheeks, a few flakes of snow in his hair, and a nice gray scarf knotted over his light jacket. When he grinned at her, she fought an urge to kiss him.

"Everything all right?" he asked.

"Of course. Why? And come in already."

"I don't know. The look on your face just now."

"Jack's here," she said as he slipped his shoes off and left them in the pile of boots, sneakers, and slippers by the front door.

"Good," he said unconvincingly.

"Hay Bale Ball?" asked Jack as they came into the family room.

"You know it," said Brian. "We've got a seat with your name on it."

"Wouldn't miss it."

Except, of course, he had.

"I've got a list of tables you helped us sell in recent years that haven't confirmed yet," said Holly, settling in on the couch and picking up her laptop again. "Do you mind giving them a call?"

"Better wait until after New Year's. Don't want to bug people when they're home with family."

Brian laughed as he sat down on a chair at the end of the couch and unzipped his computer bag. "Is that a dig?"

"Maybe," said Jack with mock seriousness. "Any developments on the bridle-path problem?"

"Nothing from the Yadaos, who seem to be wintering in Florida," said Brian. "And the trustees won't talk, of course. But I'm working a couple of angles."

Jack looked amused, as though he was thinking any effort on Brian's part was futile.

Holly sighed. "I hope this little faux controversy doesn't discourage anyone local from buying tickets."

Jack dropped his tablet on a side table and stood up, rotating his neck to get the kinks out. "Are you kidding? Put it front and center in your appeal."

"But we've always used the horses themselves as our selling point. People identify emotionally with abused animals."

"And kids. The whole point of the easement is to connect kids with horses, and horses with kids, right? Win-win. The controversy, as you call it, is a strength, not a liability."

"I think he's right," said Brian.

Jack began dictating an imaginary letter as he slowly made his way out of the room. "Dear friend of Horse Stability: As you may have heard, our proposal to create a unique resource for young people and rescue animals in the Barrington Hills community was strongly opposed at the recent board of trustees meeting. This is a major setback for our efforts, but it is only temporary. With your help, et cetera et cetera . . ."

Brian and Holly looked at each other as Jack's voice trailed away.

"Does anyone ever say no to him?" asked Brian.

"Not that I can tell," said Holly, more pointedly than she'd intended.

Brian shook his head in either disgust or admiration. She was familiar with the dichotomy.

"The event planner's still coming?" he asked.

"She's running a little late," Holly said, surprising herself with a brief but vivid vision of taking Brian into a guest bedroom and locking the door while they waited. "But we'd better get to work."

~

Later, when Brian was gone, Holly asked, "So where did she move from?"

They were in the kitchen, and Holly was putting two chickens in a roasting pan. Jack had a half dozen bottles out, along with a cocktail shaker and an assortment of bar tools, and was poring over a cocktail book.

"Where did who move from?" he asked distractedly.

"Your lunch date. The director of medical monitoring and consulting."

Because she'd already looked her up online, found her pretty face on Cancura's "Our Team" page, and confirmed her title.

"I hired her away from our partners in Phoenix."

Which explained why he no longer needed to make monthly visits.

"So she's someone you've worked with a lot?"

"I wouldn't say a lot, but I know her pretty well."

And she was pretty. Not gorgeous, but with a wholesome, heart-shaped face framed by wavy chestnut hair. If she'd dyed it a striking color, as Sienna had suggested, it had been since the headshot was taken.

"She's going to be out of the office a lot, since we just put her on the American Healthcare Systems rollout," he added. "She doesn't realize it yet, but she's basically relocating to Omaha."

"Oh," Holly said, tired of wondering what was even true.

Chapter Eighteen

JESSICA AND HOLLY

Disagreements are inevitable. Never walk away angry.

—"How I Lied about My Name and Discovered My Truth,"
a TED Talk by Jon M. Wright

It was three o'clock on New Year's Eve, and Cancura was filled with the unfamiliar sounds of early departures as everyone hurried to get out of the office. The shift in tone from all work, all the time, to *What are your plans tonight?* was audible as even the stalwarts headed home to prepare for the evening, whether they were planning to attend parties, dine at one of the seemingly hundreds of restaurants with meal-and-party packages, or simply stay in to count down with the people on their TVs.

Jessica was in no particular rush. New Year's Eve fell on a Tuesday, meaning the office would be closed on Wednesday, and then it would be back to business as usual by Thursday. She still badly needed some catch-up time before she met Jon at home for a quiet dinner, an eastern standard time New Year's toast, and a long-overdue opportunity to ring in the New Year by making love until they both fell asleep, sated and exhausted.

She'd been out of town since mid-December—first for what had been a busy and exciting seven days in Omaha at the headquarters of American Healthcare Systems. AHS was a big, cumbersome organization with a work culture to match, but she was energized by their enthusiasm about onboarding the Revelate technology and took pride in her role as the point person for Cancura. From there, she'd headed home to Gilbert, Arizona, for Christmas with her mom and latest potential stepfather. It was a welcome week off from nonstop work, even if her mom had set an interrogative tone by peppering her with questions at the breakfast table starting Christmas Eve morning.

"Explain this whole Revelation thing again, will you please?" she'd asked, filling both of their mugs with watery coffee.

"Revelate," Jessica corrected her. "It's cutting-edge technology that can painlessly diagnose childhood cancer before there are any symptoms."

"So you've been transferred to Omaha?"

"I'm commuting back and forth."

Her mom regarded Jessica over the rim of her mug. If it was possible, her filler-plumped skin looked more sun-damaged than when Jessica had left Phoenix just three months earlier. Of course, Kent, Mom's newest flame, was a spry ten years younger. That he was currently out of work was apparently beside the point.

"I thought you said you have an apartment in Omaha," her mom said.

"Cancura is renting a corporate apartment for several of us."

"You're sharing a place with coworkers? What about Jon?"

"Everything is great with Jon," Jessica said, ignoring her mom's prying. Jon and Kent were roughly the same age, which apparently made them competitors. "There are three bedrooms, and I have my own bathroom. Various employees are in and out. As for Jon, you are the only one who knows, and it needs to stay that way."

"Mum's the word," she said, stirring her coffee pointedly. "I assume that's why he can't be here?"

"He has to be with his children this year," Jessica said. "The separation has been rough on them, and they need him."

Given her mother's three marriages and counting, she hoped that particular truth would hit home.

"So, next year, for sure . . . ?"

By next year, there would be so much more to celebrate, especially if the Revelate implementation in AHS was as successful as projected. As Kent sprawled on the couch, absorbed in a college football game, Jessica had tried but couldn't picture Jon there. Maybe it would be better, she'd thought, to invite her mom—and whoever she was married to by then—to spend next Christmas in Chicago instead.

Halfway through her to-do list, Jessica took a quick trip to the ladies' room through the all-but-empty office floor. As she passed Philip's cubicle, he stood up suddenly and startled her. He was already wearing a cap with the earflaps down and a thick scarf wound several times around his upturned coat collar.

"Happy New Year, Philip," she said warmly.

"I would like to stop and speak with you except I'm running late for the bus," he said, hurrying past. "We'll talk in the New Year."

She managed to hold in her chuckle until he was around the corner. He was truly the oddest duck in the flock. Then she continued on her way.

As she was flushing, Jessica was surprised to hear the restroom door open. She emerged from the stall to see an attractive, aristocratic woman of about forty-five checking her lipstick in the mirror. She looked familiar.

"Happy New Year," said the woman warmly.

"To you, too," Jessica said as she began to wash her hands.

Was she a new hire? And if so, had she started during the last few tumultuous weeks, or had Jessica somehow forgotten her?

"I apologize if we've already met," Jessica said, feeling embarrassed. "I'm Jessica Meyers, director of medical monitoring and consulting."

The woman flashed a practiced smile. "Holly Wright."

Jessica willed her knees not to buckle. She'd studied the photos in Jon's office, the limited public pictures on Holly's Facebook profile, and everything else she could dig up online, which wasn't much. But none of the pictures did her justice. Somehow, she'd come away with an impression of Holly Wright as taller, sturdier, and certainly crazier-looking than the willowy, impeccably groomed, gray-tinged blonde poised at the next sink.

"Nice to meet you, Mrs. Wright," Jessica stammered, grabbing a paper towel and drying off thoroughly before shaking hands.

"Doctor, actually," Holly said, still smiling. "And you've got a big job. I don't believe I've heard of you before."

Jessica had no reason to feel nervous. Jon had separated from Holly before they'd even met. That Holly didn't know about Jessica's existence was Jon's decision, not hers. She also had always known she would someday encounter the unbalanced Holly Wright face-to-face, although she had always assumed it might be outside a courtroom or even at an event for one of the children, long after tensions had cooled following the divorce. Never in a million years would she have expected their tête-à-tête to occur today, in the employee restroom at Cancura.

"I'm somewhat new, and things move quickly around here."

"There's no doubt of that," Holly said. "Where did Jack find you?"

Jack?

"I was at Mayo . . . in Phoenix," Jessica said, still feeling shakier than she should. Why was Holly at the office?

"Makes sense," Holly said cryptically. "It's getting late, and I'm surprised you're even still in the office. Do you have big plans tonight?"

"I've been traveling a lot lately, so I'm really looking forward to a quiet night at home."

"Not alone, I hope," Holly said.

"With . . . a friend. And you?"

"I'm here to take my husband out for New Year's Eve," Holly said. "We're going out for drinks at the Palmer House, to dinner with friends at the Union League Club, and then we'll watch the fireworks. Just like we do every year."

Jessica was texting Jon even before she shut herself into her office.

I just ran into Holly.

WTF are you talking about?

She was in the second-floor bathroom.

You're sure it was her?

We had a conversation. She's here to pick you up for drinks, dinner at the club, and fireworks, "just like you do every year."

There was a long moment before his next reply. *Shit! Now you see what I'm dealing with. We haven't done that dinner thing in three years.*

She doesn't seem to know that.

Well, this is fucking awesome. I see her. She's headed right for me.

Do you want me to call security? Maybe Holly Wright was crazy enough to be dangerous.

No. I've got this.

You sure?

I'll be home by dinnertime to ring in the New Year with you.

Spotting a bar on Randolph Street, Jack pulled over and said to Holly, "Let's try this place."

"What's wrong with the Palmer House?" she asked. "We do that every year."

"Exactly," he said, shutting down the engine.

Holly peered out the window. The bar's window was filled with posters and neon beer signs. It looked like the kind of place that would be frequented by what Ava called "bros and hoes."

"I don't think I'm dressed for this," she said icily.

Jack opened his door. "Let's just do something different for once."

He had seemed distracted ever since she'd surprised him at his office. Usually, they met in the Loop for drinks before dinner, but she had wanted to get a look at Jessica, and disguising that as a spontaneous visit worked well—after all, Jack *had* told her she was always welcome.

His new director of "medical monitoring and consulting" didn't look at all like Holly was expecting. Sienna had said she had blue hair, but if Jessica Meyers had recently returned to her natural, beautiful chestnut brown, her stylist deserved a medal. The woman herself had been hard to read. A little flustered, but that could have been brought on by the awkward location. Or the fact that she'd just met the wife of the man she'd been sleeping with.

The bar was cold and cavernous, with most of the light coming from several dozen TV screens. She stopped just inside, but Jack continued threading his way through an acre of tall tables. There were almost no other patrons, and the heavy metal music was deafening. Reluctantly, she followed him to a two-top in the middle of the room.

"Should we get Jell-O shots?" she asked.

"I think I'm just going to have a beer," he said, ignoring her tone.

Eventually, an amused barmaid wandered over and shouted at them over the music, "We don't have table service. You have to order at the bar."

Holly was already scooting her chair back, ready to leave, but Jack grinned, apologized, and followed the girl over to the bar to place their orders. He returned with a beer in a fancy goblet and a white wine for her.

"You didn't even ask what I wanted," she said. "What if I wanted something different?"

He smelled his beer as if it were an exotic flower and then took a swallow. "I haven't seen you drink anything but white in, what, ten years?"

Which was true, but still. "Maybe I don't like change just for the sake of change."

"So you are pissed off we're not at the Palmer House."

"Do you really think this is a better alternative?" she asked, spreading her arms. If there was a place that was the literal opposite of the elegant Palmer House Hilton, with its soaring, gilded atrium, Jack had found it.

"It's okay," he said. "Never know until you try. Excuse me for a second."

He went looking for the bathroom. She couldn't say for sure, but it seemed to her that he'd almost flinched. Probably because he'd felt a vibration in his pocket. So he was going to text.

Jessica, probably.

Who did look ever so slightly like the only other one Holly had actually seen in person. So maybe he had a type.

Give him credit, Jack only stayed in the bathroom for as long as he would if he were actually peeing.

When he sat back down, she said, "So, will this little adventure satisfy your wanderlust for the evening?"

"About that."

"Here we go."

Jack drank half his beer and then looked up as if to signal for another. Then he remembered: no table service. Holly wondered how long his forced enthusiasm for the place would last. Because Jack Wright was not accustomed to carrying his own drinks.

"You know how I feel about the club," he said, leaning forward so he could speak at an almost-normal volume.

"Do I?"

Her family had been members of the Union League Club for generations, and while it was not nearly as business minded as other old-line Chicago institutions, it had certainly provided Jack with valuable connections in the early days of their marriage. If he had noticed the subtle slights from her parents and their friends back then, he never showed it. And now that he was not her boyfriend Jonny but Jonathan Wright, visionary founder of Cancura, he was a celebrity there. Her parents had taken Holly and Jack to dinner on New Year's Eve for years, but now that they were snowbirds, Holly and Jack had taken over the standing reservation and begun including some of her old friends and their husbands.

"Those people are only interested in me because of my money," he said, drumming his fingers on the table.

"For years, you were only interested in them because of *their* money," she countered.

"What are you saying?" he asked defensively.

"Simply that you have found investors there, which has worked to the advantage of everyone, including some of our dinner dates this evening."

"Which makes it feel like work."

For some reason, Jack was spoiling for a fight, which made her only more determined not to let him have one. She finally sipped her wine, which was as terrible as she'd guessed it would be.

"That fucking Chris guy, the husband of what's her name—"

"Karen."

"He puts in thirty-five grand and thinks it makes him chairman of the board—"

"That's a lot of money for some people."

"Bullshit. He's got plenty more."

"So you're worried he's going to talk about Cancura, and you don't want to? This is unfamiliar territory."

"Can't we just do something to mix it up for once?" he said, finishing his beer and heading over to the bar.

He spoke briefly to the bartender, who was working with someone else to restock a beer cooler. In the light over the bar, Holly could see her hair was streaked with vivid magenta. *She* was the kind of person you described as having dyed hair.

Jack came back. "She's busy. She said she'd bring the drinks over in a minute."

"What do you mean, 'Mix it up'?"

"Cancel. Do something else. Have some fun."

The anger she'd fought so hard to control began to bubble like a simmering pot.

"We cannot cancel, Jack. People hired babysitters. They got dressed up. They're on their way into the city right now."

"It's not like they'll go hungry. They can have dinner without us."

The lid on the pot began to rattle. "What is wrong with you? We can't treat our friends like that!"

"They're your friends, Holly, not mine."

"This is the first time I've noticed you drawing a line between friends and investors."

He looked at her intently. "You know what your problem is? You want everything to be the same, same, same. The same restaurant on the same day with the same people. You're fucking *married* to these rituals and traditions, this idea that we do things a certain way for no better reason than because we always have. You're just like your mother, Holly, and there is no way I'm going to end up like your father."

Two things happened at once. Boiling over, Holly said, *"You asshole!"* and her hand flew out, knocking her wineglass over—just as the bartender arrived with their new drinks. White wine splashed her bare midriff as the glass fell off the table and broke on the floor.

Holly, frozen, couldn't speak as the glaring bartender set the new glasses down and said, "I'll leave you two alone."

"That's just fucking awesome," said Jack, rising again. "Call me when you get it under control, okay?"

He stopped at the bar on the way out, no doubt to apologize for his crazy wife and give the bartender a ridiculous tip. Jack cared what everyone thought of him, including people who had no idea who he was.

Everyone, apparently, except Holly.

She cursed herself for giving him the excuse he wanted to leave. He obviously hadn't planned to go through with the evening at all. All his claims rang false, because he lived to schmooze, always wanted to be around people with money, and never let personal chemistry get in the way. When he found himself around someone annoying, he just let his own charming personality fill the room.

He had made excuses before, had even canceled at the last minute, but never anything like this. Never left her alone in a bar. Never told her to call him when *she* had it together.

Holly had a fleeting fantasy of racing out to the sidewalk, hailing a cab, and telling them to follow Jack's Porsche SUV. Tailing them, no doubt, to Jessica's apartment.

But what then?

And anyway, by the time she reached the sidewalk, he was gone.

Jon came home for New Year's Eve dinner a little late but still in plenty of time to enjoy the standing rib roast and new potatoes Jessica had prepared.

"I'm so sorry for this insanity. I've already left a message for my lawyer."

"She calls you Jack," Jessica said, pouring him a glass of wine.

"As in jack-of-all-trades," he said nonchalantly. "It was a joke from med school that sort of stuck."

Later, while they ate, Jessica said, "She seemed surprised she hadn't heard of me."

Jon looked perplexed. "How would she have?"

"Maybe she keeps in touch with people at the office?"

"I find that hard to imagine. If she called anyone, it would be Olivia, and I'd hear about that immediately."

Over the tiramisu, which turned out perfectly, Jessica returned to the subject. "I hope she's not putting things together. She definitely took note of the fact that I was from Phoenix."

"It probably rang a bell because I traveled there all the time."

Part of her ached to see him worry more, drink far too much, even break down over what his soon-to-be ex-wife had put him through. He didn't, though, and she felt she had to play the whole thing off as another uncomfortable inevitability. "She's pretty."

"Yes," said Jon, nodding. "But the things I liked most about Holly were her intelligence, drive, and what I mistakenly thought was total stability."

Which was exactly how Jessica would have perceived her had he not told her otherwise. "She certainly doesn't seem as crazy as—"

"That's the problem with this whole damn situation," Jon said mournfully. "Just looking at her, nobody would believe it."

They rang in the New Year on eastern standard time and were making love at midnight, knowing he'd be out the door again by midday—first to the office, and then off to the airport for a presentation at Duke, of all places.

"Just think, I'd be plucking you out of the crowd in Durham this week if we hadn't met in Phoenix," he said, his arm around her.

"Maybe that would have been better," she said.

"You don't really mean that, do you, Jessie?"

"Life would certainly be less complicated."

Jon pulled her close. "Everything is as it's meant to be."

"Maybe you wouldn't have noticed me, anyway," she said, wishing she weren't being such a downer.

"Impossible."

"I would have been an oncology fellow, not a doe-eyed resident."

"Playing hard to get, are we, Doe Eyes?"

"Maybe," she said, as she felt him harden against her hip. "It wouldn't have been so easy to lure me away."

"You didn't stand a chance then," he said. "And you don't now."

~

Holly showed up at the club for dinner, of course, not because she was like her mother but because people didn't treat each other that way—blowing off plans, walking out, seeking private pleasures. She made an excuse for Jack, caring less than usual whether anyone found it plausible that he had an emergency call with an investor in Shanghai who didn't observe the Western New Year.

If she was believed, it was because she'd been practicing for years. As the waiter brought their menus and directed a busboy to remove the sixth place setting, she wondered whether the lies she'd been forced to tell on Jack's behalf had compromised her, too. Because once someone stopped caring about the truth, didn't everything else crumble?

Karen, whose husband Chris's small investment had so offended Jack, had been Holly's roommate at Glenlake Academy, and they had maintained their friendship out of comfortable force of habit. Tina and her husband, Lane, were friends from the University of Chicago. It was an odd mix, now that she thought about it—stay-at-home mom, real estate investor, medical school provost, and plastic surgeon—the disparities made more noticeable without Jack to plaster over the cracks.

Holly willed herself to be lively, to ask everyone questions about their kids and jobs, wanting to prove—to her absent husband?—that social niceties mattered, that maintaining connections made a difference. But as drinks and appetizers led to soups and salads, she found it harder and harder to maintain focus. By the time the entrees had arrived (she ordered rack of lamb, because she always did, and because her father had been so proud of her when she announced "I'll have what he's having" at eleven years old), she was drifting. Barely there. Nodding and smiling and looking interested while in reality she couldn't have told anyone what they were talking about.

For years after what she thought of as the Bachelor Party Incident, she had watched Jack closely, worried about a repeat. They were often together in those days—he didn't travel much yet—and she didn't see anything that particularly troubled her. And when he did begin traveling, and his itineraries and business deals became too byzantine to keep track of, it all happened gradually. He spoke excitedly of so many people in so many cities that to have given in to jealousy would have driven her insane. She listened dutifully, trying to share his excitement for the big idea while still wondering whether it was even possible. And eventually she lost track of the particulars.

Lost track of Jack.

Until one night, shortly after they'd moved to Barrington Hills. Ava was five, Paige was two, and Holly was four months pregnant with Logan. Their Lincoln Park town house was newly on the market and the Realtor informed them, with an open house scheduled for the next day, that they had overlooked a considerable amount of clothes and toys in the girls' closet. Jack, holed up in his new home office in front of a glowing screen, had irritably said he was too busy to take care of it. After making him promise to look in frequently on Paige, who was running a fever, Holly put some empty boxes in the back of her car and drove into the city.

She had cleared the closet and stacked the boxes on the back porch when the doorbell rang. Puzzled but not thinking too much of it, she opened the door to a pretty, younger woman with a heart-shaped face and light-brown hair. Taller than Holly, which would bother her later, as would her much larger breasts and curvy hips.

Her face was neatly made up, but her eyes were red from crying. She held a small bouquet of flowers to her chest.

And looked utterly shocked to see Holly.

"Is this . . . does Mitch Wright live here?" she asked, suddenly unsure of herself. "I might not have the right address."

Everything became clear in an instant. "Mitch" had a piece on the side, whether in Chicago or somewhere else. They'd fought, or broken up, who knew—and somehow, she'd found his address. Come there to apologize. Make up. Make love.

What stayed with Holly most, perhaps, was how calm she'd been. How, as the moment elongated, she'd thought quickly of so many people—Jack, their daughters, their unborn son, her parents, their friends—and thought about what would happen if the truth came out. Though it would take months and years of rage and self-doubt, somehow in that moment she had already decided she wouldn't let this woman tear her family apart.

"I'm sorry," she told the woman simply. "There's no Mitch Wright here."

At home, she confronted Jack—so he'd know she knew—and endured his weeping explanation that he'd been drunk, that it had been a onetime thing, an accident he desperately regretted. He cried convincingly as he said he couldn't get the woman to leave him alone and she'd stalked him until he threatened her with a restraining order. Holly let him believe she accepted it—and let herself believe he would be too chastened to repeat himself.

No one else had knocked on their door, at least.

Against her better judgment, she asked the woman's name, and he told her it was Kim. Which for some reason Holly found disappointing.

Dessert came, along with the coffee everyone insisted they needed to stay up past midnight. The plan had been to bundle up and watch the fireworks over the Chicago River, but Holly begged off, saying she'd promised to meet Jack at home to at least pop a bottle of champagne. The other couples, suddenly disconnected by the departure of their mutual friend, debated whether they should just call it a night, too.

Holly urged them not to let her be the reason the evening ended, but she truly didn't care.

As she said good night and collected her coat, as she waited half an hour for the Uber that would deliver her back home, she knew this time Jack's cheating was different. Because this time he'd brought it to work. Actually *hired* his mistress—whether the relationship began before or after Jessica started at Cancura, it was as far from a drunken one-night stand as it was possible to get.

Holly also knew she was going to do something about it. Even if she didn't know what, exactly, that would be.

They were rolling along the Kennedy Expressway when she got a text. Not from Jack, apologizing.

From Brian. With a little emoji of toasting champagne glasses.

Happy New Year.

Chapter Nineteen

LARK

Celebrate each success with every member of the team.

—"How I Lied about My Name and Discovered My Truth,"
a TED Talk by Jon M. Wright

Lark hung up the phone, pounded her desk until her palms hurt, and let out a yell that probably startled the shit out of someone upstairs.

She picked up her cell and called Trip. Straight to voice mail.

She texted, *TARGET SAID YES!!!!!*

A moment later, she added, *22,000 units, and more if they start moving.*

He didn't answer right away, which meant he was on a flight. It was frustrating how often he was in the air lately. And now, finally, she had good news to share!

Unfortunately, Sandro, her part-time assistant and first hire—he hadn't even met Trip yet—wasn't in the outer office because he was on an audition. Highly personable, hyperarticulate, and fanatically organized, he was also a talented dancer trying to piece together a living in show business. Lark knew he would have been more than happy to toast the first big success of Larkspur Games, but he wouldn't be back until tomorrow morning.

Lark grabbed her phone and keys and practically jogged out of the office. She texted Callie as the elevator made its slow, one-story descent.

Meet me at my office ASAP. Big new$!!!

Her response came after Lark had made it down the block, turned the corner, and was crossing the street to the liquor store.

Congrats! So exciting! Just got home . . . was going to put my feet up for a few.

Callie's job as an apartment leasing agent had irregular hours. Lark suddenly wondered whether she could hire Callie to do something. Larkspur would definitely need more people right away, and her roommate—who happened to have a degree in marketing and communications—deserved a reward for putting up with her this whole time. She would definitely have to think about it. Meanwhile: celebration.

Girl PLEASE?!? This is HUGE. I mean it!

Callie responded with an emoji of an arrow hitting a target and a question mark.

Lark, standing in front of the liquor store, which looked kind of sketchy now that she thought about it, sent her a wink.

After a beat, Callie replied, *Be there as soon as I can.*

YAY!!!

Lark felt a twinge of regret at cajoling her roommate into coming out when she was tired, but good news like this didn't arrive every day. It might happen only once in a lifetime. And she didn't want to celebrate at home—she wanted to celebrate in her new office. After Trip, Callie was the person she wanted to be with.

The glass door to the liquor store was protected with serious-looking security bars, and when she went inside, an old-fashioned bell jingled over an electronic beep. They were covering all the bases. The cooler up front was stocked with comically large cans of beer, suggesting much of their business was day drinkers chasing a cheap buzz, but farther back there were rows and rows of wine and liquor that included some expensive bottles on the dusty top shelf.

There were exactly five kinds of chilled wine to choose from: a cheap pinot grigio, a moderately priced muscatel, a popular rosé, a six-dollar Cold Duck, and, bizarrely, a bottle of Dom Pérignon. Who knew how long it had been there—but it didn't go bad, right?

Before she could talk herself out of it, she hauled the antique-looking bottle to the register, where the startled clerk practically dropped his phone. With tax, it came to well over $200, but thankfully she had shoved her card into the chip reader before she could back out.

Somehow, she knew Trip would approve.

She was carrying the bottle out in a brown paper bag when she stopped. "Do you have cups?"

Because she was damned if she would drink $200 champagne out of a rinsed-out travel mug.

"Red Solo and also the fancy kind," said the clerk.

She bought the "fancy kind," which ended up being two-piece plastic champagne glasses and cost another eight bucks for a pack of ten.

Back at the office, she assembled two of the glasses, stood them next to the sweating bottle on the reception desk, and waited for Callie. If she had jumped in the car right away, she'd be there in fifteen minutes or so. Trip still hadn't answered, so he was likely in transit somewhere. Hopefully, he'd be able to come celebrate in person soon.

She definitely wanted him to advise her on the next steps in hiring. She had Sandro to answer calls, manage her schedule, run errands, and do other odd tasks. A freelance web designer was nearly finished with her new website, but she probably needed a full-time marketing expert and someone to oversee production and the supply chain. Eventually, she'd need a good sales rep and another entry-level person to handle orders and customer service. She wondered how many people she would be able to squeeze into the outer part of the office suite before they needed more room.

She pushed open the door to Trip's office, which looked exactly the same as the day he'd removed her blindfold to show her the space. He'd been there for an hour or two on two different occasions, using it as a place to park himself while he waited for Lark to finish work. She hated to ask, but if she didn't put someone in here, she might have to let someone work in her own office. Which was fine. But wouldn't it be weird if they had this big empty office next door?

A good problem to have. She also had to figure out how to deal with individual orders that came through the website. There were probably ways to outsource it, but maybe there was a small office in the building that could work as a small supply and mail room. So.

God, she wanted to pop that cork. She scrolled through Instagram, looking to see if Trip had posted anything new—of course he hadn't, not since the *Sweet home, Chicago!* picture he'd taken from the plane the last time he landed—and quickly liked a few posts from the friends she didn't see often enough in real life.

Finally, the outer door opened, and Callie came in with a bottle in a reused gift bag.

"Congratulations!" she said, rushing across the room to wrap Lark in a big hug before handing over the bottle.

Lark was pulling it out of the bag when Callie saw the Dom.

"Now I'm embarrassed," said Callie, reaching for the bag. "Give it back."

"Nothing wrong with a good bottle of prosecco," said Lark, not wanting Callie to feel bad. "We can save mine for later."

"Like hell we can. I've never had Dom Pérignon, and if you're buying, let's forget I even stopped at 7-Eleven. In fact, this bottle isn't for you at all."

They both laughed at that. Relieved to be off the hook, Lark peeled off the foil and popped the cork, which hit the acoustic tile ceiling hard enough to make a dent. Whether it was because she'd walked too fast coming back or the bottle was too warm, the champagne geysered forth, forcing a frantic scramble to get their cups under the spout before too many ounces of the precious stuff soaked into the carpet.

Once their glasses were filled, Callie gamely put her mouth under the bottle and gulped until finally it stopped overflowing.

"Well, damn," she said, wiping her chin. "Our family always celebrated with Cold Duck."

Lark took a sip, then a mouthful, savoring the bubbles. She had no idea how food writers managed to separate so many different flavors when describing wine—all she knew was that it was somehow bold and delicate at the same time. It somehow made her think of a cool, dark cellar in a big, old mansion. It tasted like *success*.

They quickly finished half their glasses before refilling and toasting again, this time posing so Callie could share the moment on Facebook "for the folks back home."

"So how big is the deal?" Callie asked.

"Pretty big. Twenty-two thousand units. I think that equals roughly a dozen per store."

"What does it mean, moneywise?"

Lark had definitely run the numbers.

"At a retail price of $44.99, if every single game sells, they're looking at almost a million dollars in gross receipts. Of course, Target pays us half that for the games and can return unsold units."

"So a half million bucks?"

"Minus production and overhead. The games cost ten bucks each, so that's almost a quarter million. And I definitely need to hire more staff to deal with this."

Callie looked at her glass and grinned. "I don't mean to be a killjoy, but maybe we should have opened my bottle instead."

"This is all about getting started and scaling up," said Lark. "The more games we make, the cheaper they'll get. And if they're successful at Target, we'll pitch other chains. There are direct sales to think about, institutional sales to schools—"

"What happens when everyone who wants their own Activate! has one?"

"By then we'll have four new games in development."

"You have more ideas already?"

"A couple. But they don't all have to be my ideas."

Callie shook her head. "You are amazing. Most people would have just done a Kickstarter and left it at that."

Lark didn't bother telling Callie she had wanted to leave it at that until Trip convinced her otherwise.

"I'll bet Trip is over the moon."

"He doesn't even know yet," confessed Lark. "He's on a flight somewhere."

"That sucks. I feel like I've hardly seen him lately."

"Me too. We had that weekend in Chicago, but he spent the holidays with his brother's family."

Callie took another drink and set her glass down. "I hate to bring this up, but Dylan has been texting me."

"Dylan? What about?"

"Well, apparently, ever since his plan to woo you back with a song was such a disaster, he's become a little bit obsessed with Trip Mitchell. Googling him, even doing database searches at the library."

"Unfuckingbelievable." Lark didn't even try to conceal her irritation.

Callie looked pained. "He says he can hardly find anything. Which he thinks is somehow suspicious. Trip doesn't even show up as ever having been enrolled at Indiana University. You have to admit it's kind of weird, if Trip is such a big shot."

Lark felt a flash of anger at her usually sweet and supportive friend. "It's over with Dylan. I can't believe you're ganging up on me with him, of all people."

"It's not like that. The only time I even answered was to tell him to knock it off. I just . . . Dylan got me thinking, so I googled Trip a little bit myself, and heck, there are more results for *me*, and I'm anything but a wealthy financier."

"Well, the reason neither of you are finding results is that his real name is Jonathan. I mean, his friends have called him Trip since he was a kid, but obviously he wouldn't use his nickname for business deals and stuff like that. He also told me he intentionally keeps a low profile because he doesn't want people hitting him up for money all the time."

"I'll bet there are a million Jonathan Mitchells," said Callie.

"If you want to keep Dylan really busy, let him search for *that*," said Lark.

Because she had done that very thing, back when Trip first offered her a contract. Once she'd gotten past his frustratingly nonspecific website, the list of authors, politicians, lawyers, athletes, and scientists who shared his name had seemed endless.

"I won't tell him anything at all," said Callie. "I know you and Trip are crazy about each other, and I'm so happy he's making you happy. Just keep your guard up a little, okay? It's only been three months, after all."

"You're a good friend, even if you're kind of a cop," said Lark, regretting the remark when Callie winced. "I'm sorry."

"No, I'm sorry. I shouldn't have brought it up." Callie set her glass down half-full. "I've gotta go. I have to go back to work, and I shouldn't drink too much."

"So glad you came. Love you."

"Love you, too."

Then Lark was alone in the office, feeling a little buzzed but with half a bottle to go. There was no fridge and no way to put the cork back in the bottle. And she didn't want to go home until Callie was out of the house.

She texted her parents to share her news but wasn't surprised when they didn't answer right away. Her mom was probably in the classroom, and her dad was so old school he didn't even check his personal cell phone at work.

"It's you and me, buddy," she said to the bottle, filling her glass.

~

She was drunk, sleepy, and about to take an Uber home when Trip finally texted.

YES! YOU DID IT! CONGRATULATIONS, BABY!

I had help. Thank you.

You closed the deal. Time to celebrate.

I already did. Callie helped me drink a bottle of Dom. Not telling him she'd done the heavy lifting herself.

Attagirl.

I want to celebrate with you, too!

We will. Soon.

When? Resisting the urge to put it in all caps.

I've got to put out a fire. Then I'll come, even if it's just for 24 hours. I miss you so much.

I miss you, too.

Callie left and it's weird to be alone in the office after something so big happened, she added.

It's lonely at the top, baby.

It certainly was.

Chapter Twenty

Jessica

Underpromise and overdeliver isn't just a cliché—it's a philosophy.

—"How I Lied about My Name and Discovered My Truth,"
a TED Talk by Jon M. Wright

Randy Warner, AHS vice president of technology implementation, stepped into Jessica's field office. "Sorry to hit you with this first thing on a Monday, Jessica, but I believe we have an issue."

"What's wrong?" Jessica asked.

Randy closed the door and handed her a folder. "The Revelate picked up nothing in two cases where a CBC showed low platelets and a high white blood cell count. If this is indicative of the accuracy—"

"Were all these patients prescreened according to our parameters?" she interrupted pleasantly, trying to slow his momentum. Feeling déjà vu as she flashed back to her confrontation with Kate.

"Of course."

"And the blood tests?"

"They were run simultaneously."

"Were the patients given the Revelate nano pill exactly twenty-four hours before scanning?"

"I've already confirmed that we followed your protocol precisely." Randy seemed exasperated. "I thought the whole point of the technology was painless diagnosis?"

"It is," she said.

"Try telling that to the kids who had to undergo bone marrow biopsies anyway."

"We all know we're still a ways off from making tests like that obsolete," she said, as fine beads of sweat formed on her face, back, and under her arms.

"But you agree these numbers are off?"

"On the page, yes, but I don't want to jump to conclusions. There are variables we need to explore."

"I'm not the only one questioning whether this technology is ready for prime time," Randy said, leaving the folder and backing toward the door. "Some people are saying we need to halt this rollout."

"I'm going to reach out to my team right now," Jessica said, picking up the phone and dialing Marco back at Cancura headquarters.

The call went through to voice mail.

After leaving a message, she sent him a text, then an email, and spent the next hour trying not to chew her nails to the quick while her thoughts went in circles. Why was she the only person who seemed to stumble into problems with the Revelate technology?

Jon, not Marco, called her back.

"I'm on the next flight," he said. "Set up a meeting for late afternoon."

"I'm sure I can handle this myself," Jessica said. "I just need some—"

"I just need some of you. Tell Randy not to wet himself. I'll be there soon."

Though she was looking forward to the unscheduled time with Jon, Jessica felt slightly stung that he'd been so quick to saddle up his white horse and ride to her rescue. If she was the face of Cancura as far as AHS was concerned, couldn't he have just given her the information she needed to save the day? Did his lightning-fast mobilization reveal how worried he was?

Marco called shortly after she hung up with Jon. "AHS has buyer's remorse, which is more common than you'd think when someone drops a shit ton of money like this. And the solution is always to deploy our most powerful weapon: the famous visionary Jonathan Wright. Just ask him."

Although the note of sarcasm in his voice helped to assuage her bruised ego, Jessica realized Marco was right. It was Jon's company, after all, and she was fooling herself if she thought the clients didn't merely see her as his intermediary.

Just before four o'clock, she met him outside the building as he climbed out of a black car.

"They're waiting in the boardroom," she said as he drew her in for a stealthy kiss.

"Let's go put their minds at ease," he said.

Jessica had seen Jon work a room before, but his performance as they made their way through the building was truly remarkable. No one would have ever guessed he was sweating a $50 million deal as he greeted everyone, from nursing assistants to doctors, with confident warmth. Truthfully, most of them probably had no idea who he was, but they could tell he was *someone*. Heads swiveled in their wake as people tried to guess the identity of the good-looking, confident man.

Once they were seated at the long conference table—with Jon in the center, not at the head, and Jessica to his right—Randy went around the room, introducing everyone from the AHS CEO to heads of departments. There were more than two dozen people in all, and when Jon began speaking, he repeatedly addressed people by name to powerful effect.

Apparently, he'd just been getting started.

"Ten years ago, I gave my first TED Talk, which had the unfortunately hokey title of 'Nanotechnology: The Molecular Miracle Worker,'" Jon said, getting a laugh. "I told the audience that everything from the common cold to cancer could be detected, repaired, or cured by nanotechnology. When I announced my plans to pioneer nanorobots that would identify tumors, deliver multiple drugs in precise ratios without adverse side effects, and destroy them without leaving a single cancerous cell, the applause was lukewarm, because I happened to be addressing an audience of elite medical professionals who were sure I was delusional. Come to think of it, you might have been there, Manish."

Manish Sharma, head of oncology, chuckled and held up his hands. "I wasn't there, but I did think you were crazy."

"You had good company," said Jon, taking a sip of water. "And when I founded Cancura with a ten-year goal of identifying disease via an easily chewable pill, I was told by a former surgeon general of the United States that the idea was—and I'm quoting here—'sci-fi stupidity.'"

He pushed his chair back, stood up, and looked out the window as Jessica wondered why he was spending so much time highlighting his detractors.

"We can videoconference using a device that fits in our pockets. Driverless cars are quickly becoming consumer technology. Not that long ago, a guy literally crossed the English Channel with a *jet pack*! A few decades ago, this *was* all fodder for sci-fi novels and movies. It turns out the biggest limitation we face as humans is that of our own imaginations."

Jessica took a sip of water. Her mouth was as dry as her underarms were damp. But if the AHS executives and administrators had looked tight lipped and guarded to begin with, their body language was starting to relax.

Jon began to slowly circle the table. "Thankfully, a few forward-thinking investors believed in both the science and my ability to assemble a team of the best and the brightest. Seven years later, I stand before you to address your valid concerns about a few inevitable hiccups in—"

"Hiccups?" interrupted Randy. "The Revelate failed to diagnose two full-blown cases of acute lymphocytic leukemia."

His expression was almost fierce, unlike CFO Sharon Montgomery, who couldn't take her eyes off Jon.

"All of you at American Healthcare Systems knew you were partnering with Cancura at the beginning of what will be a revolution in health care. The solution for this issue, and truly every problem we've encountered so far, is in tweaks, fine-tuning, and small adjustments. The technology is sound. More important, the data you've given us, which will be studied without delay, is exactly why we're so excited to partner with you." Jon paused. "But one of the reasons I wanted to be with you in person today was to share two big announcements."

As people murmured and shifted in their chairs and Jon bit his lip like he couldn't wait to share the good news, Jessica wondered what it could possibly be.

"First, Henrik Bergland, a former director-general of the World Health Organization, will be joining the Cancura board of directors. Second, we have almost completed phase two testing of specially designed nanoparticles that are sending back an amplified signal when they bind to cancer cells in the brain."

Jon looked directly at her as the room filled with excited whispers.

"I'm counting on all of you to keep this confidential until we're ready to make an official announcement," Jon said. "But if all goes according to plan, the Revelate will be enabled to detect brain cancer markers, including glioma and neuroblastoma, by the end of the year."

"That's definitely great news," Randy said, now looking reluctant to continue pressing Jon. "But—"

"Randy, this is the first time we've allowed people outside a lab to operate our machines. I think the next step is to move a team of our techs on-site to analyze performance in a working environment."

Bill Nelson, the CEO, cleared his throat, quieting the room. "We have faith in Cancura, Jon, but I'm wondering if we were somewhat premature in bringing the machines into a clinic setting. For both our reputation and yours."

"The FDA certainly doesn't think so, Bill," Jon said. "But if this isn't right for you, that's fine. We'll go to the people who are already number one and looking to retain their spot. Or we can help you knock them off their perch."

The CEO was a cool customer, but Jessica realized he'd stumbled into an awkward position—a sales negotiation in front of his most trusted staff. She wasn't a mind reader, but she had a sense that the room was on Jon's side, and nobody wanted to be part of the team that passed up medical technology that made biopsies and spinal taps look like diagnostic tools from the Middle Ages.

But why hadn't Jon or Marco mentioned to her either the new brain cancer detection advances or that Cancura had other big suitors besides AHS?

"We certainly don't need to make any hasty decisions," said Bill. "After all, the Revelate pilot program isn't replacing anything just yet. We're looking forward to having your techs on-site and continuing our great relationship."

～

"It's not lying," Jon said, working his way down the buttons of Jessica's blouse. "They just needed some incentive to choose their own best interest."

"But there isn't another company that wants the Revelate?"

"There are many," he said, reaching the last button and gently pulling the sleeves over her arms. "All I have to do is make a call."

"What about Dr. Bergland?"

"We're in advanced talks, and I expect a favorable conclusion."

As appealing as Jon's confidence was, she wished she felt as comfortable as he did about playing so fast and loose with AHS. "What about the comparative test results between the Revelate and—"

Jon kissed the small of her back. "Don't worry, my love. AHS was well aware there would be a shaking-out period."

"Well, they were definitely feeling shaky," Jessica said, enjoying a rather pleasant quivering sensation herself.

He unfastened her bra. "Which is why you're there to hold their hands until they're comfortable implementing. Lucky bastards."

"I had no idea we were so far along with brain cancer markers."

"I'm full of surprises," he whispered, unzipping her skirt.

"I'm afraid that—"

"You need to learn to live a little more dangerously, Jessie."

"Aren't we doing that right now?" she asked as he led her to the living room couch in the Cancura corporate apartment. "What if someone comes here tonight?"

He slipped off her panties as she raised her hips. "Someone is definitely going to come tonight."

Chapter Twenty-One

HOLLY

Don't let people use your history to predict your future.

—"How I Lied about My Name and Discovered My Truth,"
a TED Talk by Jon M. Wright

"I think we're ready. Do you?"

Brian looked at Holly and nodded. "All systems go."

She leaned back and let herself laugh. "I thought this day would never come."

"I had faith," he said, before smiling and sipping his coffee.

They were sitting at Holly's kitchen table with their laptops open and paperwork scattered all around. Holly's own coffee was down to the dregs, and she was resisting the urge to cut off a second piece of the amazing apple strudel Brian had brought all the way from Bennison's in Evanston. The kids were back in school after winter break, Jack was out of town, and Galenia was shopping and picking up the dry cleaning. Holly and Brian had the place to themselves.

For propriety's sake, it would have been better to meet in a coffee shop, but Holly wasn't sure how much she cared about that anymore.

The Hay Bale Ball would take place in three weeks, and thanks as much to Brian's efforts as her own, everything was set for a drama-free evening. They had given a final head count to the caterer (slightly padded to account for any last-minute additions); sent in the liquor order; delivered the down payment for the bartenders; confirmed the tables, chairs, and centerpieces; printed programs and place cards; booked the jazz band; and created a schedule with duties for Horse Stability volunteers, all while attending to a host of other essential details she'd already forgotten. Every year, she thought the job would become more routine, but somehow each time was just as hard as the last.

"We sold eight percent more tickets than last year," Brian said. "I'd call that respectable growth."

"Very respectable growth," said Holly.

"Jack's idea to put our challenge with the Yadaos front and center seems to be paying off," he said. "It'll be ironic if I'm able to solve it before the party. I think the thing to do is find something Larry wants. He's a real estate developer, you know."

She tried hard not to let anything show, but apparently the sour look on her face after hearing Jack's name was too obvious to ignore.

"What's wrong, Holly?"

She opened her mouth, closed it. Thought, *Don't tell him.* But suddenly it was either that or she would burst out crying, which would have been exactly the same thing.

"Jack's having an affair," she heard herself say.

"God, Holly. I'm so sorry." Then, while she fought to control her breathing, Brian asked, "You're sure?"

"The signs are all there," she said, her eyes welling. "I haven't told anyone . . . it's so strange to say it out loud."

Brian was out of his seat, coming toward her. He guided her to the living room, discreetly snagging a box of tissues on the way.

"Tell me," he said, as she sank into a corner of the couch and he pulled a chair into place opposite her.

"I don't know too much about her except that she works at Cancura, she's from Phoenix, and apparently she likes to change the color of her hair." Holly dabbed the corners of her eyes, not letting the tears actually fall. "He picked a fight on New Year's Eve so he'd have an excuse to storm out and leave me alone."

Brian looked stunned. "You were alone on New Year's? I had no idea. We could have—"

"Invited me over?" she said, shaking her head.

He ran his fingers through his hair and laughed ruefully. "We could have both watched Nancy sleep on the couch."

"I wasn't completely alone. I had to make his excuses and suffer through an intimate dinner with two other couples. I left early and got home in time to share some popcorn with the kids. Jack stayed out all night, but the next morning he began the apology tour. Flowers, jewelry, promising a special trip sometime soon. He said he spent the night alone in Cancura's corporate apartment in the Loop."

"But you don't believe him?"

Holly looked across the living room at Jack's reading chair, the place from which he held forth like the benevolent patriarch of a happy family when he was home. Which was almost never these days.

"He's with her now. He told me he was in Omaha, which could even be true. I don't know. But it means they're together."

"And you're sure," said Brian, looking pained. "Absolutely sure."

Suddenly, she ached to be held. "Sit with me?"

Very slowly, as though he were thinking about each movement before he made it, Brian sat next to her on the couch. Inches away. Holly shifted until their thighs were touching and leaned her head on his shoulder. She laced the fingers of her left hand through the fingers of his right. Her heart pounded so loudly she wondered if she was feeling his heartbeat, too.

"He had a one-night stand the night before we were married, and then he had an actual affair when the kids were little. When I confronted him, he confessed and cried and swore it would never happen again. He called it a moment of weakness and said he despised himself. He's just so . . . believable . . . he almost makes you feel sorry for *him*. And as angry as I was, I also had this feeling that I was damned if I was going to let another woman take my happy life from me. I didn't want my kids to grow up in a broken home. And so I found a way to look the other way. I've done a lot of that, over the years."

"But this time, you want to know?" he asked.

One tear escaped, rolling hotly down her cheek. She wiped it off with the back of her hand, forgetting momentarily about the tissues. "He hired her to work for him. How can I look the other way?"

"I'm so sorry, Holly."

She looked at him. "I'm sorry you have to hear this."

"It's okay. I mean, this is nothing like what you're going through, but Nancy and I have our own problems. As you know. I don't suspect her of anything"—he laughed wryly—"at least, I didn't until now. But it's more like things have just . . . stopped. I can't remember the last time she looked at me and I thought, *This woman loves me.* It feels like we're colleagues whose project is our children."

"That's awful in its own way."

They were facing each other, inches apart. It was so easy and so natural to just lean forward and kiss him, and once she had, her anxieties suddenly melted away. They kissed intently, hungrily, holding each other close like they were afraid to let go.

Brian pulled away. "I don't want this to be because you're angry at Jack."

"I'm not—"

"Of course you are. I'm furious at him, too."

Her body was telling her to keep kissing Brian. To take him upstairs to her bed. But was he right—was she giving herself permission because of what Jack had done? Was she using Brian to take revenge on Jack?

Now the tears came freely, silently, as she realized that Jack had once again outfoxed her. He was doing whatever he wanted, and she was still bound to him.

"I'm not going to let him get away with it this time," she told Brian. "But I don't know what to do."

"I assume you have evidence that he's cheating?"

"Not exactly."

"You don't destroy a marriage without facts. You need to play this smart."

"I'll get proof," she said. Worrying what she'd see when she found it.

Chapter Twenty-Two

LARK

*There have always been people who doubted me, but
I've never for one second doubted myself.*

—"How I Lied about My Name and Discovered My Truth,"
a TED Talk by Jon M. Wright

Gregory Zapatka, who insisted his name was pronounced Greg-ORY, sat in his chair like it was a throne. He had flamboyant sideburns and purple aluminum ear gauges, and he had chosen to come to the interview wearing cargo shorts and a black concert T-shirt that barely covered his belly. Lark thought of herself as musically knowledgeable, but she couldn't even read the band's name due to its runic font and abundance of umlauts. Gregory had a weird body funk that smelled like a mix of Axe body spray, Red Bull, and spicy Indian food.

The moment he'd taken his seat opposite them, Lark and Callie exchanged a silent look that said, *Unless he's some kind of eccentric genius, let's keep this short.*

Gregory, however, had other ideas, and had spent the last fifteen minutes interviewing them—as though he were a prize they'd be lucky to win.

"So let me get this straight," he asked now. "This Activate! game is your only product, and you're six months from market?"

"That's correct, although we do plan to develop more games," Lark said.

He looked around, practically sneering at Lark's ironic *Hang in there, baby* poster. "And this office is where I'd be working?"

"Actually, in the group area just outside," Callie said.

The idea obviously did not appeal to Gregory. "You know, I was on the team that developed Vikings: Gamma Horde and Star Cowboys: Wizard Edition. I worked with Lionel Rex and Bianca Grenoble when they were starting up Game Horizon Studios, and even back then they had a cool loft."

"That's a very impressive résumé," Lark said, and it would have been, if she were creating fantasy role-playing games for hard-core gamers instead of fun and educational experiences with mom appeal. "We'll be in this space for at least a year, and then we'll see what comes next."

"Do you mind if I vape?" asked Gregory suddenly. Without waiting for an answer, he produced a device that had been designed to look like a tobacco pipe from a hundred years ago. Lark was perhaps more relieved than she should have been when his exhaled vapor smelled like passion fruit, not cannabis.

"We're smoke-free and vape-free at Larkspur," Callie informed him.

Gregory wrinkled his nose, sighed theatrically, and stowed the vaporizer in the side pocket of his cargo shorts. "If I decide to come here—*if*—what's my salary?"

While Callie stalled for time, Lark surreptitiously texted Sandro: *Knock.*

Fifteen seconds later, her part-time assistant did exactly that, rapping discreetly on the door before opening it and sticking his head inside. "I'm terribly sorry to interrupt, but your next interview is on their way up."

Lark and Callie were out of their seats before he finished his sentence, thanking Gregory for his time and reaching out to shake hands. They both immediately regretted it: his hand was doughy, warm, and moist.

"I'll let you know my decision," he said as he gathered his messenger bag and tucked in a dangling headphone cord.

The moment they heard the outer office door close, both of them burst out laughing.

"He looked great on paper," Callie deadpanned.

"And I liked the arrogance in his cover letter, but it reads a little differently now," added Lark.

Sandro came back. "Not a good fit, I take it."

"Not a good fit," they both confirmed.

"Coffee run?" he suggested sympathetically.

"Yes, please!" said Lark. "I presume the next candidate is not, in fact, here?"

"Not for twenty minutes," said Sandro.

He left, and Lark and Callie fell back into their chairs.

Gregory's condescension aside, Larkspur Games was looking and feeling like a real place of business. Lark had felt it the moment she arrived in the morning and saw Sandro's neatly designed Interviews Here sign on the door and Callie already hard at work inside.

Her roommate had resisted the idea of being Lark's first full-time hire—and had outright refused the position of marketing director, insisting Lark owed it to herself to find someone with experience in the world of games. Callie's counterproposal was a role as general manager, playing jack-of-all-trades "until real professionals were in place." She would update the website, handle initial production and supply issues, coordinate customer service, and so on.

Lark realized eventually that Callie was right: the marketing director was probably the most important hire she would make. She needed to find someone who could guarantee Activate!—and future games—made a splash.

As Callie reached for her phone and Lark swiveled toward her computer, there was a knock, the door opened, and Trip walked in.

"I know I'm not on the schedule, but I saw this, and I'm here to apply," he said, grinning and holding up the Interviews Here sign.

Lark wanted to crawl over the desk, tackle him, and smother him with kisses—but with Callie in the room, she just stood for a quick peck. After so long apart, the mere sight of him gave her goose bumps.

"Why don't you have a seat?" she said instead, playing along. "We'll be happy to discuss your qualifications."

Trip put the sign on her desk and sat down. "I'm afraid I don't have a copy of my résumé on me."

"That figures," said Callie. "Do you have any references?"

He cocked his finger at Lark. "I'm in pretty tight with the boss."

She really, really wished she didn't have a full day of interviews ahead. Because what she wanted to do was take him home and pretend they were just waking up together . . .

"And what is your relationship?" asked Callie, still with a straight face.

"We're business partners. Also partner partners. I won't beat around the bush: we're romantically involved. If that's a crime, I'm guilty as charged."

"Are you a hard worker?" asked Lark, just to say something. Callie seemed to be taking her role a little too seriously.

"I've been told that's my greatest fault," said Trip.

"We've actually been keeping a big office open for you," countered Callie. "Yet you never seem to be in it. Do you have any intention of putting it to use?"

Lark thought Trip looked a little wounded, but he did his best not to show it and responded breezily. "My work requires more travel than I'd like, but I'm a loyal soldier, and I go where and when I'm required."

"Other employers seem to be putting a lot of demands on your time," said Callie intently.

Trip finally seemed to be at a loss for words. He held up his hands, palms out: *Take it easy.*

"Are you willing to relocate?" asked Lark, trying to keep it light and bring it back to their faux interview but inadvertently continuing Callie's line of questioning.

Trip met her eyes. "I'll certainly consider all reasonable offers."

"I think there's already an offer on the table," said Callie, standing up and heading for the door. "I'll give you guys a minute."

When they were alone, Lark went around the desk and sat in Trip's lap, wishing they had a couch or something more comfortable.

"It's good to see you," she said, after a quality kiss.

"You have no idea," he said. "But what's with Callie?"

"She thinks it's her job to be suspicious of everybody. I guess we were both scarred by Dylan."

"She couldn't possibly think there's anything wrong with my intentions?"

"Of course not." She kissed him again, thinking he looked, smelled, and tasted very fresh for having gotten off a red-eye. He'd probably already gone to his hotel to shave, shower, and brush his teeth. "Also, the office space may literally be an issue."

Trip laughed. "*That's* what's bugging her? Well, if it will put her mind at ease, she's more than welcome to have it."

"She doesn't want it herself. We're interviewing marketing directors, and that might be a useful perk to offer."

"Well, that's fine, too. Use it however you want. We can get more space on this floor if you need it."

"But where will you work?"

Trip lifted her chin. "Baby, I'm not the important one here. You are."

The phone on her desk trilled. She tugged on the cord until it was close enough to pick up.

"Your coffee and your next interview have arrived, Miss Robinson," said Sandro. "May I send them in?"

"One minute," said Lark, hanging up and sliding off Trip's lap. "How long are you in town?"

"Just until tomorrow, so we'd better make it count."

"I'm busy all day, unfortunately."

"Me too. Dinner in Santa Monica? Walk on the beach?"

"Deal," Lark said, kissing him one more time and showing him to the door.

Neither he nor Callie acknowledged each other as he left.

Chapter Twenty-Three

JESSICA

Always stay the course.

—"How I Lied about My Name and Discovered My Truth,"
a TED Talk by Jon M. Wright

Now that a team of Cancura techs was working on-site to troubleshoot the performance of the Revelate in a hospital environment, Jessica was winging back and forth between Omaha and Chicago. One day, she was in Omaha, and the next she was back at headquarters triaging tasks that seemed only to increase in number no matter how much work she did remotely. The pace and the promised payoff were exhilarating—if only she didn't feel like a human pinball, hitting spinners and bumpers and dropping into kick-out holes. She hoped she was headed for a flipper and not the drain.

The advisory boards Jessica had formed per her job description, during her first weeks on the job, were either deadly boring or further unfocused her view of the big picture. Particularly the client-experience board, of which Kate and Arjun were cochairs.

How could she have missed that they were a pair? They were usually together, agreed on everything, and, when they were in the same room, were always within arm's reach even though they never actually touched—not at work, anyway.

Watching them made Jessica wonder what people would say about the body language between her and Jon when they found out.

If they ever found out.

She was starting to wonder about that almost as often as she thought about the Revelate's alleged inability to detect the one cancer for which it had FDA approval.

"The fundamental problem is that AHS wants the Revelate to do something it was never truly designed to do," said Arjun.

"Shouldn't a test that identifies precursors to a disease also be able to confirm when the actual disease has manifested?" asked Jessica.

"Not necessarily," Arjun said. "Nanotechnology, by its very nature, is strictly targeted and infinitesimally precise."

"We weren't trying to reinvent a process that already exists," Kate said flatly.

"There have to be modifications we can make," Jessica said, hearing a pleading note in her voice.

"We aren't in the business of performing parlor tricks for some hospital exec who needs to assuage an overcautious board," Kate added.

"We are investing our time, research, and money in the discovery of formerly undetectable proteins, as well as antibody, DNA, and RNA fragments," Arjun said, slightly more diplomatically and definitely playing the good cop role. "Not working backward."

"That's our mandate from on high," Kate said.

Jessica rubbed her temples. "Meaning from Jon?"

They nodded in unison.

~

Jessica willed herself to focus on a particularly complicated cost-benefit analysis of multiple hardware parts suppliers during her next meeting, which was with the finance committee.

Three-quarters of the way through the discussion, Philip appeared outside the conference room window, as though instinct had told him he was missing a gathering of his tribe.

Lorna, the chief financial officer, waved him in. "I asked Phil to brief us on the financial ramifications of transferring the production of gold nanowire from Tarius in Palo Alto to Deacon, here in Illinois."

Phil, as Lorna called him, brushed his hair out of his eyes and stepped tentatively into the room. He fumbled open a red binder and began to rattle off facts and figures in his oddly deep monotone.

Jessica lost track almost immediately as her mind went back to the meeting with Kate and Arjun. How would she address client concerns when the same issues became even more pronounced once new tests came online? Why was Philip the only person at Cancura who seemed willing, however reluctantly, to acknowledge a potential problem?

Without looking up from his notebook, he stopped as abruptly as he began and then stood there as if waiting to be dismissed.

"A very succinct summary," Lorna said, looking at him appreciatively. "Thank you for taking on that little side project."

"I had the time to do it," he said, eyes still downcast.

"It sounds like there are multiple benefits to changing suppliers, once we determine the right time to do so," Jessica said. "If there are no further thoughts or comments, I think we can adjourn."

As everyone stood to leave, she asked Philip, "Do you have a second?"

"Can you stop by my office, Phil?" Lorna asked, collecting her papers, electronics, and water bottle.

He nodded noncommittally.

"I just need a minute," Jessica said, wondering if she'd interrupted plans between yet another stealth couple that she and everyone else had failed to identify.

"What did you want to talk to me about?" he asked.

Jessica took a deep breath. "You remember when I asked you about some discrepancies I found in test results from that leukemia study a few months ago?"

"And Jon employed a third vendor to run another series of tests, and they matched our in-house results?"

"Exactly," she said.

"Too exactly," he reiterated.

"What would you say if I told you I've learned the Revelate was never truly designed to detect disease that is already identifiable through traditional means of testing?"

Philip turned toward the glass window and checked in both directions. "I would have nothing to say that would be of help."

"I don't understand," she said, wondering what had rattled him. "Who do you think I should talk to about something like this?"

"Graham," he whispered.

"Your friend who used to work here?"

Philip tilted his head and scrunched his face. "Until he was fired."

"Fired? I was told he was lured away by another med-tech start-up."

"That's not what happened."

"Then what did happen?"

"He didn't understand that there are some things you just don't say out loud here," he said, turning to leave. "Lorna is waiting for me."

Like what? But he'd already hurried out the door and down the hallway.

∿

"Did you know a data analyst named Graham?" Jessica asked Marco over lunch. "He left right before I came."

Marco looked up from the salad he was splitting between two plates. "Of course. Why do you ask?"

"Philip made kind of an odd comment about him."

"Philip made an odd comment?" repeated Marco, feigning shock. "About his friend who kept vintage ThunderCats action figures on his desk? *Quelle surprise.*"

"They're probably worth a fortune," Jessica said, trying not to judge. "In any case, Olivia told me Graham was poached by a Silicon Valley start-up, but Philip said he was fired."

"They're both right," Marco said. "When Jon discovered Graham was talking to someone else, he was let go."

"Just like that?"

"At the risk of repeating myself, everyone wants to cure cancer, but nobody thinks about the level of security that requires," said Marco. "Graham had a big mouth and needed to be reminded of the strength of our confidentiality clause."

"Gotcha," she said, pushing her half of the truffle mac and cheese around her plate. It made sense.

"You're barely eating," Marco said. "Don't tell me you've developed a taste for the soggy tuna salad and withered carrot sticks at the AHS cafeteria."

Jessica half-heartedly speared a few noodles. "I'm just not all that hungry. It's been a long morning."

"Second Wednesday of the month, which means you were communing with Komodo Kate."

"I managed to avoid being bitten by her or Arjun," Jessica said, even though she felt like they'd ripped a chunk out of her.

"I can't say I'd mind being nibbled on by Arjun," Marco said with a giggle.

Mindful of how closely Jon had held the secret, Jessica stopped herself from telling Marco that Arjun was a willing victim of Kate's venom. Her friendship with Marco had relaxed to the point where he shared personal details about life and love while she offered tidbits about her past while maintaining that work was her life for now.

Which wasn't exactly a lie.

"I have a question," she said.

"The answer is yes. You should set up a Tinder profile in *both* Chicago and Omaha. Though now that I say that, the very idea of Omaha Tinder makes me shudder."

"Very funny."

"And I'm not kidding, Jessica. You're so smart and good-looking, I really do find it hard to believe you're sleeping alone. You would tell me if there was someone, wouldn't you?"

"Seriously," she said, shutting him down. "Did you know Jon instructed Kate, Arjun, and their team to devote all their time and resources to getting the new tests up and running—"

"Why is that even a topic of discussion?"

"—without making any modifications that will enable us to confirm the results in patients with already detectable disease?"

"Hold up," Marco said. "What do they suggest we do about Randy and AHS, or the FDA, for that matter?"

"Talk to Jon, naturally," Jessica said.

Now it was Marco's turn to push his mac and cheese around on the plate. "Well, we can only assume Jon has this all worked out and is three steps ahead of everyone else, as always."

"And if he's not?"

"It hasn't happened yet."

∾

Jessica came home expecting the apartment to be dark and empty but was surprised to find Jon sitting on the couch with his feet on the ottoman, watching CNN.

"Hi, babe," he said, sending an air-kiss in her direction.

He had never beaten her home on a weekday before. Not only that, she had never actually seen him relax and watch TV. She would have felt badly about disrupting his stolen moment of peace and quiet if she hadn't spent the whole afternoon continuing to obsess about her conversation with Kate and Arjun.

She set her purse down on the counter and walked into the living room, preparing for the worst. "I'm sorry, but I need to talk about work."

To his credit, Jon simply muted the TV and patted the couch beside him. "What's up?"

She didn't sit. "I have questions, and I need answers in order to do my job properly."

"Sounds eminently reasonable," Jon said. "Talk to me."

Instead of thinking before speaking, which she'd long found to be the most successful way to make a point without sounding emotional, irrational, or *too much like a woman in a man's world*, she said, "Why didn't you tell me the Revelate was never designed to detect full-blown diseases, only specific precursors?"

"Because that's not entirely true," Jon said.

"Not according to Kate and Arjun," she said.

"They don't know the whole story."

"Which is?"

"A few months ago, when I told you I employed another vendor to run a third set of tests—"

"That matched our in-house results?"

"The real story is that those results matched those of the lab we fired," he said. "Ours were the outliers."

"But what you showed me—"

"What I showed you was simply a copy of our in-house data."

Which Philip must have suspected when he spotted the identical numbers. "My god, Jon. Why would you do that?"

He looked down. "A lot of people have sunk their fortunes into Cancura and staked their futures on what I promised. I couldn't afford to let them know something was wrong."

"Which is why you got so angry at me when I brought it up."

"I was panicked," he admitted.

"You lied to me," she said, finally voicing her growing fear.

"I had to. I couldn't tell anyone."

She felt like she'd been stabbed. "Even me?"

"Especially you," he said, still unable to meet her eyes. "My earnest, honest, principled love."

"What am I supposed to tell AHS? That—"

"You can tell them they've made the best possible decision for themselves and their patients."

Jessica's head was spinning. "In one breath you say the Revelate doesn't work properly, and in the next that AHS has invested their fifty million dollars wisely? Forgive me if I don't understand."

"I didn't, either, until I realized our original model was entirely irrelevant," Jon said, finally looking up, that unmistakable luminescence returning to his face. "There's no need to *confirm* disease in patients where it's already known to exist. That's never been what we've been about anyway, and there are already tests for that. The whole idea is, and has always been, detecting and curing cancer before it ever presents itself, much less has a chance to metastasize."

"Once again, I have to ask why we pursued a partnership with AHS, knowing our technology had such a significant limitation."

"It's not a limitation. It would be nice if the Revelate worked the way they want it to, but Arjun and Kate are right that it's not necessary. We just need to keep identifying nascent cancer markers, and we all win. Humanity wins."

"The deception really bothers me," Jessica said. "Not to mention the fact that you kept me in the dark when it's my job to know exactly what's going on."

"What I don't like is that we'll be able to identify all these cancers but only cure one of them for now," said Jon.

"What do you mean, *cure one*?"

Jon raised an eyebrow teasingly. "You heard what I said."

She fought the impulse to be taken in immediately like she always was, like everyone was, by his sheer enthusiasm. "Are you telling me—?"

"Why did you come to Cancura instead of heading to Duke for that fellowship, Dr. Meyers?" Jon asked. "That is, besides the opportunity to make your boss the happiest man ever?"

"Leukemia," Jessica said, her heart racing. "Are you telling me you've figured out how to do targeted therapy using nanotechnology?"

"Will that piece of information help you in your role as director of medical monitoring and consulting?"

"Oh my god, you've figured it out?"

Jon drew her over to the couch. "I'll take that kiss you've been withholding now."

"Yes, sir," she said, treating him, and herself, to a lingering smooch.

"That's more like it," he said. "And now I have an important question for you: What are your thoughts on Cancún?"

"Cancún?" she repeated, wondering if she'd somehow misheard the word *Cancura*.

"I have to speak at a bullshit conference there next weekend. All I need to do is wow them with my keynote, shake hands at a reception, and show up for a breakout session or two. We can get a romantic weekend out of it—that is, if you'll come with me."

Chapter Twenty-Four

HOLLY

Avoid loose ends. A single stray thread may well be your undoing.

—"How I Lied about My Name and Discovered My Truth,"
a TED Talk by Jon M. Wright

Playing detective was a hell of a lot harder than it looked. Especially after having spent the last two decades studiously avoiding clues.

Which wasn't to say Jack was sloppy. His phone would have been the obvious place to look for evidence, but he was scrupulously careful with that. His notifications were sometimes set to chime, sometimes to vibrate, but no messages appeared on his lock screen, and he never let go of his phone without locking it and placing it facedown. The most recent night he'd slept at the house, Holly had lain awake until he came to bed, then waited until his breathing was deep and even before trying to break his phone's password. But apparently he wasn't sentimental enough to use their anniversary or the birthday of anyone in the family. After a few more far-fetched efforts, she'd simply run out of ideas.

Now, with the kids gone and Galenia working away downstairs, Holly decided to try again. Opening the top drawer of his bureau, she carefully lifted socks out, planning to put them back the same way. Then she plucked the two-key ring out of the small wooden bowl at the bottom.

Jack's office was furnished with built-in bookcases, a plush Persian rug, leather club chairs, an immaculately restored antique wooden desk, and a fully stocked bar cart that was really just for show. A narrow table against one wall was crowded with etched crystal paperweights connoting various honors and recognitions—the kinds of things clubs and organizations had made up so they'd have something to hand to their illustrious speakers. On the walls were photos of Jack with various senators, representatives, and captains of industry, many of them signed with personalized messages.

Go get 'em!

Jonathan—you are the man.

Proud to shake the hand of the man who's going to cure cancer.

Though Holly rarely came in here, Jack's visits weren't much more frequent. Some weeks, he spent a half day here plus a few odd hours. Other weeks he didn't use it at all.

But he did have a two-screen computer setup, along with an expensive webcam he used for videoconferences, webinars, and the occasional cable TV appearance. Approaching the desk from behind, she draped a handkerchief over the webcam, which was aimed at the office chair. She was probably just being paranoid, but spyware was a distinct possibility.

Holly sat down in Jack's chair and unlocked the drawers. A cursory search revealed mostly outdated paperwork. The lower-right-hand drawer was stuffed with old Cancura swag: pens, notepads, sticky notes, and stress balls. Hardly the place to squirrel away evidence of an affair.

Tapping the keyboard, she woke the computer from sleep. On the desk was a single framed photo of the whole family that was woefully out of date. Logan appeared to be still in kindergarten.

The computer demanded a password. This would be no four-to-six-number PIN but could be anything: a word, a sentence, a randomly generated sequence of letters, numbers, and special characters.

Holly tried for twenty minutes before quitting, utterly defeated. She couldn't even access his desktop. It would probably be the same story with his laptop and tablet—not that they were in the house. They went with him everywhere.

She had already spent hours googling him, using his full name, adding *Cancura* and *Jessica Meyers* as search terms, but there just wasn't anything to find. Her heart stopped for a moment when she spotted a result from Facebook—until she realized it was her own page and the *Jessica* and *Meyers* came from their unconnected friends Jessica Ames and Dan Meyers.

Real detectives had access to secret databases no member of the general public could use. TV detectives talked to people. Sometimes pretending to be someone else.

Did Olivia know? Though it had been years since they worked together, she still thought of Olivia as a friend. The thought that Jack's executive assistant could be aiding and abetting him in an ongoing affair—or affairs—made Holly want to vomit. Then again, if Olivia knew from observation, not because Jack confided in her, why would she sacrifice her own job by going to Holly? Even if she mostly owed her career to Holly?

Maybe Olivia could help her another way. Using her cell phone instead of Jack's desk phone—caller ID—Holly called the office, silently rehearsing what she'd say.

Jack's been going on and on about what a great job Jessica Meyers has been doing. I'd love to send her some flowers!

No, to her home address.

Why not at work? No reason.

She was trying to disconnect when Olivia answered. "Hello, Holly!"

"Olivia—I'm so sorry," said Holly, stammering while she stalled for an excuse. "I misdialed. You're next to Jack in my favorites."

"I think he's in a meeting. Do you want me to try to put you through?"

"No, no. It's not urgent."

"I'll tell him you called, then."

Great. Now she needed to think of some mundane reason she might have called. *Don't forget to get Dave O'Connell to come to the Hay Bale Ball!*

She wished now she had raced outside that godforsaken bar on New Year's Eve, hailed a taxi, and followed Jack to Jessica's apartment. To the *love nest.* God, it sounded like one of her mom's potboilers she used to read when she was twelve years old, thinking the adult characters' forbidden desires and tangled relationships were so wonderfully exciting.

But maybe literally following them would be the easiest way to do it. Following Jessica, who had seen Holly only once and hadn't recognized her on sight. She had no idea what Holly's car looked like. And in any case was unlikely to be checking her rearview mirror like a fugitive as she made her way home from work.

～

Holly drove into the city and was in place for her stakeout by four thirty. After circling the block several times, she found a spot on the other side of the one-way street from Cancura. She could see the side door that led to the parking lot, and when Jessica pulled out, there would be only one direction she could go. Holly could easily pull in behind her.

Though the late-January sun was already almost down, she was wearing sunglasses and had driven her Range Rover because it had tinted windows. Keeping the engine running and the heat on full blast, she lowered the passenger window halfway until she had a clear view and then reluctantly ditched the sunglasses.

How long would she have to wait?

Quite a while, as it turned out. Jack modeled an always-working leadership style his subordinates were highly motivated to emulate. Holly sat, listening to NPR on low volume, until she'd heard the same news repeated three times and rush hour had come and gone as the neighboring buildings emptied out. She'd texted apologies for running late to Galenia, then did her best to manage the kids' homework remotely, all the while keeping an eye on the Cancura entrance. Her legs and feet were hot, and her head and shoulders were chilled from the frosty air whipping in the lowered window. If she raised it, though, she might not recognize Jessica.

Only a dozen cars were left in the lot, Jack's among them. Would they be so obvious as to leave together? She wished she had a camera with a telephoto lens.

Finally, she saw her, recognizing that lovely chestnut hair in the security light over the side door as Jessica came out of the building, hunched against the wind, and scurried over to an anonymous silver sedan that was at least ten years old. Apparently, Jack hadn't gotten around to giving her a nice new car yet.

As Jessica waited for the gate to open, Holly saw the silhouette of a cactus on her front license plate. Arizona. Holly raised her tinted side window. And when Jessica pulled into the street, Holly gave her a half-block lead and then followed along behind.

With traffic getting lighter, it was easy enough to keep track of the car. Jessica drove cautiously, as though she were still new enough to Chicago streets to be intimidated by them. And the route was simple enough: after heading east toward the lake for a few blocks, Jessica turned north on Halsted and then followed the stop-and-start traffic out of the West Loop, under expressways, and over the river into Lincoln Park, then Lakeview, where she turned left on Belmont.

A short distance and a right turn brought them to a picturesque one-way street crowded with tall three-flats and small apartment buildings. In summer the leafy canopy would connect overhead, filtering the streetlights with a soft green glow.

Suddenly, theirs were the only cars moving on the block. Her heart thudding, Holly lifted her foot off the accelerator. Had she been following too closely? Did Jessica suspect anything? Or worse, had she seen Holly's license plate and committed it to memory?

Impossible. Still, Holly let Jessica pull ahead, then regretted it when the silver car turned right at the end of the block without signaling. Holly stepped on the gas, crunching over a speed bump, and followed.

When she rounded the corner, Jessica was nowhere in sight.

Panic. Anger. Then a realization.

Holly pulled up to where an alley bisected the block. Looked left and saw nothing. Looked right—there. The sedan pulling into an off-alley parking spot.

She made herself wait a full minute before following slowly, navigating by her parking lights. Halfway down the block there was parking for a half dozen cars. Jessica's, empty and dark, was one of them. The building number, 3201, was spray-painted on a dumpster.

Holly hoped for a further clue, like unit numbers painted on the pavement, but the dirty crust of ice and snow obscured even the lines of the parking spaces.

Tapping the gas, she continued down the alley and was about to turn right again to view number 3201 from the front—it must have been the building on the corner—when Jack's Porsche streaked past.

She froze, feeling caught, exposed, and completely panicked even as his car disappeared around the corner, following Jessica's route to a parking space.

He hadn't seen her. Had he?

Every fiber of her being told her to flee the neighborhood and hurry back to Barrington Hills. But slowly reason overpowered her flight response. Jack couldn't have seen her. He had no reason even to be looking for her or to expect her car to be idling in an alley behind Jessica's apartment building.

He had waited until Jessica left Cancura, giving her a few minutes' lead to ensure no one saw them leaving together. Then he'd followed, driving the way he always did, fast and recklessly, taking any shortcut that would save him a few precious seconds. Because Jonathan Wright hated to waste time.

Especially when he was eager to see his lover.

Breathing steadily, feeling her pulse begin to drop, Holly resolutely turned right and right again, halting in front of 3201. It was a squat three-story building, probably over a hundred years old, whose gray exterior gave little hint at what lay within. Lights were already on in several windows, and a giant TV flashed on the wall in one of the second-floor units.

Jessica was in one of them. Jack was making his way upstairs. Holly waited, half expecting to see their silhouettes embrace in a front window. But she didn't see motion in any of the units.

Picking up her phone, she texted, *What's your schedule tonight?*

His answer came quickly. *Still at work. Going to be a late one. Sleeping downtown and headed to that conference in Cancún tomorrow.*

Don't work too hard, texted Holly.

Thinking that this time, his absence gave her room to move.

～

The next day, after getting Ava, Paige, and Logan off to school, Holly searched the address of Jessica's apartment building and found an open listing. She had a full morning of patients at the clinic but made an appointment to view an empty unit at three o'clock, ample time to get there and back with no chance of encountering Jessica. She'd confirmed Jack was actually in Cancún—the website for the four-day "Envisioning Medical Futures" conference featured him as the keynote speaker, and he wouldn't blow them off the way he'd blown off his own wife on New Year's Eve—so there was no chance he'd be dropping by for some afternoon delight.

Through her appointments, a mix of annual checkups and sick visits, Holly struggled to stay focused, to make small talk with the moms (it was always moms) who accompanied their kids, to compliment the kids on growth spurts, to keep alert for signs that a rash or fever might actually be something other than the obvious childhood malady.

She failed miserably.

Instead, she was consumed with a desire to see inside the apartment, to see whether there were clues as to how far things had progressed. Did Jessica cook for Jack? Did he keep a change of clothes there—or more than one? His own toothbrush? How many hours had they spent together there while Jack claimed he was hard at work at the office?

Jessica Meyers was a cipher. The handful of photos Holly had been able to find online—from graduate school, the Cancura site, and a rarely used Twitter account—didn't even hint that she was a free spirit who streaked her hair with primary colors. Her smiling, wholesome face gave no hint that she was the kind of person who would carry on an affair with someone she knew damn well was married.

But Jonathan Mitchell Wright III was not just a random not-quite-silver fox. He was rich, widely respected, and almost famous. Any ambitious young woman would be drawn to him.

Finally, Holly's appointments were done. After a hurried lunch, she headed into the city and made her way from the expressway back to Jessica's apartment. She parked two blocks away, not wanting to risk anyone seeing her car or license plate. She'd even taken the precaution of making the appointment from the house's landline, a number no one used with a voice mail no one checked.

The leasing agent climbed out of his Ford Focus as she came down the sidewalk. A young man with wavy, light-brown hair and a friendly, open face, he introduced himself as Evan.

"Elizabeth Isles," she told him. "Call me Liz."

Recalling the fake name Jack had used with his long-ago fling, she'd decided two could play that game. Unfortunately, she wasn't much more creative than Jack, and all she'd been able to come up with was her middle name and her maiden name.

"You want to see the two-bedroom loft, correct?" asked Evan.

"I'm divorcing my husband," Holly told him, the words surprising her as they came out of her mouth.

Evan looked momentarily stunned. Then, gamely, he said, "Well, I can see why you need your own place."

As he let her in and led her through the lobby to the elevator, Holly glanced at the mailboxes: 205 was labeled MEYERS. She had no idea what possessed her to start inventing a story, because she'd told herself to say as little as possible. But following Jessica to the building, and now being inside it, had left her emotionally raw.

"Please forget I said that," she said. "It's not your concern."

"I'll keep that in mind if you start hitting on me," said Evan, grinning. "It hurts being the rebound guy."

She laughed gratefully.

The building, once used for some forgotten industrial purpose, had been completely gutted and refurbished. The elevator was clean and quiet, the halls were carpeted in a tasteful neutral pattern, and the hardware throughout looked sleek and expensive. Evan explained that, while there were some studio and one-bedroom apartments, the most desirable units were the four two-bedroom, two-story lofts, such as the one she was looking at.

"These don't stay vacant for long," he told her, turning the key to 204 and pushing the door open so she could enter first.

The space, brightly lit by the winter sun and with a living room ceiling that soared to the roofline, was a designer's dream of sandblasted brick, massive wood beams, and gleaming countertops. Unfurnished, its hard surfaces made it feel beautiful but stark and cold.

It was literally cold, too. Seeing her shiver, Evan apologized that the heat had been set so low.

She toured the unit while he dutifully pointed out all the features of the 1,400-square-foot unit, from the gas fireplace to the walk-in closet off the master suite to the in-unit washer and dryer. Holly tried but couldn't picture Jack and Jessica there.

"This is lovely, Evan," she said. "But I'd feel a bit claustrophobic in a middle unit with windows only on one side. Is there a corner unit available—maybe 205?"

"I'm sorry," he said, fear he'd already lost his commission written on his face. "Both corner units are leased."

"Do you think they'll be there long term?"

"I have no idea about 201, but the lease for 205 runs until August 31—I know because I closed that one myself. I only met the man, but I know a couple lives there because he told me his girlfriend was relocating from out west to be with him."

Before letting her go, Evan insisted on showing Holly the parking spaces behind the building, informing her they were a steal at $200 a month. She froze when she saw Jessica's silver sedan sitting where she'd seen it only last night.

Either Jack's lover had been home all this time, or she'd gone with him on the trip.

Chapter Twenty-Five

LARK

I'm well aware that I'm always being watched.

—"How I Lied about My Name and Discovered My Truth,"
a TED Talk by Jon M. Wright

A few months ago, the idea of Lark needing a break from her stressful job would have been a novelty—unimaginable that she'd be working at her own brand-new business. It was happening nevertheless, and her days had been beginning earlier and earlier—and ending later and later—as she worked through the multitude of challenges facing Larkspur Games. Lark was making a growing number of big decisions on her own as Trip's more pressing business interests limited his visits to the West Coast.

Wanting to unwind and reconnect with her parents—and, truthfully, take a break from Callie—Lark had proposed a Sunday-morning visit to the Beverly Hills Farmers' Market, the location chosen with her father in mind. Leroy Robinson may have been tall and broad shouldered, and carried himself with military bearing, but he was also completely starstruck and thrilled by celebrity sightings, which was a never-ending source of hilarity to Lark and her mom. Outside of a red-carpet premiere, there were few better places to spot famous faces.

Her mom, Kalani, already had standing plans with her women's hiking group, but Lark was just as happy for some father-daughter time. With a general plan of picking out some fresh veggies for dinner, neither of them was feeling the least bit hurried.

Despite the gray day, her dad was wearing mirrored aviator sunglasses to make his gawking less obvious.

"Don't look now, but I'm pretty sure that's Eva Mendes," he whispered out of the side of his mouth.

"If I don't look, what's the point?" asked Lark, even though she was no more than mildly curious to spot famous actors. Maybe it was a generational thing, or maybe it was because her dad had grown up in a neighborhood famous people never visited. She'd seen enough of them over the years to realize star power wasn't something they necessarily radiated in the frozen-foods section of the grocery store.

"Okay, you can look now. She just turned the other way," said her dad.

Lark did her best to follow his vague nods and was successful in locating the dorsal view of a highly toned shopper wearing yoga pants—meaning she looked like almost every other woman at the market.

"Wow," Lark said appreciatively, glad they were off to a good start. "Kombucha?"

He grimaced. "Knock yourself out. I just hope someone here sells Diet Pepsi."

As they headed toward a white tent offering fermented beverages, fresh-squeezed juices, and coconut water, he added, "You know, I've got a bottle of unfiltered apple cider vinegar at home. You could save yourself eight bucks."

"Sounds good, but I'm thirsty now," she said, jabbing him with an elbow.

"How's work?" he asked, once Lark had gotten her drink. "Have you hired a marketing director yet?"

Their preferred choice was still making them wait for an answer, but both Lark and Callie had been delightedly horrified when Greg-ORY Zapatka had emailed to announce that, after careful consideration, he had decided to accept the job they had not offered him.

Your loss had been Gregory's two-word reply after she corrected his assumption.

"Our first choice will let us know by tomorrow," she said.

"Fingers crossed. Oh, I think that's—never mind." Words her dad said with some frequency in the city as he realized an attractive woman or man wasn't the celebrity he thought he had seen.

Stopping to buy a cookie the size of a salad plate, he broke it down the middle and offered her half.

"You do realize that's vegan and gluten-free, right?" she told him.

"Ah shit," he said, crestfallen.

After the first bite confirmed his suspicion, and Lark told him she didn't want any, he discreetly slipped the remains into a nearby trash can.

"And are things going okay with Trip?" he asked, brushing crumbs off his hands.

"Definitely."

"Seeing a lot of each other?"

"When we can. It's a bicoastal relationship—I'm here, and he lives on Lake Michigan."

"It's getting a little weird that your mom and I still haven't met him. He's obviously a very important part of your life."

"I know, Dad, and I'm sorry. He wants to meet you, too."

A white lie. It wasn't like Trip didn't want to meet them, but neither he nor Lark had made it top priority for their increasingly rare evenings together.

As they slowed down to navigate a small cluster of people in front of a tent selling naturopathic products, her dad craning to scan every face, there was a clopping behind them, and they had to move out of the way for a pony led by a man in a John Deere T-shirt. On the pony was an adorable little girl in a frilly blue princess dress, and following along behind were a familiar-looking man and his familiar-looking wife.

"Did you see that?" her dad breathed as the procession went past. "John Legend and Chrissy Teigen."

Even Lark had to admit it was a pretty good celebrity sighting, though she didn't whip out her phone and surreptitiously start taking photos like he did.

"I think you're mostly getting horse butt," Lark told him.

"I got some Chrissy Teigen butt, too," he said. "Don't tell your mom."

Lark waited patiently until he was done and then talked him into splitting an open-face bagel sandwich with avocado and harissa. They ate as they went, walking carefully and watching for pony poop.

"So, is it serious?" he asked. "It sounds serious."

She nodded. "Very serious. Almost too good to be true. Callie's not so hot about him, though."

"She's probably just looking out for you. I know he's . . . a bit older than you."

"Uh-huh." Thinking: *Way to keep a secret, Mom.*

"You told him your dad is a six-foot-one killing machine, right?"

"*God*, Dad. How did you ever end up with a hard-core feminist like Mom?"

"You know I'm kidding, Lark."

"I know. But answer the question anyway."

Her dad looked thoughtful as he finished his bagel in two huge bites, chewed, and wiped his mouth with the back of his hand. "When I met your mom, I thought she was too good to be true, but she didn't feel the same way about me. She definitely took some convincing.

Sometimes opposites attract, and sometimes the appeal is being with someone just like you. I think the most important thing is that you give yourself to someone who allows you to be you. Even better, more you than you were before."

"Very profound, Dad."

He grinned. "I think so. Now I seriously need that Diet Pepsi."

They left the farmers' market half an hour later, planning to reconnect and cook a family dinner that evening. Her dad's presence had been reassuring in a way Lark couldn't quite put her finger on. Maybe it was just knowing that true love could last.

The only problem with Trip, she thought, *is that there isn't more of him to go around.* She had no idea how someone who made her feel so good could be so unconvincing to Callie.

She called him while she drove home.

He answered on the third ring. "Larkspur Games, field sales."

"This is your boss calling."

"If it's about those expense reports, I can explain."

His connection seemed staticky. There was a surging noise that rose and fell.

"Where are you?" she asked, breaking character. "It sounds like the beach."

He laughed. "I wish. Just traffic. How are things at the home office?"

"I'm okay, I guess. I miss you, and I'm frustrated because we're not together."

"I'm sorry about that."

"Don't be," she told him, trying to mean it. "The most important thing is that we allow each other to do what we need to do and be who we need to be."

"Beautifully said. But you sound worried."

"I guess I kind of am," she confessed. "Do you ever get the feeling that what we have is too good to be true?"

"You do realize there's no logical weight behind that phrase, don't you?"

"I know. I'm sorry. It's been hard being alone so much."

"We're in this together," he said, with an earnest tone that helped her believe it. "And there's no such thing as too good to be true."

Chapter Twenty-Six

JESSICA

I have a passion for mergers and acquisitions.

—"How I Lied about My Name and Discovered My Truth,"
a TED Talk by Jon M. Wright

Jessica had been to dusty Nogales several times and vacationed in laid-back Puerto Peñasco once, but she'd never had any particular desire to visit Cancún. Part of it was that she'd grown up surrounded by sand, sunshine, and Latino culture in Phoenix. Mostly, though, she associated the place with the pre– and post–spring break chatter of party-hearty sorority girls whose conversations were peppered with, "Cancún is, like, so lit!"

But as Jessica relaxed in her own private cabana on the white-sand beach, sipped a slushy mango margarita rimmed with smoky chili powder and salt, and gazed out at the honest-to-god turquoise sea, she had to admit those ditzy girls with Greek letters on the asses of their underbutt-baring shorts were onto something. And *they'd* stayed at the seedy strip of downtown hotels known for hosting weeklong, all-you-can-drink bacchanals for horny college students, not the stunning White Sand Resort. Jon had lifted her out of blustery, arctic Chicago and set her down in an all-inclusive, five-star heaven.

"Your job," he'd told her while he knotted his tie and she headed for water yoga, "is to relax and recharge while I give this speech and shake a few hands."

"And what if I want to watch you in action afterward?" she'd asked.

"Trust me, you've seen it before. When I'm done, it's time to dine, dance, and romance."

Once she was nearly horizontal on the cushioned chaise, even those activities sounded like too much effort. Which must have been the last thing she thought before the crashing waves and the potent margarita lulled her into a peaceful nap.

She woke to Jon's voice, carried to her on the gentle breeze.

". . . you sound worried . . . You do realize there's no logical weight behind that phrase, don't you? . . . We're in this together. And there's no such thing as too good to be true."

Talking business. Always business, even here in paradise.

Hearing Jon's footsteps crunching toward her in the sand, she closed her eyes and pretended to be asleep until she felt a soft kiss on her lips.

"Water yoga in the infinity pool must have been even harder than it looked."

"It's impossible to balance on those floating mats," she said drowsily, looking at him.

Jon had changed out of the suit he'd worn to the conference at the three-star resort next door and into blue bathing trunks. How he looked equally good in both was a mystery for the ages.

"Sounds like a decent workout, anyway."

"How was the conference?" she asked.

"The speech was the speech. At the reception afterward, I learned that Farber Nanotech is a mere ten years behind us in diagnostics, and their technology sucks. I also talked investment with a guy who may or may not have been a member of the Saudi royal family."

"So, an arms dealer?"

"Gone legit," Jon said. "Or trying to."

"A successful morning, then."

"All I could think about was getting back to you."

"Objective accomplished," Jessica said, pulling him in closer for a longer kiss. "What should we do next? There are some amazing ruins we could tour, but I've always wanted to swim in a cenote. Or we could—"

"Jessie," Jon said, sitting down on the edge of her chaise, suddenly serious. "My divorce came through."

"What?" she said, certain she'd misheard him over the surf.

"There are a lot of logistical details to be worked out, and things are definitely going to be difficult for a while, but the papers are signed."

She had been waiting for this moment for so long. Even though she'd suspected he would surprise her, she was utterly dumbfounded.

He took her hands and held them between his. "I'm officially single, and I have no intention of staying that way for long."

"Jon," she whispered, her pulse racing.

He slid off the edge of the chaise and knelt in the sand. "Let's get married."

Her heart beat so hard it almost hurt as she struggled to process what was happening. She'd abandoned her fellowship and followed Jon to frigid Chicago in the fervent hope that this moment would come—but had always assumed it lay just beyond the horizon. She'd never imagined it could happen so fast.

A shadow crossed his face. "Is it too soon?"

"Yes," she said, tears suddenly streaming down her face. "I mean no, it's not too soon. Yes! Let's get married!"

"Perfect," he said, tilting his face upward to kiss her. "They have the most stunning area for weddings, and I reserved it for us."

"Tonight?" she gasped.

"I've never felt so impulsive or vulnerable, but I can't think of a better way to officially start our life together than to exchange our vows right here, in this beautiful place."

"I . . . I just don't know what to say. I can't even find the words."

"Follow my lead: I love you. I want to marry you. Right away."

"I love you, and I want to marry you right away," she said, trying to regain her composure. "But what about my mom and my family? I feel like they should be here."

"We'll have a second ceremony or a big celebration after the dust from the divorce settles. Whatever you want. But today is about us."

"What about rings?"

"I'm having them custom made in Antwerp."

"So you've been planning this—"

"Since my lawyer emailed yesterday. It caught us both by surprise. Now that we're here, I can't pass up an opportunity like this."

"I can't believe this," Jessica said, her whole body electric.

"Believe it," Jon said.

"I need a dress! I didn't bring anything I can get married in."

"Come as you are," Jon said. "All we have to do is show up, and the El Oro wedding package will take care of the rest: flowers, music, officiant, and the most beautiful setting you can imagine."

"I love you," she told him.

"I love you, too. But if we don't stop gushing, you're going to be late." Standing up, he reached for her hand and helped her off the chaise. "You're due at the bridal salon in thirty minutes."

Jessica really did feel dizzy. "This can't be happening. I'm still asleep in the sun."

"If that's what you want to believe."

~

Jessica wasn't one of those girls who'd grown up planning a picture-perfect big day, going over all the details in her mind until all she needed was a willing groom. She had always assumed there would be a billowing white dress, a church, and a car with JUST MARRIED written on the back window in shaving cream, but she found the idea of starring in a big production much more intimidating than, say, defending a thesis. Though she'd expected a traditional wedding, she preferred the idea of an elopement.

Somehow Jon had managed to give her both.

Of course.

Her only regret was that her mom would miss it. But, really, there was no need to fret about how her thrice-married mom would handle it when she learned her daughter had gotten married in Mexico on the spur of the moment.

With that thought, Jessica relaxed into the prewedding pampering Jon had arranged and slowly accepted the reality that she was truly a bride.

Her anxiety about a dress evaporated when a van from a nearby bridal shop arrived with a rack of choices in her size, all of them perfectly suited to a beach wedding. She did feel a fleeting moment of loneliness as she tried on dresses in the hotel—the saleswoman was a warm and encouraging stranger—but that vanished, too, as soon as she came out wearing the dress that made both of them say, "Yes!" It was a Jenny Packham column dress with beaded straps bedecked in ivory embroidery and matching beadwork over a sandy-hued lining.

Fortunately, she'd brought along something old, a necklace that had once belonged to her grandmother that Jessica still wore regularly. With her stunning new dress and a blue garter belt borrowed from the bridal salon, she was ready.

At exactly sunset, a solo violinist played the first notes of the "Wedding March." Jessica emerged from her private bridal suite holding a bouquet of roses, orchids, and assorted tropical blooms. *It's odd,* she thought, *that no one will ever see me as a bride in the most beautiful dress I've ever worn.* But when she locked eyes with Jon, standing beside a robed minister beneath a white gazebo overlooking the ocean, she realized she was seen by the only one who mattered.

Orchids, roses, and assorted greenery overflowed the white pots lining the aisle as she walked toward him, their heady fragrance nearly overwhelming her senses.

"You're even more breathtaking than I imagined," Jon whispered into her ear as she reached his side.

A delicate breeze cooled the heat rising in her cheeks. "I still can't believe this is happening," she said.

"If it's a dream, do you want to wake up?" he asked.

She shook her head.

The minister, who she presumed was nondenominational from his simple attire, opened a slender book and beamed at them over its pages. Pushing his glasses up on his nose, he began to speak in lilting, lightly accented English.

"Dearly beloved, we are gathered together here to join Jessica and Jon in the union of marriage," he said. "This contract is not to be entered into lightly, but thoughtfully and seriously, and with a deep realization of its obligations and responsibilities . . ."

Jessica was more sure than ever that she was still asleep, that any second she was going to wake up on the lounge chair with only a melted margarita by her side. Yet she'd never felt so awake and alive.

"Do you take this woman, Jessica Rae Meyers, to be your lawfully wedded wife?"

"I do," Jon said.

Jessica's heart soared as the smiling officiant turned to her.

"And do you, Jessica, take this man, Jonathan Mitchell Wright III, to be your lawfully wedded husband?"

"I do."

Chapter Twenty-Seven

HOLLY

Remember that white horse? Sometimes, you're going to get saddle sore.

—"How I Lied about My Name and Discovered My Truth," a TED Talk by Jon M. Wright

Halfway through cocktail hour and Jack still hadn't shown up. The Hay Bale Ball was finally underway: the band was playing, guests were arriving, and she still hadn't gotten more than a few stray texts from her husband since the day he left for Cancún.

Who knew where he'd spent the week after his return?

Jessica had been with him on the trip—that was certain. Her car hadn't left the space behind the apartment building, and a nonsense email Holly had sent from a made-up Gmail account to jmeyers@cancura.com triggered an out-of-office reply:

> Thank you for your email. I am out of the country attending a conference with sporadic access to email and my response may be delayed.

Holly wondered whether Jack knew his girlfriend was being so sloppy. She was tempted to ask him, if and when he ever showed up tonight, but had resolved not to tell him everything she knew. To see if she could trick him into making a mistake.

"No Jack?" asked Brian, passing by with a stack of programs that had had to be reprinted due to a typo and that a volunteer would now distribute to every place setting before guests were seated for dinner.

"He wouldn't dare disappoint us," she said, wishing she felt as confident as she sounded.

Brian gave her forearm a discreet squeeze and hurried off.

Holly, standing at the top of the stairs leading into the ornate, vaulted Preston Bradley Hall, turned to greet more arriving guests, pointing them toward the coat check station and the several bars scattered throughout the room. It was snowing outside, and melted snowflakes glittered on their shoulders, sleeves, and hair.

To get through the night, she told herself, she would think of Jack as professional party help.

And then he was there, newly tan, head thrown back in laughter as he came around the corner onto the landing with . . . Theresa and Larry Yadao?

Holly was so flabbergasted she couldn't speak or move a muscle as the trio made their way toward her up the final flight of stairs. The Yadaos did not share Jack's level of hilarity but were smiling and did seem at ease.

After a fifteen-second eternity, they were in front of her.

"Theresa . . . Larry . . . what a pleasant surprise," said Holly with effort.

Jack squeezed Larry's shoulder. "I took the liberty of inviting our neighbors. In a way, I think it's our fault they haven't been fully welcomed by the Barrington Hills community. I asked if they would be willing to let us buy them dinner and drinks so they could get acquainted with some truly fine equestrians—and they bravely said yes."

"He was very persistent," said Theresa.

"Fortunately, we happened to be back in town for another event," added Larry. "We usually don't come back until March."

"Well—welcome," said Holly, recovering. "Jack certainly has a way of bringing people together. I'm so grateful we'll have this chance to get to know you better."

"We're happy to be here," said Theresa politely.

"Let's get out of these coats and into a few cocktails," said Jack, gesturing toward the coat check.

As Theresa and Larry moved on, Holly whispered, "Do you think this is really going to work?"

Jack winked. "We're halfway there."

So many thoughts were racing through her head. She was grateful she hadn't put anything about the bridle-path issue in any of their written materials, although she was going to have to amend her welcoming remarks to make *a shortsighted challenge to a beneficial community program* something like *an opportunity to bridge differing points of view.*

And she was furious with Jack. This move encapsulated everything she hated about him—keeping her in the dark, assuming he knew better, using his charm to get what he wanted, and trying to defuse justifiable anger with a grand gesture. Giving her something she actually wanted while yet again withholding the one thing he'd promised all those years ago: himself.

Drinks were drunk, food was eaten, speeches were made, funds were raised, and fun was seemingly had by all. Jack worked the room as usual, shaking hands and slapping backs, but remained attentive to the Yadaos, sitting with them during dinner, checking on their drinks, and circling back every so often to introduce them to *someone you just have*

to meet. Though they didn't strike Holly as social butterflies, they had to be enjoying the warm bath of attention and goodwill.

Brian worked just as hard but to different effect. Supervising the caterer and the volunteers, he seemed to be everywhere at once, making sure the party went off without a hitch. Holly wasn't even sure whether he managed to eat dinner—she had managed only a few bites herself. From time to time he appeared at her side to update her on something or to pause silently and follow her gaze to wherever Jack was currently schmoozing.

"A bold move, bringing the Yadaos," Brian said, catching up with her while Jack chatted up their state senator by the bar. "Did not expect that."

"Me neither," said Holly.

"My impression of Larry is that he's not a guy who measures things in warm fuzzies. Also, his guard will be up now, which may screw up the end run I was trying to make around that easement."

"Are you serious?" Holly asked, her stomach sinking.

He waved it away. "Hopefully, I'm wrong. How are you holding up?"

"I feel a little numb," she confessed.

"It doesn't show," he said softly, his eyes warm. "You look beautiful and in control."

"Thank you, Brian."

She wanted so badly to embrace him. They parted reluctantly.

Finally, the night began to wind down. Guests trickled out in twos and fours as the jazz sextet eased into some smoky, slow ballads. Through the arched windows at the end of the room, Holly could see the snow had stopped and the night was still. Alone for a moment, her throat raw from constant talking, Holly went to the nearest bar and ordered a second glass of wine.

Then, as the waiter handed her the glass, she changed her mind.

"Make it a whiskey on the rocks," she said, adding, "I'm sorry."

Chuckling, the bartender set the wine aside. "No need to apologize—I'm not paying. Bourbon or Scotch?"

"Scotch," she said, because Jack sometimes drank bourbon.

She carried her drink to a table at the edge of the room and sat down, watching as Brian and other volunteers began to gather the goods from the silent auction, which would be shipped later to spare the winners the awkwardness of carrying them home. The cater waiters were clearing coffee cups and dessert plates from tables, and only a few knots of people remained.

Jack appeared at her shoulder, nodded at the band, and asked, "May I have this dance?"

She shook her head, and after waiting a beat to confirm she meant it, he pulled out the chair next to hers and set his napkin-wrapped beer on the table.

"Whiskey's new," he said.

"Maybe it's time to try new things," she told him. "Are the Yadaos still here?"

"I tried to bring them over to say goodbye, but they were worried about missing their Uber."

"How did it go?"

"Very well. I managed to introduce them to several people who would most likely be galloping past their house, and I could feel the goodwill in the room. I didn't put the hard sell on them, of course, but I feel confident they're going to withdraw their objection to the bridle path."

"I guess we'll see," she said.

Holly sipped her whiskey. It was so strong it almost burned her mouth. But she wanted something that burned right now. She took a bigger drink and closed her eyes, concentrating on the taste.

When she opened them, Jack was looking at her intently. "I thought you'd be happier to hear this."

"You're having a relationship with Jessica Meyers," Holly said flatly.

"Whoa, hold on—"

"You're sharing an apartment in the city, and you went away together to Cancún," she continued. "You brought your mistress to Chicago to work for you."

"Holly, have you been drinking like this all night?" he asked, with a meaningful look at her glass.

"I'm sober. Don't try to deflect."

Jack shook his head. Then he took a deep breath, as if he were summoning some deep, inner reserve of strength and patience. "Yes, Holly, I brought Jessica to Chicago to work with me. Yes, I found her an apartment because Olivia had severe morning sickness and someone needed to do it. And yes, Jessica came to Cancún for the conference, but it's all professional. It's all for work."

It amazed her that his first instinct was not to ask where she'd gotten her information. "You stopped going to Phoenix after she moved here."

"Which is why I go to California now. The Phoenix partnerships are self-sustaining, and it was time to look for new opportunities for Cancura."

"After you left me alone on New Year's Eve, you went to see her."

She was bluffing and had no proof but stated it with a certainty that clearly had him wondering how she knew.

Jack broke off eye contact and took a drink of beer. The bandleader announced that the next song would be the last of the night.

"I can see why you'd think these things," he said, sighing heavily. "And it's at least partly my fault. When I was recruiting her for Cancura, I guess she got the wrong idea. You know me, I try to be personable. She thought relocating to Chicago meant . . . something else. She's obsessed with me, and I need to shut it down, but it's hard because she's brilliant and absolutely essential to Cancura. I guess I thought she'd move on. There's not exactly a shortage of handsome and talented young guys in Chicago."

"Have you been having sex with her?"

"What? No! We've—I mean, she tried to kiss me, after a work thing where people were drinking a little too much. I regret that I didn't pull away a bit faster, but that's all that happened."

It was almost identical to the way he'd explained away Kim, all those years ago. Either he didn't remember, or he didn't care enough to invent a new scenario.

"You're sure that's all it is?" she asked.

He nodded a little too vigorously.

"You need to deal with this now, and you need to start by staying away from her so people don't get the wrong idea. I'd hate to have to see you take out a restraining order against a valued employee."

If he heard the sarcasm in her voice, he didn't acknowledge it. He reached out and gripped her closest hand in both of his.

"Holly, I'm so sorry I haven't handled this better," he said, choking up. "Things are so crazy in both our lives right now, but you're my touchstone, and I'm afraid I've been taking you for granted. Can you forgive me?"

Not this time, she thought, so revolted by his touch she almost yanked her hands away. But until she figured out how to provide security for Ava, Paige, and Logan—and to make sure her parents' finances were safe—she would refrain from telling Jack.

Closing her eyes to make it easier, she leaned forward and gave him a dry peck on the cheek.

His relieved expression told her it was enough.

Chapter Twenty-Eight

JESSICA AND HOLLY

Events will not always be under your control.

—"How I Lied about My Name and Discovered My Truth,"
a TED Talk by Jon M. Wright

Jessica had now been secretly married for exactly thirteen days, one hour, and twenty-six minutes. In that time, she'd been a blushing (and tan) bride in Cancún and enjoyed a week's worth of married bliss. She'd been delighted when Jon sent Marco back to Omaha in her place so they could spend their second week of married life together at home, but that plan was scuttled when Ellen McBride, the head of marketing, came down with walking pneumonia and Jon told Jessica to fill in for her at a medical innovations symposium in Germany.

"Send someone else," Jessica had said. "Anyone from marketing can give the Cancura spiel as well as I can."

"If that were all that's required, you know I would," Jon had told her. "Jessie, you're in the inner sanctum now. You need to expect to be called on at a moment's notice. But more than that, you're one of our rising stars. The visibility is crucial for you."

"I'm sorry," she said, torn between his praise and her frustration at being separated so soon.

"But we wouldn't be together all week anyway. I just found out I have to go to Japan to discuss an IP swap with the head of Tangyo Bio-Innovations."

Her sigh had been heartfelt. "We should be on our honeymoon, not headed to opposite sides of the globe."

"We will have a honeymoon, and we'll go around the world if you want," he'd said, touching her cheek tenderly, even though Olivia was just outside the glass wall and definitely would have noted it if she'd been looking up. "I promise."

Now that she was back in her own time zone, and despite missing a week of what would surely have been newlywed bliss, she had to admit that Jon was right. She'd spent the entire week building relationships with company heads who were full of enthusiastic questions about the Revelate's seemingly endless potential. Not to mention that Gunnar Andersson from Genovis and Hans Möller from Siemens Healthineers were politely competing for the chance to wine and dine her.

She glanced at her ring finger. Ironically, she'd flown home over Antwerp, where her absent ring was currently being crafted.

She'd landed only a couple of hours from bedtime but felt jittery, wide awake, and compelled to go grocery shopping so once she finally did crash, she'd wake up to fresh coffee, milk, bread, and fruit.

As she parked at the Whole Foods on Ashland and headed into the store, however, the overly alert sensation gave way to a foggy, slow-motion feeling. And maybe it was the lighting, the comforting din of a familiar language, and the uniquely American colorfully packaged abundance, but she kept thinking she spotted familiar faces among the other customers.

She felt accompanied, likely by her own shadow, as she made her way through the produce section toward Pink Lady apples that, although organic, somehow looked larger, more colorful, and obscenely healthier than their mildly bruised European counterparts. Batting away a brain-dead thought about the underbelly of Big Agriculture, she collected four apples in a compostable bag and a bunch of bananas, grapes, and salad fixings.

As she made her way to the seafood counter to pick out a piece of salmon for tomorrow night's dinner, when Jon returned from Japan, and then went up and down the aisles to collect a pound of coffee, the cardboard-tasting granola Jon loved, and a few other odds and ends absent from their pantry, the jet lag really started to get to her. She spotted Yulia's wild red hair—but it wasn't her, unless she'd gained sixty pounds in the past two weeks. She veered around Marco's partner—if he happened to be taller and Asian. Not only did her limbs feel heavy and the floor seem like it wasn't flat, but the uneasy sensation of shopping with her shadow gave way to a feeling she was being watched.

Clearly, it was time to go home and climb into bed, but the aromas of wood-fired pizza, barbecued meat, and savory soup made her stomach growl. Before she headed to the register, Jessica made her way into the labyrinth of prepared foods. While she usually went straight for the salad bar or perhaps to the ready-made sushi, her unwanted friend jet lag insisted on comfort food: mashed sweet potatoes, seasoned roasted corn, and, oddly, saag paneer.

All her exhaustion-inspired culinary potpourri required now was dessert. She was reaching for a cup containing layers of whipped cream and chocolate pudding—something she'd never even look at, under normal circumstances—when she spotted yet another familiar shopper. The tall, slim, fortyish blonde wore black pants, stylish flats, and a cashmere sweater.

Jessica dropped the pudding cup as Holly Wright stepped toward her.

~

Holly had decided she needed to talk to Jessica herself if she was going to get to the truth. Whether Jessica Meyers was indeed pursuing Jack or it was the other way around, she didn't trust Jack to let Jessica know he was no longer available. That he had an ironclad responsibility to his wife and three children. Holly was finally allowing herself to think the word *divorce*—but she had to make sure it was on her terms, not Jack's. She had no intention of allowing Jessica or anyone else to be the recipient of Jack's attentions and gifts, or the family's money.

But how and where to confront Jessica? Not at Cancura, for obvious reasons. Reluctantly, she had decided on the *love nest*, because she simply didn't know where else to find her.

The day after Jack's admission at the Hay Bale Ball, Holly had asked what he intended to do about Jessica and learned she'd been exiled to Munich while he "thought about how to handle things best for Cancura." Next, she visited the office to bring him a surprise lunch— something she knew would aggravate him—where she casually queried Olivia about "our wonderful director of medical monitoring" and learned the date and general time of Jessica's return.

Holly was waiting in an empty space behind the building with her engine running, thinking how little time it had taken for her to adapt to this new routine of surveillance and pursuit—even wondering wryly whether she should have been a private detective instead of a pediatrician—when Jessica's sedan came down the alleyway, slowed, and then continued past without turning in.

Puzzled, Holly had followed her to a nearby Whole Foods before realizing that confronting Jessica in a grocery store was even better than at her building. There would be witnesses in case Jessica's obsession with Jack was actually something dangerous. And the shock factor would be useful, too. Caught completely off guard, who knew what Jessica would confess?

But it was more crowded inside than Holly had expected, even on a weekend evening. As she prowled from aisle to aisle without catching sight of the attractive young woman with chestnut hair, she began to fear Jessica had already slipped out.

Her calm evaporated as she walked faster and faster. If Jessica left and made it back to her building, Holly would lose control over the situation. She pictured herself standing in the lobby, buzzing the intercom again and again while Jessica simply watched her on the camera over the door.

She was almost running by the time she reached the prepared-foods section. There, just across from the hot bar, reaching for something in a nearby cooler: Jessica.

Holly stopped suddenly, drawing the attention of Jessica, who dropped a dessert cup and yanked her hand back as if she'd been stung. Unlike their previous encounter in the bathroom, when Holly was calm, almost detached, she now felt like her nerves were sparking and smoking live wires.

"You've been having an affair with Jack," she said, not at all the words she'd rehearsed. *I think we have something we need to discuss.*

Jessica straightened, smoothed her hair, and took a deep breath. She looked left and right as if searching for an escape route, putting one hand on her little grocery cart before letting it fall.

"Mrs.—Holly," she said, "I don't think this is the time or place for us to talk."

"You don't get to decide that. I do," said Holly, taking a step closer.

Jessica shrank back. Holly had a fleeting sensation of the power she'd tasted the morning she asked Jack about Jessica. Then she saw a box of Jack's favorite cereal in the cart and deflated again.

"I don't know what you think is—"

"I just told you what I think, Jessica."

"I know you've been under a lot of strain."

That one set Holly back. She stopped, tried to laugh, and heard herself make a strange sound. *Strain?*

"What do you know about my *strain?*" she croaked.

"I know things have been difficult for a long time between you and Jack," continued Jessica, eyeing her cart and seemingly deciding to abandon it as she took yet another step backward. "I know you care a lot about Ava, Paige, and Logan."

Her children's names came out of the woman's mouth and struck her like blows, staggering her. Holly found it suddenly hard to breathe. Jack and Jessica's pillow talk. About her?

"And you know this . . . how? Because Jack told you?"

"Jack . . . Jon . . . I know he loves all of you so much."

And now Jessica was treating her as though she were a fragile child the truth would shatter.

"Because he *tells* you?" Holly demanded, her voice suddenly a screech that caused shoppers to turn their heads. People were watching. A man raising his phone—was he FaceTiming a friend or getting her on video? The grocery store had not been a good idea after all.

At least Jessica was trembling. At least she seemed afraid.

"Divorce is awful, even under the best circumstances," she said haltingly.

Holly felt a sudden chill. "Why would you say that?"

"Because my parents. When I was still in grade school, they—"

"They split up and hurt you? If that's the case, I have to wonder how you justify getting involved with a married man—a family man."

"I would never do that," Jessica protested. "Separated isn't married."

Holly's head whirled with rage and bafflement. Jessica's conviction seemed genuine. "He told you we were *separated?*"

Jessica glanced fearfully over her shoulder before nodding. "He told me it's been hard for you to accept the way things are now."

Holly, unsteady on her feet, had the sense a stout, frowning woman nearby was on the verge of intervening. She wanted to leave. She wanted the truth.

"And how, exactly, are things now?"

"We're together," Jessica whispered. "Jon and I are together."

Holly imagined throwing herself at Jessica, raking her fingers down those youthful cheeks, slapping that pretty face until her palms burned.

Instead she gathered herself, taking a step back and standing up straight. She waited a long moment until she had command of her voice. "You should be ashamed of yourself for what you've done to our family."

"I told you. We didn't get together until after he left you."

The whole point had been to remind Jessica her lover was still married. But Jack had, astonishingly, told her he and Holly were separated. Disowned her. In that moment, Holly no longer wanted to claim him, either.

Her chest ached. "Jack has been lying to me for years. What makes you think he's not lying to you?"

Chapter Twenty-Nine

JESSICA

The three Rs: roll with it, reassess, and recover.

—"How I Lied about My Name and Discovered My Truth,"
a TED Talk by Jon M. Wright

"Your ex accosted me at Whole Foods last night," Jessica said as Jon came into the apartment the next morning, not even waiting for the door to close behind him.

"Shit!" Jon let go of his suitcase, and the plastic clatter of its wheels echoed through the apartment. "What happened?"

"I was headed home from the airport but decided to stop for some groceries. She must have been stalking me, because she suddenly appeared and made a scene in the middle of the prepared-food section."

"Jesus," Jon said as he stepped toward her and wrapped her in his arms. He looked worn out from his trip.

Despite her own bone-deep exhaustion, Jessica had spent the night tossing and turning with fragments of the crazy conversation repeating on an infinite loop.

You've been having an affair with Jack . . . Separated isn't married . . . What makes you think he's not lying to you?

As he held her tightly, the tears finally began to flow.

"I tried to stay calm and defuse the situation while she caused a huge scene," she choked out. "I really did."

"It's okay," he said.

"She basically accused me of wrecking your family. Everybody was watching."

"You didn't tell her we were married, did you?" he asked, releasing her from his embrace and looking at her intently.

"You told me not to tell anyone. Of all people, why would I start with her?"

"What did you say then?" Jon pressed. "Tell me everything both of you said."

Jessica wiped her eyes. "What scared me most was her anger. She was literally shaking with rage."

"That's how she manipulates people," he said. "But what words did she use?"

"I . . . I'm not sure I can remember word for word."

"Try." Jon's voice had an unexpected but somehow familiar edge.

As Jessica recounted the exchange, starting with her feeling of being followed, Jon began to pace back and forth from the entryway to the living room. His phone chimed, and he glared at the lock screen before silencing it and shoving it back in his pocket so hard she thought it would rip out of his coat. His expression grew darker and more intense as she added every detail she could remember, reiterating that she'd told Holly, "We—you and I—didn't get together until after the two of you separated."

Jon put his head in his hands. "Oh god."

"Should I not have said that?"

"She shouldn't have chased you down," he said, not entirely answering her question and sounding even angrier than before. "This is a fucking nightmare."

"Jon, she really seems to believe you two are still together."

"Because she's a lunatic."

"What do we do?"

"*You* do nothing," he said pointedly. "You've had your last-ever conversation with Holly. If she comes near you again, we're getting a restraining order."

"Do you think it's going to come to that?" Jessica asked, dreading another encounter with his deranged ex-wife.

"I won't let it," Jon said. "Besides, if I know Holly, she's done with you for a while. I'm the one who's on her hit list."

"Could she be dangerous?"

"You never know," he said. "I have to go deal with this."

"You're leaving? Right now?"

"Don't worry, I'll get this all under control."

"But when will you be back?"

He kissed her on the forehead. "As soon as it's safe."

Chapter Thirty

HOLLY

I'm going to let you in on a little secret: no is a transitive word.

—"How I Lied about My Name and Discovered My Truth," a TED Talk by Jon M. Wright

Long before dawn, Holly dragged herself out of bed, her head cloudy from a third glass of wine, and dressed in barn clothes using arms that didn't seem to work quite right. She fed Mini-Me first, then tramped through the yard and across the dirty snow to the barn, where she fed the horses and, one by one, turned them out to the pasture. They didn't like the chilly gray morning any more than she did; Alderman, who had finally shed a few pounds, stood morosely in the barn door before reluctantly following the rest.

She saved Wags for last. Ever since he'd kicked her, Holly had been more determined than ever to help him rediscover his gentle inner nature. And though her head still sometimes throbbed involuntarily when she entered his stall, she never flinched, showing him only love and affection. In a strange way he was becoming her favorite.

Now she cooed to him as she stroked his flanks, resting her cheek against his muscular neck and feeling his strength and warmth as he playfully tossed his head.

"Go on, get," she said fondly, urging him outside.

Who knew? Maybe she'd keep him after all.

She tackled the rest of her chores as if in penance before going in to find Paige, her early riser, at the breakfast bar with a cup of the extremely sweet and creamy coffee she was experimenting with, and Galenia already packing lunches.

Glancing at her phone, Holly saw a new text from Brian, adding to the two unanswered ones from last night. Barely ten hours since she'd made a fool of herself in a grocery store and she'd spent the night wallowing in self-reproach and self-pity. Self-reproach for her loss of control. Self-pity for the loss of her marriage.

Today she planned to cancel everything. To throw herself into being present for the kids she'd been neglecting while chasing Jessica Meyers. To stop anesthetizing herself with second and third glasses of wine.

Today was the day she took back control.

Pouring herself a cup of black coffee, she sat down next to Paige and gazed lovingly until her beautiful daughter dramatically turned, rolled her eyes, and said, "Mom, *what?*"

"I just love you, that's all," said Holly, tucking an unruly strand of hair behind Paige's ear.

"Is everything okay? You and Dad seem . . . I don't know."

"It's nothing for you to worry about. Everything will get worked out."

"It's because he travels so much, right?" Paige said, pleased with her own maturity and knowledge.

Holly forced a smile. "He travels far too much."

After giving Paige a grudgingly accepted kiss, Holly went up to her room to shower and dress for the day. She slipped off the stiff

Carhartt overalls she wore for morning chores, began to unbutton her wool Pendleton shirt, and stopped. Picked up her phone.

She texted Brian first.

Sorry I've been out of touch. Having a rough time. But your messages made me feel better. Talk soon.

Then she called Jack, who would have gotten back from his trip to Japan. It rang twice and went to voice mail.

She left a message: "Don't bother coming home."

And pondered the timing of the email she would send to Jessica.

Chapter Thirty-One

LARK

Your assets can never be too diversified.

—"How I Lied about My Name and Discovered My Truth,"
a TED Talk by Jon M. Wright

Trip looked like he was running on fumes. He had always seemed like the Energizer Bunny, ready to go go go, but when he'd shown up unannounced at her apartment this evening, the faint smile lines at the corners of his eyes seemed more deeply etched, and there was a slight puffiness under his eyes that wasn't quite hidden by his winter tan.

She liked it. It made her feel like, for once, she could take care of him. She was glad he had a surprise weekend getaway planned. He needed it. They both did.

"What idiot decreed that golf was the game of business?" he groaned as she kneaded his shoulders. "In fact, I'm not so sure I wasn't invited there to fill out a foursome, because seventy-two holes later, I still don't know if there's an opportunity for me."

"Where were you?" she asked, working on his spine with her thumbs. She had taken a massage class and still knew a move or two.

"God, that's great, please don't stop," he said, his head drooping as he ignored the TV across the room. He was seated on the floor between Lark's legs while she sat over him on the couch. "Miami."

"What's it like there?"

"The golfing is excellent, if you like that kind of thing."

"I don't, but I'll bet you're good at it."

"I'm smart enough to feign enthusiasm and good enough to let the other guy win."

Lark stopped for a moment. "Really? I can't imagine you letting anyone else win."

"Well, it depends on the situation."

The door opened and Callie came in. She still worked some evenings at her old job, and while she told Lark she was just helping out, Lark couldn't help but wonder if she was keeping one hand on an escape hatch. Callie had refused to discuss a future at Larkspur Games beyond her initial six-month commitment.

"Oh," she said, seeing Trip. "It's been a while."

"Too long. It's nice to see you," he said gamely.

Lark appreciated how hard he worked to be nice to Callie, even when Callie was in a mood.

"Are you staying for long?"

"I came for my follow-up interview," he said.

"That position's been filled," Callie said with a fake smile before going into her bedroom and closing the door.

"Really?" asked Trip.

"The candidate finally accepted this morning," explained Lark. "We're small time for her, but she loves the game and sees a real opportunity to position Larkspur as 'Smart Games for Strong Girls.'"

"That's great," said Trip, wiggling his shoulders until she started rubbing again. "Sometimes all it takes is finding someone who's passionate about what you have to offer."

Lark worked his neck with her fingertips for a minute, then said, "I'm sorry about Callie. She's been moody lately."

"I hope she hasn't changed her mind about me. I thought we got along really well."

"It's . . ." Lark sighed, unable to continue. Unwilling to tell Trip that Dylan had played even the slightest role by stoking Callie's suspicions. Or that those doubts had taken on a life of their own.

"She's probably still protective and afraid she's losing a friend," said Trip. "It's normal."

Lark leaned forward and kissed the top of his head. "Thank you for being so understanding and patient."

"She's important to you, so she's important to me, too." Trip reached back and grabbed her hands, held them tightly on his shoulders. "How quickly can you get your bag packed?"

Twenty minutes later they were headed east on Interstate 10, with Lark's overnight bag next to Trip's still-packed bag in the trunk of his rental Jaguar. It never ceased to amaze Lark how many different models were available, and Trip rarely seemed to repeat his choice of transportation. When she'd quizzed him about it early on, he'd said, "It's always been my lifelong compulsion to try all the flavors."

"Where are we going?" she asked now.

"Palm Springs okay?" he asked in return.

"More than."

He seemed fidgety and distracted, checking his mirror and changing lanes more often than necessary, which she thought was probably a sign of his fatigue. Wanting to help him relax, Lark synced her phone to the car and queued up a series of beautifully moody songs, which soon had the desired effect. They were comfortably quiet as the car rolled through the heart of LA in stop-and-start traffic, then finally began to pick up speed as they passed Pomona and Ontario. After Redlands, Trip put the pedal down, and they began flying.

The sudden departure, the cool winter night, and the peaceful easiness between them . . . *The only bad thing about my relationship with Trip,* Lark thought, *is that he isn't around more often.* And yet maybe that was part of the magic, too. Maybe spontaneity and separation were the very ingredients necessary to keep a relationship healthy and vibrant long term. She had seen Dylan every single day until she couldn't stand the sight of him. So.

She thought about saying something to Trip, but the silence was too sweet to break. There would be plenty of time once they'd arrived.

Lark had been wondering what kind of glamorous, high-end resort Trip had reserved for them—he'd stepped outside with his phone while she was getting her things together—so she was surprised when they turned off East Palm Canyon Drive into a small, nondescript parking lot in front of a low building. The sign on the front had no name, only an image of two birds.

The lobby was fun and funky, the pool was small, and their secluded cabin at the back of the property was somehow cozy and airy all at once, a gorgeous blend of red-stained wood and stone walls. The similarly decorated bar was about to close, so Trip ordered a bottle of champagne and a plate of cheese and crackers, and they pulled on their jackets and headed outside to the flickering firepit, where they were the only guests. Pulling two Adirondack chairs as close together as possible, Trip plunked the champagne bucket down on the ground between them, and they settled back with their feet near the fire. The darkness erased all traces of his weariness.

Lark was amazed at how many more stars were visible only two hours away from the city.

"Your timing is perfect," she told Trip. "Everything is going great, but I'm definitely starting to feel some stress about work. And, of course, we're overdue for some time together."

He squeezed her hand. "More than overdue."

"Do you ever think about what's next for us?"

"All the time."

"And?"

Trip swallowed champagne and nervously tapped a fingernail on his glass. "I've done my best to let you drive things, but it's hard."

"I appreciate that, but it can't be all about me—that's a little old-fashioned, Trip."

He winced. "Ouch. Well, what do you want?"

"I want you to tell me what you want. To let me know how you want to be in my life."

Trip turned his body so he could look directly at her. "I don't want to scare you."

Lark felt a shiver of anticipation, wanting him to say something big. Wanting him to commit to more than wonderfully dramatic appearances in her life.

"You can't scare me."

"Well, in that case . . ."

Setting his glass on the stone rim of the firepit, still holding her hand, Trip slid out of his chair and knelt in front of her. His eyes were black gemstones in the flickering firelight.

A thousand butterflies beat their wings furiously. She felt dizzy as she suddenly understood why he'd been acting differently.

"Lark Robinson, will you marry me?"

Chapter Thirty-Two

JESSICA

*I don't claim to have the best ideas, just the ability to
spin gold from straw.*

—"How I Lied about My Name and Discovered My Truth,"
a TED Talk by Jon M. Wright

"I left Chicago last night," Jon said when he finally called her at work
on Monday morning. "Things didn't go well with Holly, and I just need
to clear my head."

"Where are you?" Jessica asked.

"The desert."

"Sedona?" Jessica asked, thinking it was code for their charming
getaway spot when she'd lived in Arizona. "Should I meet you there?"

"You need to go to Omaha. Tonight. If the ticket price is ridiculous,
have Olivia authorize it with accounting."

Jessica's pulse quickened. "Why? What's wrong?"

"Randy Warner is apparently in Bill Nelson's ear again. Somebody
spotted Randy, Bill, and Sharon Montgomery coming out of a huddle
looking unhappy."

"Can't I at least wait until I hear what's going on from them? Marco is there."

"Marco's just a salesman. He needs backup."

If she weren't married to the boss, she'd be flattered to be sent off to save the day for Cancura. Instead, she wondered why Jon hadn't thought to take her with him to the desert in the first place. Why did he get to clear his head while she kept her nose to the grindstone?

She was still sitting at her desk, ready to call him back and ask him, when an email popped up in her in-box.

From Holly Wright.

> You need to know that Jack and I are still married.
> We never separated.

Jessica's irritation was swept aside by a torrent of sudden fear. She needed to get the fuck out of town and put as much distance as possible between her and Jon's batshit-crazy ex-wife.

She dialed Jon, now to tell him about the email and let him know she was going to have to take out a restraining order against Holly.

He didn't answer.

Instead of leaving a message that would only leave him feeling as stressed out as she did, she decided to book her ticket first and call him again when she was safely on her way to Omaha. As she logged in to Cancura's travel booking site to search for flights, her fingers froze on the keyboard.

Holly and *Jack*, as she called him, couldn't still be married, because he'd already gotten remarried. To Jessica.

He'd been living with Jessica for months.

It was Holly's words from the grocery store that cut like glass.

What makes you think he's not lying to you?

She knew Jon lied when it benefited Cancura. And himself?

Jessica rubbed her throbbing temples. Jon had said over and over that Holly was a master manipulator, and this was only her latest mind game. Jessica couldn't let herself get drawn in. The way to win was to refuse to play.

After a brief glance at the ticket prices, she got up and walked down the hall to talk with Olivia, the one person who could authorize her flight and confirm how disturbed Holly Wright truly was.

∾

"Completely off the subject," Jessica said as Olivia authorized the override for the accounting department. "*And* off the record . . ."

Olivia looked up from her screen, rested her hand on her basketball-round belly, and sipped from an insulated cup that probably contained a "natural suicide," her nausea-abating soda mixture. "The way you came down the hall, I wondered if something was on your mind."

"This is a little awkward," Jessica said. "And please don't tell Jon that I asked you."

"Promise," Olivia said.

"What do you think about Holly Wright?"

Olivia pointed to a crystal paperweight with distinctive purple flower petals suspended within. "Love her. She knows I like hydrangeas, and when she spotted this incredibly rare variation on a trip to Asia, she had this made for me."

"That is very thoughtful," Jessica acknowledged. "But is she also . . . I don't know . . . a little wacky?"

Olivia looked incredulous. "Wacky? Holly Wright?"

Feeling like she owed Olivia an explanation for her suspicion, Jessica scrambled for a believable story.

"We met briefly in the ladies' room on New Year's Eve, and she seemed amazing," Jessica stammered. "But then this morning, out of the blue, she emailed me to welcome me to the company like we'd never even met. I've been at Cancura for over six months now."

"She's usually more on top of things, but it sounds like she didn't really know who you were or how important you are around here until recently," Olivia said. "She did mention you the other day when she stopped by with Jon's lunch."

Jessica bit her lip so she wouldn't blurt, *She did* what? Then, attempting a nonchalant smile and a breezy tone, she asked, "What did she say?"

"I think she referred to you as our *wonderful new director of medical monitoring*, so Jon must have been talking you up. She wanted to know if you were around, but I told her you were in Germany until Saturday."

Which explained how Holly had known her schedule.

"It would definitely be worth your time to get to know her, because she's brilliant."

"Brilliant how?"

"Total superwoman," Olivia said, handing her a flight schedule and carefully standing to stretch, mindful of her stomach. "She hasn't been around as much the past few years, but when Jon was getting started, she was a mom with three little kids who maintained her medical practice and was basically the de facto VP of Cancura. I mean, she came up with the idea for the Revelate in the first place."

Jessica put both hands on Olivia's desk for balance.

She heard Jon's voice. Saw him speaking on the stage in Phoenix. Remembered the way he seemed to be looking at her as he said it.

Years ago, I had a simple idea.

"Are you okay?" asked Olivia.

"I'm fine. It wasn't Jon's idea?"

Olivia chuckled. "Oh, you mean, 'Years ago, I had a simple idea: What if detecting childhood cancer was as easy as getting kids to take chewable vitamins?'"

Her imitation was dead-on, right down to Jon's humble–not humble smile when captivating a room.

"Jon may have run with it, but it was definitely Holly's idea. Not that she's the kind of person who needs credit."

"You're absolutely sure?"

"My first job was as a receptionist at Holly's pediatric office. That's how I eventually got this job. I was there when she said it the first time, before she ever said it in front of Jon. Are you sure you're okay? You look like you don't feel good, and I should know."

Jessica was light headed and dizzy and wanted to throw up.

"This is total gossip," Jessica said dully. "But someone told me Jon and Holly were recently separated, maybe even getting a divorce."

Now it was Olivia's turn to look shocked. "That would be news to me. I'm guessing it would be news to them, too."

~

When Jessica got back to her office, there was a text message from Jon.

You called but didn't leave a message. Everything OK?

Not knowing what else to do, she wrote: *Hey—you never mentioned that Holly brought you lunch while I was in Germany.*

I don't think the food was poisonous, but she was up to something, he wrote back immediately. *Needless to say, I didn't eat it.*

Gotcha. Just letting you know I'm leaving for the airport.

Call me when you get there.

Will do.

Jessica spent the whole flight processing everything she'd heard from Olivia. Should she let Jon know about Holly's latest email? Demand his explanation for everything she'd just learned? Her whole body felt leaden with dread as the Uber rolled toward the corporate apartment. When she got out of the car, she still didn't know what to do. She probably would have forced herself to call Jon and at least let him know she'd arrived if Marco hadn't been kicking back in the living room with a glass of wine.

"Here I am, to save the day," she said, putting her bag down with a weary sigh.

Marco got up to grab another wineglass from the kitchen. "If you say so. But let the record show, I told Jon I had things completely under control."

At that moment, Jessica decided not to call Jon at all.

Chapter Thirty-Three

HOLLY

Always be true to yourself.

—"How I Lied about My Name and Discovered My Truth,"
a TED Talk by Jon M. Wright

Somehow, Jack had become even more of a presence since she'd told him not to come home. For starters, the kids—who were so used to his absences they barely batted an eye at a two-week trip—were suddenly keenly interested in what was happening. Judgmental Ava was furious with both her parents but seemed to be reserving the silent treatment for Holly while maintaining an open line of communication with Jack via text. Paige continued to attempt heart-to-hearts, her wise and knowing looks sometimes making it hard for Holly to keep a straight face. And even the usually oblivious Logan had been asking whom he'd live with if there was a divorce.

"You will always be welcome with both of us, and neither of us is going away," she'd told him, privately certain Jack would love nothing better than to have them one weekend a month so he could fully capitalize on being the *fun* parent.

And while Jack had respected the physical boundary she'd set, his calls and texts were so frequent she'd more than once considered blocking him. Even though she wasn't picking up, the notifications alone were a constant distraction.

Especially now, as she drove to lunch with Brian, where her plan was to update him on the latest developments without crying or falling into his arms.

Just in case, she'd suggested Bob Chinn's Crab House in Wheeling. It was fifteen miles away, it was dark inside, and nobody they knew would go there for lunch. Brian had accepted the location without comment, just one of the many things she appreciated about him.

As she rolled up to a stop sign at a deserted intersection, her phone buzzed four times in a row, and the lock screen filled up with messages from Jack. It sounded like a wasp. She hesitated before she picked it up, dreading a sting.

Call me, please, Holly, he had written. *I want to do better. I want to BE better.*

She turned left onto Otis Road, leafy in summer but now a tunnel of stick-fingered trees with skirts of dirty snow. The asphalt was clear, and with a careful check of her mirrors, she unlocked the phone and texted back, keeping her speed right at the limit.

Where are you? she wrote. *With her?*

NO. I'm alone.

Where?

I'm in an intensive therapy program.

What kind of therapy? she asked, thinking Jack's definition of *alone* didn't match anyone else's.

She dropped the phone and put both hands on the wheel as one car came toward her, then another, while her phone buzzed with his answer. Then there was a car behind her, and she couldn't look until it turned off at Hawley Woods. Texting and driving was just as stupid as giving more attention to Jack. But therapy? That was new. It was almost as if he'd finally realized mere apologies were not enough.

Almost.

She turned right on Hawthorne Lane and picked up the phone again.

It's a residential program, he'd written. *Only wish I had done this years ago. Without you and the kids I'm nothing.*

There it was. Unmoved, she wrote back, *Therapy for what?*

Then traffic got just heavy enough to make her worry whether texting and driving would leave her children motherless as well as, for all practical purposes, fatherless. While Jack thought about what to write next, she synced her Bluetooth so notifications would come up on the dashboard screen. She could use voice recognition to reply. A call would have been easier, but she didn't want to hear his voice. Especially after his next message.

It's to address the problem of my unfaithfulness, the root cause of which is typically low self-esteem.

That made her laugh out loud, which made her swerve, prompting a panicked honk from an oncoming driver.

If Jack has low self-esteem, she thought, *what hope is there for any of us?*

Funny, I never thought of you as insecure, she replied.

It's different from that. I think I've never felt worthy of you, of your family.

Don't put this on me, she warned.

It's all on me. I have a problem and I want to get better. I want things to be like they used to be. I understand and accept that you're angry. Just PLEASE don't write me off. Our kids still need us.

Their kids were exactly why Holly hadn't done anything about this sooner. They needed to be provided for now and in the future. And she did, too. After all she'd given up for him—all she'd given him—it was only fair. And until she had that sorted out, there was no need to give him a definitive answer on anything.

"I'm not writing you off," she said out loud, watching the words form on her dashboard screen. "But right now, I'm having a hard time thinking of our marriage as anything more than a business relationship."

She would maintain just enough communication to keep their affairs in order and to coparent the kids as much as he was inclined to do. And this afternoon she would call the highest-priced divorce lawyer in Chicago to begin discussing her options.

It is so much more than that to me, but I know I need to prove it, he wrote contritely.

As she drove on autopilot along Dundee Road toward Wheeling, Holly tapped satellite radio, which immediately began playing her favored nineties stream. But those songs were songs from the era when she and Jack had begun dating. She changed it to Today's Pop Hits, the station Ava and Paige preferred. The music wasn't to her taste, but at least it was new.

~

Brian's Volvo was already in the lot. Inside, the restaurant was practically empty. He stood up from his corner table and gave her a hug she gratefully accepted.

"I'm sorry, I don't know why I picked this place," she said. "I haven't been here since my dad's birthday years ago."

Brian raised his eyebrows. "What's wrong with it?"

It took Holly a moment to put her finger on the problem. "It's the kind of place you go on a special occasion."

"Time with you—I'd say that qualifies," he said with a wink.

She smiled as the waiter came and took their drink orders. Holly wasn't hungry but imagined she could manage some soup and salad.

"Jack's attempt to woo the Yadaos seems to have fallen flat," Brian said.

"I guess you called it. Did he make things worse for us?"

The word *us* hung in the air between them.

"I don't think he did too much damage. A developer friend of mine told me about something Larry needs, so we might have some leverage. But we can talk about that later. I've missed you. How are you doing?"

She was summoning the energy to tell him the latest developments when her phone vibrated. She glanced at it irritatedly, assuming Jack had yet more to say, then realized it wasn't a text but a call from a number she'd recently found on the Cancura directory and entered into her phone.

Jessica Meyers.

"I'm so sorry, Brian, but I have to take this," she said, standing up so quickly she bumped the table and spilled some water. "Just give me one minute."

She hustled out of the dining room to the dim, overdecorated entryway, where rope lines awaited the dinner rush, and answered the call just before it went to voice mail.

"Hello," she said, trying to quiet her breathing.

"This is Jessica Meyers," said the familiar voice on the other end. "I got your message."

"Obviously."

"I have a question for you: Whose idea was the Revelate?"

The question was so startling and unexpected that Holly momentarily lost track of her surroundings. Jessica was not pleading her case or staking a claim to Jack. Instead, she was asking about something that went back a decade and had implications far beyond the marriage of Jack and Holly Wright.

"Why are you asking me this?" Holly finally asked.

"Because I need to know what's true," Jessica said. "And what isn't."

Also completely unexpected. She still didn't want to answer, because the woman had already taken too much from her and knew too much about her. Had made her—Jack's wife!—into the other woman.

Then again, it sounded like Jessica was waking up. And if so, who was Holly to withhold the truth?

"I had a patient, an eight-year-old boy whose leukemia wasn't detected until it was too late," Holly said, remembering Preston Gaertner's freckled face and wide blue eyes. "It was a hard day. I was talking to Jack that night, and I said I wished I had a diagnostic tool that could catch cancer before my patients even knew it could hurt them. Something as simple as a chewable vitamin, so everyone would use it."

"Then why does Jon—?"

"If you want to know more, you'll need to hear it in person."

Chapter Thirty-Four

LARK

When you're happy, they're happy.

—"How I Lied about My Name and Discovered My Truth,"
a TED Talk by Jon M. Wright

The first day they'd spent in bed, making love, dozing, ordering room service, and listening to music while she tried to get her head around the fact that she was *engaged*. None of her close friends had gotten married, and she hadn't even been to a wedding since she was a teenager. The whole idea seemed so strange and old-fashioned. And exciting. She felt like she was holding a ticket for a trip around the world, but she didn't know the route.

Though she had spent a lot of time thinking about long-term relationships, she had literally never pictured herself as a bride. The fact that Trip wanted to take that step with her felt—and she couldn't think of another way to put it—like an honor.

Several times throughout the day she was overcome with a fit of giggles. Shaking herself out of it, she thought, *I can't believe it.*

That night, they went to the bar, and when a friendly couple nearby asked them what they were doing in Palm Springs, Trip had politely shut them down before leading Lark back to the firepit.

"Today is just about us," he said. "I'm not sharing you with anyone."

~

The second day was similar except that Trip started picking up his phone again. He texted and emailed with such intensity that she finally had to ask.

"Is everything okay?"

"Work," he groaned. "I've got deals in two different places and stages, and I thought they could all survive a few days without me. I thought I'd empowered everyone sufficiently, but maybe I didn't get the job done."

"Or maybe you're irreplaceable," she said, dropping her paperback on the rumpled sheets and rubbing his back.

He locked his phone and set it facedown on the nightstand. "I'm certainly one of a kind."

She was more than happy to help him take his mind off the constant churn of investment and oversight by walking her fingers down his back, along his side, and inside the waistband of his pajama bottoms.

"On the other hand," he said, sucking in a sharp breath, "there's more to life than work."

~

The third day, he seemed even more distracted, more tied to his phone. She'd been waiting for him to announce their next move—a ride on the aerial tramway? a museum visit?—but if they were going to be married for however long, she saw no reason he had to do all the travel planning. So.

"Time to go," she announced.

He looked startled. "I figured we'd stay here a few more days."

"That's fine, but not in this room. We have to let them change the sheets and clean the bathroom, at least."

He leaned across the table and kissed her. "You're right. We shouldn't stay cooped up." A short while later, they were hiking along a trail in Palm Canyon, shaded by the leafy fronds of towering palm trees. The green cleft in the parched hills was a perfect reminder that they were truly in an oasis.

"So what kind of wedding should we have?" she asked, squeezing his hand.

"What kind of wedding do you want?"

"The smaller the better."

"Perfect."

"But not, like, at the courthouse. And definitely not in Vegas."

"No."

They stopped to watch a small bird flitting around the canopy, then waited until some faster hikers passed them before continuing on. The air was so clean and the scenery was so beautiful that Lark suddenly knew exactly where she wanted to get married.

"Hawaii," she said.

Trip's face lit up. He obviously liked the suggestion.

"And I want my parents to be there. My mom still has family on Oahu, and it's perfect, because that's where they met."

"I love it," he said.

"And Callie, too. I want her to be my maid of honor. I'm guessing most of my friends won't be able to afford to come, but that's okay."

"The smaller it is, the more perfect we can make it," he said. "I'm happy to fly your parents and Callie out."

"God, I can't believe you haven't met my mom and dad yet," she said as a plan began to form in her mind.

"I'm ready when you are."

"Who's going to stand up for you?" she asked, realizing with sadness his own parents wouldn't be able to be there for the happy day. "What about your brother?"

"Well, of course I want Matt there. His wife and kids, too. My nephews."

Hearing his brother's name, Lark yelped involuntarily. Trip raised a quizzical eyebrow.

"I'm such an idiot," she confessed. "I thought you'd said your brother's name was Mike. I'd better not screw that up at the wedding."

"No, Matt," he said, smiling and shaking his head. "There is one big obstacle, though: he's terrified of flying."

Lark's heart sank. "We don't have to have it in Hawaii."

"Of course we do," he said, squeezing her hand back. "Hawaii is perfect. I'll work on Matt. Maybe his wife can help talk him into it. A couple of drinks and a sleeping pill might get him on the plane."

"How did he handle flying to Florida for your cruise over Christmas?"

"He drove down, if you can believe it."

Hearing running water, Lark pulled Trip along until they had reached a small, rocky stream flowing down the bottom of the canyon. Water in the desert. She slipped off her shoes, sat down on a smooth, flat stone, and plunked her feet in the cool shallows.

"I want the wedding to be outside," she said. "Like really outside. In a forest, or at the base of a volcano, next to the ocean. Not at a resort. I don't care if it's really simple."

Trip kept his shoes on. "We can bring a canopy and catering anywhere. Don't worry about that."

"And we'll write our own vows. We don't even have to write them. We can just say what we're feeling in the moment."

"Works for me."

"But I do want music. Live musicians. Local is okay but not some cheap luau band."

"I think Ed Sheeran owes me a favor," he said.

Lark flicked water at him. "Ha!"

After her feet had dried, they continued on, climbing up a ridge and looking down on the canyon while they worked their way back to the trailhead. Without the shade, the sun felt hot even though the temperature was probably just under seventy degrees.

"We'll get married in June," he said suddenly. "Things should have calmed considerably down for me by then. I need to wrap up those projects before I can relax."

"And after?" she asked.

"After what?"

"The wedding. Where do we live?"

His sneakers crunched gravel as he squinted off into the distance. "I assume my California girl doesn't want to come to Chicago."

Lark pictured the plastic shopping bag caught in the icy wind outside Trip's apartment window and thought of the Chicagoans huddled into their coats right now, as the sun warmed her arms. "Well, it's not my first choice, but it's where you are."

"Wherever you are is where I am, from now on."

Chapter Thirty-Five

JESSICA

*I wish I had done a better job confronting some
hard truths.*

—"How I Lied about My Name and Discovered My Truth,"
a TED Talk by Jon M. Wright

When Holly suggested not only that they meet in person but that she
"come out to the house," Jessica's first thought was *no way in hell*. She
couldn't imagine setting foot in the place without Jon, and even then,
only in the distant future and for an extremely special occasion. Ava's
wedding, for example. But after a few nights of tossing and turning,
picturing a meeting within earshot of enrapt Starbucks patrons—*He's
not your husband anymore, he's mine!*—Jessica decided that, even if Holly
was mentally ill, she had too many questions to leave them unanswered.

Jessica told both Jon and Marco she had a family situation to deal
with and might be gone for a few days.

It wasn't a complete lie.

As she drove down Merri Oaks Road and spotted the silver address numbers on the black mailbox, she thought about the airsickness bag she'd taken from the plane and tucked into her purse, just in case.

She pulled into the circular driveway and parked in front of the rambling, ivy-covered brick-and-stone mansion, thinking that for safety's sake she should have told someone where she was going. But who? Only her mother knew she and Jon were together. No one knew they were married except for the minister in Cancún. As she exited her car and forced her legs to carry her up the brick walkway to the imposing front door, she felt like a horror-movie bimbo who, despite multiple warnings, insisted on marching headlong into mortal danger.

A home-wrecking bimbo at that.

She pressed the doorbell, half expecting an eerie creak and an ominous greeting by an elderly housekeeper whose wicked smile would foreshadow an unhappy fate. Instead, the door opened silently, and Jessica found herself face-to-face with Holly.

She'd been immaculately groomed, manicured, and coiffed the last two times they'd met. Today, Holly wore no makeup, and her blonde hair was limp, stringy, and in need of washing. Her jeans looked as though she'd just dried her hands on them, and her T-shirt, though certainly Michael Stars or some other designer, looked like it had been balled up in a dresser.

Jon's descriptors jangled in Jessica's head: *manic . . . delusional . . . needs to be hospitalized . . .*

On the other hand, Jessica knew she probably didn't look much better. Even though she'd tried to make herself presentable by wearing nice slacks and an angora sweater, she had come straight from the airport. Worse, she'd barely slept in days and didn't own enough concealer to mask the dark circles under her eyes.

"You have guts, coming here," Holly said.

"I don't feel very brave," Jessica told her. "I'm scared out of my mind."

"I guess that makes two of us."

Had Holly not made that admission, Jessica might have turned around and run when Holly motioned her inside. Instead, she went hesitantly through the door and found herself in a traditional but charming entry hall full of custom millwork. It was almost as large as the lower level of the apartment she shared with Jon.

"Can I get you anything? A glass of water?" Holly asked reflexively.

"No, thank you," Jessica said, despite barely being able to swallow.

Holly seemed to falter. "Well then."

"I need you to know," Jessica began, not wanting to forget the words she'd rehearsed on the plane and during the drive out to Barrington Hills, "that I am truly sorry to add any additional pain to what I know is an already difficult situation."

Holly gave a small nod.

"I haven't stood in the way of Jon going back and forth to be with your family, and I promise I never will."

"Back and forth," Holly repeated, shifting her weight on the oriental rug. "When, exactly, did you and Jack get together?"

"There was no overlap. I would never do that," Jessica reiterated. "We met in April, almost exactly a year and a half ago. When he gave a speech at a Mayo Clinic symposium."

"The week we got Mini-Me," Holly said under her breath.

"Mini—?"

"The kids' favorite horse."

"I understand you have quite a few," Jessica said, desperate to lighten the mood.

Holly stood up straighter and pushed her hair back from her face, speaking with dignity even as her voice cracked. "I suppose Jack has told you a lot about me. Us."

Jessica didn't answer, not ready to navigate that minefield.

"Why did you ask me about the Revelate when you called?" Holly asked.

"Jon always said it was his big idea, so when I heard that wasn't necessarily the case, I wanted to know—"

"Whether he was telling the truth."

Jessica nodded, unable to look away from Holly's pale-blue eyes.

"Would you take my word over his?"

"I don't know," she confessed.

"But he doesn't know we're talking."

"He wants me to stay away from you."

"And yet here you are."

Telling Holly she doubted Jon felt like the ultimate betrayal. And if Jon had been telling the truth about Holly's ability to deceive and manipulate, then she was playing into the hands of her worst enemy. But something told her to go on.

"I guess I want to hear your side of the story."

Holly's response was so unexpected that Jessica wondered whether she'd made a monumental miscalculation. "I presume you've never seen the house before."

"No, of course not," Jessica said.

"Then why don't I show you around?" Holly's face was inscrutable.

Jessica had known this encounter would be awkward, fraught, and possibly even dangerous. She'd pictured any number of different scenarios—including shoves and slaps—but never one that included a house tour.

Maybe Holly really was Annie Wilkes brought to life, intent on pushing Jessica down the basement stairs so she could lock her down there forever.

The voice in Jessica's head shouted, *Run!*—but was it hers or Jon's?

Unsure of whom to trust, she followed Holly into a spacious, elegant living room, her senses so overloaded she barely registered more than a blur of designer furniture and horse-themed art. She had googled the address more than once, hoping for a glimpse of something not shown in the framed family photos still prominently displayed in Jon's office, but to be inside felt like an out-of-body experience.

"This is my favorite part of the house. It's full of light, and it's the only place where you can see the stables, the guesthouse, and the pond," Holly said, gazing through one of the three sets of french doors that opened onto a patio and the seemingly endless grounds.

"Beautiful," Jessica managed.

"I would normally show you the horses and the gardens, but everything is starting to thaw, and it's just too muddy. I wouldn't want you to ruin those slacks."

Jessica was glad she wouldn't have to pretend to admire Holly's horses while watching out for open root cellar doors or remote locked sheds that happened to be part of the outdoor tour.

"The original structure and the barn were built in 1922 by a steel magnate, as a wedding gift for one of his children," said Holly, proceeding to a library full of books and exquisite cabinetry. "Many of the original architectural features are still intact."

Her spiel was well practiced, and as they passed through a dining room with elaborate wainscoting and crown molding, she pointed out the chandelier, which was "original, and supposedly a gift from William Wrigley himself." In the thoroughly renovated kitchen, she explained, "The kitchen, of course, had already been redone several times by the time we got here, so we didn't feel we were tampering by going all new. Jack always preferred clean lines and contemporary, so this place was a big change from our town house in Lincoln Park."

Jessica nodded and tried to hide her skyrocketing anxiety. She passed the basement stairs without incident as they walked into the family room, "an addition designed by the grandson of the original architect," still with no idea why this encounter had become a tour.

Holly led them up to the second floor via a set of back stairs she said was "originally built for servants and unfortunately convenient for stealthy teenage exits." As they made their way down a wide hallway,

Holly opened the doors to Ava's "aerie," Paige's "ocean," and Logan's "disaster area."

"What I would have given for a fireplace and a window seat in my bedroom," Jessica said as she peered into Paige's room, which was painted and upholstered in calming blues and greens. "All three kids' rooms are so peaceful."

"Much as we all love this house, the stark realities of the outside world always have a way of intruding."

The pointed comment was the opening she'd been waiting for.

"I hope you don't think I have any intention of trying to compromise your right to this house, or the lifestyle you've enjoyed all these years," Jessica said.

Holly smiled thinly. "I'm not particularly concerned about your intentions, to be honest."

"Then why the house tour?"

"We both have questions. I think this is the best way to answer at least one of them."

Holly headed toward a set of double doors, reached for the matching pewter handles, and pulled them open. "This house features more than a master suite: a private wing with his-and-hers walk-in closets and matching studies."

"I really don't think I need to see your personal—"

"Oh, you definitely do," Holly said, taking her hand and leading her through the doors.

Despite Holly's calm, almost curatorial air, Jessica's nerves felt like arcing electrical wires.

A sitting room served as an antechamber to the master bedroom, with doors and hallways leading to the adjoining rooms that made up the private wing. It was all certainly remarkable in its grandeur, as Jessica expected. The decor was elegant and flawlessly appointed—just like everything else in the house.

And then Jessica noticed the nightstands.

Specifically, what was on top of them. On one side, a pair of glasses rested on an e-reader in a pale-pink leather case next to a bottle of hand cream. On the other were a tube of lip balm—Kiehl's, the brand Jon swore by—and a bestselling book offering a new theory about dinosaur extinction. A book she'd given him herself after the museum visits of their Chicago staycation. He'd told her he was reading it in stolen moments of business travel.

"Jack told you we were separated," Holly said, noting her sharp intake of breath. "Yet he's lived here the whole time you've been involved."

Jessica resisted the urge to rush over and open the book to check for the *XO, Jessica* she'd written inside. "I knew he stayed here sometimes—so he could be with the kids. He told me you have separate living spaces."

"There's never been a night when Jack's been home that he didn't sleep in our bed. Although he does sometimes nap on the couch in his home office."

Holly pointed her down a short corridor toward an open door. Jessica forced herself to take a look.

Unlike his glassed-in office at Cancura, which was sleek, modern, and unusually neat, this one contained an oak desk and matching credenza, a leather club chair, and an oversize sectional with dark-blue velvet upholstery that was nearly identical to the couch he'd rented for the apartment.

"You're here today because you have questions," Holly stated. "Questions you felt *Jack* wouldn't answer truthfully."

Jessica nodded dumbly.

"Which then made you wonder if there were other things he wasn't being truthful about," continued Holly.

"Yes."

"For example, whether he really was the poor, misunderstood victim in a troubled relationship. How am I doing so far?"

"He said you were mentally ill," said Jessica, needing to stop the interrogation, wanting to defend herself. "He told me he was trying to have you institutionalized."

"*What?*" Holly turned pale and sank onto an upholstered bench.

"Every time he left me to see you, he said it was because you were manic, fighting with your kids, making threats. He even had a nickname for you: Annie Wilkes."

Holly looked at her uncomprehendingly.

"Kathy Bates's character from *Misery*. The psycho who breaks James Caan's ankles with a sledgehammer to trap him in her home."

Recognition came into her eyes, and Holly groaned.

"I'm so sorry," Jessica said, remembering how she'd laughed when he said it.

Holly looked up. "What did he tell you on New Year's Eve, when he left me to be with you?"

Jessica swallowed, remembering the calm and collected Holly she'd met that evening. How, like always, she'd bought Jon's version of events.

"He told me you were having a break with reality. That you thought you were still married."

"But we are married," said Holly simply. "When he picked a fight on New Year's Eve, it seemed to come out of nowhere. The next day he told me he slept at the corporate apartment by Millennium Park."

Head spinning, Jessica had to tell her. "He was with me. But *we're* married. We got married in Mexico."

As she said it, Jessica felt her own tears start to fall. Realizing that either everything was true or none of it was.

"I'll be making arrangements to have his things moved to your place," Holly said, tears now streaming down her face. "The sooner the better."

"I . . . I don't even know where he is right now, exactly," Jessica stammered. "He's in the desert somewhere."

Holly seemed to regain command of her voice. "Those intensive inpatient therapy programs are always somewhere warm. Apparently, treatment for sex addiction—excuse me, low self-esteem and infidelity—requires an ideal climate."

Jessica steadied herself on the wall. "He told you that?"

"Who knows what's really true?"

Chapter Thirty-Six

LARK

*Bringing new people on board alters your
risk-reward ratio.*

—"How I Lied about My Name and Discovered My Truth,"
a TED Talk by Jon M. Wright

Uncharacteristically, Trip was in no hurry to leave Palm Springs. Claiming their hike had inspired him, he'd begun looking into other activities, from riding the aerial tramway to visiting the art museum. As she watched him methodically researching options on his laptop, Lark felt like she was peeking behind the curtain to see the hard work behind his seeming spontaneity. It was endearing and she loved it. She also loved the time he was spending with her. The long, uninterrupted hours of time together felt like an early wedding gift and a happy preview of their life as a married couple.

Only now she was the one itching to leave. Because Larkspur Games was calling. With a new hire needing direction and only Callie to provide it, Lark felt like she'd already been gone from the office too long.

"This is a bit of a role reversal, isn't it?" he joked, looking disappointed when she told him.

She kissed him. "We're both hard workers, which is why we understand each other so well."

"Damn straight," he said.

As he closed his browser, she noticed that he had more tabs open than she'd thought possible, each of them so tiny it was impossible to see what website it was from. Her big-plans fiancé definitely kept a lot of things in his head at once.

Trip glanced at his watch and grimaced. "If we leave now, we'll be just in time for rush hour."

"Perfect," said Lark, smiling.

An hour later they were driving into the setting sun with visors down and sunglasses on. It was time to spring her surprise.

"It's time you met Kalani and Leroy Robinson, Trip."

"Completely overdue," he agreed, frowning at a tailgater in his mirror.

"Lucky for you, they live in West Covina. It's on the way."

He looked over at her, surprised. "*Now?* But they don't even know we're coming."

"They're my *parents*. It's fine. And we're engaged. If we put it off any longer, it's going to be weird."

Dragging his eyes back to the road, he chewed the inside of his lip. "I don't have a ring for you yet."

"I don't need a ring," she told him, laughing, finding his consternation sweetly hilarious. "I suppose you're also worried because you didn't ask my dad *for my hand*."

"Maybe a little," he confessed.

"Maybe we shouldn't get married after all," she groaned. "You're so old-fashioned!"

He pretended to pout. "That hurts."

"If I have to have a ring, buy me one of those candy rings. Or we can find a vending machine and get a plastic one for fifty cents. I honestly don't care."

He continued to brood while they drove past Ontario, so a few miles later, she said, "Exit here," pointing to a mall called Montclair Place.

"What's wrong?" he asked.

"Let's get a ring so you can feel good about meeting my parents," she told him. "Kay or Zales—take your pick."

"I can't buy your ring at a *mall*," he muttered.

"My ring, my choice."

He sighed but exited the freeway. "We'll just get something for now, and we'll get a nicer one later."

"No takebacks," she needled him. "This is permanent."

After they parked and found the store, she took the lead, asking the clerk lots of questions while Trip hung back, communicating mostly with nods. Imagining herself as a newly engaged, gum-snapping, ring-obsessed girl was a fun game, and Lark leaned into it, targeting Trip with her cheerfulness and knowing he'd come around.

Eventually, she settled on a tasteful diamond surrounded by tiny blue sapphires—despite Trip's urging to get something bigger.

"I like it," she told him. "It's me."

"At least the blue matches your hair," he said, lightening up a little bit.

The clerk—who was almost beside himself to have such motivated buyers—told them the ring could be sized and ready in half an hour. Over Trip's objections, Lark insisted they kill time at Cinnabon.

When the ring was ready, they took the jewelry box to a little bench next to a sparsely filled planter, under an atrium skylight glowing faintly red. Lark sat down primly and told Trip to kneel.

"What?"

"You heard me. On bended knee."

Trip glanced both ways, tugged up his pant leg, and knelt. Opening the box, he took out the ring and slipped it onto her finger.

"I do!" said Lark loudly, trying to make Trip laugh and hoping someone would notice.

She helped him up and took a selfie of the two of them with her left hand splayed on her chest and the ring prominently displayed. Then she posted it to Instagram with the caption, I SAID YES.

"Montclair Place has taken a lot out of me," said Trip. "I'm not sure I'm in the best shape to meet your parents."

"You'll do fine," she assured him.

Lark may have been playacting during the ring purchase, but now that the glittering band was on her finger, she couldn't stop looking at it. She even knocked on the door of her parents' bungalow with her left hand, just to see the jewels sparkle in the porch light.

If she were alone, she would have simply walked in, but it didn't seem fair for them to suddenly discover Trip in their living room. They were in for a big enough surprise as it was.

"Well, well, well," said her dad, looking Trip over as he opened the door.

"Is Mom home?" she asked.

"Oh, she's home," he said, giving Lark a mischievous grin before calling over his shoulder: "Kalani! Lark's here!"

He ushered them inside, waiting on introductions until they were all present in the cluttered but homey living room. Lark's dad kept the garage and his basement workout room shipshape, a habit from his navy days, but happily allowed her mom to clutter the main areas of the house with books, magazines, yarn, and small dogs, one of whom began yapping at their feet.

Lark had just a moment to register that her dad was about two inches taller and thirty pounds heavier than Trip—he was only ten years older—before her mom came in from the kitchen wearing one of the flowing, Hawaiian-print housedresses that had made her cringe in middle school. Her mom was still willowy and slim with perfect skin, but her hair had turned gray prematurely, something she always laughingly blamed on her students at Mt. San Antonio College.

"At last we meet," she said, offering a hand to Trip. "I'm Kalani Robinson."

"Leroy," said her dad when it was his turn.

"Trip Mitchell," said her fiancé, holding the handshake just long enough that Lark could tell it was competitive.

"What a wonderful surprise," said Kalani.

"You have no idea," said Lark, grinning so widely her face hurt.

She could read so much in the eyes of her parents as they took in Trip's age, whiteness, and wealth, which was obvious from the silver Rolex Submariner. Lark had focused her updates on how fun and spontaneous he was, but now, standing in the modest living room of the house they'd moved to when she was in sixth grade—and about to break the biggest news of her life—the differences seemed a little more pronounced.

Before she could say anything, her mom spotted the shine on her ring finger.

"Oh my god," she said. "Is that . . . ?"

Lark nodded, her eyes suddenly wet, as her mom swept her up in a fierce hug.

"I feel like I owe both of you an apology," said Trip.

"For what?" asked her dad, playfully gruff. "Proposing to my daughter? Is there a reason you shouldn't have done that?"

"No—"

"You're not married yet, right? Just engaged?"

Trip laughed, unable to get a word in edgewise.

Her mom shushed her dad. "Leroy, let him speak."

"I'm just sorry that I haven't been here to meet you sooner," said Trip finally. "Things have been moving fast, obviously, and I honestly think we're both a little bit overwhelmed. I know it's a lot to find out your daughter's boyfriend is also her fiancé the first time you meet him."

"Damn straight," said her dad, still playing with him, not that Trip could know that. "You didn't even ask for her hand, either."

Trip glanced at Lark and took a breath. "Knowing your daughter, that would have been completely the wrong move. I'm not sure she would have forgiven me."

Her dad guffawed and slapped a visibly relieved Trip on the back.

"I certainly wouldn't have," said her mom. "Women choose for themselves. But are you done apologizing, Trip?"

"I think so?" he said, raising an eyebrow.

"Good, because I believe we're supposed to celebrate."

After hugs and handshakes, her parents went into the kitchen to see what they could pour for a toast.

"How am I doing?" Trip whispered.

"Just fine."

Her dad came back to report on the options. "Here at Chez Robinson, we can offer a bottle of sauvignon blanc that is not chilled but can be enjoyed over ice. We also have cold Miller High Life, which is not champagne, but has been called the champagne of beers."

"Beer sounds perfect," said Trip.

"I'll have one, too," said Lark.

"Beers all around then."

Retrieving a six-pack, her dad twisted each cap with a flourish before distributing the bottles.

"Here's to my beautiful, headstrong daughter, and the man she's chosen to take this journey with," said her mom.

Lark sipped her beer, the taste of it instantly taking her back to high school, when she had raided her dad's supply before heading out to shows.

Trip raised his bottle. "To Lark, for making me the happiest man alive, because, honestly, I was afraid she'd say no!"

That got a chuckle.

Now it was her turn, and Lark had no idea what to say as she looked at the faces of her mom, dad, and Trip. Once again, she felt a little weepy.

"To us," she said. "I'm sorry, but that's all I can manage, or I'm going to cry."

Her mom squeezed her shoulder.

"To Lark and this guy Trip, whoever the hell he is," said her dad, and they all laughed.

Chapter Thirty-Seven

HOLLY

Do you have an exit strategy?
Because your partners will.

—"How I Lied about My Name and Discovered My Truth,"
a TED Talk by Jon M. Wright

Holly sat at a burnished wood table in the offices of Eerdman, Fellowes, Mancini, and Shulman, on the thirty-third floor of a muscular new tower that swaggered over the Loop. The building was four blocks from Jack's corporate apartment and less than a mile from the Cancura offices, something she'd been acutely aware of as she hurried inside.

She'd chosen the long-established firm because they'd never done business with Jack, because they had the go-to divorce lawyer for the Chicago elite, and because they also specialized in business law and litigation. Suspecting Jack's finances would prove an especially tricky knot to untangle, she'd asked for a business attorney to sit in on the initial interview.

Now, in this warmly lit conference room with boxes of tissues placed discreetly at hand as though she were at a therapist's or a funeral parlor, she faced Francesco Mancini Jr., the founder's son, who was now a principal, and Mark Todd, a handsome younger man she'd been assured was "the best we have." Francesco asked most of the questions, scribbling illegible notes, while Mark listened intently and made only occasional interjections.

If she felt nervous at first, Francesco's no-nonsense professionalism had her warming to the task. Middle-aged and almost startlingly unattractive, he nonetheless oozed such power and self-confidence that it was easy to see him commanding a courtroom. He didn't ask her how she was feeling and didn't hint that she was in any way over her head. Focusing on the facts, he spoke to her strictly as an equal.

For her part, Holly did her best to act like this wasn't the hardest thing she'd ever done in her life.

Leaving Jack.

Believing Jessica.

They had covered the basics—names, spelling of names, places of employment, children's names and ages, wedding dates (Holly almost choked on this one, thinking of what Jessica had told her about Mexico), prenuptial agreements (there wasn't one)—and were moving into more difficult territory.

"Have you ever undergone couples therapy or marital counseling?" asked Francesco.

"No."

"I'm not judging, but it could become relevant. Has either you or Jack asked for—or refused to participate in—counseling?"

It felt odd to realize it had never come up. There had been precious few acknowledgments of their difficulties from either of them. If she were sworn to tell the truth in a court of law, could she look a judge in the eye and say she'd actually wanted their marriage to get better?

"No," she said. "He recently claimed to have checked himself into inpatient therapy, but I'll need to see the receipt before I believe it."

Nods. Pens scratching.

"Do you expect him to fight you for custody?"

"I sincerely doubt it, given how rarely he's home now."

"In my experience, people will often fight over things they don't even want. Just to win."

"Can we talk about his business?" asked Mark, almost hungrily. "Cancura?"

"Of course," Holly said.

"Were you privy in general to his finances?"

"No. His accountant pays most of our bills, and I put household expenses on a credit card that is similarly taken care of. I've always been led to believe there is plenty, so I haven't concerned myself with specific numbers."

"What about your income as a doctor?"

"It's very modest in comparison to his. I'm part time."

"Do you have investment properties, retirement plans? College funds for the kids?"

"Jack always said he would just pay for college out of pocket. I do have a retirement plan through Cancura."

Francesco cut in, sounding surprised. "How is that?"

"I was an employee for a short time when the company was founded. I remain on the board, although in confidence I have to tell you it's really in name only. Jack always said he was allowed to offer me benefits because of it."

Mark smiled. "Provides a nice write-off."

"He's always played loose with the rules. I'm embarrassed for not knowing, but I suspect all of our cars are registered to Cancura. I want to proceed very carefully, because I don't want him to freeze assets that can benefit my children."

"And yourself."

"And myself. Our family's financial well-being is completely tied to the company. Jack holds fifty-one percent of the stock. My parents own roughly eight percent. I believe I even have three and a half percent in my own name, due to options that have vested."

"Do you have any knowledge about the health or weakness of Cancura?" asked Mark. "Any reason to believe its fortunes will rise or fall in the near future?"

Holly caught her breath and hesitated. For years, she'd wondered how much of the buzz surrounding the Revelate came from its true potential and how much was wishful thinking on the part of Jack and his check-writing true believers. Jessica and her questions about Cancura had only intensified her suspicions.

Instead of admitting her concerns, she asked, "I presume there are laws about hiding assets from a spouse in a divorce?"

"Of course," said Francesco.

"At what point is a person's net worth determined for the purposes of a divorce? Would it be the moment a divorce petition is filed?"

"Well, hypothetically, let's say you file for divorce and his sole asset is ten thousand shares of Cancura stock. We would argue in mediation, and in court, if necessary, that five thousand of those belong to you. And we would probably win. But you get the stock, whatever it's worth when we sign, not its original value. So it could be more or it could be less."

"I see," said Holly.

"A savvy operator might even manipulate the value of his own stock," said Mark. "If you're concerned he may hide money, then it's important that we document as much as possible before filing papers. That could include hiring a forensic accountant to determine as much as possible about his assets based on public filings."

"We're getting ahead of ourselves here, and we need to better understand where Holly is coming from," said Francesco gently but firmly. "Holly, as simply as you can, tell us why you're seeking a divorce from Jack."

While the men nodded and scribbled, she told them everything she knew and everything she suspected about Jack's infidelities, saving the showstopper for last. Both men raised their eyebrows when she told them about the apartment Jack shared with Jessica. And when she added that he'd married his new girlfriend in Mexico, Mark was unable to suppress a "Damn!"

Francesco gave him an almost imperceptible frown.

"Sorry," added Mark.

"Bigamy is a Class Four felony in Illinois," explained Francesco. "If we're looking at a criminal proceeding—that is, if he's charged and convicted—that will have a favorable impact on your divorce suit. While creating more hardship for your family, of course."

Holly couldn't help picturing Jack in an orange jumpsuit. Behind bars. At a long metal table with Ava, Paige, and Logan on the opposite side.

"Would he go to jail?"

"Illinois requires a minimum of one year in prison and no more than three."

Holly's head began to throb exactly as it had after being kicked by Wags.

"What about Jessica?" she asked. "Does she have any claim on his property?"

"If she was truly unaware he was already married, she is legally entitled to all the rights of a legal spouse, including maintenance. Practically speaking, though, you don't have much to worry about in divorce court. And the marriage is easily invalidated."

"What do we do now?" Holly asked, her voice faint to her own ears.

"We have to move cautiously, for sure," said Mark, while Francesco nodded soberly. "Your husband is a public figure. The moment any of this gets out, there's going to be a media circus, so we need an airtight case and a detailed plan of attack."

"Would this Jessica Meyers be willing to provide an affidavit or testify if we go to trial?" asked Francesco.

"I don't know," said Holly.

"Do you have documentation regarding this second marriage, or infidelities with other women?"

She shook her head, then realized she felt unsteady in her chair, like she had vertigo.

"Are you feeling all right?" asked Francesco.

"I just need a moment. A drink of water and to splash some water on my face."

Solicitously, Francesco directed her to the ladies' room while Mark headed out for some bottled water. In the restroom, Holly sat down on a padded bench and collected herself.

She'd walked in feeling strong and ready to end her marriage and secure her family's future, wanting only to minimize the trauma for her children. It hadn't even crossed her mind how public the process could be for all of them. The thought was almost paralyzing.

Did she really want to send her children's father to prison?

Leaning back against the wall, hearing voices passing in the hall, Holly closed her eyes and realized she needed to stop thinking of Jack as her husband and start thinking of him as a partner in a failed long-term venture. And what would he do in that situation if the roles were reversed? Jack had never had an ounce of sentiment about business. He would coolly do whatever was best for his enterprise and move on.

Her panic passed as she realized she would do exactly the same thing.

Chapter Thirty-Eight

Jessica and Holly

No secret is ever truly safe.

—"How I Lied about My Name and Discovered My Truth,"
a TED Talk by Jon M. Wright

Catfished? Gaslighted? What was the word for being taken in by a brilliant, handsome, wildly successful man who had not only swept her off her feet but moved her across the country, gave her a job to die for, and then married her—despite already being married himself?

Other than *screwed.*

And how had Jessica, the girl who aced every test and made all the right choices, fallen head over heels for it?

Two and a half days after she left Barrington Hills, Jessica was still in bed, unable to focus on the blabbering TV and getting up only to go to the bathroom or refill her glass of water. Food was out of the question, as was just about anything else except marshaling her energy to lie to Jon about "Nana's slow recovery."

Thankfully, he'd mostly texted, calling only twice, and if he'd noticed the distress in her voice, he hadn't mentioned it. But how much longer could she hold back from voicing her dozens of questions, the answers to which would surely pierce her heart?

Did you ever really love me? Was anything about us real? Why did you do this? Where are you?

The idea that he might actually be at a clinic turned her stomach. Her gorgeous, sexy, and brilliant Jon was a liar and a bigamist in therapy for sex addiction?

Because of her.

Didn't his "cure" necessarily imply the end of their marriage?

And then the end of her career at Cancura?

The last thing she expected was the front door buzzer.

She dragged herself out of bed to the video intercom and saw a uniformed man standing in the front vestibule.

"Registered mail," he said. "I need a signature."

Exceedingly conscious of her stale sweatpants and unshowered state, she went downstairs and signed for a padded envelope from Belgium. Back upstairs, she tore it open and found herself staring at a stunning two-carat, horizontal-cut diamond surrounded by a subtle but glittering halo set in nineteen-karat platinum.

The dazzling sparkler couldn't have been more to her taste. As she held it up to the overcast daylight filtering in through the window, she wanted to tell herself the last few days were nothing but a bad dream. Why would Jon have ordered a costly, custom-made ring if he was already married?

Her phone rang. As she walked over to grab it from the kitchen counter, she tried to convince herself Jon had somehow known she was home and was calling to see if she loved the ring as much as he had loved picking it out for her. That there was a logical explanation for everything . . .

But it wasn't Jon on the other end of the line.

"Do you have the marriage certificate?" Holly asked.

"What difference does it make?" Jessica countered, her voice scratchy from lack of use. "We're not really married if he's still married to you. It's all a big—"

"Bigamy. Exactly. A crime he committed against both of us."

Jessica took one last look at the ring before putting it back in its elegant velvet box. She started sobbing.

Holly allowed her to go on longer than she deserved.

"I'm sorry," Jessica finally said. "The man I thought was my husband and the love of my life is apparently just a sex addict." She began to cry harder, uglier, choking out the words. "Even worse, he's my boss. At least you can divorce him. I'm literally screwed. I haven't been able to get out of bed since I left your house."

Holly's voice maintained perfect control. "Jessica, my situation is just as bad. I have kids I made with Jack, the man I fully intended to spend my life with. I have four futures at stake."

"I have no idea what I'm going to do. My career is dependent on him."

"My whole family is dependent on him, and I have no choice but to act."

Jessica grabbed a handful of tissues and mopped her face. "How will prosecuting him for bigamy do that? He'll bring all of us down with him."

"I'm not talking about a simple prosecution," Holly said. "I'm picturing something bigger than that."

"I haven't seen the marriage license since I signed it after the ceremony," Jessica admitted, glancing at the bills on the front table and scanning the flecked white countertop she loved so much. How soon would she need to move out?

"I'll stay on the phone while you look around."

"I just want to go back to bed," Jessica groaned.

"And how has that worked out for you so far?"

"I just feel so . . . weak. Stupid and gullible."

"I've spent two decades pretending not to believe things I knew to be true."

"How could he have married me when he was already—?"

"There have been other women, but he's definitely never gone this far before." After a moment, she added, "If I know Jack, he needs you for something, and I'm afraid it's not just sex."

"I'm so confused. What should I do?"

"I've decided that since he thinks of me as Annie Wilkes, I plan to live up to the name," Holly said. "I suggest you do whatever it takes to answer that question."

Jessica wondered which movie monster she could possibly channel as she got up and shuffled into the office, where she riffled through the paperwork on top of the desk and in its drawers.

"His file-cabinet drawer is locked," she told Holly.

"Check in his sock drawer. That's one of the places he hides keys."

Woodenly, Jessica went into the bedroom and checked Jon's half-empty drawer of socks and underwear. It didn't take long.

"Not there."

"Try the closet."

She entered their shared walk-in closet, where he kept exactly four Brioni suits, ten tailor-made dress shirts, and a handful of ties, all organized by color. His closet in Barrington Hills had contained five times the clothing.

"Where in the closet?" she asked helplessly.

"Try his shoes," Holly said.

Although the thought of sticking her hand inside each shoe of the four pairs lining the closet floor suddenly repulsed her, Jessica did as she was told and found a key in the toe of a Cole Haan wing tip.

"I think I've got it." Jessica went back into the office, where the key fit smoothly into the round lock and opened it with a gentle turn. "Yes."

The cabinet held only three files: miscellaneous paperwork related to the apartment, a sheaf of what looked like some kind of stock certificates, and a lease for office space in Culver City, California, which, at the very least, explained why he was going to the West Coast so regularly.

"There's nothing here," Jessica said, half-relieved not to see the document she'd signed back when she'd felt so happy and certain of future bliss. "Maybe it's at your house."

"I'll look as soon as I get home," Holly said. "In the meantime, can you call the minister, or judge, or whoever married you, and request a copy?"

"I can try, but we got married in Mexico."

"Yes, I know. Cancún." Holly's voice was leaden, distant.

"I'm so, so sorry. I—"

"I don't know how anyone could have anticipated anything like this."

"I'll call the resort right now and see what I can come up with."

"Take a shower first," Holly said. "Get dressed and make yourself feel better."

"Why are you being kind to me?" Jessica asked.

Holly sighed. "I've tried hating you, but it just doesn't make any sense. The only way to get through this nightmare is together."

Holly turned off her engine, got out of her car, and walked over to Jack's massive workbench while the garage door rumbled down behind her. A gleaming array of tools hung neatly on a pegboard, carefully arranged and, to her knowledge, never used. The workers she hired for improvements and repairs brought their own toolboxes filled with implements that were chipped and dusty, spattered with paint and Spackle. She lifted a solid black crowbar off its hooks, thought for a moment, and then picked up a claw hammer, too.

Upstairs in Jack's office, she opened the cabinet that concealed the safe where Jack kept his most important personal papers. Though it was just a fire safe, not a secure banking model, it was still sealed with a five-digit combination lock. She didn't even bother trying to guess. Placing the chisel end of the crowbar next to the lock, she struck the back end of the crowbar with the hammer. Her fingers stung as the cold metal jumped out of her hands and clattered on the floor, but at least she had made a satisfying dent in the safe. She picked up the crowbar and tried again, swinging the hammer carefully, keeping her grip despite the intense vibrations. The high-pitched clangs hurt her ears.

Two dozen blows later, the lock had sprung, and she was able to open the door of the safe. Inside was a foot-tall stack of papers, envelopes, and manila folders, along with a few rubber-banded stacks of hundreds.

She dragged everything out onto the floor and went through it, quickly sorting deeds to the house and their summer home in Union Pier, and records for various insurance policies. There were stocks and bonds, birth certificates for the whole family, and, almost touchingly, Jack and Holly's wedding license. But nothing to indicate Jack and Jessica had tied the knot in a clandestine ceremony in Mexico.

She took her wireless earbuds out of her jacket pocket, put them in, and dialed Jessica so she could talk hands-free.

"There's nothing in the safe," she said as soon as Jessica answered.

"I left a message with someone at the resort who said she'd try to track down the minister, but she didn't sound especially eager. Is there anywhere else he might have put it?"

"His desk, but I don't think he uses it much. It's mostly full of old work stuff."

Holly heard Jessica exhale before asking, "What, exactly, does Jon tell you about how things are going with the Revelate?"

A memory came to Holly so vividly that she could almost smell the wax in the flickering candle as Jack, his eyes alight, tried to convince her over a restaurant table that disrupting early detection of childhood cancers was what he'd been put on earth to do. That particular anniversary dinner had been woefully short on romance.

"Why do you ask?"

"Let me guess, he always says everything's going just great," Jessica continued.

Holly chuckled bitterly. The woman obviously knew her husband. "From your tone, I'm guessing it's not."

"I wanted to believe it was. Now I'm not sure."

"And you have reason for your suspicion?"

"For one thing, our biggest client is upset because the machine doesn't do what we promised, and the only reason they're not breaking their contract is because Jon doubled down and told them he's about to deliver more than they ever dreamed."

"Will he?"

"That's what I'm wondering."

Had Jack indeed married Jessica for reasons that had nothing to do with romance? Did Jessica offer something incredibly special to Cancura—or did Jack think she could keep something very bad from happening to it? Either reason might explain why he'd taken such a drastic step.

"When I originally said it—when I told Jack we needed an easy way to diagnose leukemia, lymphoma, and other cancers earlier—it wasn't a big idea, and it wasn't anything ten thousand doctors before me hadn't thought, too," said Holly. "I was just wishing out loud, because the technology wasn't there, and I had no idea if it ever would be. But to Jack, it was like a revelation. I was never sure whether he really thought he could pull it off, or he was simply selling the idea, to be honest. Either way, he had a way of making true believers out of everyone."

"Every time I find a piece of data or a scrap of information that contradicts what I've been told is true, Jon concocts a hasty explanation or tells me there's something so spectacular on the horizon that my concern seems suddenly moot."

"Just like he does at . . . home."

"Yes," Jessica said, the word sounding like a sob. "What happens if it just never works?"

"A lot of people will have their careers and financial futures ruined, for starters. Which is why people aren't too eager to ask questions."

"I think it would be more important that people know the truth. We of all people know what it's like to live in false hope."

Unfolding her stiff limbs, Holly raised herself from the carpet and stood up. "I'm going to look in his desk."

"Do you have a key?"

"Yes, but I don't need it."

Jack's sock drawer was too far away. And besides, what would Annie Wilkes do?

Holly picked up the tools and kicked Jack's desk chair out of the way. With one strong swing of the crowbar, she sent his elaborate computer setup crashing to the floor. Working the crowbar into the gap between the pencil drawer and the frame, she wiggled it until she had purchase, then pulled up hard until the wood splintered with a deeply gratifying crack. She did the same to the lower-right-hand drawers, using the hammer on the bottom one, striking the crowbar again and again until the wood facing fell off and rattled on the floor.

"Mom?"

Holly whirled. Ava was in the doorway.

"Just a minute," Holly told Jessica.

"Who's there?" Jessica asked.

Ava's eyes took in the battered and broken safe, the splintered desk, the papers scattered on the floor, the hammer, and the crowbar. "What the *hell* are you doing, Mom?"

"I know this looks bad," Holly said, hearing her own ragged breath.

"Bad? It's totally insane!"

"I needed some information, and your father wasn't getting back to me," said Holly.

"Oh shit," Jessica whispered in her ear.

"You couldn't, like, wait for him to just call you back? You're breaking into his stuff?"

Holly took a step forward as Ava retreated into the hall. "It's *our* stuff, Ava."

"So you're obviously getting a divorce. Like, it's happening."

Holly reached out, realized the futility of hoping for an embrace, and let her hands drop to her sides. "I don't want to talk about it without your brother and your sister present."

Ava stared, fury masking her confusion. Holly ached to hold her but knew one more step would cause her daughter to turn and flee like a wild animal. It turned out not to matter, because Ava left of her own accord, her final retort a strangled, *"Whatever."*

"I'm sorry, Holly," said Jessica after Holly returned to the call. "Do you need to go after her?"

"When she cools down."

Her heart breaking, Holly pulled the chair back to the desk, sat down, and started emptying drawers. Everything looked exactly the same as before.

"I'm going through the desk now," she told Jessica. "It's all just old work stuff. Outdated contracts. Cancura swag with the original logo."

"It was probably too much to hope for."

Frustrated, Holly started digging through the notepads and stress balls, tossing them aside. Underneath everything was a hard drive that must have at one time fit into a computer tower.

That was strange. She picked it up and turned it over in her hands. On the bottom, Jack had written with a Sharpie:

DON'T USE.

"What if I find something that could be important?" she asked, suddenly hesitant to admit what she was holding. "To Cancura."

"Send it to me. We can decide together how to proceed."

Holly had a random thought and made a sound that was almost a laugh.

"What is it?" Jessica asked.

"You're so serious—somehow I just don't picture you with funny-colored hair."

"I don't get it."

"During Christmas break, Ava's friend Sienna was downtown and saw you with Jack in front of the windows at Macy's. She said you had blue hair at the time."

"That's weird," Jessica said. "We were definitely there, but I've never dyed my hair in my life. Not even a streak."

They were both silent for a moment.

"If he wasn't with you, then who was he with?" Holly asked.

"I have no idea. Do you think . . . there could be . . . someone else?"

"Once we start digging, who knows what we're going to find?" Holly said grimly before hanging up.

Chapter Thirty-Nine

LARK

Social media can make or break you.

—"How I Lied about My Name and Discovered My Truth,"
a TED Talk by Jon M. Wright

Lark woke to an empty bed in an empty apartment. After staying one more day in LA, Trip had booked a dawn flight back to Chicago after discovering all the reasonable departures were sold out and had left so quietly she hadn't even stirred. Callie had been asleep when they arrived and, as Lark discovered as she dragged herself to the kitchen for a bowl of fruit and yogurt, had already left for work. She needed to get there, too—bad form for the boss to be rolling in late. After showering, dressing, and running a brush through her hair, she took her ring from the nightstand and slipped it on her finger, laughing at herself for the pleasant shiver she felt.

Thirty minutes of stop-and-start traffic later, she walked through the door of Larkspur Games, carrying a chai latte and unable to stop the stupid smile that spread across her face as she greeted Sandro and stuck her head inside the office of Hannah, their new marketing director.

"Good morning. I promise I'm usually around a lot more than this."

Hannah looked up from her screen. "It's your company. I make no judgments."

Lark held up her left hand and wiggled the fingers. "Kind of a prehoneymoon."

"Oh my gosh! Congratulations!"

They didn't know each other well enough for anything more than that, so Lark withdrew. She wanted to check in with Callie to squee over the good news, but her general manager–slash–roommate had headphones on and was hunched intently over her screen.

Lark went into her office, sat down, and touched the keyboard to wake up her computer. Her in-box was flooded with unopened messages—she hadn't been paying much attention to work email in Palm Springs—but seeing them was more reassuring than stressful. She had work to do, which meant this thing she was creating was real.

Half an hour later there was a soft knock, and Callie slipped in through the half-open door, closing it behind her. Her face was so grave that Lark's first thought was that somebody had died.

"Are you okay?"

Callie sat down in one of the guest chairs, unlocked her phone, and handed it to Lark. "You need to see this."

Callie had shared Lark's Instagram photo from the mall on her own Facebook feed. Lark's big smile and Trip's I'm-trying-to-be-cool grin in the atrium of Montclair Place. If their engagement bothered Callie, why had she gone to the trouble of sharing it?

"I put your picture up on Facebook," Callie said haltingly, "thinking it would be fun for my family and friends back home in Lincoln to see it. I mean, some of them have met you, and they've all seen plenty of pictures of us."

"That was nice," said Lark guardedly.

"Look at the comments. My cousin Sam is a lab tech at a hospital in Omaha. He recognized Trip."

Still confused, Lark scrolled through the comments.

So happy for your friend!

Nice ring could be bigger LOL

They make a very cute couple.

Then she found the one Callie was talking about: *So weird he looks EXACTLY like this guy doing some kind of a big deal at the place where I work.*

???, Callie had written.

Replying to his own comment, Cousin Sam had pasted a link to a PDF, which, when Lark clicked it, took a moment to open in the phone's browser.

She glanced up at Callie, ready to make a joke about Trip's doppelgänger, but the miserable look on her friend's face stopped her from saying anything.

The link, when it opened, was an internal newsletter for a place called American Healthcare Systems. The picture of Trip was on the front page, part of a story headlined: *AHS and Cancura: A Revolutionary Partnership.*

Only he wasn't called *Trip.* The article identified him as *Jonathan Wright III, CEO and founder of Cancura.*

"It just looks like him," Lark said, even as she enlarged the image until his head and shoulders filled the frame.

"Unless he has an identical twin he never told you about."

"He has a brother named Matt in Ohio who works in a factory or something. Trip never said anything about them being twins."

"Lark. Trip is Jonathan Wright."

Her mind flashed back to the hotel lobby in Minneapolis. *I see a Jonathan Wright and a Jonathan Yerbinski, but no Mitchell.*

Dazed, Lark walked around the desk and sat down in the chair beside Callie. The closest thing she could compare it to was the time she'd wrecked her car, rear-ending a scrap-metal truck on the 405. It had happened so fast she couldn't understand why the airbag had deployed, why her windshield was shattered, why she was no longer moving.

"This doesn't make any sense."

Callie started to cry. "I don't want to be right."

Was she right? What did it all mean? Maybe Trip was a Cancura investor, and some distracted newsletter editor had used the wrong photo or screwed up the caption.

Lark stood up. "I'll get to the bottom of this, Callie."

Callie nodded, wiped her cheeks with the back of her hands, and hurried out after retrieving her phone.

Back behind her desk, Lark keyed in *Jonathan Wright III* and *Cancura* to a Google image search. One of the first results was a page titled "Team" from cancura.com. At the top of the page was a studio shot of Trip, hair slightly mussed, eyes crinkled in a smile she'd seen hundreds of times.

Founder and CEO Jonathan Wright.

But the short biography called him Jonathan Mitchell Wright III.

The third. Triple . . . Trip.

Mitchell.

Trip Mitchell.

Lark was still struggling to get a grip on her wastebasket when she threw up into it, not much coming out except the yogurt and berries she'd had for breakfast and the chai she'd sipped in the car. Wiping her mouth with a tissue, she picked up her phone with shaking hands and selected Trip from her contacts.

He was still in the air, so she couldn't call. She could leave him a message. Or a text.

What would she say? Hello, *Jonathan*?

How would he answer?

No, she needed to see his face.

She locked the phone and dropped it, held her head in her hands. Saw the ring on her finger and tore her skin ripping it off.

Saw the stupid kitten on the *Hang in there, baby* poster and threw her cup at it, the cup crumpling and the dregs of her tea foaming down the wall.

Still barely able to get her fingers under control, she opened a browser on the computer to a travel site and keyed in *Chicago*. There was a seat on a flight leaving midafternoon.

First class.

She put it on her own credit card.

Chapter Forty

HOLLY

It's a hard truth that no one is irreplaceable.

—"How I Lied about My Name and Discovered My Truth,"
a TED Talk by Jon M. Wright

Brian opened the door, wearing flip-flops, jeans, a long-sleeved T-shirt, and a surprised look. The heaped laundry basket on the floor behind him showed exactly what Holly had interrupted and relieved at least part of her anxiety over showing up at his house unannounced.

"Is everything okay?" he asked, studying her face.

"Can I come in?"

"Yes, of course," he said, stepping aside and seeming embarrassed he hadn't offered. "Sorry the place is so messy."

It wasn't dirty—but lived in and clearly marked by the occupancy of two lively daughters. Holly tried not to let her curiosity show as she entered the foyer, and he closed the door behind her. She had never been to Brian and Nancy's home, even though it was only a ten-minute drive away and she had long known exactly where it was.

"Maid's day off?" she joked.

He shook his head. "If my job is taking care of the kids, I'm not just going to do the fun parts. Even if I don't always do the other parts very well."

"Well, now I feel guilty," she told him. "Besides Galenia, we have a cleaning service and a lawn crew. And neither Jack nor I so much as hangs a picture on our own."

"Holly, between your medical practice and your charity work, you practically have a full-time job. You deserve all the help you can get. Now, can I get you a cup of coffee? A glass of wine? A shot and a beer?"

"I don't think my nerves can handle anything other than mineral water at the moment."

She followed him back to the kitchen, noting the family photos lining the hallway. They had taken a formal family portrait every year, but nearly all the casual shots featured the girls only, suggesting Brian had been behind the camera while Nancy was elsewhere.

Dishes were piled on the counter, and kids' books and papers cluttered the dining room table, so Holly sat at the breakfast bar and set her bag on the tall chair next to her while Brian reached into the fridge.

"The woman Jack's seeing is named Jessica Meyers," she said. "He hired her and moved her to Chicago after they started sleeping together."

Brian closed the refrigerator door and put the bottle down. He came to her and took her hands, his eyes searching hers.

"Jack told her all along we were getting divorced. And that I was literally insane." Too humiliated to choke out the worst part. *He married her in Mexico.*

"Jesus, Holly. I don't know what to say."

"The crazy thing is that I feel almost as sorry for Jessica as I do for myself. She was completely blindsided."

"Most people wouldn't be so understanding," said Brian.

"I've already spoken to a lawyer, but if Jack finds out, he could outmaneuver me. Hide assets."

"You can't let him."

"Believe me. I won't."

"You're incredible."

"Can I get that drink now?" she asked, squeezing his hands and letting go.

"Of course."

As he filled two glasses with ice and mineral water, she reached into her tote and took out the hard drive, setting it down between them.

"What is that?"

"Jessica thinks there may be some big problems with the Revelate technology."

"Do you think she's right?" he asked, eyeing Jack's handwritten scrawl.

"Possibly. She's asked me to give her any information I can find. This could be nothing, but . . . we could also be talking about the end of more than my marriage."

"That's scary. Do you trust her?"

"All I know is neither of us trust him."

"If he brought her to Chicago and got involved with her based on a lie, he's obviously hurt both of you very much. It would be good if you could help each other."

Holly finally took a drink of her sparkling water, savoring the icy bubbles in the back of her throat.

"Everything's just moving so impossibly fast," she said.

"Some things are," he agreed. "But life is long. You and I are both going to be around for quite a while."

She was so grateful she almost cried.

～

When he walked her outside, he wrapped her in a hug that lasted for several long, soul-restoring minutes. They kissed once before she got behind the wheel.

"Could my life be a bigger shitshow?" she asked, smiling and wiping away a tear.

"Yes, and I'm glad it's not," he said. "This seems unimportant now, but I do have one small piece of good news. I've been looking into Larry Yadao's business for a while, and I discovered he's had a strip mall on hold in Oswego for a long time due to an arcane zoning issue: the access road the city requires would be on land where a neighboring farmer still owns an easement."

"Pretending I understood what you just said, how is that good news?" asked Holly.

"In another life, I actually negotiated with that farmer, on behalf of a client who bought another piece of his land. He's a crusty character, but he's honest, and we got along pretty well. I was able to sit him down with Larry at the local Starbucks and help them understand each other's needs. Larry's going to pay market rate for use of the land, and the problem is going away."

"Well, I'd say I'm happy for Larry except—"

"I did make one condition of my own." Brian put his hand over hers on the open car door. "Larry said he and Theresa would drop their objection to the equestrian path running in front of their home."

Holly turned her hand over and laced her fingers with his.

"Thank you," she said. "That's not small at all."

Chapter Forty-One

LARK AND JESSICA

*Do you have a safe space? A place where you can go to
get away from it all?*

—"How I Lied about My Name and Discovered My Truth,"
a TED Talk by Jon M. Wright

Lark's thumbs hovered over the screen. Déjà vu. Once again, she'd
landed in Chicago without Trip's knowledge. Again she was about to
alert him.

But not with the words, *You free?*

The brightly lit Blue Line train clattered down the middle of the
Kennedy Expressway, packed with weary commuters. Having learned
her lesson about Chicago rush hour the last time, she'd decided against
either a rented car or an Uber. A quick google, a couple of questions for
the orange-vested CTA attendant, and she was on her way downtown
to a station just a few short blocks from Trip's building.

Or Jonathan's.

I need to see you so we can talk, she wrote.

Just say when, he replied. *What about?*

Tell you when I see you. Are you at your apartment?

A slight delay. Then: *Wait, are you in Chicago?*

Yes. Are you home?

Longer delay. *Stuck in a meeting outside the city. Might be a while. Need you to sit tight. Where are you?*

On my way to your apartment.

No answer.

I'll wait for you there.

Eventually: *OK.*

The train moved so fast she almost wished it would slow down.

~

Jessica was only able to talk herself into playing the part of her gullible, trusting, love-blind former self because of her certainty that, if Jon had even an inkling of what was going on, she'd find herself homeless, unemployed, and in need of a different career.

The two glasses of wine she'd downed for courage since he'd texted to say he was on his way *home* helped a little. So did the mostly one-sided conversation she was having with Marco, who'd called on the pretext of business but had begun complaining about his attorney husband.

"He turns into the Incredible Hulk when he's in trial. And not in a good way."

"I wasn't aware there was a good way," Jessica said.

"Those abs . . ."

"Touché."

"I swear, if he's going to be in this funk until closing arguments, I may have to make an excuse to go to Omaha just so I can hide out in the apartment there."

Which reminded her of something Holly had said about New Year's Eve. "Isn't there a corporate apartment here?"

"Theoretically," Marco said with a laugh. "The whole time the Heritage at Millennium Park was going up, Jon raved about the view it would have from the twenty-seventh floor and how we'd use the apartment to wow visiting VIPs."

"What happened?"

"I can never book it. Jon always has it reserved for when he wants to 'crash in the city,' and I have to put my clients up in hotels, like always."

Speaking of the devil, Jon was due back in Chicago anytime, so as Marco continued to work through his relationship issues, concluding that *in trial* was equivalent to the *in sickness* clause of his marital contract, she refilled her wineglass. There was a very real possibility that Jon would be all over her as soon as he walked through the door, and she needed the fortification if she was going to pretend everything was life and love as usual.

At least Holly had been able to kick him out and wasn't faced with faking her way through lovemaking. *Crazy* Holly Wright, who had suddenly become her closest confidant.

Her lifeline.

Praying for guidance and strength to the alternate universe in which she now existed, Jessica closed her eyes and tried unsuccessfully to relax.

If she weren't so close to breaking down, she'd have laughed when her call with Marco was interrupted by a text from Jon.

Rerouted from O'Hare to Indy due to high winds. Headed to an airport hotel to get a few hours of sleep before a flight at zero dark thirty. See you at the office in the morning. Love you, Jessie.

～

The doorman was one Lark didn't recognize, a bald, thin-faced dude with hair creeping above his collar.

"My name is Lark Robinson," she told him. "I need the key to 2701."

"Are you an authorized user?"

"It's my fiancé's place," she said, not meaning to be irritated with the guy but unable to keep the frustration out of her voice. "Trip Mitchell."

He looked at her dubiously.

"Jonathan Wright," she said, feeling something rip loose inside her.

He tapped his keyboard and frowned. "You're not with Cancura, then?"

"I'm not sure who I'm with," she said, pissed off. "Can you call him, please?"

"Of course, Miss Robinson. Oh wait. There's a note here authorizing your stay. Apologies—I just started my shift and didn't see it."

A minute later, she was hurtling upward in the elevator, then stalking down the hallway. She found the familiar apartment and opened it with the hotel-style key. The first thing she noticed was how nothing seemed to have changed since her initial visit. The second thing she realized was why: the framed photographs she'd so carefully hung in the entry hallway were missing.

∼

Fortified by more than half a bottle of chardonnay, Jessica pulled on jeans and a sweater, climbed into an Uber, and headed toward the Loop, thinking, *What would Holly do?*

WWHD.

The woman now seemed eminently sane, but Jessica questioned her own mental state as the driver dropped her off in front of the Heritage at Millennium Park.

Even though she knew Jon was grounded in Indianapolis, her heart raced as she strode through the glass front doors into the lobby. Should she have worn a wig, *Jessica* Bond style, just in case?

The thought made her giggle.

"Evening, ma'am," the doorman said. "How can I help you?"

"I hope you can," she said. "One of my coworkers asked me to make sure our corporate apartment is ready in advance of a visit by out-of-town guests."

"Which unit?" he asked.

"I have it right here," she said, pulling out her phone and pretending not to find the text she was looking for. "Shoot. It's registered to Cancura, and I know it's on the twenty-seventh floor."

"Twenty-seven-oh-one?" the doorman asked.

"That's it," she said. Emboldened by wine, she added, "If I can have the key, I'll be in and out."

"I'm afraid you're a little late. The unit is already occupied."

Trip arrived forty-five minutes later with flowers and champagne, a smile on his lips, and a wary look in his eye. Lark refused to accept the gifts, forcing him to set them down on the table, and kept her arms crossed when he went in for a hug.

"I wish I'd known you were planning to join me here, so we could have flown together," he said gamely.

"Are you Trip Mitchell or Jonathan Wright?" she asked.

She didn't know what she expected him to say or do. From her terse emails and sudden arrival, he had to have known something was coming. Would he deny it angrily? Meekly confess? Instead, weirdly, his face went completely blank for a single second—looking frighteningly like a mask of the man she used to know—before he recovered and gazed at her earnestly. Lovingly.

"Lark, I know this looks bad," he said. "But I can explain. It's not what you think."

"And what do I think?"

"I don't know, but I have an idea." He began taking off his coat.

"Leave it on if you want," she told him. "This might not take long."

He finished and hung it on a chair. For a moment, he looked even more tired than he had in LA, and Lark had a fleeting thought that she was sharing the room with a stranger—that she should run—and then it passed and the familiar Trip was back, leaving Lark more confused than ever.

"Hear me out—please," he said. "Sit with me?"

She shook her head, wanting to keep her distance. He sat down on the couch alone.

"I've lied to you about some things," he began, with a sad smile. "You're right: my legal name is Jonathan Wright."

"And Trip?"

"My grandpa used to call me that. My dad was a junior, and I'm a third. Mitchell is my middle name."

Lark felt so confused and angry she wanted to throw something at him, but there wasn't so much as a vase in the antiseptic apartment. Wobbling, she sat on the edge of the dining room table.

"Just . . . why?" she asked.

"I'm not going to apologize or ask you to forgive me, because this is beyond that. All I can do is tell you what was in my heart, Lark. I loved you the moment I saw you. I knew I had to be with you, but I was afraid you'd reject me because I'm older and, well, I was still technically married, even though the divorce had been coming a long time and was well underway. I just didn't want you to see me as damaged goods. I wanted to show you the best version of myself."

"Not the real version."

"My feelings for you are completely genuine," he went on. "I also had another motive because—and there's no way to say this without sounding arrogant—I'm rich."

"I know you're rich, Trip. Or should I call you Jonathan?"

"It's your choice. But I want to still be Trip to you. I want that to be your name for me."

Lark massaged her forehead with the palms of her hands. "Mr. Wright."

"I'm on the Forbes 400," he stated simply. "But I didn't want you to know who I was or how much I have because, as I found out the hard way, my ex-wife cared about my money and my social status. And I wanted to make sure you loved me for who I really am."

"Without telling me who you really were," she snarled.

He dropped his head and opened his palms. "I fucked up."

Lark got up and sat on the matching couch across from him. "When were you planning on telling me the truth?"

"As soon as the divorce was finalized . . . but then things got complicated."

"Because you proposed to me."

"I didn't think things through. Obviously."

"You're divorced now?"

"Almost. We're ironing out the last details."

"What's her name?"

"Holly."

"What else did you lie to me about?" she demanded. "Ohio, Indiana, your parents dying? You really have a brother named Matt who's afraid of flying?"

He hesitated ever so briefly. "That's all true."

She looked around the apartment, at the sleek impersonal decor with no trace of his personality. "What about this place? Do you even live here?"

"I've stayed here on and off while the divorce plays out," he said earnestly. "But it's a corporate apartment owned by my company, so I move to a hotel to make it available when necessary."

"Which is why you got rid of our pictures," she said, heartbroken at the futility of that gesture.

"They're still here!" Practically leaping off the couch, he hurried to the hall closet, where he took a banker's box off a high shelf and brought it back to the coffee table. He removed the lid so she could see the half-dozen framed photos inside.

She lifted out the top one and wiped off the thin layer of dust with her sleeve. It was the selfie they'd taken at Niagara Falls.

She remembered his caption: *People say you can't find the end of the rainbow. Not true.*

Suddenly, she was sobbing uncontrollably. Trip sat down next to her. He was crying, too.

They stayed up talking half the night. Sometimes she let him hold her. Other times she pushed him away. When she yelled at him, he took it. The one time she hit him, with a closed fist on his chest, his expression told her he knew he deserved it. She wanted to hit him again—to hit anything—but didn't.

Eventually, they fell asleep on the bed, fully clothed.

She woke up at dawn, as he was leaving.

"I have to go to the office," he told her softly. "Stay here as long as you like. I'll keep out of your way. I don't want to rush you. What happens next needs to be your decision, and I want it to be right for you. But I still want to marry you, Lark, and I want to spend the rest of my life with you. No more lies. You are everything to me."

She looked at him, exhausted. "I'm not even sure what you are."

Chapter Forty-Two

JESSICA

A lie will cover another lie for only so long.

—"How I Lied about My Name and Discovered My Truth,"
a TED Talk by Jon M. Wright

"I missed you so goddamn much," Jon said, appearing in Jessica's office and closing the door behind him.

Thankfully, an entire wall of her office was glass, so they couldn't hug or touch.

"I missed you, too," she said, more easily than she'd expected. "Did you get any sleep last night?"

She hadn't, wondering if he was really in Indianapolis like he'd said, or at the corporate apartment for reasons that didn't seem to make any sense.

"A few hours," he said, not making eye contact. "Jessie, I'm so sorry we had to be apart, especially after your grandmother's stroke."

"It was touch and go for a few days," she managed to say, barely remembering the excuse she'd manufactured for missing work.

"I'm just glad everything's okay now."

Nothing's okay, she wanted to say. Still stunned at what she'd learned in the month since they'd exchanged marriage vows.

"And how is the Holly situation?" she asked instead.

Jon sighed too deeply. "I finally got her under control, and she's receiving the help she needs. Would you believe she took a sledgehammer to my old home office?"

"That's awful," Jessica said, with what she hoped was convincing conviction.

"Ava texted me to let me know, so I had to go out to the house to repair the physical and psychological damage. I needed to recover after that."

Jessica had to admit that his pained look was utterly convincing. She gave him an understanding nod—understanding that the desk-smashing incident had happened after, and not before, he'd gone to "the desert."

"I didn't want to scare you," he said, "but that's the real reason I wanted you in Omaha."

"I understand. Where is Holly now?"

"At an inpatient residential treatment facility," he said, now looking directly into her eyes without so much as a telltale blink. "Which, ironically, is where I told her I was."

Had he really both lied to her and admitted something so profoundly startling in the same sentence?

"But you weren't?" Jessica asked, wondering how many more gut punches were coming.

"Getting inpatient counseling because my wi—ex-wife lost her marbles? Hardly." He chuckled.

"Why would you tell her that, then?"

"The only way I could get her to agree to seek help was to tell her I was working on my issues, too."

"Where were you, really?" Jessica asked.

"Palm Springs, mostly," Jon said. "And LA."

"Are you opening an office in LA?" she asked, as innocently as she could.

He looked startled. "No. Why?"

Before she could cover her mistake, Lorenzo from the mail room appeared outside her door, holding a padded mailer.

"Come in," she called.

He entered and wordlessly handed over the package, clearly uncomfortable at interrupting a meeting with the CEO. As he retreated, she read the sender's name and blanched. While written in plain black pen, it may as well have been blinking red neon.

A. Wilkes.

Although it had clearly come by courier, Holly had added a Colorado return address on *Misery Lane*.

"It's from my mom," Jessica said quickly, putting the mailer on her desk facedown. "She told me she'd send me some old photos we found at Nana's after she made copies."

"I'd love to see them, but I can't stand that close and keep my hands off you," Jon said, flashing the sexy smile that now filled her with dread.

The moment he left, Jessica collapsed into her chair. Her hands shook as she opened the envelope and removed an older internal hard drive. On the bottom was Jon's handwriting, in Sharpie:

DON'T USE.

There was also a handwritten note from Holly.

Your move.

~

For the first time ever, Philip didn't see Jessica coming. His back remained turned as she approached his cubicle, forcing her to tap him lightly on the shoulder to get his attention. "Philip?"

Startled, he jumped and turned around. "Jessica!"

"Sorry," she said.

"I'm okay," he said, taking a breath to reset himself. "I was so absorbed in checking this report that I didn't see you come out of your office."

She probably should have been more troubled by the fact that he'd admitted he kept an eye on her whereabouts. "I have something I'd really like you to look at."

"What is it?"

"That's what I'm not sure of," she said, handing him the hard drive Holly had sent. Because it came from an old tower computer, she had no idea how or where to plug it in. "I don't know how to read it, or what's on it, but I believe it's important. I need your technological know-how and your analytical skills to tell me what we have here."

"My pleasure," he said, blushing crimson.

She hated to trade on whatever feelings he possibly harbored for her, but he was the one person in the whole company she could turn to for help. He was also the most qualified.

"Thank you, Philip." She lowered her voice. "This needs to stay entirely between us—no matter what you do or don't find."

Philip looked at her with a blank expression that, on anyone else, would have indicated a lack of comprehension. Jessica now knew him well enough to realize it was exactly the opposite.

He nodded. "Understood."

Chapter Forty-Three

HOLLY

You can truly be yourself only at home.

—"How I Lied about My Name and Discovered My Truth,"
a TED Talk by Jon M. Wright

Holly happened to be passing through the front hall when she heard the telltale sound of someone using the keyless entry system. Her thoughts were still outside with Alderman, who was being rehomed next week, and whom she'd just taken for a long ride, enjoying the unseasonably warm afternoon.

Six beeps and then the door latch rattled. Access denied.

Holly raced to the back door, then the side doors, throwing dead bolts and hooking chains. She took a mental inventory of her children: all home, all safely inside.

Cautiously, she returned to the foyer.

Six quick beeps. A frustrated rattle.

Jack.

Despite his visionary brilliance, he'd never been one for detail and had never bothered to learn how to reprogram the lock. Sliding closer in her socks, she heard him insert a key into the mechanical lock and try to turn it.

The "god *damn* it" was unmistakably his voice.

When he pressed the video doorbell, she answered right away, hoping to catch him before the kids realized he was there.

"Will you buzz me in?" he said, peering into the fish-eye lens.

"Why are you here?" she asked.

"I completed my inpatient therapy. I know I still have a long way to go, but I want to share some things I've learned, and realizations I've had."

"Like what?"

Jack was working hard to keep smiling. "There's so much, Holly, but mainly, I can't imagine a future without you. We've accomplished so much together. Made a beautiful family."

Holly knew she should open the door and let him sing his song of contrition, pretend to accept it, and let him continue to think she believed his bullshit. Play the game for now. She reached for the screen and the unlock button.

And then let her hand fall to her side.

"I'm not ready to talk."

"I told Jessica I'm fully committed to my marriage and she can't expect anything from me. I can't fire her without getting sued, but, if necessary, I can open an office for her to run in Siberia. In other words, she knows she needs to move on from Cancura as soon as possible."

"What about the others?"

Jack's face froze in a rictus grin. "Others?"

"You can't expect me to believe there haven't been others," she said carefully.

"I'm doing the work, Holly. I want to make things right between us."

"I'm not ready for that."

"Then when?"

"I'll let you know."

On the screen, Jack turned and stalked to the edge of the porch, where he stopped and rubbed his face like someone trying to wake up. She could just hear his footsteps through the stout oak door. As far as she knew, the kids were still unaware, still pretending to do their homework while they texted, Snapchatted, and sneaked peeks at TikTok. Hopefully with headphones on.

Suddenly, he whirled around, lunged at the door, and started pounding on it.

"Let me in *now*, Holly! This is my house! Bought with *my* money! Do you think you don't need me to keep living like you do? To squander money on your precious horses?"

When he started kicking, she took an unconscious step backward, glancing over her shoulder and afraid that Ava, Paige, or Logan would suddenly materialize behind her. But the sprawling old house had advantages that outweighed its constant need for maintenance, including thick walls and long hallways. As far as she could tell, the kids remained oblivious.

Now practically on top of the camera, Jack's face was distorted and ugly.

"I want to see my kids," he demanded, as if reading her mind.

"I'll send them out if you can calm down."

"Calm? You want to see calm?" Seeking a target for his frustration, he spotted a terra-cotta planter where the gardeners had recently buried tulip bulbs. He lifted it and threw it onto the front walk, where it cracked into large pieces and sprayed dirt and mulch all over the pavers.

"You should go now," she told him.

He came back to the camera, panting, and wagged his finger at it. "You want to act all high and mighty. Well, Ava told me you trashed my office. So I know you have anger issues of your own."

"She was understandably upset. But we can't bring the kids into this, Jack."

"I won't let you tell me what to say to anybody, especially my own children. Send them out."

"Now isn't a good time."

"You don't get to choose!" he raged.

In a way, it was hard not to open the door. She wanted to fling it wide and hit him with every damning detail she could muster. But she was beginning to recognize the dark allure of withholding information, too. Jack had always known more than her, always kept her in the dark, and it seemed to her now that had been part of what made him feel so powerful.

Two could play that game.

If Jessica was half as clever as she seemed to be, even three.

Chapter Forty-Four

JESSICA

As it turns out, the truth doesn't always set you free.

—"How I Lied about My Name and Discovered My Truth,"
a TED Talk by Jon M. Wright

Jessica pulled up in front of a nondescript beige-brick town house with matching beige trim. That seemed to fit, but an unexpected burst of color from assorted plantings and a flower bed lawn border led her to reconfirm the address Philip had handed her on a folded slip of paper. He'd added a single sentence:

Any time after 6:00 pm will be fine.

Her head throbbed as she fought northbound end-of-day traffic toward Niles. Philip had apparently discovered something on the hard drive too sensitive to say aloud or even reference in the note. That, or he was using it as a convenient excuse to lure her to his home.

Both options were deeply troubling.

Checking inside her purse for the pepper spray she always carried, just in case, she exited the car, walked up the driveway, and climbed the concrete front stoop.

Philip answered the door before she could knock.

"Where did you get that hard drive?" he asked.

"I'm afraid I can't say," she said.

"But you know who it belonged to?"

"I didn't know for sure."

"Thank goodness our technology at the office is too updated to get anything off of it, which forced me to access it here," he said, looking past her to the street, as if checking to see if she'd been followed. "I love my job, Jessica. I don't want to lose it."

"I know, and I'm sorry to put you in this position," she said. "You're truly the only person I trust at Cancura."

He paused for a moment to process what she'd said, then nodded and opened the aluminum storm door.

She followed him through a combination living and dining room filled with coordinated furniture and so tidy it could have been a Macy's showroom, with stairs leading to the second floor. They passed a kitchen, whose farmhouse motif included rooster-print wallpaper and a ceramic-cow cookie jar, before proceeding down the hallway into the only room that met her expectations of Philip's natural habitat: an office with a battered couch, multiple computers and screens, and a coffee table littered with controllers, empty snack bags, and electronic accessories whose purpose she could only guess at.

Even Philip seemed compelled to acknowledge the state of the room. "I'm not used to having people in here. We usually close the door when company comes over."

Jessica wondered about Philip's cleaner, more organized housemate as he motioned her toward a vintage-looking computer on a prefab laminate desk. "The hard drive was from a 2010 Dell PC, which I was able to install into the tower of one of the old machines I used to tinker with."

"So you were able to read the files?"

"It took some time to determine the correct version of Windows, and then to identify and download the various compatible software, but yes. It's a large drive, and there's quite a bit of data. Without knowing what you are looking for, however—"

"Phil?" A woman's voice. Footsteps coming down from upstairs.

"In my office," he called with a tenderness Jessica had never heard from him, before turning and adding: "Melanie is working the overnight shift."

"Melanie?" Somehow, it didn't compute.

"My wife."

A moment later, a short, young, and pleasant-looking woman entered the room, regarding her quizzically.

"This is my coworker Jessica Meyers," said Philip. "She came here on a work-related matter."

"It's nice to meet you," said Melanie.

As they shook hands, Jessica noted a visible swell under Melanie's baggy hospital scrubs.

"When are you due?" she asked, still astonished by the unfolding layers of Philip's personal life.

"August," said Philip, beaming and tenderly patting his smiling wife's stomach.

As she offered her congratulations, and Melanie apologized for having to run, and Philip accompanied his wife into the hall for a tender kiss, Jessica thought there couldn't possibly be any surprises left in the day.

That was until she sat down in front of the computer and, with Philip's guidance, began to go through the folders and files on what turned out to be the hard drive for Jon's personal computer from the earliest days of Cancura.

Before there was a secure company server to protect highly sensitive data . . .

Before he kept his personal taxes separate from financial information related to the business . . .

And, to her horror, before he'd wised up about his extramarital dalliances and stopped taking intimate photos of his lovers.

Chapter Forty-Five

LARK

Don't be too proud to beg for forgiveness.

—"How I Lied about My Name and Discovered My Truth," a TED Talk by Jon M. Wright

Lark lost track of how many miles she'd walked along Chicago's endless lakefront. Despite the steady breeze, she was comfortable in her light jacket as long as she kept her hands in her pockets. The lake was an opaque teal, its surface broken by small whitecaps under scudding clouds. Something about its empty vastness pulled her onward and helped still her racing thoughts.

Jonathan Mitchell Wright III had fucked up royally, no question, starting with his impulsive use of a nickname in a hotel bar and culminating in a proposal under what could only be called false pretenses. Craziest of all was his disclosure that it had also been some kind of a test to learn whether she loved him for who he really was.

And yet.

Was their connection real? What lay at the heart of love—did societally imposed expectations drive people toward suitable partners, or was everyone just a victim of genetically inherited traits and urges? Or was it something deeper and more mysterious, like a chemical connection and an unspoken bond? People who loved each other had to forgive each other all the time . . . but when did an act become unforgivable?

Having learned so much so quickly, she was having a hard time making sense of it all and didn't know whether she could trust her initial impulse to end things forever. If she did give him a second chance, would she in any way be influenced by the fact that he was one of the four hundred richest men in America? She didn't think so. She hoped not, anyway. How shallow would that make her?

She had googled the list and confirmed his name was on it. His real name, anyway.

Lark walked and walked, with Lake Shore Drive on her right and the inland sea on her left. The park began to feel smaller and more disconnected from Chicago, even as the city seemed smaller and more spread out.

After two and a half hours, footsore and hungry, she detoured from the path, followed an outcrop into the lake, and sat down on a rough breakwater made of huge blocks of stone. She put her earbuds in and started a video call.

Callie picked up on the fourth ring, having ducked into Lark's office.

"How are you?" she asked.

Lark sighed. "It must feel good to be right."

"It feels terrible. I wish I could be your paranoid friend who was wrong about everything."

"Me too."

Lark brought Callie up to speed on all that had been said and done since she came to Chicago, skipping most of the gory details out of general weariness. Telling her how he was, as much as possible, saying the right things. Ending on his vow that he still, more than anything, wanted to marry her.

"Wow," said Callie, adding cautiously, "What do you want to do?"

"You tell me."

"I won't even try, Lark."

"I wouldn't put up with Dylan because he was immature and a little lazy. How can I live with a guy who *lied about who he was?*"

"Regardless of how I feel about him, Trip is a completely different animal than Dylan."

Neither of them said anything for a minute. Lark watched hungrily as a man twenty yards away opened a Styrofoam clamshell and started eating a sandwich and fries.

Callie brightened. "Bright side?"

"Please."

"At least now you know. You have all the information you need to make a decision. You can decide to be with him, or not, but you know the worst thing about him."

"God, I hope so."

"If you decide to be with him, you can work on things. If you decide not to, well, you're a beautiful woman with a business that is going to kick ass with or without Trip. Or Jonathan, whatever."

"All thanks to him," Lark said.

"But you own the business, don't you?"

"Yes. I mean, I'm pretty sure."

"I don't want to freak you out, but you should check with your lawyer ASAP."

Lark felt a pang of alarm. She had read the contracts so carefully, but . . .

Callie's eyebrows went up. "You *do* have a lawyer, right, girlfriend?"

Chapter Forty-Six

Jessica, Holly, and Lark

I've never been a fan of team-building exercises.

—"How I Lied about My Name and Discovered My Truth,"
a TED Talk by Jon M. Wright

Jessica would never be able to unsee what Philip had shown her on Jon's hard drive. She felt nauseated sharing the sordid, steaming mess of explicit photos with Holly, but at least the accompanying evidence of shady financial dealings would bolster his wife's case for more than 50 percent of *Jack's* assets.

Besides, Jessica was left with one folder that made all the other betrayals seem trifling by comparison.

As she plowed through the clinical trials, reports, and research in the folder (unironically titled OBSOLETE), there was no denying Jon was a visionary, and that the science behind his dream was revolutionary—if only there hadn't been file after file of evidence showing the Revelate had failed on almost every front. Worse, the results from the blood tests, biopsies, and other accepted detection protocols that had been employed alongside the Revelate were not only infinitely more accurate—they had been transposed onto dummied reports to wow initial investors and skeptical scientists alike.

Much like the test results she'd stumbled upon a month into her employment. She could only conclude her job description had been missing one important competency: *ideal candidate will top-sheet and sign any and all paperwork required to enable Jonathan Wright, MD, PhD, to deceive investors, medical authorities, and the general public.*

He had married her to keep her from testifying against him.

Nothing Jon did could surprise her anymore. But what about lead researchers like Kate and Arjun, and principals in the company like her good pal Marco? Had they fallen prey to Jon's charms as easily as she had, or were they all part of the overall deception?

Jessica had no idea how long it would take to recover from the heartache Jon had caused her. The thought that her career might be over before it started was just as painful. But confronting his false claim of being able to save untold thousands of young lives was a matter of life and death.

"What's going on here?" Kate's eyes narrowed as she entered the secure, windowless conference room where Arjun, Marco, Lorna, Ellen McBride from marketing, and Cancura's lead in-house counsel, Ross Cowan, were already seated.

Jessica couldn't go straight to the board without sounding a company-wide alert. Instead she'd invited a carefully selected group from Jon's inner sanctum. She needed to hear what they had to say. Closing the door behind Kate, she took a deep breath and gathered her remaining shreds of inner strength.

"Something of critical importance has come to my attention, and I need your help to fully understand and address it," she announced.

Jessica now knew Kate and Arjun well enough to recognize their guarded expressions as nonverbal eye rolls communicating, *Here we go again.*

"Anything discussed in this meeting needs to stay here," she continued, handing out copies of the nondisclosure agreement she'd asked Ross to draft ahead of the meeting.

"What the hell?" Kate asked, staring at the page in disbelief.

"Where's Jon?" Marco asked. "Why isn't he here?"

"Jon is in a videoconference with the Gates Foundation for the next ninety minutes," Jessica said, meeting Kate's gaze, not adding that she'd scheduled the meeting for 10:30 a.m. precisely because Jon would be engaged in what he did best: charming the pants off yet another unsuspecting mark.

At least the pants, in this instance, weren't literal.

"But I assume he's aware of this meeting?" Lorna asked.

"He is well aware of everything we will be reviewing and discussing," Jessica said carefully.

As soon as all had signed—Kate only after Arjun's urging—Jessica collected the NDAs and, before sitting down, gave each of them hard copies of key highlighted documents from the OBSOLETE folder on Jon's hard drive.

"I've approached several of you at various times about irregularities in regard to the Revelate and have consistently received pats on the head and assurances that I have no idea what I'm looking at. So I'm very curious to know what you make of these."

She leaned back in her chair, watching the coworkers she thought she liked most (Marco, Ross, Ellen) and respected most (Kate, Arjun, Lorna) as they began to grasp the implications.

Arjun spoke first, his voice tight with panic. "These reports. They can't be—"

"This—this is really old data," Kate stammered.

"The first Apollo rocket exploded on the launchpad, and two years later man walked on the moon," said Marco, ever the salesman, but his cheeks were uncharacteristically flushed.

"Setting aside any defensiveness or Silicon Valley double-talk, I think we can all agree that, according to this data, the Revelate test results were falsified from the very start," Jessica said. "Correct?"

Ross shifted in his chair, looking expectantly at the others.

"I don't claim to understand the science," said Lorna.

But this time, neither Kate nor Arjun tried to disguise the look of panic that passed between them.

"Where did you get this?" Kate rasped.

Instead of answering, Jessica reached down and pressed "Send" on a text message: *Now.*

Seconds later, Holly opened the door to the conference room.

"Holly?" Marco said, his shock speaking for everyone.

"So good to see you," Ellen said, too confused to sound earnest.

Arjun at least stood to greet her, albeit shakily. "How are you?"

"I've been better," Holly said.

With the grace that continually surprised Jessica, she strode over to the table and took an open seat between Lorna and Marco.

"The files Jessica just gave you are from an old hard drive I discovered at home," she continued. "It was originally installed in a computer Jack used for two years after he founded Cancura, and before all company business was stored on a secure central server."

"Jesus," Ross whispered, putting his head in his hands.

"For the last ten years, I've been skeptical that it was possible to accomplish what Jack assured me was happening. But I also assumed that, given the size of the investments, the blue-chip names of the investors, and the actual purpose of this project, everyone involved was adhering to the highest ethical standards."

A pained silence filled the conference room.

"What we need to know from you is what the Revelate can actually do," Jessica said. "Or, if it's easier, how many of the promised functions *can't* it do?"

"Jon has always kept everyone siloed, and I don't know if any of us knows the whole picture," Lorna said, looking down at the table.

"Not easy getting past the Great Wall of Olivia," Ellen said.

Whose maternity leave had, in fact, allowed Holly to slip in without undue attention.

"I was always assured we were dealing with bugs that would be resolved," Marco said earnestly. "Or promised that something bigger on the horizon would make the current issues—"

"Obsolete?" Jessica said. "Like a forthcoming announcement about a cure for—"

"That would be a lie," Kate blurted.

The word *lie* finally unleashed.

Freed.

Every nerve in Jessica's body vibrated as Arjun quickly added, "For the foreseeable future."

By talking at length with Philip and reexamining some of the most difficult-to-explain incidents, Jessica had slowly come to realize she couldn't have been alone in her suspicions about the Revelate. In fact, she was most likely part of an NDA-silenced majority. As the conversation continued, she didn't dare make eye contact with Holly, who had agreed that the only way to find out was to present the evidence and gauge everyone's reaction.

"And Jon knows this is the case?" Ross asked.

"The Revelate can detect a handful of biomarkers," Kate said. "But the bottom line is that the digestive process is simply too destructive for the effective introduction of nanoparticles via a chewable flavored tablet."

"Whenever we tell Jon it's not working, he reminds us that the video of him eating the Flintstones vitamin has fifteen million views on YouTube and says, 'Make it work,'" Arjun added wearily.

"Then he makes it rain more money, as if that alone will solve the problem," Kate said. "We keep hoping we'll find a breakthrough before—"

349

"Some clever scientist or journalist uncovers the truth?" said Holly.

"Which explains why it's my job to turn down all media requests except puff pieces about Jon himself," said Ellen. "I might as well have his mantra tattooed on my forehead: 'Everyone wants to cure cancer . . .'"

"But nobody thinks about the level of security that requires," everyone in the room chanted in nearly perfect unison.

"Ross, from a legal standpoint, wouldn't anyone who was aware of, suppressed, or altered bad data be liable if the truth comes out?" Jessica asked.

"Indeed."

Another silence, this one longer as each person at the table took inventory of what they knew and when.

Feeling an idea just out of reach, Jessica pushed back her chair and stood up. "So the biggest issue facing us is actually the delivery system?"

"The Revelate concept is technically viable," confirmed Kate.

"This probably seems glaringly obvious, but what about a time-release capsule?" Holly asked.

Arjun nodded. "A protective coating could keep it from disintegrating until it's in the GI tract, where the nanoparticles can be absorbed. The limiting factor is that the capsule is too large to be swallowed by a small child."

Pacing now, Jessica snorted in disbelief. "But adults could easily handle it, as well as teens and even some preteens?"

"We've pitched versions of this to Jack before, but he wouldn't agree to anything that wasn't flavored and chewable," said Kate.

"How very like Jack," Holly said dryly, with a sympathetic glance at Jessica. "To chase the sexy new thing."

Her phone, which she'd left on the table, began to vibrate, and she grabbed it and stood up. "Please excuse me for a moment."

"I still can't get over the fact that Holly Wright was just here," Marco said as the door clicked closed behind her. "How does that even make sense?"

"Unfortunately, Jon's lack of ethics extended well beyond the business realm," Jessica said. "They may have shared a marriage and kids, but they definitely don't have the same moral compass, and she felt she had to come forward."

"I feel sorry for her," Lorna said.

"She'll be okay," Jessica said, more sure of it than ever. "I think we all will, assuming we can agree on a slight redefinition of Cancura's mission."

There were nods all around.

"But what do we do about Jon?" Arjun asked.

"Trust me, he's very distracted, and he'll soon be even more so," said Jessica. "Focus on your work and act like this meeting never happened. If he asks for a status report, stall him."

"For how long, exactly?" Ross asked.

"Just hang tight," she said, smiling for the first time in weeks.

Holly ended her call with Francesco Mancini—her attorney was the one caller she couldn't afford to send to voice mail—as Jessica came out of the conference room. The realization of what came next left her feeling as though she couldn't quite get enough air into her lungs.

Jessica looked tired but grimly determined, and as they walked in silence to the elevator, Holly drew strength from her presence. Despite the steely front she'd tried to project in the conference room, she felt ashamed she'd allowed herself to assume for so long that Jack's lies were confined to his personal relationships.

"What did I miss?" she asked, pushing the down button.

"Just the inevitable aftershocks of basically good people trying to come to terms with some very ugly truths."

"I've been there," Holly said.

"I'm still there," Jessica said. "But that meeting gave me a glimmer of hope."

Holly couldn't believe it had gone so well. "Knowing Marco as long as I have, I half expected him to run out of the room and drag Jack back in. I'm glad I was wrong. Despite himself, Jack hired good people—including you."

Jessica nodded and swallowed hard, as if trying not to cry while they stood awkwardly waiting for the elevator door to open. "You do realize what this means to Jon's reputation? Cancura's, too."

"I do," said Holly, careful not to upset her new ally with a flash of indignation.

Of course she knew. Not an hour had passed without agonized thoughts about what any publicity would do to her children. But if the world deserved to know the truth about Jack, then Ava, Paige, and Logan certainly did, too. They were too old to be shielded from it anyway.

"What about our reputations?" asked Jessica.

"That's the last thing I'm concerned about, personally. I honestly think you're going to come out of this very well once the smoke clears. Cancura can still do a lot of good, once Ja—once Jon has been dealt with."

"Working around Jon worries me the most."

"At work or at home?"

"Both." Jessica removed something from her pocket and held it out. "One thing's for sure: I won't be wearing this around."

The diamond ring was stunning and had to have cost ten times the amount of the one Jack had given Holly so long ago. Gently, she folded Jessica's fingers around it. She didn't want to see.

"Use me as an excuse," she said. "You should."

"I think the elevator is broken," said Jessica, pressing the down button again.

"This is how it begins," deadpanned Holly.

Despite the suffocating pressure, they both chuckled and started for the stairs.

~

The mild weather of the previous day was a distant memory as Chicago's spring turned vicious. The wind drove Lark into a souvenir store on Michigan Avenue, where she purchased the warmest hat available, a red-and-white Chicago Blackhawks ski hat with a pom-pom on top. She then sheltered in a coffee shop for a hushed phone call with a lawyer, who had already reviewed the paperwork and confirmed that, when it came to Larkspur Games, anyway, Jonathan "Trip" Mitchell Wright III had been on the up-and-up. He stood to benefit from her profits, but she was sole owner of her company—and her destiny.

So.

Feeling more nervous than she liked, she called an Uber to take her the mile or so to Cancura to end their relationship in person.

The four-story brick warehouse was not at all what she'd expected—learning more about his med-tech start-up online had led her to picture something a little more sleek and zoomy—but the lack of street signage seemed serious enough, as did the tough-looking security guard who confronted her in the lobby after buzzing her through the glass door. The all-white lobby and the Cancura logo on the back wall? More like it.

"Can I help you?" he asked.

"My name is Lark Robinson, and I'm here to see Jonathan Wright."

"Do you have an appointment?"

"No. But he'll see me."

The guard's expression said, *We'll see about that.* He asked for her driver's license and scrutinized it carefully—even holding it under a black light—before scanning it, handing it back, and picking up the phone.

One does not simply walk into Mordor, she thought for some reason, which made her giggle.

The guard raised an eyebrow.

"I'm not used to this level of security," she explained.

He nodded curtly.

She had tried and failed to plan the words she would use with Trip, finally deciding to let them spill out however they wanted.

She waited while the guard tried one extension, then another, then resigned himself to waiting on hold.

Her head suddenly warm inside her ski cap, Lark took it off and shook out her hair. As she did, two women emerged from a frosted-glass door behind the security desk. One of them was a slightly curvy brunette with a heart-shaped face and chestnut hair whom she'd never seen before. The other was a slim, elegant, ash-blonde woman who looked somehow familiar.

"Nice to see you again, Mrs. W," said the guard, covering the receiver.

The blonde didn't seem to hear him. Staring back at Lark, she nudged her companion with a none-too-discreet elbow.

They both looked at her with curiosity.

"Love your hair," said the brunette.

"Thank you," said Lark, almost as a question.

"My name is Jessica, and this is Holly. Who are you?"

"Lark Robinson," she said, her mind spinning. *Holly W?* As in Holly Wright?

"What brings you to Cancura?" asked Holly, who in person looked exactly and not at all like the woman shown in Google images riding horses, standing beside Trip in formal wear, and posing at her pediatric practice.

Tell them? Don't tell them? Lark couldn't decide. Then, in an instant, it became clear to her that the only truth she was responsible for was her own.

"I'm here to meet my fiancé, Jonathan Wright," she told them, thinking to herself it was the last time she would use that word for him.

The two women exchanged a dark, highly charged glance.

"Still trying to get through," the guard told Lark. "His assistant is on maternity leave."

"He'll be on a videoconference call for another ten minutes or so," Jessica said.

"Lark," said Holly, coming closer and speaking softly so the guard wouldn't hear her. "Jonathan Wright is my husband."

"I know," said Lark, trying not to freak out about how totally weird this was. "But you're getting divorced . . . right?"

"He's also my husband," said Jessica.

Lark's heart misfired and nearly stopped. Staring back at the two women crowding her personal space, she felt like she was in a dream whose logic suddenly made perfectly terrifying sense.

Holly Wright turned to the guard and said, "No need to bother Jack. Ms. Robinson will come back in a little while. We're taking her to lunch."

Lunch?

"We need to talk," said Jessica.

Chapter Forty-Seven

Trip/Jon/Jack

My Achilles' heel? Love.

—"How I Lied about My Name and Discovered My Truth,"
a TED Talk by Jon M. Wright

So much has changed, thought Trip as he stepped out the front door of the new Coldwater Canyon house he was halfway through renovating and made his way toward the limo idling at the curb. The June morning was blindingly hot, and the driver was visibly sweating as he opened the back door. As the big car started to move, Trip ran a finger around his collar and told the driver to "set the AC to stun." He would not be arriving with his own suit soaked in sweat.

A $20 million piece of real estate spread was an extravagance, but with Barrington Hills off-limits, and Jessica in a holding pattern, he was sick and tired of the corporate apartment. His future was out here, anyway. All he had to do to justify Cancura's purchase of the house was lease a floor of offices for the so-called LA headquarters—and since he'd done it in Lark's building, she was welcome to use it in the meantime as her company grew. And as of tonight, she would finally leave behind the crummy courtyard apartment she shared with Callie.

Holly would come around eventually. She was still being difficult, but she needed him for too much. He'd been more than happy to let her cling to the notion that she'd passed up a promising career to raise their children, but long years together had proved to him that she didn't have the steel to run anything more ambitious than a suburban charity.

Jessica's insistence that they hit the pause button had been puzzling. Her stated reason—that they'd married too soon, and she'd rushed into it because she was frightened of Holly—was understandable enough. Had Holly gotten to her again? Holly staunchly maintained she hadn't had any contact with Jessica since their meeting at Whole Foods, but he had his doubts. All he'd been able to do was graciously accept it and move out of the Lakeview apartment and promise that soon he'd be able to provide proof Holly was no longer a threat. Things had to work out with Jessica for the sake of Cancura, but he hadn't had time to orchestrate a reunion because he'd been managing the catastrophe with Lark.

First, she'd shown up at his office, so weepy and wild eyed he'd been sure a *fuck off* was coming—but all she'd said was she needed more time to think.

Then, having thought for a few weeks, she suddenly decided they should get married after all. Only she had conditions. That they get married in LA, not Hawaii. That the ceremony be performed by her mother's friend, a lesbian Unitarian minister. That the wedding be a little bit larger than they'd discussed so Lark could invite a few friends.

It would have been safer to have a small civil service in Hawaii, easier to explain why his brother somehow couldn't make it, after all—but fine. He had to give her something.

The part that pissed him off was her insistence that they not sleep together until they tied the knot.

"Did you just crawl out of a time machine from the nineteenth century?" he'd joked.

Not really joking.

"I want to make sure this is about love, not sex," she'd replied seriously. "You tested me, and I passed. Now you need to pass my test for you."

"Lark, I would crawl on my knees through broken glass for you," he told her, believing it himself.

"Glad to hear it," she said with a wicked grin.

Waiting was harder than he made it out to be. He'd been so horny he even invented an excuse to spend thirty-six hours in Minneapolis with a surprised but appreciative Alanna, his old friend from Target.

The thought of taking off Lark's wedding dress tonight prompted a painful, unwanted erection he hoped would go away before the drive was over.

The things a guy has to do for pussy. The thought made him chuckle.

"Sir?" asked the driver.

"I didn't say anything, chief."

The traffic on San Vicente Boulevard was sluggish, the road clogged with Saturday-afternoon beach traffic. It should have been a fifteen-minute drive from here, but it was probably going to be twice that.

They had just passed Twenty-Sixth Street when his phone rang. Olivia, who had just come back from maternity leave. He answered, thinking he'd need to remember to silence it during the vows.

"I . . . I heard something crazy." Her voice was shaking so much she could hardly speak.

"Don't keep me in suspense, Olivia," he said impatiently.

"There was a board meeting. Just now. At the office in Chicago, but everyone who couldn't be there called in."

A board meeting? Jon's mind went blank as the limo passed an elderly, spandex-clad cyclist puffing away in low gear.

"Who convened it?" he asked quietly.

"There was a vote removing you as CEO."

Had he been driving, the cyclist would be dead. The cars in front of them smoking wreckage. He wished he were behind the wheel. Almost considered ordering the chauffeur to pull over and get out. Instead he pushed the button that raised the privacy partition.

"Who told you this, Olivia?" he asked, trying to control his voice and breathing.

"Jon, I'm sorry."

Then she hung up.

He stared at the phone, mind reeling.

Coups happened, but not at companies like Cancura. Not *his* goddamn company, which he'd started and built from nothing into one of the hottest start-ups ever. His mind spun through the CEOs, celebrities, and retired politicians he'd recruited for the board, wondering who was responsible and what motives they could possibly have.

Meanwhile, he had exactly 51 percent of the stock, so even if they kicked him out of his office, he still controlled the *fucking* future of his *fucking* company. They would have to answer to him as a shareholder.

The driver wove his way toward Pacific Coast Highway. The street was baking outside, but inside it was suddenly too cold. He opened a window.

"Sir, should I turn off the AC?" asked the driver via intercom.

"I'll let you know," Trip barked.

He called the cell phone of Ross Cowan, but it went straight to voice mail. Tried the switchboard.

If you know your party's extension . . .

Called Jeff Nowak, his personal lawyer. One ring and voice mail. Probably communing with nature on a golf cart.

As he switched his phone to vibrate, a text came in. *Jeff,* he thought, saying he'd call after the eighteenth hole.

Not Jeff. Jessica.

This isn't going to work out between us. I'll be returning your ring. I don't want anything from you.

"Fuck!"

A text. She told him she wanted a divorce by *text*.

He called her back. No answer, of course. Why would anyone talk to him? He was only the reason for everything.

Hot again. He rolled the window back up. The air-conditioning was arctic—the driver's nuts were probably ice cubes by now. Good.

Any other day and he'd head for the airport, fly to Chicago, and set Jessica straight. Now he needed her even more. He did love her, and for a while he'd wondered if she really was his perfect match. Someone who understood the thing that drove him and could help him reach his biggest goal. But she had too many questions and not enough answers. It had been a mistake to mix work and pleasure.

And he'd soon have Holly back. He did love her, too, even if she'd annoyed the fuck out of him lately. She was a good lover, and a great mom, and he needed her to keep being one, at least until the kids were all out of the house. They could summer in LA if they wanted, but it wasn't like Lark was going to help them with their homework.

Jesus. Could he postpone the wedding, at least until he figured out what was going on at Cancura? He'd be inconveniencing what, a dozen people? Two dozen? Lark had handled the guest lists.

No, it was too late. Better to get it over with and then do damage control. Someone with ideas above their station believed that they could go toe-to-toe with Jonathan Mitchell Wright III. That someone was going to regret it.

Worst-case scenario, if he really was out of a job, he still had the stock. He could call in favors from enough board members to make sure the new CEO was compliant and run things from backstage. Meanwhile he could start something new. Empowering girl scientists or something. Get Lark to say how important he'd been to Activate! Do another TED Talk and hit the speaking circuit.

Which was a great way to meet people and make new friends.

They had turned onto PCH. Endless Pacific blue off to the left. A hell of a lot nicer than Lake Michigan. A hell of a lot warmer than Lake Michigan. Fuck it. Fuck Chicago and screw Illinois.

Focus. Breathe.

He called everyone again. Called a couple of board members. No answers.

The driver turned right and climbed slowly up to the club. Lark had spent the morning there getting ready. Soon, a team would arrive at the house to set the stage for their return that evening. Rose petals leading the way from the driveway to the master suite. Candles on the staircase. A bottle of champagne chilling in hand-chipped ice. When he texted from the road, someone would light the candles and get the hell out.

The limo pulled up in front of the club. More cars than he expected.

The driver opened the door, and Trip got out, blinking at the sun. Then the driver put an envelope in his hand.

"You've been served, sir."

The man's face was expressionless behind his sunglasses, but Trip heard a *fuck you* in his voice. He stared at the envelope. His name was handwritten on the front. A return address from Eerdman, Fellowes, Mancini, and Shulman in Chicago.

"What is this?"

"You've been served, sir," he repeated.

He tried to give it back, but the chauffeur raised his hands like he was innocent. Trip threw the envelope at him, but it fluttered in the breeze like a leaf and landed on the asphalt.

The limo rolled away.

A grinning, tuxedoed flunky appeared at his side. "You must be the groom! Please come inside."

Trip bent over and picked up the envelope, ripped it open, and scanned the first page.

Divorce. Holly.

Trip put the letter back in the envelope with shaking hands, folded it in half, and shoved it into the breast pocket of his suit.

"Let's get out of this fucking heat," he said. "And get me a glass of champagne."

"Right away, sir."

It was dark, cool, and empty inside. The lackey literally summoned a glass of champagne by snapping his fingers three times. The sound was so crisp Trip felt envious. Wasn't that the goal, to simply snap your fingers for what you wanted?

The champagne was cold and good. He drained the glass without removing it from his lips.

"Where is everybody?" he asked.

"Outside, Mr. Wright. They're waiting for you."

"Am I late?"

"Of course not."

Alone, he passed through the cool, dark interior of the 1920s Mediterranean-style building, where the tables were already set for dinner, and through the doors to the lanai overlooking the ocean. A little like that place in Mexico. Neat rows of white chairs flanked the aisle, all of them full. Maybe fifty people in all. A lot more than he'd been expecting. In the back row, one of the guests turned and saw him. It took Trip a moment to place the face, but then he remembered the guitar and the candle on the steps outside Lark's apartment.

Dylan.

Dylan?

Why she was wasting Trip's money on her loser ex was utterly beyond him, but maybe she just wanted to let the chump see firsthand she was truly off the market. Probably the least weird thing that had happened today.

Lark was standing under a green trellis, the buzz-cut minister waiting just off to the side. As a string quartet launched into one of the mopey millennial songs she was constantly playing, he wished he'd had a moment to wash his face or at least take a piss. Fortunately, he'd already put his phone on vibrate.

Lark smiled. People began to turn around. He stood up straight, threw his shoulders back, and pasted a shit-eating grin on his face.

He gave Dylan a consoling pat on the shoulder as he went past.

As he walked, he studied faces. Lark's parents. A trio of hot women Lark's age. Callie, following him with her phone to capture his every move.

Why was he the one walking up the aisle, anyway? Wasn't he supposed to be up front while *she* made the stroll? Was this a feminist thing?

Then it was just the two of them. Lark looked so good it almost outweighed every shitty thing that had happened so far that day. She was wearing a formfitting sheath dress that must have cost twenty bucks per square inch. Her hair was elegantly curled, and she was holding a small bouquet of tropical flowers. She looked . . . what was the cliché? Radiant.

"You look fucking awesome," he whispered.

"I know," she said.

Lark turned to face the audience, so he did, too. For some reason, the butchy-looking minister remained off to the side.

Then Trip saw who was sitting in the front row.

Holly. Her parents, Walt and Charlotte.

Jessica.

And his own mom and dad. Who he'd told Lark were dead. Who could tell her he had never had a brother named Mike or Matt or anything else. If they hadn't told her already.

He couldn't breathe. His heart was pounding so hard he thought it would break his rib cage.

Was he hallucinating? He hadn't seen his parents in years, but here they were, his simpleminded mom sitting there proudly like the queen of the ball, his dad looking back at him like somehow Trip had disappointed him once again.

It made no sense at all.

"I need to sit down," he told Lark.

"You'll be okay," she said sweetly as Callie held up her phone even higher. "Smile. This will all be over with in a moment."

Trip knew he was totally fucked when the minister stepped forward, opened her bible, and said, "We are gathered here today in the sight of God and the presence of friends to celebrate one of life's greatest moments—in this case, our beloved Lark's decision to *not* get married."

Chapter Forty-Eight

LARK

I've made enough mistakes for all of us. Trust me.

—"How I Lied about My Name and Discovered My Truth,"
a TED Talk by Jon M. Wright

Hotel bars still were not Lark's scene. Over the past few years, however, she had logged so many thousands of miles of business travel that hotel rooms, lobbies, business centers, conference rooms, and even bars had lost all novelty to become spaces she passed through without a second thought. Now, as she rewarded herself for a job well done with a vodka martini in the lobby of the undulating Radisson Blu Aqua Hotel, she felt so comfortable in her wingback chair that she could have been in her own living room.

The invitation to keynote the Chicago Toy and Game Fair had been completely unexpected and, to her mind, premature—even despite the popularity of Activate!, Codemaker, and Archi-types. Then again, many people in the gaming industry knew they still had an image problem, so it couldn't hurt to have a multiracial millennial female pictured prominently at the podium. If her track record wasn't quite long enough to warrant the invitation, Lark was more than happy to provide a role model for game-loving girls who wanted to join the club, too.

And Larkspur Games was by all measures successful. Who knew parents were so desperate for analog, hands-on games that taught chemistry, coding, and engineering with no batteries required? The hard part had been making them fun, but apparently Lark had balanced seriousness of purpose with enough silliness to please the nine-through-eleven-year-olds who were her target market. There was a steep drop-off at twelve as girls joined their peers and turned to screens, but Lark liked to think she was planting a seed of experience that would flower later. She'd already hired some STEM kids as her little company reached its current size of fifteen employees and expanded into several adjacent offices.

The speech—if not the cheesy opening joke Callie had insisted was necessary—had gone well although her nerves had been so tightly wound that she wished she'd had the martini first.

Unlocking her phone, Lark scrolled past new emails to a very old one she'd saved without sending a response.

Its subject line: Thought you might like to know.

Lark had indeed liked to know. Now, copying the address from the body of the email, she pasted it into the Uber app and, before summoning a ride, savored another sip.

When she opened her eyes, her martini's identical twin had magically appeared on the low table in front of her.

"From the gentleman at the bar," said her server discreetly.

"Please send it back," said Lark, smiling. "Tell him I said thanks, but no."

She could have held up her phone, mouthed an apology to the man about having a ride already on the way. But she didn't owe anybody anything. Standing up, she pulled on her coat, called the ride, and walked out of the lobby without even bothering to look at whoever had sent the drink.

~

The black car joined Lake Shore Drive and headed south, with the driver explaining that the Dan Ryan Expressway was "all red on the app." Out the window to her right, Trip's building towered over Millennium Park.

It was impossible to visit Chicago without thinking of him. Even when she was elsewhere, few weeks passed when he didn't cross her mind. They had been bound together more closely by YouTube, Facebook, and Twitter than they would have been by marriage. Her decision to have Callie livestream her vow of independence had been designed to make him infamous—and it had—but she hadn't considered the consequences for herself.

Jonathan Mitchell Wright the Third seduced me under the name Trip Mitchell and eventually proposed to me without revealing he was already married to both Holly and Jessica. Both of these brave women are sitting in the front row.

It had been the first time she'd ever seen him lost for words. Ashen, he'd wobbled unsteadily as his shit-eating grin slowly faded into a confused smirk.

Trip, you gave me a head start in business, for which I remain grateful. You told me then, "It's only weird if we make it weird." Well, it's officially weird, and you can take all the credit for that. I'm paying back every cent you spent on my behalf, plus interest. You may need it. I understand you may soon have a cash flow problem.

Putting the envelope full of begged and borrowed money in his hands had been more than a relief: it had made her feel powerful.

To all the guests, I know this isn't what you expected. There will be no wedding today, but we will have a party. Please join Holly, Jessica, and me as we celebrate our new beginnings. And, Trip, don't worry—you're not going home alone. Or without a ring on your hand.

That was when he'd seen the two suit-wearing FBI agents step forward, one of them opening a shiny pair of handcuffs.

Restraints are optional with white-collar criminals, the younger agent had explained with a wink earlier that morning. *But I'll be more than happy to make your special day more memorable.*

With her own phone turned off, Lark remained blissfully unaware of the worldwide social media explosion until the party had run its course and, more than a little drunk, she'd shared a ride with Callie back to their apartment. Over the next week, the video had racked up eighteen million views, hundreds of thousands of tweets, and become such a viral phenomenon that every late-night television host had made jokes about it. All but one of them men.

The best line came from the lone woman on late-night TV: *Finally, a man willing to change his name for marriage.*

Most people lost interest after a week, but articles followed in newspapers and magazines—then a podcast led to a streaming documentary series and a made-for-TV dramatization. Somebody even wrote an opera and staged it in a storefront theater. Each flare-up stung Lark, but then again, longevity had been exactly the idea: that Trip's falsehoods would be forever in view, just a quick internet search away for every woman he bought a drink. Social media shitstorms lasted a week, and they also lasted forever.

Who knew? Maybe her keynote invitation had something to do with her social media celebrity, too. She wasn't going to lose sleep over it. Everything that had happened was just a part of who she was now.

So.

⁓

Eventually, the driver left Lake Shore Drive and took them through a rough-looking neighborhood into a depopulated area bordered by decaying industrial hulks on one side and a windswept marsh on the other.

"Are you sure we're going to the right place?" Lark asked.

"No idea," said the driver. "But this is the address you put in."

And then, suddenly, it appeared. They drove under an arch with a sign reading **HORSE STABILITY**, past two corrals or whatever they were called, and pulled up in front of a large new building that had been designed to look like a storybook farm. A banner across the front proclaimed **GRAND OPENING**.

Lark went up the walk, thinking that providing free horseback rides to poor kids was a rich person's almost stereotypical idea of charity—but not a bad use of Holly's ex-husband's money, either. Better than spending it on herself. And people had to help however they knew how.

Inside, the party was in full swing as Chicago's wealthy elite mingled with South Side community leaders and noisy local kids. Lark smiled as she watched a small group of boys raiding the heavily laden dessert table. She shouldn't have been surprised to see the kids there: Holly was a mom, after all.

Jessica noticed her first and beelined over.

"I didn't think we'd see you," she said.

"I got lucky on the timing," Lark told her. "I had to be here for work, and all I'm missing is a dinner where a bunch of dudes will mansplain my own success to me."

Jessica grinned ruefully. "Hard to miss that."

"How are you doing?" Lark asked.

"Really well. Still at Cancura and kicking ass. The first two years post-Jon were a slow-motion nightmare. Half our people left, and our stock lost most of its value, but we didn't quit. And lo and behold, our new CEO, Kate, led us to the promised land. The technology is doing what it purports to do, and the shareholders—who now include a lot more Cancura principals—are happy again. My first stock options have vested, so . . . I'm never going to be Holly wealthy, but I'm doing okay. More importantly, we're going to save a lot of lives."

"Do you have time for a personal life?"

"Almost," said Jessica, grinning and holding up her left hand to show off a simple gold wedding band. "Happily married to a guy who wouldn't know an IPO from a post office. You?"

"Dating but not seriously," Lark told her, which was close enough. Her experience with Trip had made it impossible for her to trust anyone for a few years, but she was working on it.

She felt a hand on her arm and turned. Holly, smiling warmly and looking so stunning that Lark hoped she aged half as well. Trip's first wife had become Cancura's largest shareholder after winning half of his fifty-one percent in the divorce and adding that to a few percent she'd already owned. Her parents were rumored to own a significant amount, too—together, they made a formidable voting bloc.

"Congratulations on all your success," said Holly. "I've been following from afar."

"How are you?" Lark asked.

"Happy, keeping busy. The kids are thriving despite it all. Ava is a junior at Scripps, Paige is taking a gap year, and Logan still doesn't shower as often as I'd like. Brian's girls are high school seniors."

"Who's Brian?"

Holly pointed out a handsome guy who was helping the cater waiters move a table. "Also divorced. We're cohabiting. I haven't moved—still in Barrington Hills. I fought too hard for that place to give it up."

"Where is . . . ?"

"Jack?"

Lark nodded.

"You mean you don't have Google alerts for all his aliases?" chuckled Jessica. "I confess I do."

"Other people alert me often enough," said Lark, not mentioning that, while the vast majority of comments had been supportive, she had also been the subject of racist slurs and disgusting comments about her looks from creepy cyberstalkers and other shitheads.

"He has a house near mine for hosting the kids," said Holly. "But most of the time he's everywhere else."

"I personally think he hangs upside down in hotel-room closets until nightfall," said Jessica. "He seems to be getting around again."

Lark knew the broad outlines. Trip had been behind bars when he fell off the Forbes 400. After serving eighteen months of a five-year federal sentence for securities fraud, tax evasion, and a touch of embezzlement, and ten months in an Illinois prison for bigamy, he had all but disappeared until about a year ago, when, despite his public humiliation and utterly destroyed reputation, he'd suddenly emerged as "Jon M. Wright" to deliver a new TED Talk, "How I Lied about My Name and Discovered My Truth." Since then he'd been a fixture on the speaking circuit.

"I had someone look into it and discovered he makes ten thousand dollars a speech, if you can believe it," said Holly.

"He's also got a new start-up that supposedly connects inventors to 'thought leaders, rainmakers, and influencers,'" added Jessica.

"I can't believe anyone would buy that," said Lark.

"The TED Talk is getting some traffic, but guess which vastly more popular video comes up with every search?"

"Sometimes I wish I could just make him go away," said Lark. "The fact that he still exists is just . . . exhausting."

"I hope this question doesn't seem rude, but why do you think he wanted to marry you?" asked Jessica. "I think I know the answer for Holly and myself, but you're still a little bit of an enigma. You're obviously gorgeous and brilliant, but I still don't believe that's why he proposed."

Holly, who was no doubt too refined to pose the question herself, raised an eyebrow.

"I asked him why, and he told me it was simply because he loved me," Lark told them. "I honestly think I was just a way to escape. I wrestled with that for a long time before deciding it didn't matter.

So instead of thinking about my life as a part of his, I'm turning that around. He was just a short chapter in my story."

"He'll never escape himself," said Holly. "No matter how hard he made life for us, he will always think he has it infinitely worse. And in a strange way, that makes me happy."

Flagging down a passing waiter for a glass of wine, Lark proposed a toast.

"We thought we wanted to be Mrs. Wright, but here's to being wrong."

ACKNOWLEDGMENTS

Author Mark Stevens, to whom this book is dedicated, is the tireless champion every writer wants as a friend, and we are lucky to count him as ours. This book was improved by the expertise of Ruth Monnig Steele, Michele Chang, Brandon Hull, Andrew Hull, and Matthew Schirber.

Special thanks to Javier Ramirez, Mary Mollman, and Madison Street Books in Chicago.

Alison Dasho, Caitlin Alexander, Shasti O'Leary Soudant, Gabe Dumpit, and the wonderful Lake Union team were once again a dream to work with.

Endless gratitude to Josh Getzler, Jonathan Cobb, and the phenomenal crew at HG Literary, as well as the fabulous Hilary Zaitz Michael at WME.

ABOUT THE AUTHORS

Photo © 2019 Mark Stevens

Linda Keir is the pen name for the writing team of Linda Joffe Hull and Keir Graff, authors of *The Swing of Things* and *Drowning with Others*. Between them, they have published over a dozen novels. For more information visit www.lindajoffehull.com and www.keirgraff.com.